BY ANGIE KIM

*Miracle Creek*
*Happiness Falls*

# HAPPINESS FALLS

# HAPPINESS FALLS

*| A Novel |*

## ANGIE KIM

LONDON/NEW YORK

Copyright © 2023 by Angie Kim Writing LLC
Author Q&A copyright © 2023 by Penguin Random House LLC

Published in the United States by Hogarth, an imprint of Random House, a division of Penguin Random House LLC, New York.

HOGARTH is a trademark of the Random House Group Limited, and the H colophon is a trademark of Penguin Random House LLC.

Grateful acknowledgment is made to the International Association for Spelling as Communication (I-ASC) for permission to reprint an excerpt from a collaborative poem entitled "It's Sure Been Quite a Year" created at the Neurolyrical Café, organized and sponsored by I-ASC, copyright © 2022 I-ASC. All rights reserved. Used by permission.

LIBRARY OF CONGRESS CATALOGING-IN-PUBLICATION DATA
Names: Kim, Angie, author.
Title: Happiness falls: a novel / by Angie Kim.
Description: First edition. | London; New York: Hogarth, 2023 |
Identifiers: LCCN 2022059340 (print) | LCCN 2022059341 (ebook) |
ISBN 9780593448205 (hardcover; acid-free paper) |
ISBN 9780593448212 (ebook)
Subjects: LCSH: Missing persons—Fiction. |
LCGFT: Detective and mystery fiction. | Novels.
Classification: LCC PS3611.I45286 H37 2023 (print) |
LCC PS3611.I45286 (ebook) | DDC 813/.6—dc23/eng/20221220
LC record available at https://lccn.loc.gov/2022059340
LC ebook record available at https://lccn.loc.gov/2022059341

International edition ISBN: 978-0-593-73063-8
B&N ISBN: 978-0-593-73161-1

Printed in the United States of America on acid-free paper

randomhousebooks.com

Special Barnes & Noble Edition

1 2 3 4 5 6 7 8 9

First Edition

*Book design by Susan Turner*

*For Jim, Carleton, Steve, and Andrew*

I lost a World—the other day!
Has Anybody found?
—EMILY DICKINSON (1896)

One sits down on a desert sand dune, sees nothing,
hears nothing. Yet through the silence something throbs,
and gleams. "What makes the desert beautiful," said the
little prince, "is that somewhere it hides a well . . ."
—ANTOINE DE SAINT-EXUPÉRY,
*The Little Prince* (1943)

It's a crazy world out there. Be curious.
—STEPHEN HAWKING,
*The Universe in a Nutshell* (2001)

# PART I

## EVERYONE'S FINE

# ONE

# Locke, Bach, and K-pop

WE DIDN'T CALL THE POLICE RIGHT AWAY. LATER, I WOULD BLAME myself, wonder if things might have turned out differently if I hadn't shrugged it off, insisting Dad wasn't *missing* missing but just delayed, probably still in the woods looking for Eugene, thinking he'd run off somewhere. Mom says it wasn't my fault, that I was merely being optimistic, but I know better. I don't believe in optimism. I believe there's a fine line (if any) between optimism and willful idiocy, so I try to avoid optimism altogether, lest I fall over the line mistakenly.

My twin brother, John, keeps trying to make me feel better, too, saying we couldn't have known something was wrong because it was such a typical morning, which is an asinine thing to say because why would you assume things can't go wrong simply because they haven't yet? Life isn't geometry; terrible, life-changing moments don't happen predictably, at the bottom of a linear slope. Tragedies and accidents are tragic and accidental precisely because of their unexpectedness. Besides, labeling anything about our family "typical"—I just have to shake my head. I'm not even thinking about the typical-adjacent stuff like John's and my boy-girl twin thing, our biracial mix (Korean and white), untraditional parental gender roles (working mom, stay-at-home dad), or different last names (Parson for Dad + Park for Mom = the mashed-up Parkson for us kids)—not common, certainly, but hardly shocking in our area these days. Where we're indubitably, inherently atypical is with my little brother Eugene's dual diagnosis: autism and a rare genetic disorder called mosaic Angelman syndrome (AS), which means he can't talk, has motor difficulties, and—this is what fascinates many people who've never heard of AS—has an unusually happy demeanor with frequent smiles and laughter.

Sorry, I'm getting sidetracked. It's one of my biggest faults and something I'm trying to work on. (To be honest, I don't like shutting it down entirely because sometimes, those tangents can end up being important and/or fun. For example, my honors thesis, *Philosophy of Music and Algorithmic Programming: Locke, Bach, and K-pop vs. Prokofiev, Sartre, and Jazz Rap*, grew from a footnote in my original proposal. Also, I can't help it; it's the way my mind works. So here's a compromise: I'll put my side points in footnotes. If you love fun little detours like Dad and me, you can read them. If you find footnotes annoying (like John) or want to know what happened ASAP (like Mom), you can skip them. If you're undecided, you can try a few, mix and match.)

So, anyway, I was talking about the police. The fact is, I knew something was wrong. We all did. We didn't want to call the police because we didn't want to say it out loud, much the same way I'm going around and around now, fixating on this peripheral issue of calling the police instead of just saying what happened.

Here goes: My fifty-year-old father, Adam Parson, is missing. At 9:30 A.M. on Tuesday, June 23, 2020, he and my fourteen-year-old brother Eugene hiked to the nearby River Falls Park, the same as they had done most mornings since I'd been home from college for the quarantine. We know they made it to the park; witnesses have come forward, a dozen hikers and dog-walkers who saw them together at

various points around the waterfall trail as late as 11:10 A.M. At 11:38
A.M. (we know the exact time from the dashcam recording), Eugene
was out of the woods, running in the middle of a narrow country road
in our neighborhood, forcing a driver who'd run through a stop sign
and turned too fast to swerve into a ditch to avoid hitting him. Just
before the dashcam video jolts from the crash, you can see a fuzzy
Eugene, not stopping, not turning, not even looking at the car or at
anything else—just stumbling a little, so close to the car you'd swear
he got hit. The screech of the tires and the sound of the car thud-
ding into the ditch, not to mention the chain reaction of the two cars
behind it, apparently caused a terrible cacophony of metallic crunch-
ing, banging, and squealing that brought people out, and bystanders
reported seeing a boy they later identified as Eugene staggering away.
It bears note that not one of the five bystanders, three drivers, or two
passengers involved in the crash saw my father precede, follow, or accompany Eugene. We confirmed this multiple times, and it is beyond
dispute: Eugene was in our neighborhood alone.

While all that was going on, I was in the midst of what I was
thinking of as one of the great tragic moments of my life. It's funny
how relative these types of judgments are, how much they can
change depending on context: that day has obviously since become
The Day Dad Disappeared, but if you'd asked me that morning, I'd
have sworn it was The Day of the Big Breakup. Not that it was as
dramatic as all that. The breakup itself had, unbeknownst to me,
happened earlier through Vic's semi-ghosting, which I'd noticed but
misinterpreted as him needing alone time. This was my first Serious
Relationship (as in, one lasting more than six months), and I thought
I was being considerate in stepping back rather than nagging for attention and insisting he open up to me and bare his soul or whatever,
but what I was apparently *actually* doing was failing a test of some
sort—how much I cared, how much our relationship meant to me,
etc. That morning's call was merely a courtesy notification of the
results.

I listened quietly to Vic's (trying a little too hard to be) cool, matter-of-fact conclusion that he thought it best we "remain separated" be-cause I obviously didn't care all that much, and it occurred to me that this call was yet another test, which I could pass by acting upset and saying "of course I care" and "it's just the quarantine and the agony of being apart, the angst of isolation," blah blah. But I don't do drama. Also, I was pretty pissed that this guy who usually extolled my "re-freshingly low-maintenance lack of game playing" was playing one himself and expecting me to participate and excel. It was juvenile, insulting, and, frankly, more than a little deceitful. Which is exactly what I said as soon as he stopped talking, right before I hung up. (I be-lieve in saying what you're thinking, as much as is practicable.) I threw my phone across the room—hanging up on an iPhone isn't nearly as satisfying as slamming down an old-fashioned phone like our kitchen landline, and besides, I had an industrial-strength titanium phone protector—but damned if it didn't land on my plush comforter.

I was contemplating picking it up to try again when I saw some-thing out the window that stopped me: a boy in a bright yellow shirt, rounding our street corner, running fast. The thing my brain couldn't reconcile was that the shirt was definitely Eugene's—I distinctly re-membered him wearing it that morning—but that running gait was definitely not. Eugene's mosaic Angelman syndrome means that he has two distinct sets of genes in his body: some cells with an imprint-ing defect and some that function normally. The mosaicism makes him "less affected," without some of the most severe symptoms that can plague AS kids, like seizures and difficulties walking and eat-ing.[1] Eugene can do some things he's been practicing all his life like using utensils, walking, and even running, but he has issues main-

---

1 On the other hand, autism makes Eugene less social and communicative than many AS kids, who crave social connection. In fact, I've heard people describe autism and AS as opposites because of the stereotype that autistic people are emotionless and not sociable. The doctor who diagnosed Eugene said that AS itself is rare enough (one in 20,000 live births), so with the mosaicism variant *and* the dual diagnosis of autism, Eugene was a "true one-in-a-million marvel," which I think was supposed to make us feel better.

taining consistent coordination and speed. It's like a tongue twister; you might manage saying it once or twice carefully and slowly, but the longer and/or quicker the utterance, the greater the chances of tripping up. Eugene needed years of therapy just to walk long distances—that's why the daily hikes to and from the park with Dad, for practice—and I'd always thought he didn't like running at all. So how was it possible that this boy who appeared to be my little brother was running the length of our long street?

It's funny with siblings, how you think of them as just there, but then something great or awful happens that unearths and makes visible what Koreans call jeong. It's hard to explain in English; it's not any particular emotion—not affection or even love—but a complex bond defined by its depth and history: that sense of belonging to the same whole, your fates intertwined, impossible to sever no matter how much you may want to. I rushed downstairs, threw open the front door, and ran outside, barefoot. "Oh my God, Eugene, look at you go," I yelled out and clapped and—God, this is so not me, but I couldn't help it—even whooped and jumped a little.

Where was Dad? I've racked my brain trying to think if this question even crossed my mind at the time. I didn't notice that Dad wasn't there, but I didn't *not* notice it either, if that makes sense. I mean, I didn't see him, but parents are like that. They just seem like they're always there, so you assume they are if they're supposed to be. I didn't give any thought to it, is what I mean, but I suppose it was in the back of my mind that Dad had been encouraging Eugene to run, and once they were in our neighborhood, Dad let him run as fast as he could. There were so many reasons why Dad might have lagged behind—he might have been slowed by an arthritic knee (he didn't have one that I knew of, but this didn't seem unreasonable given that he'd already turned fifty), or he might have stopped to take a video the way parents are always doing. Not that I consciously thought these things at the time; like I said, I thought of him the way kids think of parents, which is to say, not at all.

Maybe this is an excuse, but I think I was too mesmerized by

Eugene to think about anything else. He is beautiful. Everyone comments on it, what a gorgeous mix of our parents he is—not a hodgepodge of different features from either parent, like John and me, but a true blend, as if you morphed Dad's eyes/nose/skin color/etc. into Mom's halfway. The sunlight on his face, his huge smile, triumphant and proud, and most of all, the way he was cutting across our front lawn, his legs and arms in elegant athletic synchronization as I'd never seen before. As he got closer, I saw scratches on his knees and dirt on his yellow shirt, but those made him look even more joyous, visions of a rowdy boy traipsing through the woods with friends, laughing and not caring what scrapes they were getting into.

My perpetual annoyance with John, my hurt over the harsh words from Mom the previous night—none of that mattered. I hated that they were missing this, wished I had my phone so I could record Eugene to show them. I forgot I was annoyed, forgot about Vic testing and retesting me, forgot about Mom's ultimatum, forgot everything except how I'd never seen Eugene look so graceful, so typical, and I ran across the lawn to hug him tight.

I don't know what I was expecting—a tight hug back, maybe, for those arms that looked so strong and agile right then to wrap around and squeeze me, or even his usual quasi-hug, just standing there as if tolerating my hug, his arms rising limply, feebly, then flopping down as if he couldn't quite manage it. We hadn't hugged at all lately, and I suppose I was hoping for the excitement of this moment to erase the awkwardness between us, to undo what happened at Christmas. Hope is dangerous that way; it leads you to confuse what's possible with what's not.

Eugene kept running, and just when we got within arm's reach, with that huge smile still on his face, he raised his hands and shoved me. Eugene, my baby brother, shoved me out of the way, down to the ground. Hard.

Thinking back, I should have been on guard, with the way he was running full on, right at me. But that smile—that smile is trouble. I know it doesn't always equal joy, that Eugene sometimes smiles and laughs when he feels anxiety, pain, sensory overload, even anger; I've read about it, talked to doctors about it, seen proof of it. But some things are so ingrained in our culture, maybe in humanity itself, that it's hard to convince yourself otherwise; intuition trumps intellect, every time. A smile is one of those things. Not the tight, upturned-lip fake ones, but huge, whole-face ones like Eugene's—lips, eyes, eyebrows, even ears all buoyant. My parents and John claimed to be able to "read" the subtle differences in Eugene's smiles to figure out his true emotional state, but I'd never been able to differentiate them. Plus, I had no reason to doubt his happiness; I was so taken with the extraordinary normalcy of the moment, so happy myself, that I assumed Eugene must feel the same way, and his smile matched that, confirmed it. I was utterly unprepared for the shove, is what I'm trying to say, and I fell. My ankle twisted, and a jolt shot up my spine. "Ow," I screamed, louder than the physical pain warranted, more to get Eugene to stop, but he kept going, straight through the open front door into the house.

Why didn't I get up right then? It seems clear to me now that this was one of those hinge points in a person's life, a crucial juncture of two possible realities. Reality A: I grit my teeth, get up, go into the house to get some ice, and start wondering where Dad is and text/call/ping him; I get worried by the lack of response and call Mom and John, who immediately come home; we start our search before the storm, maybe even call the police; Dad is found—hurt, maybe even medevaced, ICU, coma, amputation, whatever, but alive—and we all learn a lesson about taking our good fortunes and each other for granted, and we go on living the rest of our lives, whatever happiness levels and lengths they may be. Reality B: I lie there and do nothing.

I chose B.

In my defense, I did try to move, and it did really hurt. I could have borne the pain and gotten up, it's true, but it seemed hard, and I didn't want hard. Plus, I was tired, and it was strangely nice being outside, the grass cool and prickly against my fingers, the bottoms of my feet. Our neighborhood's officially a suburb of DC, but it used to be part of the park and retained its rural look, with isolated farmhouses, wooded backyards, and narrow, gravelly streets. Our street had a particularly quiet, deserted feel, and sitting there with no phone and no computer, I felt a calm peace infuse me, the pain in my ankle dulling to an ache.

Eugene's room was right above me, and his window must have been cracked open because I could hear him start jumping, accompanied by his high-pitched vocals—what I call *splaughing* because it sounds like a mix of singing, laughing, and playing violin spiccato (with a lightly bouncing bow). It's what he does to de-stress: just get lost in the repetitive motion and sound to restore order when his senses get overwhelmed.

I looked up at his window. The sun was in my eyes, but through the veil of light, I could see the top of his head bopping up every second, the piercing treble right when his head reached the apex, followed by the bass tone of his feet hitting the floor. It almost sounded like a rhythm track to a song—*heee-boom, heee-boom, heee-boom*—precise and rhythmic, his splaugh a high note some coloraturas can't even hit. I have perfect pitch, so I could tell it was a D, almost an octave higher than his usual F.

I lay down on the grass and kept staring, listening, thinking. The higher pitch, the faster run, the shove. In retrospect, it seems obvious these were clues, adrenaline-fueled aftershocks of the car crash and whatever had happened in the park with Dad, but at that moment, I could focus only on how much Eugene was changing, had already changed while I wasn't paying attention. That push, in particular—it shocked me. Not just him lashing out for no apparent reason—I'd seen that before—but how strong he was, how aggressive it felt. Two arms bent, chest level, then a smooth, easy, efficient snap of the elbows to send all five foot seven inches and 130 pounds of twenty-year-old me tumbling backward and down. The last time he'd gotten physical with me was at Christmas. Only six months prior, but he'd been shorter, a skinny little kid whose arms I could hold down to keep him from clawing—though not from kicking, as I found out the hard way. Now, he was my height and definitely bigger and heavier. Fourteen: no longer child but not quite man, the awful, magical age when gawky can morph to invincible and back in a second, even coexist simultaneously. He would be fifteen soon, the age when John shot up to six feet. The bigger and taller Eugene grew, the more careful I'd need to be. Pretty soon, maybe already, he might be able to overpower even John or Dad.

My eyes were tearing up. Not crying tears—I rarely cry. It had to be the sunlight, the brightness of it shocking my entire visual system after spending 90-plus percent of the last three months of lockdown in my room, curtains drawn. Plus, my eyes were tired, my lids heavy and sore. I'd gotten into the habit of staying up, falling asleep around sunrise, being forced awake for the mandatory family breakfast, then going back to sleep, but thanks to The Call from Vic, I hadn't slept that morning. The adrenaline rush of the Vic-Eugene one-two punch had kept me going, but that and the pain were fading fast, leaving me drained.

I was getting drowsy, eyes closing, when I heard a steady crunch of gravel—footsteps coming up the driveway. Dad. I'd forgotten he wasn't home yet. I expected him to come check on me and get me inside, and just the thought of it exhausted me even more; I didn't want to move, didn't want to talk about Eugene shoving me, didn't want to have to deal with anyone or anything. Still, I have to admit it stung when he kept walking, said nothing; I couldn't help but imagine the way he undoubtedly would've run up and fussed if it had been Eugene lying here, unmoving. I almost said, *In case you're wondering, I'm not dead. Thanks for the concern, though,* but it felt more satisfying to say nothing, just lie there and blink back tears, luxuriating in my righteous indignation about being semi-ghosted, shoved to the ground, and now ignored by the people who are supposed to love you. I realized even then that my doing and saying nothing was a passive-aggressive test of the sort I'd just, not ten minutes prior, accused Vic of, but there was something wonderfully indulgent about it, almost romantic.

The footsteps continued down the driveway, around to the back of the house. As I heard the faint *squeak* of the porch screen door opening, I wondered if Dad was avoiding me on purpose, the way he had the previous night after my fight with Mom. It wasn't a big deal: she found out I changed majors—from philosophy and music to computer music, with a concentration in algorithmic composition—and had just gotten approval to graduate college a year early, which I hadn't told Dad or her about yet. It wasn't like I was keeping it a secret; it just didn't occur to me to discuss it with them. I talked to my professors and academic advisors, and honestly, I thought my parents would approve of my choosing a more practical field, not to mention be happy about saving a year's tuition.

"That's not the point," Mom said. "It's not the substance of the decision, but that you didn't bother telling us about it." I said sorry, but with the ridiculous course load I was carrying to pull this off, I was distracted and forgot to bring it up.

"But you've been back for months, and we've been together every day, at least for breakfast and dinner. Honestly, Mia, you act like a tenant. I know so much more about what's going on with John's life."

Oh, please. First: we didn't talk during dinner, due to mandatory daily Family Movie Night + Dinner, part of our parents' campaign to use the pandemic to bring us closer together. Second: I'm sorry, but John was a bit too much, with this weekly melodrama, breaking up and getting back together with his girlfriend, whom our parents *adored*. Between detailed reports of that, plus the family's collective angst about Henry's House—Eugene's therapy center and John's summer internship—battling to stay open through the quarantine, all I did during breakfast was listen and eat.

I thought for sure Dad would come into my room after Mom left, a combination of expressing his own hurt and smoothing things over between Mom and me, but he never did. Mom said at breakfast she and Dad wanted to "sit down with me" later, which sounded omi-nous. I thought about preempting the whole thing with a teary recital of the agony of the Vic breakup drama, but no, I was fairly certain I hadn't mentioned Vic to them, which would make it worse, add to Mom's point about my not telling them anything.

I closed my eyes and placed my face directly in the blinding sunbeam. The world turned blank. A bright orange. A kaleidoscope of phosphenes swirled, replaced by bursts of red that exploded like translucent fireworks, turning the palette darker and more intense, into a deep crimson. I squeezed my eyes tighter, and black pinpoints oozed into blobs like inkblots on wet paper, bouncing up and down in the same rhythm as Eugene's head in the window, the visual echoes of his jumps matching the *heee-boom* from above me. I lost myself in the rhythm of it all, the sun warming my eyelids, and let myself fall asleep.

# TWO

# Heuristics Traps Galore

THERE'S A CONCEPT IN HEURISTICS CALLED SELECTIVE PERCEPTION, a type of confirmation bias that describes the powerful human tendency to make assumptions and even perceive things differently based on how they align with our expectations. You expect $x$ to happen, something happens that's consistent with $x$ (although also with $y$ and $z$), so you decide $x$ has happened. I expected Dad to come home with Eugene, so when I heard footsteps on the driveway five minutes after Eugene got home, I thought, Dad. I felt this so easily, deeply, intuitively, that if you'd asked me (as Mom and John did four hours later) if I actually saw Dad, I'd have answered yes (and did). I didn't think of it as an assumption or decision or belief; it just *was*. Dad was home. Of course he was. Where else could he be, and besides, who else could it be?

Once you make that first assumption, another cognitive bias takes over: the anchoring bias, people's tendency to rely too heavily on the first piece of information we get on any given topic. Any subsequent information, we interpret in a skewed way, stubbornly clinging to the original assumption despite indications it may not be correct (like why would my dad, who's always been annoyingly inquisitive, just walk by his unmoving, supine daughter?). My Footsteps = Dad equation became a powerful anchor for all my later thoughts. When assumed-Dad silently passed by, I constructed an unlikely narrative about him not wanting to bother with me rather than rethink my assumption. When I heard Eugene still jumping in his room later in the day, I didn't think, *Hmmm, that's strange, Dad never lets Eugene jump that long, maybe that wasn't Dad I heard earlier,* but rather, *Thank God Dad's giving Eugene a break today, maybe he's finally learning to relax a little.*

As more time passed, the anchor sank deeper, and I hooked in others as well. When Mom texted later to ask if I'd seen Dad and Eugene because she was worried they got caught in the rain, I said yes, they got home way before the storm. After Mom and John got home, when we couldn't find Dad anywhere in the house, I said he must have lost his phone in the park and gone back to find it. It's almost frightening to think back on my hubristic certainty and my family's unquestioning acceptance even as the day went on and Dad's having returned home became more and more unlikely.

The reason I'm so focused on the why and how of my Footsteps = Dad assumption is that this, even more than my falling asleep, dictated when we started our search, a factor I've since learned is the single most predictive element in finding missing persons alive, regardless of age, circumstance, or setting. Based on a timeline I constructed using phone records, weather data, and timed re-creations, I've calculated how much time we lost by virtue of my erroneous assumption: four hours, give or take five minutes. Here's how I figure it: I hung up on Vic at 11:41 A.M., which means I went outside and fell around 11:45 and heard the footsteps around 11:50. If I'd made the tiniest effort to say a perfunctory hello or even look up, I would have realized it wasn't Dad, called or texted him, and then called or texted Mom and John. Mom and I are coolheaded—we don't panic, as a general matter—but John would definitely have freaked out and come home (a six-minute drive from his internship) and started searching immediately, which puts the beginning of this hypothetical search in earnest around 12:15 P.M., more than an hour before the storm.

So against this 12:15 P.M. benchmark, here's what actually happened: I woke up around 1:30 to raindrops on my face, slow and spaced apart but heavy in that ominous way you know means it's about to pour, and then a gust of wind whipping my hair into my eyes, simultaneous with a nearby *thunk,* which I thought was a tree branch falling onto our roof but have since realized must have been the wind slamming shut the front door. I staggered to the door closest to me (the side kitchen door we thankfully never lock), not quite making it inside before the sky opened up.

At 1:34, as I was hobbling into the shower, I heard my phone's text alert. I would have ignored it—I'd seen eight missed calls and a whole screen of texts from Vic, iterations of *You hung up on me? Seriously?!?!, Call me back!!!,* and *Hello?!?!* (Vic is big on serial exclamation and question marks)—but it was Mom's special *Twilight Zone* text tone and I was trying to get in her good graces after last night's fight, so I replied, assuring her that yes, Dad and Eugene had beaten the storm home and sure, I'd be happy to go around the house and close all the windows. I really did mean to do that, but I was already undressed, so I texted Dad to close the windows (*Please, per Mom,* I specified—I'm working on seeming less bossy) before I stepped into an extra-long, extra-hot shower.

We texted five more times. All family-logistical requests to Dad in his role as family shopper and cook—for more coffee and vodka (Mom), ice cream and frozen pizza (John), and sushi for dinner (me). Multiple unanswered texts, and it didn't occur to us to be concerned. Dad was our caretaker; *he* did the noticing, the paying attention, the rescuing from trouble. That was his job. (It was also arguably Mom's job, but only quasi when she was at home, not at all when she was working, the same way Dad was prior to their switching places four years ago.) If we noticed his nonresponse, it was out of annoyance, not concern, but honestly, I never noticed. The Vic situation was getting out of hand; I tried my best to ignore the barrage of calls and texts, but I ended up getting so fed up, I had to block him, leaving me seething about being forced to become the kind of person who blocks her ex-boyfriend.

At around 3:30, Mom and John got home early for some Zoom meeting about his now-canceled fall semester abroad. Mom went straight to Eugene's room as usual to give him a *hello-I-missed-you-today* hug. (No comment on the lack of a similar routine for me, except to say it's fine, I prefer no hugs anyway.) They both barged into my room within five minutes, John to say he couldn't find Dad anywhere, where was he?, and Mom to say Eugene was still wearing his muddy clothes and hiking shoes and he wouldn't stop jumping—what in hell was going on? I pointed out that I wasn't the no-shoes-in-the-house enforcer and perhaps Dad had gone out for errands. Mom said no, his car was here, and John added that Dad's phone was "off the grid."

"Off the grid? What are we, undercover spies?" It makes me cringe to remember this, how I rolled my eyes and laughed at John. I pulled up Dad's location on my phone: current location unknown, last known location at 11:12 A.M. along the waterfall trail, one of the few spots around the park with actual (albeit intermittent) cell coverage. It was obvious what had happened. "Look, his phone was in the park earlier. He's been home since then, so he must have left his phone in the park. That explains why he never texted us back. At some point, he realized what happened, so he went back to find it. It makes perfect sense."

"What? That makes no sense at all. Why would he leave without telling us?" John said.

"Umm, because he couldn't? He didn't. Have. His phone. That's what it means to lose something." I spoke slowly, overarticulating the way I do when John's being stupid. He hates that.

"But why didn't he leave a note? Or tell you in person?" John said without a hint of annoyance at, or mention of, my sarcasm, which was both unusual and troubling. He really was worried, which, in turn, worried me.

"A note? What century are we in? I'm sure he thought he'd be gone for like half an hour. He's probably on his way back right now."

We both looked to Mom. It was her policy to never get involved when we were bickering, but this was different. She sighed. I know her sighs well, and this particular one—short and loud, with a frown and a shake of the head—meant, *You two are too old for this juvenile bullshit*. She looked at me. "When's the last time you saw him in the house?"

Was there an inkling in the back of my mind, a trifling doubt, that I hadn't actually *seen* Dad, much less *in* the house, since they left for the park? But I could picture him—frowning and shaking his head at my lying around all day, and then giving me a wide berth by walking around to the back porch to go inside. I said, "When he first got home, like eleven-thirty or something."

"*Eleven-thirty?*" John said. "So for all we know, Dad twisted his ankle or something, and he's been sitting there for five hours, wondering why we're not coming to help him."

I wanted to tell him to chill out, mock his math skills, point out that 11:30 was *four* hours ago, but Mom said, "Let's calm down and talk through this. Now, Mia, when Dad got home, did he say anything about his phone? Did he look worried? Was he limping or hurt in any way?" Mining my three-second memory for clues, that's when I started thinking—did I look up? I saw his legs . . . or shoes? Right when it was dawning on me that I didn't actually see his face or hear his voice, Mom said she'd texted Dad to bring in the package we got that morning—did Dad do that? Did anyone else come by the house? Neighbors?

Ever since Mom and John walked in, the mood in the room had been changing gradually, our worry deepening bit by bit, question by question, small steps down a slight hill. The moment these two re-alizations converged—1) I did not see or hear Dad, and 2) there was another person (and therefore other feet) walking up our driveway that morning—that wasn't a little step down; it was a cliff, a fucking free fall.

"What package?" I asked. "When did it come?"

Mom frowned, shook her head. "Sometime this morning. Why?"

"What *time*? And where did they leave it? Can you please check?"

Mom checked the package-alert email, but I already knew. Inside the screen door to the back porch at 11:47 A.M., when I was lying outside, under Eugene's window, drowsy in the late-morning sun.

I told Mom and John. I felt strangely numb—I'm not sure if from the embarrassment of realizing my mistake or from a premonition of this being the start of something significant—and I used the numbness to feign a lightness I didn't feel. I spoke matter-of-factly, stuck to the facts: Eugene's push, hurt ankle, lying down, sun in my eyes, footsteps. I said there was still a chance it was Dad but probably not, in which case . . .

"In which case, Dad never came home. Eugene came home by himself, and Dad's been missing the whole frigging day, and you never even noticed," John said.

This was fair. Not only didn't I notice, but I actively impeded others in *their* efforts to notice. If John hadn't said it, I might have said it myself. But there's something about a sibling accusation—particularly from a twin—that triggers an instinct of denial. It went back to our toddler days, probably to the womb, elbowing each other. *Did not. Did too. Did not.*

I went on the offensive, said in as much of an amused-pity tone as I could manage, "*Missing?* You're blowing this way out of proportion. I'm sure Dad's fine. There are a million explanations." I rambled on with the first I could think of, a variation on my earlier lost-phone-search theory in which Dad went back to the park after escorting Eugene safely back to our neighborhood, but honestly, I wasn't buying it myself and I was struggling for something better, when it came to me: Eugene must have run off in the park. Yes, of course, that made sense, especially with the way he was running so fast this morning.

Dad searching for a phone for four hours through an awful storm—
that was crazy, I could admit that now. But if he thought Eugene was
lost in the woods, he would stay all day and all night, check behind
every tree, around every boulder, down every street in the surrounding neighborhood, until he found him. He wouldn't call us—he
couldn't anyway because of the spotty cell coverage, but even more,
Dad had this thing about being the family protector, bearing burdens
himself to spare us pain and worry. And he wouldn't even consider
the possibility of Eugene getting home on his own. Crossing streets
terrifies Eugene, and that four-lane quasi-highway separating our
neighborhood from the park, there were days it took Dad a good five
minutes to coax him to cross. No way he thought Eugene was home.

Later, on hold with a local emergency room, it would occur to
me: How *did* Eugene get home? I knew roads were much less busy
with the pandemic, but even so, Eugene crossing that road alone was
inconceivable, which meant Dad must have walked him across it to
our neighborhood and told him to run home only once they were on
our safe, familiar streets. This, of course, was the first time it occurred to me: Could Dad have run away intentionally?

In any case, at the time, we didn't stop to consider Eugene's route
home. What mattered was that we had a plausible explanation, one
consistent with a reality in which Dad was fine, out there looking everywhere but the one place where Eugene had safely been for hours.
Seen this way, it was almost comical—silly Dad!—and at one point,
I even said, "I can already tell—we're gonna be laughing about this
over dinner tonight, and Dad's gonna be so embarrassed. We should
make him do the dishes to pay for worrying us."

I don't want to give the wrong impression here. It wasn't all mirth
and merriment, or even a little. We weren't delusional; we knew it
wouldn't be as easy as going to the park and finding Dad wandering
around calling Eugene's name, running up to tell him Eugene was
home, and all hugging and laughing, TV-sitcom style. We didn't have
to say what was obvious, that a (if not the) likely reason for Dad's
long delay was that he was hurt. Mom merely said we should go look

for him and bring a first aid kit, just in case, and I said I'd call the nearby hospitals, just in case.

That was when John brought up calling the police. He said it like we'd already discussed it and made a decision. After I said my ankle was still sore and I didn't want to slow them down, so I should stay home, just in case Dad got back before they did, John said, "So when you call the police, give them our—"

"The *police*?" I said.

John looked at me, then at Mom, then back at me. He looked confused, like he couldn't figure out if he or I was the crazy one. "Umm, Dad is missing. That's what you do when people go missing—you call the police."

There he went with the "missing" again. "Stop saying he's *missing*. Dad's a grown man who's late getting home from somewhere he didn't even have to drive to. It's still daylight outside, for God's sake, and we haven't even taken five minutes to look for him. Besides, you can't report a missing person unless it's been twenty-four hours."

"What? Where'd you hear that? Some TV show?"

"I read it. In *The New Yorker*." (I hadn't. I'd seen it on *Law & Order: SVU*.)

I could see doubt creeping in, his face softening, his eyes looking down and to the side as if trying to remember if he'd read that. (He hadn't; he never reads the articles, only the cartoons.)

"Besides," I said, looking to Mom to settle our spat, "if the police get involved, you know they'll try to talk to Eugene, maybe take him to the police station. Do we really want that?"

The answer was no. Eugene didn't do well with strangers or new environments. It wasn't just a matter of Eugene's comfort—though that *was* paramount to us, especially Mom—but also the fear of the added stress making it harder to communicate with him. Before leaving for the park, Mom managed to get him to stop jumping so she could help him out of his dirty clothes and shoes, but the minute she asked what happened to Dad, hoping to glean something from his body language, facial expressions, gestures, *anything*, Eugene ran into his closet and refused to come out. Mom wanted to try asking again later, using these YES (smile), NO (frown), and I DON'T KNOW (shrug) picture cards, the latest in a long line of alternative communication tools Eugene's therapists had tried with him over the years. To preserve any chance of Eugene calming down enough to tell us something useful about Dad, we needed to keep the police away. That's what I said, and I won. Mom decided we should search for Dad ourselves for the time being.

I know what you're thinking. I'm thinking it, too. John was right; I was wrong. If we had called the police right away, they would have searched the water, looked for blood on the rocks, interviewed witnesses—all the stuff they did anyway, but early enough to have made a difference, for the trajectory of the investigation to change. Maybe.

But sometimes, when something happens, or rather, when something might have happened, you can keep your fear at bay by denying it. Confirming its seriousness by saying it out loud—"Hello, we have an emergency. Our dad is missing"—is not only terrifying but seems unwise when there are still two ways this might go. The moment hangs in balance like a seesaw, and the slightest wind could be the deciding factor between up or down, found or lost, safe or dead. I saw in Mom's eyes the same thought: calling the police would mean this was a big deal. Laughing it off as silly Dad might be just what we needed to make it fall the other way, tell the universe to leave it alone, let us be.

You don't have to say it; I know—wishing, pretending, doesn't make it so. We knew that. Maybe it was plain old-fashioned selfishness, a desire to sustain the relative tranquility of our lives a little longer, for Eugene's sake if nothing else. I could almost hear it, Dad saying, *I'm fine, don't worry about me; worry about Eugene—he's the one you have to take care of.* So that's what we did, and of course, looking back, it seems clear: buying ourselves this half day of ignorance—hardly blissful; let's call it pre-painful—brought us so much more trouble later.

WE STARTED OUR SEARCH FOR Dad in earnest at 4:04. Three hours and forty-nine minutes after we should have, would have, if only . . . you know. The park is four hundred acres of woods and creeks, bordered on the north by the Potomac River. The plan was for John to bike all around, using the trails to cover as much ground as possible, while Mom drove and walked around the park's perimeter and surrounding neighborhoods. I was to stay home with Eugene, give him a snack, keep him calm, maybe try asking him about Dad again, and call local hospitals.

I called eleven. I didn't realize we had so many ERs nearby. I told myself it was a waste of time, I was only doing it because Mom asked me to, but every time I asked whether an Adam Parson or a John Doe had been admitted that day, my chest muscles constricted, squeezing my stomach acid up my esophagus, and with every *no,* a release, everything unclenching and rushing back to its place. Between calls, I kept checking my family's location, waiting for something to change—refreshing John's location and Dad's old one, seeing the two dots get closer, closer together, then move apart, John's dot circling all around the park, Dad's ghost dot from this morning unchanging.

It was 6:03 when Mom called. I was lying on the floor in Eugene's room, next to Eugene, who was under a weighted blanket on a beanbag. His iPad was on a repeat loop of a Manhwa cartoon video he'd watched nonstop back in Korea. Mom had suggested this whole setup to comfort him and keep him regulated, but honestly, the video was helping me, too. We lived in Korea for eight years, from when I was five to thirteen, and this video still immediately transports me back to our Seoul apartment—something about the mellifluence of the animated children's informal banmal style of conversation—and I needed that just then. I answered Mom's call and talked first: "Okay, I checked with every hospital in a fifty-mile radius and there's no sign of Dad. And yes, I remembered to check John Doe."

Mom didn't say anything, and I almost hung up, thought it must be the spotty cell coverage. I said, "Mom? You there? Any updates?" before Mom started speaking. She said they looked everywhere. She said she drove all around, John biked all around—on trail, off trail, around the woods, along the river, in the neighborhoods—and there was no sign of Dad anywhere, and the whole park was empty and eerie, mud puddles everywhere from the storm earlier, no one around.

"Mia," Mom said, and I remember sitting up at that, the way she said my name. It sounded like an important announcement. "Mia," she said again. "We can't find him. We're afraid. . . ." She cleared her throat. "We need to call the police."

I nodded. Said okay. Said come home and see you in a few minutes and hung up.

I looked out Eugene's window. It was strange—it wasn't even 6:30 on a summer evening, and looking at the sky, you'd have sworn it was sunset. It must have been the post-storm clouds—the sky looked dusky, the sun peeking through a break in the clouds near the horizon, casting a fiery glow. The clouds looked like a distant mountain ridge, a bluish gray the color of a fading bruise, the sky around the sun a soft red, too uniform to be real. I wondered if this was a dream, the product of my sleep-deprived mind processing the melodrama with Vic.

The Manhwa children were singing a happy ditty in G major punctuated by high-pitched chortles that pierced and grated, the cartoon-video equivalent of nails on a chalkboard. "Eugene, sweetie, that's really loud. Let's turn it down, okay?" I reached for the iPad. Eugene brought the screen closer to his face, gripped it tighter. His thumbs blanched from the pressure, and looking so close up at the moons of grime and dirt under his nails, I noticed a crescent of dark red under his right thumbnail.

I sat up. Leaning in and craning to look at his other fingernails, I saw the same slivers of red under his right index and middle fingernails. I got up to look for the yellow shirt and the shorts he'd been wearing earlier and found them on a pile of dirty clothes behind his bathroom door. Just as I held up the shirt to inspect a blot of dark red on the shoulder, the doorbell rang.

Even before I saw the police uniforms through the peephole, I had the feeling of everything changing. Their flashing lights must have been on, the red-and-blue strobe beams slicing through the faux-sunset backdrop and setting my senses on edge. I don't remember seeing the lights, but I must have. That's the only explanation I have for what I did next. I scooped up the pile of Eugene's dirty clothes and rushed to the laundry room to throw them into the washer with heavy-duty detergent. I pressed Start. As the doorbell rang again, I ran back to Eugene, whispered "come on," and led him into the bathroom. I turned on the shower and told him to get in. I put soap on a sponge and handed it to him, pointed to his fingernails. I mimed scrubbing, told him to scrub hard. Get everything off. Wash it away, clean.

# THREE

# This Could Get Bad

IT TOOK ME A LONG TIME TO ACTUALLY OPEN THE FRONT DOOR. YOU'RE probably guessing (the way John did when I told him everything later) that I was freaking out, second-guessing what I'd just done and wondering if I'd destroyed evidence that could lead us to Dad. But I wasn't. I was 99 percent positive what was under Eugene's nails and on his shirt: the dried remnants of Dad's blood. It wasn't a big deal. It happened from time to time during difficult therapy exercises. Dad is goofy, and to reward Eugene for working hard, Dad would throw him up in the air, which Eugene loves. Lately, with Eugene getting so big, it became more like Eugene jumping, with Dad half-supporting, half-boosting him. Sometimes, their timing would be off and Eugene would end up kicking or scratching Dad by accident. That had to be what happened. But if the police saw it, they would misunderstand, and God knows what they'd do to Eugene.

So, no, the blood wasn't the problem. The problem was what I'd read while researching the can't-file-police-report-for-twenty-four-hours thing I'd bickered about with John. I looked it up and it turned out he was right: it's a myth. "Given how critical the first twenty-four hours are in locating missing persons, why would we forbid missing-person reports for the first twenty-four hours? It's nonsense," some FBI specialist was on record as saying. Experts blamed Hollywood, speculating that 24 must have made it up to cover some plot hole. One blog post addressing this went on to discuss another TV-propagated myth as being true: when someone is dead, the police show up at your house unannounced to notify the next of kin.

I don't tend to believe in things like kismet or fate or whatever, but the co-occurrence of 1) the police showing up without my having called yet 2) within an hour of my reading this article 3) while my dad was un-locatable—it seemed too remarkable to be coincidence. It occurred to me that I'd called all the hospitals but none of the morgues. I stood there, sick, like I might throw up, with cramps in my stomach (I hadn't eaten since breakfast, had no idea if it was hunger or stress or maybe my period starting— What day was it? What month?), and I took yoga breaths because I was light-headed but then I was breathing too loudly, and shit, the police were saying, "Hello? Is someone there?" I was seriously contemplating tiptoeing into a closet, but out the side window, I saw Mom's car turning in to our driveway and John's bike right behind. I had to pull it together, for them, handle some of the hard parts myself. I opened the door.

"Hi, we're here about a car accident that occurred this morning in this neighborhood," the female cop said, and I saw Dad on our narrow, winding road, a car smashing into his body and catapulting him up, Eugene freaking out and running, running, running. Of course. That's how Eugene had crossed the road; he hadn't been by himself, not at first. I couldn't imagine the trauma. No wonder why he'd jumped nonstop for hours, why he'd run into the closet.

"Is he dead?" I said, my words coming out in a rasp I didn't recognize.

The police seemed taken aback. The woman said, "I'm sorry,

who's dead?," the same time the man said, "What? No. Everyone's fine."

A lot happened right after that, which I tried to focus on, but my brain was stuck on *everyone's fine*. The surge of relief was like a riptide that whips you around. Mom and John ran up, talking over each other—Did we know anything yet? Was Dad home?—and the confused officers clarified they were here about a boy, identified by neighbors as a resident of our house, who may have caused a car accident. They said they needed to talk to him and his parents, not only for accident-reporting purposes, but for, as the female cop put it, "child welfare and protective purposes."

That phrase was the verbal equivalent of a slap; it stopped everything—Mom's and John's overlapping blathering, the *everyone's fine* relief chant in my head, the ground swaying. We knew what those words meant, had heard enough horror stories about Child Protective Services investigations of child endangerment, neglect, and abuse from other special-needs families. A kid with Eugene's disabilities running around public streets unsupervised—it was the kind of thing that gets kids taken away. For a second, I even thought, Dad had better be in trouble because if he's not, this could get bad, quick. And then a more sobering follow-up: he *was* in trouble, real trouble. No way he'd let what happened to Eugene happen if he wasn't.

John, Mom, and I looked at one another, and I felt that same certainty zap through and unite us. John started to stammer something, but Mom cleared her throat and stepped forward, squeezing John's arm as if to say *I got this,* and I saw something I can only describe as a don't-fuck-with-my-family oomph come over Mom's face. "I'm Dr. Hannah Park, mother of the boy you're looking for," Mom said, which surprised me; she usually omitted "Doctor," reasoning that most people equated that title with an MD, rather than the PhD in applied linguistics she has. More than that, though, what surprised me was how authoritative she sounded and looked. I realize this isn't the type of thing one should fixate on at a time like this, but it was really something, the change that came over Mom. It was like she became a real person. Not that she's not a real person, obviously, but I didn't think of Mom as existing outside the sphere of being our mom, with qualities beyond that nondescript mom-ish mix of caring and perpetually tired. And it's not that I didn't know she was smart— I'd read her dissertation on the inadequacies of the existing romanization systems for Korean and used the phonetic-spelling approach she proposed for my own thesis—but the way she talks sometimes made me forget. She speaks English like an immigrant—with an accent and a too-perfect syntax that sounds awkwardly geeky, foreign. It usually embarrassed me, but watching her as an outsider might, I was struck by the impressiveness of her formal diction, the regal dignity of her hyper-articulated syllables. She explained Eugene's condition, taking care to emphasize that Eugene was safe at home—loved, cared for, and closely supervised by Dad and her, of course, but also by us, his twenty-year-old siblings—and also explained the "confluence of events exacerbated by Eugene's inability to speak" that led us to not realize until recently that Dad hadn't returned home.

She said all this calmly, quickly, but describing her and John's search of the park, her voice started to break. "I know you came here about the car accident involving my son, and I will take full responsibility and cooperate . . ." Mom blinked, like she was trying not to cry, and I reached for her hand and squeezed. Mom swallowed and continued. ". . . but I'm asking you to delay that investigation until we find my husband. Please. We need your help."

Things happened very quickly after that. The police responded with a systematic and urgent efficiency, gathering Dad's information and pictures and calling them in. Within fifteen minutes, an interjurisdictional search involving the police and park rangers was under way. The two officers said they were leaving to coordinate, but not to worry, a detective had been assigned to the case, someone with "expertise in these matters." John wanted to go with them to show them his own earlier search sites, Dad's favorite trails, the picnic tables he liked to use, but they said no, he'd already shown them on the map, and besides, they needed us to stay to talk to the detective.

"I won't tell you not to worry because of course you will," said the female officer I'd decided I liked, "but take care of yourselves. Take care of Eugene. Go inside. Sit. Eat. Leave things to us for a while."

I'm not good at leaving things to other people. John routinely accuses me of being a control freak, and I know myself well enough to know that's not entirely unfair, especially for things I consider important. But at that moment, the police officer's words were a salve. Sometimes, it's a relief to cede control.[2] All responsibility, decisions, and analyses transferred to people with expertise—such a beautiful word, *expertise*—who are promising to take care of the situation, to do a better job than you could on your own. It shamed me that I'd been so against calling the police. John never even called me on it. As the officers were leaving, he thanked them for starting a search even though it hadn't been twenty-four hours, and they said no problem, there was no twenty-four-hour rule or anything like that, and that was that. I stood nearby, waiting for John to say something, to gloat or maybe casually and subtly work it into conversation, but he never did.

John went to make us something to eat, and I went upstairs to tell Mom the police were gone. She'd gotten Eugene out of the shower and was helping him get dressed for the detective, who was due soon. I stuck my head into his room and saw Eugene, out of the shower and dressed in the dressiest clothes he'll tolerate: a polo shirt,

---

2 This is one of the things I sometimes miss about being little: having to do whatever your parents tell you to do. Don't get me wrong, John and I did our share of rebelling, but at the end of the day, we trusted and respected our parents. I remember when Eugene first got diagnosed with autism (we found out about Angelman later), Mom and Dad sitting me down, saying how responsible and mature I was, so they were going to give me more independence and rely on me to do more things myself. I was nine, and I was so proud—I'd been complaining I wasn't a *baby*, to please just let me deal with my own life—but I also remember the slight panic that came over me. Like, okay, now what? And after that, every time I was confused and wanted to ask them what I should do, I'd think back to our conversation and remind myself how I couldn't let them down, how proud they'd be to know I dealt with it all myself.

long pants, and even socks, which he usually hates. Mom was combing his wet hair into a neat part, standing behind him, looking at him in the mirror with so much tenderness I wanted to cry.

"Hey." My word came out in a whisper. "You look so handsome, Eugene."

Mom looked at me in the mirror and smiled, finished combing his hair, and straightened his collar. It occurred to me that Eugene probably couldn't scrub his hands by himself, at least not well. As furtively as I could, I looked down at his fingers, his nails. Clean.

Downstairs, John was yelling that the detective was here, calling us down. Mom brushed my hair to the side, out of my eyes. She took Eugene's left hand, and I took his right. Before we started walking together, she smiled at me as if to say, *It's okay. It'll be okay. Everything will turn out fine.*

# FOUR

# Snowflakes, Rainbows, and the Vortex of Overanalysis Hell

I KNEW THE DETECTIVE. OR, RATHER, I'D MET HER, REMEMBERED HER six-foot-tall figure and super-short, super-red hair from three years ago when she spoke at our high school after three student suicides in two months. Detective Morgan Janus. As we introduced ourselves, she looked at me, narrowed her eyes like she was trying to focus, and said, "The importance of semantic connotations? River Falls High School?" At my embarrassed nod, she said, "I thought I recognized you, even with your mask on."

She explained to Mom how I'd come up to her to discuss the police officials' use of the phrase *committed suicide*. I'd argued the phrase was inherently judgmental, connoting guilt—you commit a crime, commit fraud, murder, sin; you don't commit strokes or depression. "Mia reminded us these were their friends who'd died, how it hurt to feel like we were victim-blaming them," Detective Janus said and turned to me. "We changed the departmental policy on that. It's part of our sensitivity training now. So thank you."

I always thought I'd been pretty obnoxious, lecturing adults—worse, the police—all strident with that self-righteousness of youth. It was the kind of thing that made me blush to remember once I was in college and made me more careful, wondering what I was doing or saying that would shame me in ten years. Still, I can't deny that her show of appreciation flattered me. Now, knowing what she'd just discovered and was hiding from us, I suspect that was her point—to play good cop, get us to trust her—but at the time, I thought she was simply being nice.

She continued her warming-up-to-us spiel (not that I thought that at the time), emphasizing her background as a licensed social worker and how she'd started out as a family therapist. She didn't say, "So you can trust me," but that was the clear implication. She emphasized this background so much I didn't even think of her as a cop—more as a counselor, to help us through the emotional difficulties. We clearly had a hero-worship thing going on (especially John, who's considering going into social work) because when I picture her now, with the persistent I-understand-your-pain frown between her brows and eyes so wide she looked perpetually surprised, I can't understand how I didn't immediately spot her fakery.

For an hour, we sat at our screened-in porch table (even Eugene, although she allowed him to watch videos with headphones) and answered questions. She asked us about that morning, to catalog for her what was usual and what was not. The usual part was easy. We're a family that depends on routine and schedules, and the broad strokes of our mornings had been the same throughout the pandemic. We even had a laminated chart for Eugene, with corresponding alarms set on his iPad. At 7:30 A.M., Dad woke us up; we showered, got dressed, and came downstairs by 8:00 to help Dad make breakfast; at 8:15, we sat at the fancy dining room table for family breakfast, a tradition Dad started when he realized how much calmer Eugene was in the mornings, before he's gotten overwhelmed by all the sensory inputs of the day; we went upstairs at 9:15 to brush our teeth; at 9:30, we dispersed—John to his internship at Henry's House, a nearby therapy center (one of the few jobs exempt from the lockdown), Mom to the empty office space she started renting in early June to focus on her translation work, Dad and Eugene off to the park for therapy exercises, hiking, and a picnic lunch, and me to my room for "thesis research," consisting mostly of sleeping, listening to music, and trolling music composition discussion forums ("Smart music is neither smart nor musical. Discuss."). Step by step, functionally, this morning was like every other morning, down to the minute.

Detective Janus is one of those people who nods the entire time you're saying something, like a bobblehead doll. "That's very help-ful," she said in a tone that made me think it actually wasn't. She looked at us—really gazed at each of us in turn as if to forge personal connections—and said, "Your mornings are the same the way snow-flakes are the same." It sounded vaguely Confucian, like one of those fortune-cookie non-fortunes I hate—the first flicker of suspicion—but I knew what she meant.

"Focusing on differences," she said, "is there anything out of the ordinary from this morning, anything at all, even minor things?"

Abnormality was a big thing with Detective Janus. Anytime we told her something we remembered, she'd ask, "Is that unusu-al? Atypical in any way?" If the answer was yes, her interest level quadrupled. Mom and John were annoyed by it, I could tell, frus-trated by her dozen-plus follow-up questions about Dad wearing gym shorts instead of his usual khaki shorts, for example. But—and this is what I blame for so stupidly and entirely letting down my guard—it made me feel a kinship with her. I share her obsessive fascination with small changes that have drastic implications. In my experience, studying variances is the best way to gain a full understanding of the norm. And sometimes, it's the tiniest difference that can make the most difference.

Take DNA, which taught me this lesson during a field trip to the Smithsonian in middle school. "Humans have more than ninety percent of their DNA in common with apes and ninety-nine percent with other humans," the guide said. The class oohed and aahed, and

John and the other boys got all hyper and did this frantic jump-dance resembling a gang of chimpanzees on crack. The guide was delighted by our delight, and she elaborated on the similarity of all humans, how in fact you could have more DNA in common with someone of a different race and gender than with someone who looks like you. To illustrate, she pointed to John and me—we were standing next to each other—and said, "So you, a girl of Asian ancestry, could share more DNA with this boy of European ancestry than with this other girl who looks like you," and here, she pointed to Becky Nguyen.

Our classmates guffawed, and someone yelled out, "But John and Mia are twins!" The guide laughed, an oh-you-crazy-kids chuckle, but with an uncertain look, like she wasn't quite sure if we were messing with her, and looked at me.

I felt my cheeks burn with humiliation—I still have this distinct memory of trying to convince myself I should feel embarrassed *for* her, not *by* her, and failing—but I managed to look her straight in the eye, serious and dignified, and say in the most you're-a-dumbass-but-I'll-deign-to-talk-to-you tone, "It's true. John and I are fraternal twins. Also, we're half-Korean, and Becky is Vietnamese, and I think we look nothing alike."

At home that night, I looked through our family's genetics report in Eugene's medical files. Until Eugene was seven, his sole diagnosis was autism. But at some autism conference, Mom was talking about Eugene's smile and how grateful she was he's so happy, and someone brought up Angelman syndrome. The geneticists who confirmed it tested the whole family to figure out comorbidities, and they included an analysis of John's and my chromosomal differences in a three-page footnote, which, given the super-small font, was probably longer than the main report itself. Extrapolating from the details, I calculated that John's DNA and mine are 99.97 percent identical.

For people who are only 1/3333rd different, it's remarkable how dissimilar we look. We must have gotten opposite genes from our parents with no overlap, the maximal disparate DNA combination possible for siblings. John got the pretty parts—Dad's round, deep-set moss-brown eyes framed by Mom's delicate bone structure and dainty nose—while I got the angular leftovers—Dad's Roman nose and thick unibrow, Mom's narrow-set eyes. We both have black hair, but John's is wavy with a reddish tint, whereas mine is a straight, sassy black with a blue sheen.[3]

We have one identical feature, our unusually long, thick eyelashes, but even that accentuates our differences. John does this thing where he stares into your eyes, blinks in slow motion, then looks askance like he's shy, leaving you to marvel at the beauty—the sheer length and sheen—of his lashes. It's nauseating, and I put up with it only because it hypnotizes our parents into a Jesus-like, all-transgressions-forgiven mode. I, on the other hand, have been told I have a tendency to blink rapidly while frowning, like a little girl trying on too-long, too-heavy false eyelashes for the first time.

And if the ramifications of our 0.03% DNA variance—girl versus boy, musical versus athletic, hyperlexic versus (relatively) monosyllabic—seem drastic, think of Eugene, how a nick in one of three billion DNA strands has so profoundly impacted his life. Things many people consider fundamental to the core of a human existence—the ability to will your face to match and express your feelings, to expect your body to obey your commands, to use words to communicate—these are things this infinitesimal partial defect in 0.00000003% of Eugene's genes has ripped away from him.

So the point I'm getting at is that I, of all people, know about microscopic differences. I know they matter, and my family knows they matter. We've thought about and lived with this reality more than

---

3 It's always irked me that the gender mismatch in our looks has girls swooning over John's "pretty-boy" face, whereas people call me "handsome," which I've learned is not a compliment. Whenever men have features deemed "feminine," that makes them more attractive to women (thus, the sensitive male who isn't afraid to cry and the pretty-boy thing girls love), whereas women with "masculine" features (like my strong jaw and nose, and my no-nonsense get-stuff-done attitude) seem to repel men. Proof that women are less rigid about gender conformity and heteronormativity than men? Discuss.

most, and normally, I would have applauded Detective Janus's scrutiny of minutiae. But time was limited; daylight was dwindling. We didn't want to sit around our house talking—about that morning, our family, or anything else. We wanted to be in the park—we wanted *her* to be in the park, searching the woods, the trails, everywhere. An hour into this, our minute-by-minute accounting and Detective Janus on a repeat loop asking if that was unusual/atypical/uncommon/unexpected, I noticed the moon becoming visible in the darkening sky. I looked at the clock. 8:15.

Mom said something about Dad wanting to have family dinner in the dining room that night, and I thought, Oh please please *please* do not ask if this was "out of the ordinary in any way" one more time or I will scream, but of course Detective Janus did, and I wanted to yell that yes, goddammit, our entire lives were out of the ordinary, the whole fucking world was these days, so would you mind pretty please just focusing on the thing that was most not-ordinary of all, my dad's disappearance, and just go out there and find him instead of wasting time talking to us?

I managed to say rather than yell this (minus the *goddammit, fucking,* and *pretty,* with an extra *please* at the end). But even with the tonal and phraseological muting, it came out pretty bitchy, and John and even Mom looked unsure how or if to respond. Detective Janus didn't react, though, just kept nodding and said not to worry, they had a dual parallel process, and even as she was talking to us, multiple teams were canvassing the park, including several canine units.

"Canine?" I said.

"Dogs, to pick up scent," she said. I wanted to shout that I knew what canine meant, did she think I was stupid?, but all I could think was, this was serious. You didn't have canine searches unless . . .

"My dad's allergic to dogs," I said, the same time John said, "Scent of what?"

Detective Janus looked at me the way people look at Eugene when he jump-splaughs in elevators, and then turned to John. "Blood, in case he's injured. But just human scent, too—he could be lost or fallen somewhere. Your mom gave us some of his clothes earlier for that. But bear in mind: usually, when people don't come home, it's intentional; they're not in distress. Something happens and they get called away—a friend has an emergency, or they just want to get away and clear their head, and they forget to tell their family or they can't because something happened to their phone, that type of thing. So that's why it's important we talk to you, friends, trace credit cards, geo-locate, ask about domestic squabbles, and so forth."

"Squabbles?" John said. "You think Dad's fine and he left because he's mad at Mom?"

Mom shook her head. "Adam would never do that. He would never leave Eugene alone, no matter what other things *came up*."

"Of course, of course," Detective Janus said, but in the tone you use to placate an unreasonable child, a throwaway as she pivoted to logistics, handed Mom consent forms to sign.

"No, not *of course*." Mom dropped the papers on the table and sat up taller. "I need to know you're taking what we're telling you seriously. This isn't a man late getting home for dinner because he's off somewhere with some woman and forgot to call. He was with our child who can't talk. Who almost got hit by a car. This is not a *usually* case. Something is terribly wrong."

"I understand, and I assure you, I'm not treating this lightly, and neither are my colleagues who are coordinating with the park rangers and rescue crews and preparing to work all night if they have to, as will I. But I've been doing this for a long time, and the worst thing we can do is jump to conclusions too early. So I'm going to keep an open mind and try to gather as much information as possible, both to help my colleagues searching the park *and* to consider why else he might be missing, if for no other reason than to rule those out."

She asked Mom to sign the consent forms for accessing phone and banking records and life-insurance policy information.

"Life insurance? Why would you need life insurance?" Mom

scanned the form. "Wait, are you thinking . . . Do you specialize in suicides? Is that why they sent you?"

"No, I handle all types of cases."

"But suicide . . . that's something you're considering?"

She peered at Mom, not blinking, and said, "At this early stage, it's my job to consider *all* possibilities."

*All possibilities.*

That phrase set the constituent parts of my body bursting and racing—my thoughts, my nerves, my blood. This tall woman, a detective, thought Dad might be dead by suicide. And who knew what else was among the "*all* possibilities" she was considering? Maybe that Dad was like those moms who get sick of their kids and run away—did stay-at-home dads do that, too? And if suicide was on the table, why not homicide?

I thought of Eugene's shove, the blood under his nails and on his shirt. I thought of the way Detective Janus had asked us several times in a (carefully calibrated?) throwaway tone, evenly spaced throughout the evening, why we didn't call the police right away. Was she wondering when—*if*—we would have called if the police hadn't happened to come by about the accident?

My worry for Dad, lack of sleep, guilt and confusion, concern for Eugene—those were swirling into a jumble of panic and paranoia that was messing with my judgment, what was left of it, and all of a sudden, I was mad at Dad, furious with him, for not being here, for causing this mess, and then furious at myself for being disloyal and self-centered and awful. Which may be why I downplayed what happened next.

Mom was asking about the car accident—any injuries, if she could talk to the driver—and Detective Janus took out the accident report. When she read, "Driver reports proceeding slowly after full stop at intersection," I noticed Eugene squeeze his eyes shut and shake his head as if in an emphatic *no*. I thought something in his video must be upsetting him, but when Detective Janus placed the report on the table, he lowered his iPad and craned his neck, as if reading it. I almost said something, but Mom picked up the report and Eugene turned back to his show, and I told myself Eugene couldn't read.

On her way out, Detective Janus reminded us to write down anything unusual we remembered. It was funny how all along, I'd insisted—not just said, for show, but actually believed—there was nothing like that, but now with her "all possibilities" backdrop, everything changed, every facet of our breakfast taking on a sinister overtone. It was like when I first got contact lenses, how once I put in those tiny discs of plastic, those fuzzy orange blobs on our wallpaper morphed into intricate red-and-yellow geometric patterns. Details were jumping out at me, from the way I grabbed salt at breakfast and Dad said, "Mia, you should taste it before you assume it needs salt" (trying to teach me one last life lesson?), to him making real bacon instead of our usual tofu bacon (a last-meal treat, knowing cholesterol issues would soon be moot?).

But even more than those specifics I noticed only in retrospect, there was a different feel to the breakfast as a whole—a bit off, or rather, too on, everything 5 percent brighter than usual. Eugene's smile, for one, seemed less nebulous, directed at and connected to specific comments and people, his happiness rising and waning in waves rather than remaining steady at one level. Once, he laughed at a joke Mom told. He often laughed when everyone else laughed, but that morning, I noticed him looking at Mom directly, his eyes in focus, like he got the joke and was laughing at *that* rather than due to some contagion effect.

Also, Dad and Mom were nice to each other—not married-twenty-five-years ho-hum nice but first-date *nice* nice: Dad complimented Mom on earrings she'd been wearing for a month straight, and Mom thanked Dad for making coffee, which he'd done every day for four years, maybe more. I wondered if they'd fought, exchanged words of the regrettable-but-not-so-awful-as-to-require-a-full-on-apology variety. I kicked John under the table to see if he noticed, but he just said, "Ow, stop," and then *he* was overly nice to Dad, thanking him for getting the peach yogurt he mentioned liking the previous week, saying, "It's so thoughtful of you to notice, Dad. You're such a great dad. You do so much for us. Thank you, Dad. Truly. Thank you."

Okay, if it weren't for the over-the-top *truly* (truly!) and the second "thank you," I might have made it through, but I couldn't not laugh, which, given the coffee in my mouth, led to my near-choking. Once my coughing fit was over, I was about to tell them all to cut it out, it was too much saccharine for this early in the morning—my family needs my over-bluntness from time to time—but it occurred to me that maybe I was the problem. Sure enough, Mom and John were frowning at me, Dad was shaking his head in a disappointed-but-not-surprised way, and no one asked if I was okay. I thought of Mom's words the previous night, that I needed to try to be (or at least act like I wanted to be) a part of our family, not a tenant. I looked down at my food and mumbled, "Sorry." I was tempted to say "truly" and a second "sorry," but I didn't. I just ate.

I think Dad felt bad for me, or maybe he wanted to fix the awkwardness. He patted my arm and said, "It's okay. Truly. It's okay," and winked. Eugene looked straight at me and laughed—again, not a social-contagion, going-through-the-motions laugh—which made *me* laugh. Dad said to John, "And *you,* I *really* appreciate your appreciation. *Truly,*" making John and Mom laugh, too. At this moment of maximal warm gooeyness, Dad lifted his glass. Dad is very into giving toasts, loves using them to get all philosophical and orate about life and family and sometimes the universe, how far we've come, blah blah. But he didn't; he placed his crystal water goblet into a pinpoint beam of sunlight coming through the window, creating tiny rainbows on the table, and said, "Look, Eugene, your favorite." Eugene was already smiling, of course, but he looked up (at the ceiling, for more rainbows?), down, and then back at Dad, and they both chuckled. If I didn't know better, I'd have said he was joking around, rolling his eyes at Dad's corniness like a teenager.

After Detective Janus left, I replayed this scene in my head, trying to figure out how to interpret it. If this breakfast turned out to be our last together, was it a lucky coincidence that we gained a memory filled with kindness and laughter and even rainbows—these ridiculously wondrous things we can savor? Or was it a clue to be mined, a sign of a man who sensed or perhaps planned some coming doom and wanted to say goodbye? And the (possible) eye roll from Eugene—was that a sign of something going on with him?

I wished I could talk through these micro-anomalies with Mom and John, ask if they noticed them, if they were worried about the implications, if these were even anomalies to begin with. But they hated what Mom called my "vortex" mode (as in, "Warning, warning: you're sinking into a vortex of overanalysis hell")—Dad was the one who most indulged me—and besides, we were too busy to sit around speculating. Mom called everyone—friends, neighbors, Eugene's therapists, other special-needs families—and went through Dad's things, files, bills, looking for anything unusual, per Detective Janus's instructions.

John decided to work with Eugene, explain to him what was happening and try asking what happened to Dad using the YES-NO picture cards, as well as other alternative communication cards and apps featuring pictures of activities, foods, and toys Eugene could use to tell us his needs and wants. It was a long shot. Eugene hated picture-based systems; he'd never managed to pass tests for pointing to the correct picture, and recently, he'd apparently been flat-out refusing to cooperate. Besides, how could anyone use this limited array of preschool-level pictures to say what happened to someone they love? There was no picture for *lost* or *kidnapped* or *attacked and hurt and lying in the middle of the woods, waiting desperately for help.*

Mom assigned me the job of hacking into Dad's laptop, email, cloud, and phone accounts. They both used this top-security password app, so Dad's passwords were all on his phone (which, of course, we didn't have), but she thought he might have kept old passwords on some accounts. For two hours straight, I tried various birthday, anniversary, Social Security, name, and initial combinations, but nothing worked. I was about to give up when I remembered the 1-terabyte portable hard drive I'd gotten Dad for Christmas, which he used to back up his laptop.

I found it in Dad's desk, in a drawer under a manila folder. A handful of loose pages fell out, and I was putting them back in the folder when I noticed what looked like code. Each page had questions in Dad's handwriting, followed by letters in his neater block print with numbers off to the side:

Form of energy widely used today?
    BMAK                                     2:31
Layer of atmosphere our lesson's about?
    MYOOF                                  4:28
Tell me 1 of 5 types of alt energy? (Switch to full)
    WUGXFHQL                           6:23

What the fuck? The questions seemed easy, like basic science questions meant to hide code in those espionage movies Dad loves. Was Dad a spy? Or maybe Dad put his random passwords in a form undecipherable to anyone but himself? On the inside of the manila folder itself, Dad had written *LOGIN—UYV@1019.* Login for what? A portal for covert ops agents?

I brought both the hard drive and the manila folder to my room. Sure enough, the backup drive wasn't password-protected; plugged into my computer, it opened right up to Dad's desktop view. A bunch of folders—Bills, Insurance, Taxes, Kids, Eugene-Medical, Eugene-Therapy, Eugene-School, Eugene-HenrysHouse, all standard stuff— and one file. A PDF named *2018_LifeInsPol_AJP.* Dad's life insurance policy? Why was it not in a folder? What did it mean that it was the only file not in a folder?

I was trying to calm down, force my uncooperative hand to move the mouse to click it open, when I noticed another unnerving thing: a column of folders separated from the others on the right, and translucent, as if meant to be hidden. HQ-General, HQ-Research,

HQ-Hypotheses, HQ-Experiments. I double-clicked HQ-Experiments. It asked for the password. Shit. I tried with the other HQ files. Same thing. All password-protected. I right-clicked, looked at the properties. Twenty-four subfolders in HQ-Experiments alone. What was this? What was HQ? Headquarters was all I could think of, but experiments? Hypotheses?

Wait. The login written inside the manila folder. *UYV@1019*. It was eight characters, and the password input required . . . yes! Eight characters! My fingers kind of shook as I typed in the letters—I really hadn't slept or eaten, I was freaked out and scared, and the world was woozy in a very unpleasant way—and I pressed Enter.

Nothing.

I found and tried all the 8-letter codes on the pages inside the manila folder, all the 4-letter codes in combination in different orders, UYV + 5-letter and 1019 + 4-letter combos, 7 letters with numbers and symbols. Nothing, nothing, nothing.

I took a deep breath, told myself to keep working. I was going through the codes again to enter in reverse order when Mom knocked and popped her head in to say she and John hadn't found anything useful—nothing from Dad's friends, nothing from Eugene—and how were things going? I opened my mouth to tell her about the hard drive, but something stopped me. It was the way Mom looked—dejected and weary, a heavy sagginess infusing every part of her body from her eyebrows to her ankles—and I didn't want to burden her with yet another unknown, unknowable thing.

But no. Mom had told us earlier how Detective Janus had taken her aside to warn her about marital issues coming out and ask if she'd like to receive updates without John or me around. "I told her there's nothing like that," Mom said. "Our lives just aren't that interesting. Besides, we can't afford to waste time right now. We have to tell one another everything. John, no holding back, worrying about hurting my feelings. Mia, no shutting us out and trying to do everything yourself. We share everything. Agreed?"

We did, and not just because Mom was in scary-dictatorial-do-what-I-say-or-else mode. If we learned anything from the murder mysteries Dad chose for Family Movie Nights, it's that one person always holds some seemingly irrelevant information that's key to solving the puzzle, but only if combined with some bit someone else knows. How many times did we collectively yell at the TV, "Oh my God, just *talk* to each other already!" and want to bonk their heads through the screen?

I said, "Actually, I found some stuff that . . . Here, let me show you. I'm not sure what to make of it," and Mom was walking in when we heard the *thwack-thwack* of a helicopter approaching. We heard helicopters all the time—our house was apparently in some flight path for the White House—but this sounded different, closer, as if it were headed right to us. Mom walked into the hallway, and I followed. John and Eugene came out, too, and we all looked out the hallway window toward the park. We couldn't see beyond the trees, but the helicopter noise was settling into a steady chuff, circling and hovering over one area. It was hot in the house—I'd never closed the windows like Mom asked—but I felt cold, my arms and hands starting to shiver.

We looked at each other. Mom opened her arms and pulled us into a group hug like when we were little, squeezing Eugene between all of us the way he loves, the deep pressure calming him, calming all of us. We stayed there like that, huddled in one another's arms, feeling the warmth of our bodies together, our breaths in synchrony, until we could no longer hear the helicopter.

# FIVE

## Requiem

THERE'S THIS MOMENT RIGHT WHEN YOU WAKE UP AFTER SOMETHING horrible has happened, and everything seems normal. A halfway point between asleep and awake, where both worlds seem equally plausible. You're no longer in the dream world, but your memory clings, its vestiges fast overtaken and displaced by the sensorial realities of the moment—the feel of the pillow, the smell of your breath under the blanket, the cracks of light around the curtains.

I don't understand people who pop out of sleep at the first alarm. I love snoozing. A push of a button, elongating the surreal haze of that liminal phase, letting me linger in the delicious afterglow of the dream world where anything is possible, where I can think something and it's suddenly there the next moment, no transition, no explanation, no logic. It's like sitting in the theater after a great movie has ended, listening to the score as the credits scroll, giving you time to reflect before you head back to the real world.

On most days, I snooze God knows how many times. But on

June 24, the first morning after Dad didn't return home, I didn't snooze at all. I'd kept working on the passwords and had barely slept, so I should have been exhausted, but as soon as the alarm went off, I was awake. For a glorious three seconds, I didn't know anything except that I was in my bed.

At once, I remembered about Dad. All of it in a single rush, from normal to devastating in a zeptosecond. Once, when we were helping Mom wash the car, John turned on the water hose by accident. I'd been humming my latest composition, mindlessly soaping the hood, when I got hit in the face, close-up. That's what this felt like: a shock of adrenaline and fear in a blast so unexpected and intense, I couldn't breathe and had to clutch my bed. Everything seemed more awful, maybe because this changed reality had solidified overnight, and waking to the risen sun, indifferent to our plight, seemed cruel. Or maybe it was the element of betrayal, the guilt that I'd fallen asleep and escaped into pleasant blankness.

Or maybe I'm conflating that shock of returning to reality with what happened next, the sound that terrified me.

To properly explain what this sound was and why it upset me so much, I have to go back more than ten years, to when we lived in Seoul with Harmonee, our grandmother.[4] We moved from DC to Korea when I was five—because Dad's consulting firm opened a Seoul branch, my parents said, but really, I think it was because Mom was pregnant with Eugene and wanted help with the new baby. (Dad was working crazy hours, and we were apparently "a handful" then: John had mild ADHD, with an emphasis on the H, and because I was

---

4 Harmonee isn't her name but how you say *grandmother* in Korean, converted into English using my mom's own Korean-to-English transliteration system. Mom has numerous reasons why she loathes standard Korean romanization systems (she literally wrote a dissertation on the topic). I personally hate English spellings that suggest Korean words sound different from how they're actually supposed to sound, like *halmeoni* (which I would pronounce hal-mee-oh-nigh instead of the more correct har-mo-nee) for *grandmother* or *babo* (which might be pronounced bay-bo instead of bah-bo) for *silly fool*.

hyperlexic and didn't like playing with kids, doctors thought I had Asperger's syndrome.) Eugene was a perfect newborn, with puffy cheeks and fat thighs and eyes that looked straight into yours. He did all the baby things—sleep, eat, poop—on time and in vast quantities. But he never cried. Even when he should have been unhappy—when he startled awake or had a dirty diaper—he didn't fuss. We called him the happiest baby in the world.

Harmonee adored Eugene, carrying him everywhere on her back, traditional-Korean style, and spoke to him exclusively in Korean. (She disapproved of John and me not speaking Korean well.) Mom said bilingual kids often take longer to talk, so no one worried about him not talking. But around Eugene's second birthday, we noticed him sometimes opening his mouth and moving his lips, as if he were talking, but with no sound coming out, like a guppy.

He made his first sound when he was three. He was watching TV with Harmonee after dinner while John and I were cleaning up. It was eleven years ago, but I still remember the moment: John was handing me Mom's martini glass—he was rinsing; I was drying—and as my fingers squeezed the slick stem, I heard a high-pitched scream, not a normal human scream but a hundred pigs squealing and an ensemble of out-of-tune violins screeching above the highest A7 combined into a piercing cacophonous note that hurt my ears. Between us we dropped the glass, shattering it. Ran to the other room.

It was Eugene, standing over Harmonee's dead body. A stroke. What made it awful—more awful, I should say—was Eugene's smile. It was the first time we noticed Eugene smiling when he clearly should not have been happy, and it freaked me out, made me wonder if something was wrong with him on some deep, fundamental level.

Eugene made that sound again the following morning right as he woke up. It was as unbearably intense as the previous night, but there was a warbly plaintiveness, too, like a farewell aria in a changgeuk, a traditional Korean opera. I heard in it what I couldn't see in his smile the previous night: the pain of witnessing Harmonee's death but being unable to tell anyone, the grief and fear—an entire requiem in a single dissonant, frenzied note.

After that, he continued making sounds, but nowhere near the pitch or intensity of those two screams—a full octave and twenty decibels lower. More singing and laughing than screaming, with a touch of melodic sweetness, in short, repeated bursts like spiccato, the bouncing bow technique I'd been working (but sadly failing) to master on violin. After his autism diagnosis, we considered it a repetitive behavior typical of autistic kids. That's when I started calling it a *splaugh*, which John hated but our parents thought was cute and used.

So my point is, Eugene's high-pitched vocals have become normal for us, relatively speaking, something we don't even notice anymore. It got to the point that when I remembered the ferocity of those two original screams, I told myself I must have made it up, allowed each remembrance to magnify it over time. But waking up that first morning after Dad went missing, Eugene screamed that original requiem scream, and even down the hallway and through his closed door and mine, hearing it brought me right back.

I ran to Eugene's room. Mom was already there, and she'd managed to calm him. She was holding him tight, eyes squeezed shut—trying her hardest to keep it together.

"What's going on? What's wrong, Eugene?" John ran past me.

Mom opened her eyes. They were red and puffy, her lids swollen. "It's okay," Mom whispered, still holding Eugene tight, patting his hair gently in a repetitive pattern. "It was just a nightmare. Why don't you go get some cereal out? We'll be down soon."

John started to say something, but Mom turned her head and looked at him. We knew this look. It didn't matter if she was smiling, frowning, silent, yelling, whatever. She looked, and it pierced. You knew to shut your mouth and obey.

As soon as we closed the door, John started to say something.

"Shhh," I said and motioned for him to follow. We went downstairs and turned on the kitchen fan.

"Are you thinking what I'm thinking?" I said.

"I have no idea what you're thinking, but I'm thinking I need coffee, ASAP. I can't believe we haven't heard anything yet. I really thought we'd wake up and Dad would be here with some perfectly innocent explanation."

"I'm talking about Eugene, screaming like that. Remember the last time he did that?"

"Yeah, yesterday."

"Oh come on, even you're not that tone-deaf. You know it was different. That's why we all ran into his room just now. He normally splaughs—"

"I hate when you say *splaugh*. It's so immature and pretentious, at the same time."

"Whatever. I'm talking about . . . Don't you remember the last time he woke up sounding like that? It's the same as the morning after Harmonee died."

John didn't say anything, just walked to the coffee maker. But as he did, I saw it: a brief moment, his eyes darting back and forth like he was remembering. He shook his head no, but it was like he was trying to convince himself, not me.

"I think we should tell the police," I said.

"Tell them what? That he made the same sound he always does when he wakes up, but we think it might have been louder than usual? What the fuck does that have to do with anything?"

"He woke up exactly the same way as the last time something bad happened to someone he loved and no one else knew. Maybe the same thing's happening now, and he's frustrated he can't tell us something important, maybe that Dad is hurt or trapped somewhere or kidnapped or . . ."

John shook his head. "We're all stressed and freaked out, and Eugene is picking up on that and reacting to it, that's all. I'm sure Dad's fine. It's like that detective was saying last night. There's some explanation we're not thinking of right now. I'm positive everything will turn out fine. Dad is fine. He has to be."

What did that even mean? Dad didn't *have to be* anything. Chances were, something horrible had happened to Dad, and only Eugene knew about it. The pain of that, the frustration and fear—that's what made that unbearable sound. It was obvious. "Dad is not fine, and your saying that just makes me wonder if you're being delusional. Don't you even care?"

"Don't *I* care? I'm not the one who didn't notice he didn't come back. I'm not the one who insisted we shouldn't call the police. Has it occurred to you that if something bad's happened to Dad, it might be your fault?"

I closed my eyes. Finally. Blame. Those words washed over me, settling and seeping into my skin.

I heard John sigh. "Mia, I . . . I didn't mean that. That's not—"

The kitchen phone rang. Our eyes locked on each other. It rang again, breaking the paralysis of the moment. We jolted up, ran to reach for it. John got it first.

For all his talk of Dad being fine, it was remarkable how much John's voice shook just saying "Hello?" I breathed in, reminded myself that the police always told the family any bad news in person. On the other hand, hadn't I learned my lesson about the way the police "always" handled things?

John didn't say anything, no indication of who, what, why—nothing. He just nodded, kept nodding, and I wanted to scream at him to fucking say something, that people on the other side of the phone can't see you nodding, you have to say "uh-huh," "sure," *something*—when he opened his mouth. No words came out, and I thought how much he looked like Eugene. He finally said, "Okay, thank you," his voice cracking a little, and he hung up.

"What? What is it?" I said before he even put down the phone.

"The search team, they found . . ." His voice cracked and he cleared his throat and blinked, hard, like he couldn't see, and my stomach dropped in a free fall. ". . . they found people who ran into him and Eugene yesterday. Detective Janus is talking to them now, and she's coming with some specialist in an hour to try to figure out how to interview Eugene."

I breathed. Pressed my stomach to get it to settle. I got out coffee and cereal.

———

YOU'D THINK IT WOULD HAVE been a big deal the first time we sat down for breakfast without Dad. I think more than anything, though, we were worried about keeping Eugene calm for his upcoming interview, plus Mom and John had to find people to sub for them at work, which left me to deal with canceling all of Eugene's therapies. I wished we could just be together and not have to deal with other people, but in some ways, all that logistical busywork was a blessing. It wasn't until after Eugene's timer went off for toothbrushing that we all looked up from our phones and turned to one another.

We had this routine Dad made up after John lost two baby teeth while brushing his teeth. He decided he was never brushing his teeth again, and in a spirit of solidarity, I joined the strike. To coax us out, Dad sang us a silly pre-toothbrushing song he and I "composed" and held a toothbrushing contest, complete with a countdown, a purple three-minute hourglass from our dentist, and funny noises and commentary ("Oooh, I like Mia Parkson's style and panache in brushing her bottom incisors!"). Dad tried to get Mom to take over for him, but thankfully, she declined. (Mom's a horrible singer, one of those unfortunate people who thinks volume can make up for atonality.) Dad worked crazy hours back then and rarely saw us, and she encouraged him to make it a daily thing: a special father-kids bonding time, every morning, whenever he was home. Mom relished this time, too, with a ten-minute ritual of her own: sitting by the window with her coffee, reading one short poem in English and in Korean she'd chosen earlier, considering the rhythmic and subtextual differences between the two versions.

The routine became bare-bones over time—the countdown, the

hourglass, and sometimes the scores at the end—and I'm sure we would have stopped eventually if it hadn't been for Eugene. It was one of the few group activities that allowed Eugene to be a truly equal and active participant, and besides, it was an easy thing we all had to do anyway. Even after we started college, Dad sent group texts with a countdown for the brushing ritual, in case we happened to be in the bathroom getting ready anyway (three times in two years for me, weekly for John). This is the kind of invisible everyday thing that, to me, made us an atypical family, because what normal twenty-year-olds still called in to their family's corny little-kid toothbrushing ritual?

That morning was the first I'd been home and not heard Dad say, "Get ready, set: one, two, three, BRUSH." I'd brought my phone into the bathroom, and I almost expected to hear the custom ringtone I'd downloaded for Dad—Darth Vader breathing and saying, "*I . . . am your father.*"

I started to pick up my toothbrush, but I couldn't do it; my chest ached, like my lungs were cramping up, unable to expand to take in air. I picked up my phone again, went to my text chain with Dad, and typed *One, two, three, BRUSH!* I turned over the purple hourglass and watched the grains of pink sand fall and settle into a tiny dune.

Just as I was reaching for my toothbrush to try again, that's when I noticed my phone screen. My last message—*One, two, three, BRUSH!*—moved slightly up, and under my text bubble, READ 9:24 A.M. appeared.

I picked up my phone. Gripped it in both hands. My heart beat faster, harder, setting my fingers, toes, head, *everything* tingling.

My now-read message slid up the screen, and a gray text bubble popped up on the bottom. Dot, dot, dot. Blinking, blinking, blinking.

The tears came fast. A deluge. Dad was okay. He was writing a message. He was *alive.* I'd been afraid to say it, to think it, but I'd really thought Dad might be dead—God, what a horrible word, I felt nauseated thinking it, and I wanted to call Dad, couldn't wait to hear his voice, couldn't wait to yell at him and laugh and have the last twenty-four hours be done with, but I was sobbing, my hands shaking so hard I couldn't move them, and why wasn't his message coming through already?, and fuck, I dropped my phone into the fucking sink.

From the sink, I heard Darth Vader's ridiculous heavy breathing—Dad's text tone—and I laughed out loud, picked up my phone.

On the screen, in bright white letters against the dark background of my phone, it read: *Who is this?*

# SIX

# A Mere Seventy-seven Degrees

I CAN GUESS WHAT YOU'RE THINKING. YOU'RE GUESSING I MUST HAVE been devastated by the *Who is this?* message, taking it to mean it wasn't Dad but some rando who found his phone somewhere, or— soap-opera-ish, but possible—it *was* Dad but he was suffering amnesia, wandering around, wondering who this "Mia" was, popping up on this mysterious rectangular thing in his hand. Not good, either way.

But here's what you don't know: this had happened before. In fact, this was a semi-regular occurrence due to the antics of a certain immature twin of mine who liked to break into our parents' phones and change my contact name to something childish—"Crew L. Ah" and "Ghee Key Nurd" were his standbys, although recently, after I pooh-poohed one as particularly sophomoric *and* generic ("P. Brane"), he changed my name to "Sesquipedalian Pleonast," which impressed me until I found in our family computer's search history, *pretentious big words for annoying people who use pretentious big words.* (This is the problem with Google—the democratization of intelligence and knowledge. It's also the great thing about it, but it's problematic when you're trying to win an argument with your less studious sibling.) I retaliated, of course, with something equally asinine—I try to avoid juvenility, but John brings out the worst in me—with the result that our parents sometimes couldn't tell who was texting them, John or me. Mom usually looked up the associated phone number to figure it out, but Dad always played along. We got carried away with daily name-change attempts at first, but that got old pretty fast, so we ramped it down to a few times a year. Mom and Dad pretended to be exasperated by it, but I think they secretly loved it. For one thing, they found the names we picked to be funny and even informative on occasion—for a brief peak-escalation period, we used this to cheat on our usual no-tattle policy (e.g., "The One Who Got a C– on Math Test"). Also, neither had siblings, and they seemed to find our interplays of mutual torment comforting, a paradoxical sign of sibling closeness, similar to how extreme cold can mimic, and even result in, burns.

If I'd stopped to think when I saw *Who is this?* I'd have cut through the shenanigans and answered *Mia* or *M.* But I was too giddy to think. I reacted by instinct, typing in my standard response, an inside joke: *The most average and not-at-all-special person you've encountered.*

Dad's reply was instantaneous, almost simultaneous with mine: *Mia?*

————

YOU KNOW THAT PROVERBIAL FROG that doesn't realize it's in boiling water until it's dead? (Okay, obviously, it can't realize anything when it's dead, and in any event, experiments have proven this to be false—frogs will jump out when the water reaches a mere 77 degrees Fahrenheit—but you know what I'm saying.) Imagine that frog being placed into cooler water and it's not until that moment of relief that the frog realizes it's been in peril and in pain. (Again, I know frogs don't have the cerebral cortex development to make these realizations; this is obviously a metaphorical *and* proverbial frog.) The minute I read *Mia?* I became that frog. I felt this sudden release, and I realized I hadn't quite believed my own bravado about Dad's text actually being from Dad. That, maybe, my text reply was a test of sorts. Like, please *please* know who I am without my having to say *Mia, your daughter.* And the reply proved it—it was from Dad.

His *Mia?* message moved up.

Another text box. Dot, dot, dot. Blinking, blinking, blinking.

The gray box went away, and the *Mia?* message moved back down to where it had been. I waited for the new message to appear—sometimes, there can be up to a five-second lag, which I hate, the not knowing of whether it's about to appear or whether the person you're texting changed their mind and decided not to write anything after all. The problem is the expectation. Zero response is so much better than an unfulfilled, retracted text bubble.

*Dad?* I texted. It didn't go through. What the hell? I called. Straight to voicemail. There was only one explanation I could think of: his phone battery died. Frustrating, yes, but a minor problem now that Dad had gone from possibly dead to unquestionably alive. What else mattered?

I ran out to the hallway, calling for Mom, John, Eugene. I sounded maniacal, even to myself, and they all bounded right out as I ranted about Dad's messages. I showed them my phone screen.

Did I notice Eugene's reaction in that moment? It was so fast, what happened, that maybe I didn't. I think his usual smile must have blended with the teary laughter of Mom and John, our collective relief overtaking us. When Eugene snatched my phone from my hands, though, I noticed that even as his lips were upturned into the familiar approximation of a smile, his eyes weren't crinkled with joy; they were wide with fear, his eyeballs bugging out cartoonishly.

"Eugene, what are you doing?" I tried to grab my phone back, but he held it tight in both hands and moved it out of my reach. And it happened again—his looking intently at the screen, the same way he'd done at the police report the previous night. Except not for a few seconds, so fleeting I suspected I'd superimposed something imaginary onto an otherwise meaningless moment. Eugene wasn't just glancing toward the direction of the screen. He was *reading*. He didn't look the way most people did, with their eyes moving left to right and up to down, but more like he was taking a picture of all the words together as a whole: his eyes fixed on the screen, squinting as if to bring the words into focus, and then, *click,* a hard blink, that smile of his remaining on his lips but accompanied by a look of pure confusion and panic in his eyes, *around* his eyes, his eyebrows rising and rising, the wrinkles across his forehead deepening at a matching rate.

There was no doubt in my mind: Eugene, my little brother who had never given any indication that he even knew the alphabet, was reading the texts between Dad's phone and mine, processing the words, and becoming distressed by them. It was mesmerizing, wondrous, and puzzling, all at the same time.

"Eugene, are you . . . is he . . . are you *reading*?"

I remember hearing those words in John's voice and being disoriented at my thoughts coming out of someone else's mouth, wondering if maybe we were trapped in some surreal dream dimension. Eugene started squeezing his eyes shut as if he couldn't bear to look at the words on the phone clutched in his hands.

"Sweetie, what's wrong? Here, can Mommy see? Give that to Mommy." Mom said this slowly, carefully, as if he were a bomb about to go off. A flash of annoyance swept through me. I didn't know why at the time, couldn't even say who or what, precisely, was annoying me—everything happened so fast—but looking back, I see this as a turning point, when my conception of Eugene started to change. He was no longer the baby brother I'd always known, devoid of words, but a stranger capable of reading, comprehending, *cogitating*—all the things the doctors said he'd never be capable of.

Eugene seemed to feel this way, too. He shook his head from side to side, a violent objection, its incongruence with his upturned smile adding to the sense of his lips being painted on, a nightmare clown act. Still with his eyes shut tight, he opened his mouth and let out a wail. It was a sustained version of what I'd so glibly labeled his usual "splaugh," but that word, with its connotation of playful cutesiness, was all wrong to describe what it was—the only sound Eugene could produce to communicate his pain, indignity, suffering, incredulity; an emphatic *no*—and I understood all of a sudden why John's always hated it. Eugene threw my phone like it was a snake he just realized he'd been holding, digging his fingers into his scalp as if to claw through his skull to reach something at its core and crush it to bits.

I must have yelled for him to stop, and John must have, too, but all I remember is Mom crying out, "Eugene-ah, what's wrong? Come here; Umma is here," but in Korean, which stopped us all. She told us once that for her, speaking in English requires three steps: think in Korean, convert to English, speak aloud. The process is quick, the utterance nearly instantaneous with the thought, but the point is, speaking in English requires thinking for Mom. Speaking in Korean, her native tongue, on the other hand, is pure instinct. When she can't think—when she's overcome with fear or anger, something acute—she reverts to Korean; it's a useful gauge, a clean-cut measure of how mad your mom is at you and, at times like these, how worried you should be. Eugene seemed to know it, too (although how? I'd never considered whether he knew the difference between English and Korean), stopping everything and looking at Mom, at the panic contorting her face, before falling into her arms.

The kitchen phone rang.

"It's Dad!" I said and started hobbling downstairs to get the phone.

"What? Why would he call the landline?" John said, even as he ran past me. It was obvious why: Dad's phone died, so he had to use someone else's phone, and he hasn't memorized any new numbers since switching to smartphones, so he called our house phone, one of the few numbers he knows off the top of his head. But I was too busy running to say any of this. John's way taller and faster, especially given my ankle, and he got to the phone first, but this was *my* call. I snatched it out of his hand. "Dad? Dad!"

"Mia?"

A woman's voice.

"Detective Janus," I said. "Listen, my dad texted—"

"Mia?" she said again, and something else, too, but the connection was bad—she must have been in the park with its spotty cell coverage, which I used to find quaint, in line with nature and all that, but was now realizing was sheer inanity—and her words were cutting in and out, sounding like "M-ah, I . . . your da . . . back . . . here bu . . ." before the call dropped. "Hello? Hello?" I said into the drone of the dial tone, the dissonance of the almost-A-and-F quasi-chord setting my eardrum itching intensely.

"What did she say? Is Dad there?" John asked as I fumbled with the phone, the caller ID, and dammit, where was the stupid Callback button? "Mia!" he yelled, and I yelled back, "I don't know! I couldn't hear!" and I finally found the button and hit it, heard the out-of-tune autodial beeps that usually vexed me but felt strangely calming at that moment. I breathed and said, "I think she said Dad's there, but I could only hear like every third wo—"

Finally, ringing. Come on, answer, I thought, maybe mouthed, maybe said; who even knew anymore? Four. Five. Six. "Come on, *answer*," I definitely said out loud that time, and as if on cue, I heard a *click* and Detective Janus's voice, but ugh, it was voicemail— "Greetings. You have reached . . ."—and I lost it. "*Greetings?* What are you, the Borg talking to *humanoids?* Who in hell says *greetings?*" I yelled into her infuriatingly serene outgoing message and slammed the phone onto the base. "None of this would be happening if we had some goddamned cell service around here. I mean, what century are we fucking living in? John, I'm warning you, if you say one word about my protesting that new tower, I swear—"

"Dad's dot has moved," John said, looking at his phone.

"What?" I stepped next to him. Dad's dot on the family locator app was still grayed out, indicating an old location, but had changed to the park's parking lot, with the time stamp of six minutes ago. When he was texting me. What's more, his archived phone battery icon displayed a sliver of red—nearly empty. I was right; his battery had died mid-text.

Oh my God, I thought. Or maybe said. I was dizzy; it was hard to tell. I blinked to bring the blurring dot back into focus. I reached out my index finger to John's phone screen, touched the dot. It felt warm.

We both looked up from the phone. Turned to each other. Was Dad still there? We didn't have to say it; I could see the question on his face, knew he could see it on mine. I squinted; he raised his eyebrows—both slowly, our faces in harmony rhythmically, tonally, even though our movements were different. I opened my mouth, saw his open, too, and I knew what we were both going to say.

"The park."

Those words were like the starting shot for a race. We both ran, John to the garage shouting "I'll get shoes" and me upstairs shouting "I'll tell Mom," the adrenaline dulling the soreness in my ankle. I got my phone off the floor, yelled to Mom we were going out and would text to explain, ran down to the garage, got in the car, buckled in, and slipped on the shoes John had put on the floor mat as he backed out and drove toward the park. The whole thing took maybe sixty seconds, a triumph of ingrained fraternal coordination. We used to be like this all the time, but we stopped at some point, and I'd forgotten how magical it felt, the simple pleasure of effortless synchrony and simultaneity.

I picked up my phone to text Mom, and I flashed back to Eugene reading from it, how huge that had seemed just five minutes ago. No, I couldn't think about that. It needed to wait. If I'd learned anything from the 331 episodes of *ER* I marathon-watched when I had strep, it was about the relativity of emergencies, the need to triage.

My phone opened automatically to my text chain with Dad, and I touched Dad's words, started to smile, but sliding my finger over the text bubbles—*Who is this? . . . Mia?*—I felt pressure in my chest, like I was breathing in something heavy.

I turned to John. "Hey, did you change my name this week? You know, in Dad's phone?"

"No, I have a good one saved up, but Dad changed his passcode. Why? Because it's weird for Dad to say 'Who is this?' to an old name?"

That was precisely why, and it disturbed me how he said this so casually, like it was obvious. It made me worry about my judgment—the whole delivery guy thing, now this. How had this not occurred to me before? What else was I missing?

"You think so, too?" I managed to say.

"Of course. That's the first thing I thought when you showed us the texts, but I figured it's just Dad being Dad. No weirder than you playing games, too. Whatever, it doesn't matter. What matters is that he knew that meant you."

Did he, though? "Then why the question mark? It's like . . . like he was guessing but he didn't *know*. Like he kind of remembered my name but kind of didn't, like . . ." As I said this, it popped into place, what had been lurking in the periphery of my memory: movies. Specifically, movies featuring this admittedly dubious kind-of-but-kind-of-not-remembering-your-child's-name-in-a-text-due-to-dementia story line, two of which we'd watched in as many months due to Mom's recent obsession with Alzheimer's and dementia.[5] These

---

5 It started when Mom read about an immigrant Alzheimer's patient who lost all English skills and reverted to his native language, which he hadn't spoken for sixty years. Every time she picks one of these movies, I wonder: If she lost the ability to speak English, how would she connect to Dad, who barely speaks perfunctory Korean? Would mere shared existence in the same house be enough? And on the flip side, would that bring her closer to Eugene, being able to truly understand what it's like, being unable to communicate with the people you live with, unable to form the emotional connection that comes from the sharing of stories and ideas, from intimate confessions to the logistical exchanges and casual jokes that fill everyday silences?

movies always have an early scene featuring the first disturbing flash of memory loss, and in two recent movies, the obligatory scene involved the character's (adult) child texting *I love you* (which, let's get real, was a clear sign these were fictional because what child older than ten does stuff like that, unprompted?) and the parent feeling a vague familiarity with the child's name but not sure why. Somewhat prophetically, Dad and I joked about this, with me pointing out the implausibility of this setup and Dad agreeing that if he got a random note of affection from me, he'd immediately think I was kidnapped and demand to know who was texting.

"Helloooo, earth to Mia," John said, singsong, which I hate. "Like what?"

"It could be Alzheimer's."

"Oh God, we have got to stop watching those movies."

"Okay, look. I know it seems ridiculous, but that's because the movies were cheesy. If they were like Oscar winners or, no, like Sundance or Cannes or"—John was sighing audibly—"okay, whatever, forget the movies. Here's the point: early-onset dementia is a real thing, and Dad's over *fifty*. It all fits. He's been acting strange lately, all distracted and—"

The car jerked, screeched to half its previous speed. John grabbed my shoulder to keep me from flying forward. "Sorry, but that just . . ." He motioned with his chin to the road in front of us. A boxy gray sedan just like Detective Janus's was driving toward us, coming from the direction of the park's parking lot. No sirens, no flashing lights, no speeding, seemingly all business as usual, but of course it wasn't, and I understood John's slamming on the brakes.

Was Dad in that car?

It was strange how our car seemed to be moving in slow motion, but my heart was beating triple its normal speed, thrumming so hard I could feel it in my neck, my ears, my temples.

I wanted John to stop the car, wanted to get out, run to Dad. I reached for the door handle and squeezed—my palm thrummed, I could *hear* it—but just as I was about to pull, I saw. A girl practicing driving with an older man, the neon STUDENT DRIVER sign on the side of the sedan coming into view.

We drove in silence the rest of the way. It wasn't far to the park entrance, to Dad's dot, just a few hundred yards. I don't think I breathed.

# SEVEN

# Something Beautiful and Dangerous

A ROW OF ORANGE CONES BLOCKED THE ENTRANCE TO THE PARKING lot, a sign saying CLOSED. "Oh shit," John said. "The quarantine." There was no place even to pull over. "That street up there has parking, I think," John said, backing up, but I unbuckled my seatbelt and opened the car door, got out. "Mia, what the hell?"

Whatever. He was going like two miles an hour. I moved the cones out of the way. This was an emergency. Let them arrest me. "Come on," I yelled and ran in.

The lot wasn't big—enough space for maybe sixty cars—but it was wooded, with a thick row of tall pine trees dividing the lot in two, so it took me a few seconds to check both sides. Empty. My legs felt weak, and I had to lean against a tree trunk. Of course I knew it was a long shot, had told myself he wouldn't just be standing around a parking lot on the offhand chance his kids happened to see his ghost dot and come get him.

I opened my family locator app, saw Dad's dot—now sixteen

minutes ago—and walked to the spot, my blue dot and Dad's gray one getting closer and closer until they formed one perfect circle. Dad had been standing where I was standing, looking down at his phone like I was at mine, reading my text, maybe chuckling, remembering when he said to me, *Fine, from now on, I'll call you the most average and not-at-all-special person I've encountered,* after I got annoyed at him for embarrassing me with his over-the-top speech at our high school graduation dinner. Where did he go?

John parked next to me, got out of the car. "Dad must have been with the police, because no one else is allowed here. Maybe they took him home."

"No, we would have passed them." There was just one way to our house from here. But John was right—only the police and the like would park here. Someone official, something for an emergency, like . . .

"An ambulance," I said. "I can't believe we didn't think of this. They found him, but of course he's disoriented, dehydrated, he gets an IV or whatever but he's still woozy, gets my text, is like, 'Who is this?,' then he gets my average blah blah text and is like, 'Hmmm, is it Mia?' because he's still fuzzy, then the phone dies." It made perfect sense.

"Maybe," John replied, but his face said, *Highly doubtful.*

"*Or,*" I continued, "maybe the EMT had Dad's phone, and they're like, hey, you got a text from Sesqui-something—because they can't pronounce it, who can?—and Dad's like, 'Who?,' so they text, 'Who is this?' and they tell him what I said, and Dad's like, 'Oh, that's Mia,' and they go, 'Mia?,' you know, to verify, then the phone dies, and they're like, 'Okay, we should go to the hospital.' See?"

"Maybe," he said again, his frown getting deeper. It pissed me off, his lack of support when he couldn't even offer up an alternative of his own.

A small creek separated the lot from a large picnic area and whitewater scenic overlook. I ran across the wobbly wooden footbridge, surveying the area for people I could ask about an ambulance they might have seen. No people, but I spotted a MISSING flyer with Dad's picture at a vista point. It was a formal headshot, Dad's old work picture from his firm's website. Clean-shaven, short hair neatly parted, suit and tie. Yesterday morning, he'd had on a T-shirt, hadn't shaved in a day, maybe two, and his hair was long and wavy, uncut in three months at least. How would any-one recognize him? is what I was focusing on, not on the sign right above the flyer in bold red lettering—THE RIVER CAN KILL! STAY OUT!—warning people to stay on the trail and off the slippery rocks, the so-called Death Counter sign directly ahead reporting the number of fatal falls and drownings since the park's opening in the 1960s.

I took in the view directly ahead, a series of whitewater rapids forming mini-waterfalls popular with kayakers, the water churning, colliding into and around jagged rocks, the mist and spray forming a thick, ever-present fog on top. I leaned against the waist-high guard-rail, which tourists sometimes jumped for a better picture, standing on a boulder next to the river. Little kids sometimes did that, too, for that thrill of nearness to something beautiful and dangerous.

Could Dad have been here? Was he—

No. Eugene loved water, was attracted to it to an inexplicable degree, a hallmark of Angelman syndrome, but he also couldn't stand loud noise. In situations involving both, the noise sensitivity trumped the water obsession, hands down, the reliable constancy of this Hate > Love inequality being why Dad felt safe bringing Eugene here. They always stayed far away from whitewater danger spots like this area, stuck to the peaceful, calm stretches.

"Mia, look who I found," John yelled. He and a woman who looked vaguely familiar were hurrying my way. She reached out as if to hug me but stopped. "Oh, Mia, I'm so sorry about your dad, I wish I could give you a huge hug." A rare upside of the pandemic: the prohibition of uninvited, unwelcome bombardments of physi-cal affection from parental acquaintances you barely know and can't quite place. "I was telling John—I came by to help with the search;

the whole playgroup's supposed to meet up at ten." At the mention of *playgroup*, I remembered. She was the mom of one of the kids in Eugene's socialization therapy group at Henry's House.

John said, "Susan was saying she saw police cars leaving. . . ."

"Right, when I was walking here, around twenty minutes ago. Maybe I missed it, but I didn't see an ambulance. Definitely no sirens."

I swallowed. "Maybe the police took him directly to the hospital. We should go check."

"Of course. Please let your mom know I'm praying for you. You're dealing with so much already, I can't believe this, after the horrible news last week—"

"What news?" John and I said at the same time.

The woman blinked, her eyes darting from John to me in what I could have sworn was a look of surprise, confusion, and assessment. But it was so fleeting and subtle—and more importantly, her next words betrayed nothing. "Oh, your dad told me about your colleges being virtual next semester and your family trip being canceled," she said, then continued on about things being so upsetting for everyone but especially for us special-needs families, the extra burden. Knowing now what she was covering up, I find it impressive how smooth she was, the quick thinking. The substance of the excuse not as much—Were virtual college classes "horrible"? How was a trip cancellation causing "extra burden"?—but the perfect tone of her voice with the Goldilocks amount of concern: not so rambly and anxious she seemed guilty, the way a bad liar sounds, but not so nonchalant it seemed fake. I now marvel at how expertly she distracted us from her error and got us itching to leave—and we ran to the car, mumbling thank-yous.

A few steps from our car, right around Dad's dot point, my phone sounded. *Twilight Zone*, Mom's text tone. Her group text to John and me popped up on the screen: *GUYS! ANSWER! WHERE R U????* I texted back: *Sorry forgot to text. At park. Will call soon.*

As I opened the car door, Mom's text tone sounded again. Not just once, but like ten times in a row, no pauses, simultaneous with short buzzes from John's phone.

> Can u come watch E? My
> bathroom. I started bath 2
> calm him down

> Bring cup of juice for E

> Hello? Guys?

> Calls going to vm. Where r u?

> Car gone. Did U leave house?

> Whats going on? WHERE R U??

"You didn't text Mom? How could you—" John was calling Mom. "Mom? Mom? We're fine. Mom, calm down. We're okay. Mom? Can you hear me?"

I shouted into the phone, "Mom, I told you we were leaving, did you not hear?"

John was shushing me. "I can't hear you. Mom?" I could hear bits of a high, hysterical voice.

I texted Mom: *Coming home now.* I said to John, "I texted her. Hang up so she gets the text."

John said, "Mom? Check. Your. Text." He sounded unhinged, halfway screaming. He threw his phone down. Started the car. Couldn't look at me.

"I know. I really screwed up," I said. John said nothing. "It's to-tally my fault, I'm sorry," I tried again. Nothing. He just blinked, started driving. I thought of the snippets of Mom's voice I overheard. Was she crying? She never cried. A dull ache radiated from my chest, thinking of Mom sitting by Eugene in the bathtub, unable to leave, her husband gone, and then we disappear, too. She must have sent these texts and called when we were in the park. How long were we in there?

Mom's texts were all time-stamped 9:52 A.M. Bizarrely, Mom's last *WHERE R U??* text was marked 9:51 A.M., one minute *earlier*. I felt a faint tingling in my scalp, growing as it traveled through my arms to my fingers clutched around the phone.

Dad's *Mia?* text came a second after my most-average-person-you've-encountered text, which I'd taken as proof that Dad was the one replying, per our inside joke. But what if it was written *before* mine?

Here was the scenario forming in my head: Someone finds Dad's phone and brings it to Detective Janus in the parking lot, where there's intermittent data. At 9:24 A.M., she gets my *One, two, three, BRUSH!* text, in real time, and replies, "Who is this?" As I'm writing my response, all my previous texts from the past twenty-four hours come through. Based on those texts, Detective Janus reasonably guesses it's me and sends "Mia?" at the same time I send my stupid inside joke.

I told John. He didn't say anything, which I took to mean he agreed it was plausible. Probably probable.

We were five minutes from home, but I couldn't wait. As soon as we got cell reception, I did what I should have from the beginning: called the police station, asked the receptionist to relay an urgent message to Detective Janus asking if she sent the text I got from my father's phone, gave my number.

My phone rang within thirty seconds. I answered on speaker.

"Mia," Detective Janus said, and I knew. "I sent the text. I'm so sorry."

John pulled over, stopped the car, closed his eyes, and slumped over the steering wheel. So many questions came up, jumbled and fighting for dominance: Why didn't she identify herself? Why didn't she call back earlier, keep trying me, so I wouldn't be caught up in this delusional fantasy? How could I have believed even for a minute that Dad would play *games* with me—how could *I* have played games with *him*—in the middle of this crisis? (Answers, which I figured out later: she meant to but Dad's phone died; she didn't have my cell-phone number; a combination of two heuristic biases—the normalcy bias and the ostrich effect.)

She was providing an excruciatingly detailed explanation—how they found Dad's phone, they couldn't unlock it (none of us knew his passcode), and when a text popped up from someone they didn't recognize, she jumped at the chance to reply from the lock screen—when John's voice broke through: "Did you . . . you found Dad? Is he . . ."

His pause stretched out over time, and I could almost hear him trying out the words fitting in that sentence—*dead, alive,* and every-thing in between. "Is he okay?" I finally said.

She said, "No." Before she could say more, there was all this hubbub with someone shouting her name and her saying she had to go and would be over in ten minutes to explain everything. She hung up.

"I can't believe she didn't tell us anything," I said. "She just said *No.* No what? No, she didn't find him? Or she found him but no, he's not okay, in which case *how* not okay is he, like, is he just stuck somewhere or is he, like, is he—"

John hugged me. A bear hug, like one of Dad's. When we were little, we used to sleep hugging each other, but I couldn't remember the last time we'd hugged like this—for more than a second and just us, not a family group hug. Even when we left for college, it was quick, both of us annoyed at our parents for making it feel performa-tive and evaluated, with their picture- and video-taking and *See? You guys are going to miss each other* style commenting.

John said, "I know you're freaking out. I am, too. But we have to keep it together. For Mom and Eugene. Okay? We have to."

I managed not to cry until we got home. Mom was pacing in our driveway, and I ran out to hug her tight, tell her over and over I was sorry, I'd never scare her like that again. She kept pulling out of the hug to look at me, touch my face, my cheeks, my hair, then John's cheeks, his hair, then pulling us back into a hug. What made me cry was the fear in her face. It was manic and crazed, her hair messy all around her head like she'd literally pulled it out, or tried, like she hadn't quite believed we were coming home even though we'd tried to tell her. I hugged her tight, John and I both did, and she put her arms around us, but feebly, like she was sapped of all her strength, like she was fighting gravity and losing.

It occurred to me at some point: if Dad isn't found, if he doesn't come home, or maybe even if he does, this will be what happens to us from now on. For the rest of our lives, every time one of us goes somewhere and doesn't return on time, doesn't let the others know where we are, we will remember this time, what can happen. And we will fall apart.

# EIGHT

# Just Tell Us

FACING DETECTIVE JANUS AT OUR PORCH TABLE, I HAD THE MOST IN-tense déjà vu. They say déjà vu is a memory-sequencing miscue, an eerie byproduct of your brain trying to reconcile the accidental activation of the wrong memory bank. But sometimes it's not a processing error at all, but just a sign that you are, in fact, doing the same thing over and over.

The feeling ended as soon as she spoke: "We could not find him."

She wasn't unkind. Her blunt statement—no sorrys, no preamble, no softening, nothing—might sound insensitive, but I've always preferred nurses who give shots with no warning. We'd been tortured enough; we didn't want one more minute of dreading bad news or, even worse, hoping for good news.

She checked each of our faces for questions, but none of us said anything, and she went on. She said their initial search was complete, including the infrared helicopter search, thermal scans, and canine teams, and they could not find Dad anywhere in or around the park.

She paused and said they found his backpack in the middle of the river—at the word *river,* I remember hearing a sharp intake of breath, wondering who was being so histrionic, and realizing it was me, John's hand clutching mine and squeezing tight as Detective Janus said the bag was a half mile downstream from the park trail where he was last seen. That, as we know, the water is fast-moving around the many jagged rocks, and luckily—I remember inhaling again at *luckily,* squeezing John's hand reflexively—the bag's strap had caught on one. That the phone seemed fine—Dad's military-drop-tested, water-, sand-, snow-, and dust-proof case apparently worked—but everything else was drenched, being processed by the evidence lab.

At this point, Detective Janus walked across the room to get a file from her bag. It seemed to take her an inordinately long time to perform such a simple task, but looking back, it occurs to me that she was giving us time to process the news, for it to sink in that Dad wasn't just lost or hurt, but *gone,* possibly permanently. Not that they were giving up—they were organizing a volunteer search party to "re-comb through all the nooks and crannies"—but there was no denying that the initial search results had tipped the scales on Dad being found from above a 50 percent chance to below. A subtle shift in terms of numbers, maybe, but crossing that 50 percent line meant a 180-degree turnaround in outlook from likely-found to likely-gone.

Sitting back down, she studied us, her face expectant as if in anticipation of a bombardment of questions. And there *were* questions, of course—so many, small and big, from the logistical to the existential. But I didn't dare ask. No one voiced them, all our breaths on hold, the unasked questions swirling around the core of our need, our plea: Don't force us to ask. Don't make us have to string together and say out loud unutterable, unthinkable words about Dad in the water: *drowning, body recovery, divers.* Just tell us.

A chilling thought: Was her silence a test? Was our silence atypical, and in the same way she'd questioned why we didn't call the police, was she wondering why we weren't ravenous for information?

I spoke up. "Given the backpack in the water, what are the ramifications for the person who owns . . . I mean, who might have fallen in wearing . . ." This was torture and I couldn't go on, and thank God, Mom rescued me, or maybe my words had shattered our collective frozenness, but regardless, she finished my question: "What does finding Adam's backpack tell you about whether he might have fallen in, and if he did, what are the chances of your finding his . . . him?"

The crinkles on Detective Janus's forehead relaxed (was she relieved?), and I tried to focus on what she was saying, which was hard because my stomach kept lurching, forcing me to swallow back the cereal I'd forced myself to eat earlier. She said how the answer to our question was that there was no good answer, that despite the park's experience with water rescue attempts, success remained elusive, and often, bodies—it was remarkable how easily she said *bodies,* as if it were just another word—are never recovered and personal effects like shoes can turn up weeks or even months later, miles from the origin point.

"In the meantime," she said, "there are many other avenues we're pursuing. First, the items recovered from the backpack. We're still drying everything to preserve as much as possible, but let me show you some pictures to see if anything looks unusual." She spread out on the table a dozen pictures from her folder. Dad's bag, the dark green so wet it looked black. His phone, the screen a dark blank but otherwise the same as always. Granola bars, Eugene's favorite, and a water bottle. His keys and pens. A manila folder with something yellow sticking out of the top. A green spiral-bound notebook, bloated with water.

Mom touched that last picture, slid it closer. "I've never seen this. This was in Adam's bag?" Detective Janus said yes, and Mom said, "H. O. I have no idea what this could be."

I rotated the picture toward me. The writing on the notebook cover was mostly illegible, faded from the water, but the first line clearly began with H. The first letter on the second line looked like a circle, the bottom right smudged. If I hadn't been looking through

Dad's HQ files all night, I might have read it as an O, too. But it wasn't O. It was Q. HQ again.

Detective Janus said, "My team is drying the notebook to read it, in case there's something relevant in there. It'll take time because it's so wet, but we did manage to read enough to figure out the H probably stands for Happiness. They're sending a scan of the first page now."

The Q hadn't meant anything to me before. There were so many things it could be without the context of the first word: quotes, quarter, quarantine, quorum, quiche, quick, quirk, quiet, quit, query, quibble, quantify, and on and on.

But next to Happiness, the meaning of Q came to me right away. I blinked, and the words appeared in my head.

Happiness Quotient.

# PART II

## HAPPINESS QUOTIENT

# NINE

# Blue Brain

THEY SAY HUMAN BRAINS HAVE THE STORAGE CAPACITY TO HOLD everything on the internet, the equivalent of 4.7 billion books. Even if you believe that everything we experience gets stored, including dreams and in utero sensations, any of which we can access by triggering the right synaptic connections, that still accounts for only a tiny fraction of our brains. So the question is, why? Why all this wasted extra brain space we could never hope to fill?

A related question: Have you ever had a name/image/phrase pop up in your brain you don't remember ever hearing or seeing, and you think, Where in the world did that come from?

One possible answer to both questions, according to certain philosophers: all human knowledge is within us, stored in each of our brains, and as we live our lives, our experiences trigger the connections that allow individuals to access these omnipresent (but not omni-accessible) points of knowledge—similar to how individual memories work, but at a tribal or species level. It sounds very woo-

woo, I know, but elements of it undergird religions and philosophies all over the world, from Daoism and Plato's innatism to Chomsky's nativism. In fact, neuroscientists at a Swiss supercomputer simulation of brain activity called Blue Brain Project have actually proven that innate knowledge exists through neuronal interconnectivity scans. (It's complicated, but think of it as different parts of the brain lighting up than you'd expect if the knowledge was from learned experience or memory.)

When *happiness quotient* popped into my head at the police picture of Dad's notebook, I thought, Blue Brain? Because this phrase wasn't from memory, at least not a memory of mine. I'd never heard or seen it, but I *knew* that the title of Dad's notebook was *Happiness Quotient;* it was like an intuition, something I'd always known, and it confused and spooked me a little: like, was there some collective knowledge base at the familial level, allowing me to access Dad's memories?

"You know, I think this must be a Q, not an O," I said to Mom and Detective Janus, holding up the picture of Dad's notebook. "Remember, Mom? The HQ files I found last night?" I was tempted to say more, that it stood for *happiness quotient,* but I couldn't figure out how I knew that, and I'd decided long ago not to trust anything I can't explain and verify, a lesson painfully confirmed by the *Mia?* text debacle. I explained to Detective Janus: "I found these files named HQ in Dad's backup drive. I couldn't open them, but they must be important, since Dad went to the trouble of putting passwords on them."

It's not like I was expecting some sort of prize for figuring out this clue, but I expected a little show of interest. Mom kept scrutinizing the pictures, though, like she wasn't even listening, frowning slightly the way she does when I go off on a tangent. John sighed. It figured; neither of them had thought much of the HQ files or the code-containing manila folder. Detective Janus smiled—at least I think she did from the way her mask moved—as if in encouragement, and I felt a small swirl of gratefulness. She said, "Hopefully, we can figure out what it is as soon as we can read the notebook."

Mom looked up from the pictures and said, "Where's Adam's wallet? Did you not find it? I see his keys. He keeps them in the same compartment."

"We noticed that, but we figured he keeps his wallet in his pocket."

"No, he hates that, and anyway, he was wearing his gym shorts without pockets. He's really careful about keeping it zipped up because he's paranoid it might fall out."

As she nodded and wrote in her notebook, Detective Janus said, "I'll check the photos of the bag, but it's definitely possible the zipper came open and it fell out. The rapids are so strong, and with all the jagged rocks everywhere, things have a way of getting really tossed around and completely shredded sometimes . . ." She stopped writing and talking mid-sentence. She must have realized the effect of her words.

I squeezed my eyes shut to keep out the image of Dad plunging into the rapids. Detective Janus said, "I'm sorry. I wasn't thinking of . . ."

Her phone rang, and the way she bounded up, looking at the phone like a long-lost friend, I could tell she was relieved not to have to finish that sentence. She said it was an important call and she'd take it in her car.

"It's really hot and muggy," Mom said. "Let's go inside, cool off."

It wasn't that hot, but that reminded me. "Mom, why did you have Eugene put on long pants and socks? You know he hates that."

Mom looked genuinely puzzled. "He picked it out," she said, turning to Eugene. "Sweetie, are you hot? Want shorts? Hot?" she said in that high baby-talk voice, which I couldn't believe I'd never noticed was so irritating. I wanted to tell her to cut it out, just talk to him like a normal person. But who was I to scold? I did that to Eugene, too; we all did. Eugene ignored her, his eyes focused on his screen. He ignored stuff all the time, but this was deliberate, his message as clear as if he'd said it out loud. Mom got it, too, and dropped it, but then said under her breath in a barely audible monotone, as if to herself, "Okay, well, I need coffee, let's go in," which would have seemed demented except that John, who was across the porch, seemed to hear that fine and replied in an equally muffled monotone, "Definitely need coffee."

It annoyed me, their matching strangeness, and I said loudly—not quite yelling but with the same level of inappropriate loudness as their inappropriate quietness—"NONE FOR ME, THANKS." Mom and John startled and exchanged glances of the not-sure-whether-to-be-concerned-or-annoyed variety, and I thought how Dad would guffaw if he were here, join me in making fun of them. "I'm gonna hang here with Eugene. I probably shouldn't have more coffee," I said in a quiet-ish voice.

"Eugene, what do you know about happiness quotient?" I said in as normal a cadence, tone, and volume as possible. He glanced up, looking surprised but in a good way—because of how I was talking to him?—and then peered at the picture of Dad's notebook. I felt a fluttering in my chest, the heaviness of the last half hour lifting. Calm down, it may be nothing, I told myself, but I continued. "Did Dad talk about it with you? Because he's never mentioned it to me, and I don't think Mom or John have heard it, either. But I have this weird feeling that's what this notebook is about." Eugene glanced up at me, then down again at the notebook—I swear, that looked like a nod—his gaze fixed on that particular picture, not on any of the dozen pictures nearby, not on his iPad.

Looking back, I wish I hadn't done what I did next. But I couldn't help it. My assumption that Eugene couldn't understand pretty much anything had been ingrained for more than a decade. It was too much for me to just accept that he all of a sudden knew what *happiness quotient* signified.

I jumbled up the police pictures, spread them out randomly, and said, "Eugene, can you point to happiness quotient for me?" His face sagged, what I could have sworn was a flash of disappointment—maybe anger? I blinked, and nothing. He was focused on his iPad like always.

Had I made that up? Read too much into meaningless things? "Eugene, sorry, I know pointing's hard. How about just look? Look at happiness quotient. Look. At. Notebook. Eugene?"

He didn't even blink. He was done with me. I know now that he was pissed at being doubted and tested like a lab rat. Patronized. But I couldn't fathom that at the time. All I could focus on was how I'd just seen, not even an hour prior, how false hope can wreak havoc, not only for me but for John and Mom. I was trying to learn from that experience, doing my best not to get my hopes up this time with Eugene, but it wasn't working. Optimism is like ice cream: as much as I try to remind myself it's bad for me and I should stay away, I'm human, can't help a tiny taste, and the next thing you know, I'm digging into the whole carton, gulping it down, and it always ends with me feeling sick and wanting to throw up, the way I was feeling just then.

"I need more coffee," I said and went inside.

———

IN THE KITCHEN, I WAS tempted to tell Mom about *happiness quotient* popping into my head, as if by magic. Mom is very into the our-brains-are-all-connected theory; she's actually the one who first told me about it.[6] But truth be told, I've always hated that theory, especially Chomsky's linguistics version, nativism, which states (and I'm definitely oversimplifying here) that language is inherent to and distinguishes human brains—what makes us truly human—which begs the question, What does that make Eugene? It doesn't help that this topic reminds me of my first college philosophy class, which still makes me mad and sad to remember. The professor was talking

———

6 A quick pause for a thought challenge: What's your best guess as to why my mom believes in this idea? Is it because a) she's Asian and this we-are-all-connected thing sounds Asian in a Kung-Fu-Panda ancient-Chinese-secret kind of way? Or b) you remembered her linguistics PhD, also remembered my earlier reference to Chomsky's nativism, and figured she, like many linguistics PhDs, idolizes Chomsky? (Correct answer: b.)

about Plato and Descartes being the "grandfather" and "father" of the theory of innate knowledge, and I raised my hand and brought up earlier Asian thinkers and how it irks me that people classify innatism/nativism as epistemological schools of thought but classify the same ideas from Asian cultures as mystical nonsense. This led to what I thought was a fascinating discussion about appropriation and the offensiveness of the labels of "Eastern mysticism" versus "Western rational thought," but later, I found a class chat thread saying the professor didn't really agree with "that Asian girl's nonsense" but was obviously feigning agreement to avoid being canceled for racism.

No. There had to be a rational explanation for the appearance of the phrase *happiness quotient* in my head. I just needed to focus. I sat next to John, gulped his coffee. He drinks coffee sickly sweet, with ridiculous amounts of artificial sweetener. I can't stand it, but I needed caffeine just then, and I was too tired to get my own cup. At least it was strong, and the caffeine hit immediately; I could feel the blood vessels to my brain dilating, everything accelerating. John and Mom both looked like zombies. I needed to distract them. We needed to *do* something, not just sit around, reeling. "Quick, what does *happiness quotient* mean to you?" I said.

Mom said, "Eugene must be hot. I'm going to bring him shorts," and left the room.

"Okay, then." I turned to John. "Happiness quotient. Go."

He shrugged. "Numbers. Division. Someone who's dividing the amount of joy in someone's life in half, in other words, sucking the joy out of their life, like you're doing to me right now."

John being smart-alecky usually annoys me, but it buoyed me right then, this morsel of normalcy. All our huggy niceness was getting to be a bit too much.

I took another sip of John's vile coffee—it was strange how I couldn't stop drinking this swill—and thought, Happiness numbers, happiness quantities. They came to me almost the second I swallowed, two instances when Dad, happiness, and numbers all intersected. The first was right after the Graveyard Incident, around the time we moved back to the US, so I would have been thirteen. Here's how it went:

DAD: Imagine you're sitting on a plush sofa chair in front of a crackling fire, reading a book. Anyone in that situation would say you're content, let's say six out of ten on the happiness scale.

ME: One is the happiest?

DAD: What? No. Ten is the happiest. Why would one be the happiest on a one-to-ten happiness scale?

ME: Because one is the best. First place, first prize, firstborn (*like me,* I was thinking but didn't say).

DAD, SIGHING: No. Mia, sometimes . . . Anyway, okay, so, dry, warm, in front of fire, reading. If you'd spent the whole day like that and I asked how happy you were, you might say six. Perfectly content. But let's say you were cold and miserable outside in a storm and you just came in and sat in front of the fire, and right as you got warm and dry and started reading a great book, I asked how happy you were. You'd probably give a higher number. Because relative to what you've been experiencing, your baseline, your happiness level would be higher, see?

ME: What if you don't like reading? What if you're dyslexic? Or what if you were horribly burned or you just watched *Inferno* in 3D (I'd just watched it, and it scared the shit out of me) and just the smell of smoke terrifies you? In that case, the person who's been in front of the fire all day might be happier because they had longer to get desensitized.

That was the end of that conversation. Dad just looked at me, giving me his disappointed-shake-of-head-combined-with-sigh-and-frown-and-long-silent-stare thing he saves for when he thinks I'm being particularly exasperating. I gave him my best teenage-girl defiant stare, and he walked out of the room, still shaking his head and sighing. Truth be told, I'd been trying to pick a fight. I thought his point was interesting, and if I hadn't been in a pissy mood and feeling particularly thirteen, I'd have engaged.

The problem was not that I was a teenager (though there was that), but that I thought he was trying to torture me for the afore-mentioned Graveyard Incident. I don't want to get into the whole thing now—I don't like to talk about it, plus it's an interminably long, boring story—but the gist is that John and I secretly took Eugene to our grandparents' burial site outside Seoul, and when Dad found us after we'd been missing all night, he thought we'd been kidnapped and killed, which was not an unreasonable assumption given that we were lying on the ground, utterly still, in the middle of a grave-yard. We weren't dead (obviously), and I still remember waking up to this crumpling sound—Dad fell when he saw us; he had gargantuan bruises on both knees for days afterward—and seeing Dad as I raised my head. I'll never forget it, the way his face morphed in the dawn-ing light, like one of those tricks where a clown wipes a frown into a smile, but intensified to the hundredth power—crucifying agony, wipe, rapturous elation. Later, he said it was precisely *because* he was destroyed—"I wanted to just fucking die," he said, which I remem-ber as the first time he said *fuck* to us intentionally, no flinching or apologizing, which was cool but also disturbing—that realizing we were alive brought such an intense joy, "an almost violent euphoria," he called it. He went on and on about it, how the state of our being alive had been the unremarkable baseline of his life, but because of his momentary belief that we were dead, returning to that baseline became this extraordinary thing. So against this backdrop, when he gave that fireplace example and talked about happiness levels and baselines, you can see how I feared this might be some parental guilt-trip thing. I wanted to shut it down, and I did.

The second time was several years later, around the time of our parents' near-divorce (also when Dad not so coincidentally became a full-time dad). Dad plugged his phone into the car after picking me up from orchestra rehearsal, and some inane podcast about happiness started auto-playing. I opened his Podcasts app, and his feed was all pop-psycho-philosophy happiness stuff: *How to Be Happy, How Not to Be Unhappy, Optimism Program, Gratefulness Challenge, Take Your Happiness Temperature, 30-Day Happiness Program, Achieve Happiness in 8 Steps or Less!*, and on and on. I was very proud of myself that I managed not to say anything or even to surreptitiously roll my eyes. I just closed it out and shuffle-played Dad's eighties-rock playlist I pretend to tolerate but actually like. I didn't connect Dad's podcast focus with our previous fireplace-happiness-levels conversation; there was a whole industry around "happiness achievement," and I thought Dad had just fallen into the craze of the moment. But I do remember lingering on the happiness temperature concept, thinking how funny it was that people were trying to quantify happiness, and feeling this shard of recognition like when there's something you're remembering in the recesses of your mind. Dad asked me some scheduling question, I filed it away to think about later, and I forgot to.

These two memories told me Dad thought about happiness in terms of numbers. But the way he compared different happiness levels in the fireplace example implied a *difference*. So why a quotient, not a difference?

Quotient, not a difference. That sounded familiar; it was on the tip of my brain.

"Hey, do you remember anything about a quotient versus a difference? Something Dad was working on?" I asked John, who was pouring more coffee and fake sweetener into his cup. I swiped it, guzzled.

"No," he said, snatching his coffee back, "although didn't *you* work on something right before college? Something about calculating the saddest chord or something to impress that creepy guy who dumped you?"

I wanted to snipe at John to get his facts straight—for the record, *I'd* dumped *him* (although I couldn't deny he was creepy)—but he was right: I was working on a music-composition program algorithm to express mathematically why dissonant chords produce different harmonic functions and/or moods in different keys despite having the same interval (say, G–to–F-sharp versus D-flat–to–C). I assigned numeric values to musical notes to demonstrate that even though the *difference* between them is the same, the *quotients* aren't, that the quotient concept allows more nuance because it takes the pitch of the root note into account. It's similar to comparing 999 minus 995 versus 8 minus 4. The difference between both sets is 4, but the quotients are dramatically different, with less than 1 percent variance in the first set and 200 percent in the second.

Anyway, I was telling Dad all this because I wanted his help setting up spreadsheets—he *loved* spreadsheets and once said he thinks in spreadsheets—so I could plug in different chords and automatically calculate the varying resonances. Something came over Dad's face as he listened to my difference-versus-quotient rationale. He said, "Mia, this is brilliant. This is exactly what . . . I've been working on something, trying to capture my intuitive understanding of the relativity of emotions, but I was using subtraction and getting the same values for situations I know are not. I think your quotient insight's exactly what I was missing. You're brilliant."

I remember at his mention of "relativity of emotions," flashing back to our fireplace discussion, but I didn't say anything because I was too embarrassed (but also happy) about Dad saying (twice!) that I was brilliant. I feigned annoyance to cover up my embarrassment, saying anyone with an elementary level of proficiency in music or math (unlike *you,* I implied) would realize my "insight" was pretty reductive and, honestly, not that insightful. I lectured how "everyone knows" (probably not true) that G-major chords sound happier than, say, D-flat major chords, and D-minor chords are way sadder than G-sharp minor chords. I wasn't saying any of this to be bitchy, although I realize now that it was. Dad looked down, like he was embarrassed and maybe hurt, and he turned to the spreadsheet. I remember thinking I should say something, maybe admit my embarrassment and explain why I said what I said. But I didn't, and he never brought up happiness levels or quotients again.

Knowing what I know now, I wonder what would have happened

if I'd asked him about the "relativity of emotions" thing. Would he have opened up to me, confided in me about his happiness theories, sought my help as an assistant of sorts on the experiments I now know he'd started by then? Would he have told me about the women? The one woman in particular?

There's no way to know, because I never did.

# TEN

# Micro and Macro

SITTING BACK DOWN AT THE PORCH TABLE AFTER DETECTIVE JANUS FIN-ished her call, I noticed the picture of Dad's notebook was set apart from the others, placed neatly on the table in front of my seat, like a place mat or a gift. "Eugene, did you move this?" I whispered. He didn't look up from his iPad, but I thought I saw his mask shift up.

I picked up the picture and considered my three memories. I didn't recognize them as connected at the time, but if you considered them side by side and combined elements from each, it made sense that *happiness quotient* would pop out. Seeing *happiness* and $Q$ must have triggered the memories, which I must then have connected and synthesized instantly and subconsciously. I had the sense Eugene would appreciate my revelation more than Mom or John. Or maybe I was crazy; it was hard to know.

Mom sat down and placed a piece of paper on the table. "The detective is coming back in a minute, but she sent this scan. It's from that green notebook—they found it in the front pocket, apparently. I read it already. Go ahead."

I angled the paper so John and I could both read it and instantly understood why they'd decided the H meant Happiness. At the top, in the same block-print writing as the strange codes in the manila folder, Dad had written NEED TO DEFINE HAPPINESS. The top third of the page was a typed summary about a protein replacement therapy to "correct" the genetic errors that cause Angelman syndrome. Our parents had gone to a meeting about the medical and philosophical debate surrounding it and said they were considering signing up Eugene for a study and asked our thoughts. I remember saying, "What's to think about? If you can fix a disability, why wouldn't you?," and John saying it was more complicated, that he thought that view was ableist (a term we had to explain to our parents), akin to hearing people insisting on cochlear implants for Deaf people who didn't want them, and me pointing out that Eugene has no sign language or other way to tell us what he wants. This was right when we were applying to colleges, and John ended up writing his Common App essay about it and why he wants to go into special education.

Anyway, after the summary paragraph, Dad had written in black ink:

Normalcy = desirable. Is this assumption true? Many "normal" teens seem miserable, most Angelman kids seem happy. If we want our kids to be happy, if being happy is human goal, why do we want to "fix" AS gene?

This begs the question: How do you define "happiness"?

1) Micro-level: hedonistic, utilitarian, valueless description of a person's emotions at any given moment, OR

2) Macro-level: life satisfaction view, a longer, more Aristotelian perspective. Eating chocolates & streaming movies all day → happy hedonistically but feel emptiness under #2?

For your kids, you don't want unhappiness at either micro or macro levels. You want both. E appears happy on micro level.

Certainly much happier than M, even J—their whole HS class is miserable, stressed out. 3 suicides, how many on antidepressants? But on macro level, is E's life more satisfying? As a mosaic AS kid, he's luckier than most. No seizures, can walk, eat independently. BUT he still has reflux and constipation. Sleep issues. Can't communicate needs or wants. Crux of prob: E can't tell us what he would want. Fair to do something like this without <u>his</u> knowing consent?

Consider <u>J vs M</u>: Twins in same family, stellar IQ & grades, diff activities but both doing great. So why are they so different, happiness-wise? J is optimistic to a fault, generous in how he interprets people's motives, with a radiant happiness that is infectious, lifts everyone's moods. Why does J get so much more joy out of same experiences as M? Is it genetics? Research shows your genetic optimism makeup accounts for 40% of your happiness. Are H and me both Op for optimism gene, and M got 2 pessimism alleles, J got 2 optimism? Even if we could change M's pp to OO, I'm positive M would NOT (and should not) consent to that.

Reading this, I didn't know what to think, what to feel. Dad analyzing me, comparing me with John—maybe not unexpected given how often others did shit like that, but I have to admit I felt hurt reading his praise for John's radiance and generosity and then nothing for me, the implicit criticism. (Although he did say John was optimistic "to a fault" and that I shouldn't want to change.) But petty sibling envy aside, I thought about Eugene's beautiful run, his possibly reading (?!) the police report and my texts, understanding the phrase *happiness quotient*. Was it possible, could it be, that . . .

"Mom, is Eugene already enrolled in the study? Have the treatments started and you just haven't told us?" I said, and John said, "I wondered that, too."

Mom looked taken aback. "No, of course not. I don't think the study's even begun. Why would you possibly—"

Detective Janus walked in and sat down. She must have noticed our confused frowns because she stopped, asked if we were ready to continue. Mom said, "Yes, I was just showing them the scan you sent," and I said, "Do you have more pages we could read? I've discussed stuff like this with my dad, and I'd like to try to figure out if it could help with the search in some way."

The detective said how everything they find is evidence but also Dad's personal effects and of course they'll return it to us, and yes, they'd love my help deciphering the notes, and she'll have her evidence team send me scans of the pages as they dry. After sending my number to her team, she placed a folder on the table, laying her hands over it carefully as if to keep it from opening on its own. "Dr. Park, with respect to my running things by you first, are you sure—"

"Absolutely. We talked about it last night and agreed we shouldn't keep anything from one another."

"All right, if you're sure." Detective Janus opened her folder. "We found two things we think may be related. The first is that eight months ago, in October, Mr. Parson transferred twenty thousand dollars from his IRA to an account at your bank. It didn't match the account numbers you gave us, so we looked into it, and it's an individual checking account he opened one day before the transfer.

"The second thing is a phone number that jumped out at us during our scan of your phone records. We think it may be related to the twenty thousand dollars because it started appearing in Mr. Parson's call logs in October, a few weeks before the transfer. A cell number belonging to an Anjeli Rapari. Is that name familiar?"

I looked up and saw in John's and Mom's faces what I was feeling: I had never heard that name before, and somehow, this was scaring me, even more than before. I wanted to hug Mom, bury my head in the crook of her neck like when I was little, let her long hair drape over and cover my face like a veil.

"No," we all said, not quite in unison, one right after the other, like echoes.

"Over the past eight months, there have been numerous, frequent calls and texts between Mr. Parson's phone and this number."

John said, "Dad's always calling and texting with Eugene's therapists and the other moms at Henry's House. His schedule changes every day, and—"

"They exchanged dozens of texts and calls every day," she said. "And we cross-checked the name and number against Eugene's therapist list and the Henry's House family directory."

I wished I hadn't had all that coffee with fake sugar. It churned in my stomach. I wanted to vomit.

"Because you're the primary account holder, Dr. Park, we were able to use your authorization to access voicemail messages. This was sent to Mr. Parson's mobile phone and deleted two nights ago, the night before his disappearance, but the phone company archives deleted messages for thirty days, so we were able to retrieve it." She clicked on her phone, and the message started playing. A woman's voice, low and husky, with a slight Indian accent.

*Hi. Can you call me? I feel badly about how we left things. It's just . . . I hate sneaking around like this. You have to tell Hannah. It's not fair to her, or to me. I've never done anything like this before. And the plan you laid out . . . the more I think about it, the more I think it's wrong and really hurtful. Call me.*

As soon as the message stopped, silence set in, a heavy, oppressive pressure that pushed against my eyes, neck, chest. I wondered how Mom must be feeling, but I was too chickenshit to look. Detective Janus said, "We're trying to contact her, but her phone is off. Her home is in the county, near our headquarters, actually, and we went by this morning—that's the update I was getting just now—but no one answered the door. We spoke to some neighbors. None of them know her well, but it appears she hasn't been home in a few days, maybe more, although no one can say for sure because everyone's been isolated. We're trying to get a search warrant to go inside, but this voicemail, the frequency of their contact, and her also being unreachable—those all suggest Mr. Parson's disappearance may be voluntary, so it's unlikely we'll obtain a warrant."

She was trying to use as formal a wording as possible to shield us, but I knew what she was saying.

"Voluntary?" John was saying. "No way it's voluntary. Dad would never just leave Eugene to fend for himself. You don't know him, but we're telling you, he would never do that."

"One hundred percent," I said. "Not to mention, Dad's not the type to go around with random women. We know him." But even as I was saying it, I thought, Do we? I thought we did. I thought he was open with us, telling us all sorts of stuff about his girlfriends and drinking, drugs, and sex in college. We sometimes had to tell him it was TMI, honestly, remind him that kids do not like to hear about their parents' sex lives, premarital or otherwise. But the password-protected files, the codes, the voicemail, the $20,000, this mystery woman. I thought about the statistics people are always spouting off about how many marriages end in divorce, how many people have affairs, and I wondered how many of those people's kids assumed they didn't have the time or logistical wherewithal, let alone the inclination, for extramarital anything. How many would have sworn their parents weren't the type to cheat?

It occurred to me that Mom wasn't saying anything, wasn't coming to Dad's defense. Was she shocked into silence? And then the thought: Maybe she couldn't. Maybe she knew something we didn't.

Detective Janus's phone buzzed. She wasn't on the call for long, didn't say much, just "Uh-huh" and "Where?" When she got off, she said, "We set up pings on Mr. Parson's bank and credit cards, and we just got a hit. A cash withdrawal of one thousand dollars using your joint checking ATM card, from a convenience store ATM fifty miles south of here. Thirty minutes ago."

I wish I could go back in time, stop myself from thinking what I thought as she went on about the store's surveillance video recording. She sounded excited, which made sense—this was a possible break that meant Dad was fine, walking around a store and buying stuff—but I remember praying, Please, no. Please let this be a huge mistake, let it be someone else, let Dad be hurt, let him be dead.

Because if he did this on purpose, if he ran off with some woman and did this to Mom, to us, to Eugene . . .

Before I could finish my thought, Detective Janus said something else that stopped me. I'd been assuming that someone using Dad's ATM card—meaning, someone who knew his PIN—must be Dad. But Detective Janus asked if Dad wrote his PIN on his ATM card—something that seemed asinine but that, according to her, many people do—and/or used his birth date as his PIN—ditto—and then referred to "the potential suspect." It took me a minute to work out the implications of the word *suspect*: how would someone— a *suspect*—get someone's ATM card, the wallet of someone who's missing? Mugging? Kidnapping? Could this be a *crime* here?[7]

The minute I thought that, I realized: my going on about hoping, wishing, praying it wouldn't be Dad and how I'd rather he be dead than a man who'd cheat on his wife and abandon his vulnerable kid—that was all bullshit. When it came right down to it, dead was dead, alive was alive, and I would take a pathetic, two-faced, deplorable Alive Dad I could hit and scream at over a noble, funny, lovable Dead Dad a thousand times.

Before that moment, I'd felt disappointment, anger, grief, so many things. But all that got swept away. Shame, fierce and furious, seared everything, obliterated it. I'd actually wished for the death of the man who gave up his career to stay home and take care of us, moved us

---

7 I've been thinking about this a lot, and I think kidnapping would have occurred to me immediately if the missing person were Mom, Eugene, or John. So why not Dad? Because he's tall and strong? But John is taller, stronger. Because I don't think of him as vulnerable because he takes care of us? But Mom takes care of us, too, *and* she's a tae kwon do black belt and works out way more than Dad does. The only thing I can think of is media conditioning: adult men don't get kidnapped in the missing-person mysteries I've watched and read (unless they're spies or mafia-affiliated, which is definitely, unconditionally not applicable to Dad). But that begs the questions of 1) what is it about women as victims that makes these stories so popular? and, more importantly, at least from the standpoint of perpetuating the image of adult men as strong and powerful, 2) what is it about men as victims that makes these stories seemingly implausible and rare?

half a world away and back. No matter what he'd done, even if he was happily gallivanting around with a husky-voiced woman named Anjeli, how could I have wished for my own father's death, even unsaid, even for a moment? What kind of a person does that?

Harmonee used to say that shame is the most powerful and long-lasting emotion we have, that scanning through her seventy-plus years of memories, the moments that felt unbearably intense at the time—teenage first love, childbirth, the deaths of loved ones—have mellowed over the years, but remembering the moments she's ashamed of, even from childhood, she still feels the rise of heat, the flush on her face, its intensity not only undiminished but possibly even growing over time. I used to think this was something she made up to reinforce her lectures to us on the importance of not lying, of not being mean to our classmates, to each other, and, most importantly, to Eugene. But I've come to believe she was telling us the truth. Because now, whenever I think of all that happened that day, not only what we'd already been through but the even more awful things yet to come, my thoughts instantly zoom to these moments of shame, and I feel a hot flush spread up my neck and settle into ugly red blotches on my cheeks, there for everyone to see.

# ELEVEN

# That Summer

IT SEEMS STRANGE TO SAY IT WAS A SHOCK WHEN THE CHILD PROTECTIVE Services specialist showed up that morning because we had been anticipating it for so long. Of course, I say "so long," but it hadn't even been a day, barely eighteen hours, since the police first came to our door. Tragedies and emergencies warp your perception of time. This past day, with so much happening, our lack of sleep, the dramatic ups and downs of emotion—it felt like Dad had been gone a month.

I think maybe the shock was, paradoxically, *because* the CPS visit was planned. The one-two-three punch of 1) Dad's bag being found in the river, 2) the cryptic voicemail from the woman who may have also disappeared, and 3) the ATM withdrawal by someone who was either Dad or his mugger/kidnapper/murderer—that felt like a game changer. The idea of sticking to a previously planned schedule seemed disrespectful of the magnitude of these developments, like going in for a scheduled teeth cleaning right after getting diagnosed with cancer. I expected Detective Janus to say the CPS interview was canceled, that she needed to rush out for emergency meetings, chase down leads, no time to waste. When the car drove up and she said that must be the CPS folks, Mom said, "We're . . . still doing that?"

"Why wouldn't we?" Detective Janus said.

Maybe if we thought there was any chance of the police getting useful information out of Eugene, we would have felt differently. You could argue that it was more critical than ever for the police to sit down with Eugene, figure out what happened in the park. But we expected the interview to be a mega waste of time. It was inevitable: the interviewer would be a kind social worker who would come in with picture cards, a basic proficiency in sign language, and a deep and abiding hope that some combination of good intentions, patience, and understanding would be the key to connecting with Eugene—how many movies and shows had we watched where that was all it took to reach a previously unreachable kid? Equally inevitable was how it would end: Eugene would remain nonresponsive, and his anxiety, frustration, and withdrawal from videos would mount until he melted down and/or started jumping. They'd give up and file a report that yes, they made a valiant attempt to interview the son, and move on. Knowing this, with Dad's life on the line, it was hard not to feel impatient with Detective Janus wasting her time on a checklist item.

Yet another reason for the shock: as the interviewer was walking our way through the backyard, Detective Janus warned that we'd all need to leave so they could interview Eugene by himself. She tried to make it seem normal, like this was how they conducted all their interviews, but the fact was, she'd never asked to question any of the rest of us alone. She'd treated all of us as a team. So for her to say all of a sudden that they wanted to question Eugene without the "undue influence" of our presence?

"No, I'm not leaving," Mom said. "Eugene is my son and a minor, and I do not and will not consent to him being questioned outside my presence." Detective Janus said something about not needing her consent under Virginia law, being able to question minors as long as they themselves consent, and Mom said, "Great. As soon as he says, 'Yes, I consent to being questioned without my mother present,' I would be happy to leave," sounding like a badass lawyer. She hasn't done it in a long time, but Mom's first job was as a Korean-English interpreter. She used to talk about it a lot, how much she loved the intensity of interpreting in real time for heated political negotiations or legal disputes, and how the best interpreters were like Method actors, trying to get inside the minds of the speakers to convey their subtext and emotional intent as well as their words. That's actually how our parents met, when Dad was negotiating some deal against a Korean company; he loves talking about it, how the Korean CEO was trying to play hardball but was too bland and boring to pull it off, but Mom saved him, delivering his aggressive words with this edge, a hint of flirtatious venom that completely impressed and intimidated Dad's team. Mom's like that with us all the time, but I think we tend to discount domestic things, maternal things, see them as inapplicable to the real world. Seeing Mom stand up to Detective Janus, though, forcing this tall, scowling cop into an awkward, fake-conciliatory smile-nod with a curt "Point taken"—I could totally see the kick-ass professional Mom was, *is,* could see why Dad fell for her.

"But them . . ." Detective Janus motioned to John and me, and Mom flicked a glance to the door, a silent *you are dismissed.* We got up, went into the house, closed the door.

"Outside?" John whispered. The problem with our porch was the inability to eavesdrop; the extra-thick storm door was impossible to hear through. Our only hope was outside, behind nearby bushes.

"Nope, the prison system's on," I said, referring to our alarm system that beeps loudly when a door to the outside opens. After this morning, Mom turned it on to prevent us from leaving the house without her knowing. We usually protested these types of encroachments on our privacy and freedom, but this was not the time to test Mom. "But wait. Didn't Dad put a nanny cam in the porch?"

John ran to the home security panel and pulled up the cameras Dad installed a few years ago to monitor Eugene's therapists and babysitters after reading these horrifying stories about nonspeaking children being abused. John found it, clicked to enable video and sound. The camera must have been hidden in the fake plant in the corner, at eye level; it was full color and surprisingly high-def. "Wow, the picture quality—kind of disturbing," he said. I found the volume control, turned it up.

The CPS specialist looked to be a total newbie, not only in that she looked young (mid-twenties, tops), but in the way she dressed— navy skirt suit, white blouse, high-heeled pumps, hair in a severe bun, leather briefcase—which, instead of making her look professional, made her look insecure, like she was overcompensating for inexperience. She was seated across the table from Mom and Eugene and saying, "I'm actually not a caseworker. I'm a consultant for the county. I'm a speech pathologist, and I specialize in augmentative and alternative communication for nonspeakers—all types, but especially therapies that involve text-based communication using letterboards and keyboards."

Oh fuck, I thought as John said it out loud, though under his breath.

Was it my imagination, or was Mom's face becoming blanched? "Mom looks like she's going to faint," John said.

The therapist was giving what sounded like a canned speech about her training, her voice animated—*cheerful,* even—unaware or maybe uncaring of Mom's growing unease. I wanted to run in there and put a stop to this, yell at the therapist to stop being so clueless, or at least warn her to tread lightly, explain why this was dangerous. But maybe that was unfair. After all, it's only because of our family's history with assisted writing therapy—a history she couldn't have known about—that I was associating this woman with the ugliness that came before, the thing that nearly broke our family apart.

———

THE TIME I'M REFERRING TO is what we call That Summer. I don't think we're the only family that has stuff like this, cryptic ways of referring to things you don't want to say out loud. That Summer is code for the time our parents almost got a divorce. It's also when Mom went back to work full time and Dad "retired." (As Mom likes to point out, it's fascinating how it's called "retirement" when fathers quit their jobs, but "becoming a stay-at-home mom" when mothers do.) John and I are 99 percent sure this switch must be linked to the near-divorce, but we've never been clear on the nuances of the causal chain involved, such as: Did Mom give an ultimatum, or was it Dad's idea? Did Mom want a job, which forced Dad to quit, or did Dad volunteer to quit, which freed up Mom to get a job? As much as we'd love the details, our curiosity is outweighed by our certainty that we must never bring it up—thus, the code.

The whole thing sprang up, as does almost everything in our family, from our collective focus on Eugene's inability to talk and our desperate attempts to communicate with him. This is, of course, to be expected from families like ours. We know plenty of siblings of nonspeaking kids from Henry's House and various chat boards, and we all agree this is the focal point around which our families' lives have come to orbit. When you love someone, it's natural to want to communicate with them—to hear their thoughts, to connect and coordinate, to ask questions and get answers, to simply exchange information, if nothing else. And it doesn't help that we're a particularly verbal family, what with Mom being a linguistics specialist and all of us, even John (though he doesn't like to admit it), being really into word games and puzzles.

But as much as Dad, John, and I have always wanted to help Eugene communicate, it's nothing compared to Mom's dedication. Eugene's autism diagnosis came right after Harmonee died, right when Mom was spending a lot of time alone with Eugene (while Dad was at work and John and I were in school), and she fell into the autism world the way you might into a black hole—that is to say, wholly and inescapably, as if toward an unreachable singularity. She became *consumed* by theories, therapists, specialists, conferences, supplements.

Maybe Mom's obsession was inevitable, given her love for Eugene, her baby, mixed in with her high-achievement mindset from her academic days, plus maybe the expectation he'd be "gifted" because John and I received that label early on—but I've given a lot of thought to this, and I think there's an extra factor that seeped in and magnified all this, like in alchemy: guilt. Mom blames herself for Eugene not talking. She's always been susceptible to what Dad calls "if-only thinking," second-guessing her decisions and actions, and that went into overdrive with Eugene. The night he got the original autism diagnosis (the week he turned four), I overheard her telling Dad it's her fault, that any good mother would have gotten him started on speech therapy a year sooner. Later, for some questionnaire she was filling out while I was doing homework in the next room, Mom started reading out the "risk factor" questions about prenatal diet, toxic paint fumes, long flights during pregnancy, and on and on. "Yup, I did all these things; check, check, check," she said, her voice getting higher with each "check," until Dad said, "Hannah, stop. Don't do this to yourself."

I think Dad thought Mom would calm down as soon as we found out about Eugene's Angelman diagnosis three years later. After we came out of the geneticist's offices, he said to all of us but clearly directed at Mom, "That's it, then. We know. It's in his genes—part of him, intrinsic to who he is. We couldn't have the Eugene we have, the boy we love, without having the gene, too." And maybe that would have happened, taken away Mom's guilt, if it hadn't been for the follow-up meeting.

By that time, John and I had our phones and Eugene his iPad, so we were watching stuff with headphones on while our parents talked to the doctors. I was fascinated by DNA during this time—I was working on a genetics project for our middle school science fair—so I muted the volume, staring at the screen like I was watching YouTube, and instead listened to the discussion (a good way of eavesdropping on grown-ups).

Anyway, the geneticist was going on and on about insurance issues—he had a soporific, atonal voice, and I got so bored I started half-watching my show—but he said something about *maternal* and Mom said, "Sorry, what was that?," and he said how the Angelman genetic error comes from the mother's chromosomes.[8] I sneaked a peek and saw Dad put his hand on Mom's like he was concerned, squeezing, but Mom took hers away—not snatching, not mean, but just quietly and slowly, cupping her hands together in her lap, as if in prayer.

I suppose it's possible I'm reading too much into it, that it's all coincidence and I'm confusing association with causation. But that very next week was when Mom found an augmentative and alternative communication (AAC) therapist I'll call TFT[9] and our lives changed.

TFT wasn't actually a therapist, although she called herself one; she was a trainee who was a few months into a yearlong program on physically supported writing (PSW), in which a facilitator-therapist

---

8 I remember thinking, But Mom doesn't have Angelman herself, so was her genes' interaction with Dad's what caused the error? In which case, it's not "caused by the maternal gene" at all. Which is exactly what the follow-up research showed, although not until recently: that in some cases, the Angelman genetic error is caused by the male chromosome crowding out the female chromosome. I talked to Mom about this for the first time recently, and she said this was nothing new—the first pamphlet she got after Eugene's original autism diagnosis explained the "refrigerator mother" theory, blaming autism on cold, unloving mothers who cause irreparable psychological damage to their kids, which is an ancient, discarded theory in the US, but apparently still popular in Korea. What bullshit nonsense, this whole blaming everything on moms. Is it any wonder that women are increasingly deciding not to have children, why the birth rate is declining drastically in both the US and Korea?

9 Why the initials? It's not that I've forgotten her name; you'd better believe I remember it, as many times as Mom talked about her that year. And it's not like I'm afraid to name her, like she's Voldemort or something. It's more like when something awful happens and you don't want to raise the visibility of something/someone you'd rather not exist in your sphere of awareness. I'd rather people not know her name; it's as simple as that. TFT also has the benefit of standing for The Facilitator-Therapist (which is how she described her function) or The Fucking Therapist (which is what John and I secretly called her).

touches or holds a nonspeaker's arm or hand to help them point to letters to spell out words. The justification for the physical contact is that for some nonspeakers, the words are locked in due to oral and physical motor difficulties, so physical support is necessary to control their arms, especially at first. The goal is to fade the physical support over time and enable independent typing. All that, you can learn easily enough through Googling or Wiki-ing. What Google and Wiki can't tell you is how magical it made our lives.

I remember that whole winter/spring of PSW as the happiest time for our family. It was the hope it created in Mom. We'd seen this before—the excitement about a new treatment making its way through her circle of friends—but it had always been guarded. Mom is, at heart, an academic, someone who prides herself on cool intellectualism, and whenever she discussed some new thing that worked wonders for some friend of a friend, she'd say she planned to try it, just in case, but Eugene was very different from *xyz* so it probably wouldn't work. Limited hope, with a correspondingly limited disappointment. This was especially the case for TFT, who was working with Eugene for free in exchange for him serving as her "pilot" client. Mom seemed to regard the whole thing as a throwaway, an experiment to try with no downside.

I think what made PSW different was that it seemed to work for Eugene. As early as the second month of therapy, Eugene was able to sit through a whole half-hour therapy session without melting down or needing to jump, which was unprecedented. When he started pointing to letters and spelling things out, Mom still played the part of Rational Skeptic. She knew what we would think and voiced it first, following the truism that the best defense is a good offense: PSW's main risk is the ideomotor phenomenon, aka the Ouija Board effect—that you move without realizing it, without meaning to. She said, "Obviously, the danger with the facilitator-therapist touching the child's hand is that it's the therapist doing the communicating, not the child." She explained how this was a greater risk for TFT, who had a nephew with Angelman syndrome and was experimenting with a special hand-over-hand technique customized for him and other AS kids like Eugene with poor muscle control. Mom said TFT acknowledged that her particular variation required a lot more physical support than sanctioned by the PSW system, but that she was constantly on guard to make sure she wasn't in any way guiding or influencing her clients' letter choices.

The breakthrough—when Mom's hope took root and started growing wildly out of control—happened three months into PSW, when Eugene pointed to the letters spelling out *my throat hurts*. That night, Eugene developed a fever, and the next day, the pediatrician diagnosed him with strep.

Mom was giddy telling us about it, any trace of skepticism gone, and Dad and John seemed convinced, too, saying how amazing it was, a huge turning point for Eugene and our family. I went along in front of Mom, but later, I told Dad and John I'd read about those mediums who hold séances to help people talk to their dead husbands or whatever—how some are scam artists who go through people's trash to figure out convincing lies, but some are genuine believers who happen to be talented at picking up on subtle clues, not intending to, not even aware they're fabricating stories. "For example," I said, "TFT might have subconsciously noticed Eugene rubbing his throat. Or maybe another client just canceled with strep so it was on her mind, and since they're all touching the same stuff, it makes sense Eugene caught it."

Dad seemed intrigued, asking about the article to look it up, but John didn't want to hear it, and I can't blame him. We'd gotten used to Mom being glum, and seeing her so happy, it was infectious. You don't realize how much one depressed, stressed-out person in a house affects the whole family's mood until it's been lifted. She became a person I'd never known, her smile wide and crinkled, both rows of teeth showing, even the molars, the way it was in pictures of her and Dad, pre-us. She *hummed*. She fucking hummed! It was amazing to have every breakfast and dinner, the bookends of the day, filled with Mom telling us some new thing Eugene spelled, how they were working on "generalizing the skill"—trying to spell with other people or in other settings—and how Mom could now ask questions, communicate directly with Eugene. It was like Christmas every day, the anticipation and unbridled hope that was buoying Mom and, by extension, all of us. But even more than the happiness, what I remember the most about that summer is the fear it would end, that it had to. It's like I knew it wasn't real, it couldn't last, and I wanted it to keep going for as long as possible. And maybe that's how Dad felt, too, which is why he didn't say anything.

It all stopped the day TFT came to our house. It was one of the rare Saturdays Dad wasn't working, and he spent a long time with Eugene, just Eugene, which was unusual. When TFT arrived, I went to the basement to get them. Dad had a red ball with green stars I'd never seen. He was saying, "Eugene, remember, this is a *red* ball, R-E-D. With *green* stars. G-R-E-E-N, green. Okay? Let's do a fun game with the *red* ball with *green* stars. Here, catch." Eugene, predictably, did not. I got the ball and gently placed it in his hand the way I always did.

I guess my point is that I didn't really think about it; it didn't occur to me to think of this game as anything but Dad playing with Eugene in a fun but educational way. When we got to the family room, we sat on the couch while Eugene sat with TFT at a table by the fireplace, facing us so we could see the letters on TFT's tablet screen and their hands and all that.

Mom had said what a big deal it was, TFT agreeing to let us watch—how stressful it was for Eugene, but TFT was willing to try because the family was so excited and wanted to share in it. And I *was* excited; I had a whole slew of questions, starting with whether Eugene wanted a dog (John's and my vote) or cat (Mom's and Dad's) and whether he jumped so much because he truly loved it or he couldn't help it (similar to my biting my nails), and I couldn't wait to see his questions for me. But I remember watching her hand over his and thinking, Eugene is perfectly capable of moving his own hand;

yes, I know it's hard for him, but does she have to have her hand over his so completely (which the PSW brochures Mom had brought home specifically said was a no-no)? Also, he seemed kind of spaced out, not even looking at the letters. It really *did* remind me of the Ouija board, how she sounded out the letters and said the words. On the other hand, I'd never seen him sit still for so long without watching some sort of video. Also, Eugene/TFT were saying really specific things I couldn't figure out how she would know—for instance, how I hid Halloween candy in my old violin case (which I was positive Mom didn't know).

About twenty minutes into the session, Dad said, "I've been waiting so long for this. Is it okay if I talk to Eugene? Ask a few questions?"

I've thought about it a lot, why what Dad did was so hurtful to Mom, and I think it was the slyness—the abruptness combined with the clearly planned nature of it. The fact that he didn't give her any warning, no raised objections or hint of skepticism, but instead pushed for this at-home session, saying we needed to see for ourselves the wonder and bear witness. And the way he asked to talk to Eugene—unsure and shy, with a touch of nervousness, like he was intimidated and in awe—it was Dad at his most charming and disarming. I'm sure Mom and TFT thought he was excited to talk directly to his son for the first time, exactly the way he meant for them to. Eugene/TFT said Y-E-S.

Dad said, "What color was the ball we were playing with in the basement just now?"

TFT looked up, alarm on her face. "I'm sorry, that's not the kind of question . . . This isn't a test."

"It's a simple question. What's the harm?"

"You're trying to verify, and the insinuation that you don't believe in his ability—"

"I'm not questioning *his* ability. It's just a few questions. It won't take but a minute."

It was brutal to watch, efficient and devastating in its effectiveness. Eugene/TFT said the ball was blue with yellow stripes, which was a good guess—we have a ball like that for Eugene's physical therapy homework—and that the story Dad's been reading to him at bedtime is "Yertle the Turtle," another good guess, as that's Eugene's socialization therapy group's monthly pick. Dad didn't correct anything, just went along, breezy and cheerful.

After five questions, though, he took out a piece of paper from his pocket and unfolded it. "I suspected but I was really holding out hope. I was just praying I was wrong," Dad said and read from the paper: a list of the answers to his five questions, in order. None matched Eugene/TFT's answers. When he finished, he held up the paper, like one of those lawyers on TV showing the jury a piece of evidence.

That's the first moment I can recall thinking of Dad as anything but kind. I think it was how calculating he was, the way he had clearly prepared for a long time—not only memorizing the questions in order and typing out the answers but buying a different ball, reading Eugene a different book for the last month without Mom knowing.

There was a moment of silence as we all stared at the answers, the indelible typed words making it undeniable: Eugene was not the one who'd answered these questions; TFT was unreliable at best, an outright fraud at worst. TFT broke the silence, saying, "This is absolutely unacceptable. I've never had a client blindside me like this, which is completely unfair, not only to me but to Eugene. You owe me an apology. Right now."

Looking back, if she hadn't been so aggressive, if she had mixed in even a dollop of contrition or humility, just an acknowledgment of her human fallibility, Mom might have come to her defense with points (which we now know are valid) about the emotional strain and stress this type of testing places on memory and verbal output. But TFT's unapologetic truculence, her belligerence—it was hard to sympathize with and impossible to defend.

"Please. Leave," Mom said, slowly and firmly, enunciating each sound so you could tell she was 100 percent resolute. TFT started to say something and Dad started to cut her off, but Mom cut through both and said, "Please don't make it worse for us or for yourself. Please leave."

While TFT was still in the room, it was easy to focus our collective anxiety and anger on her, at the way she was behaving like a petulant tantrumming toddler, really, throwing the letterboard into her bag, banging it around, not even saying goodbye to Eugene on her way out, slamming the door. But after she left, it's like there was all this built-up emotion in the room that had nowhere to go and needed to be discharged, like static electricity. Dad became the natural grounding conductor, our lightning rod, all our stray emotions zapping to him and the paper still in his hand, the numbers lined up neatly: 1-2-3-4-5.

Mom reached for it, her hands shaking a little, and Dad handed it over. She held it with both hands, stared for a long time, her mouth ajar, and I thought she was trying to process that TFT had somehow been answering for Eugene this whole time. But then she focused on Dad, her eyes narrowed like she didn't recognize him, her face going saggy, and I realized I'd been reading it wrong. It was disillusionment, an ineffable sadness, but not solely or even primarily about the therapy.

"Honey, I'm sorry I had to do that," Dad said. "You probably didn't even realize, but of course you're going to inadvertently share stuff about our family routines and funny stories while you're coordinating schedules and chitchatting. And it's natural she'd repeat that later, not even remembering it, just subconsciously, and of course that seems like proof that Eugene's the one communicating."

Mom didn't say anything, and Dad continued, his voice rising. "Look, Hannah, I really doubt she did this intentionally, and I certainly don't think you guys were in *collusion* or anything like that." Mom frowned at that, shook her head a little like she was incredulous, and I thought, Oh God, stop talking, Dad. Don't make it worse.

But he kept going. He sat next to her and put his hand on her knee. "You have to know. I don't blame you in *any* way. At all." The way he said this reminded me of those Important Oscar Scenes in movies, the actor's words dripping with sincerity, punctuated by meaningful pauses, deep and tender gazes into the actress's eyes.

"Well, how magnanimous of you," Mom said, but with no sarcasm. She took Dad's hand off her knee—not huffy or mad, but gently, with a quiet dignity. I felt a spurt of fury at Dad, wanted to kick him as hard as I could.

"Come on, Eugene. Let's go upstairs, take a nice bath," Mom said, standing and holding out her hand. Eugene went with her obediently, and I thought, Wow, I almost forgot he was here, he's been so calm through all this, and I thought again about Mom saying how good PSW and TFT had been for Eugene. John went upstairs, too, pissed at Dad, like I was.

This was our usual dynamic when they fought: John with Mom, me with Dad. It wasn't taking sides, exactly, just the way it worked out. No matter who we agreed with, we both had to do our part to nudge them together, make each feel better. But not this time.

"Have you considered that was an asshole thing to do?"

Dad frowned at me. He looked clueless, had no idea. "I didn't blame her in any way. That therapist was really convincing, so of course she fell for it. I almost did, too. All I did was test her, to make sure she wasn't a fraud. You agree with that; I know you do. You've been saying that from the beginning."

I was sixteen, at the height of my rebellion stage, and God, it pissed me off, how sanctimonious he was being. "So now you're blaming me?" I kept talking, straight through Dad's protests. "Yeah, I questioned it. But I didn't go around staging this takedown. *That's* what I'm talking about. *How* you did it, planning—for what, a month?—but not saying, letting Mom's hopes get higher and higher and then doing this TV-lawyer thing to bring them down. It's like your graveyard thing, total despair to elation. You did the opposite to Mom. You let her build up hope, *knowing* it was false hope, and when she was as happy as she could be, you slammed it down, and not only that, you did it in front of her own kids, proved that this thing she's poured all her time and effort into is a total sham. Jesus

Christ, Dad, what did you expect? This is the lowest of the low for Mom. As euphoric as you were in the graveyard, Mom is now miserable. How do you not see that?"

Of course, I know now that what I said impacted his thinking about the relativity of happiness. But back then, Dad seemed to dismiss what I said, swiping it away with the back of his hand as he left the room.

# TWELVE

# Post Hoc, Ergo Propter Hoc

YOU KNOW HOW PEOPLE SAY WHEN SOMETHING AWFUL HAPPENS, YOUR spirit gets broken? I remember that summer thinking that's wrong. Mom didn't break. She shut down, like a laptop in hibernation mode. A spiritual obliteration for a week, then re-emergence into a translucent, smaller version of her former self. She talked to all of us, even Dad, but minimally, for logistical things. She wasn't cold, like she was punishing him. More like she was drained of energy and purpose. She stopped doing therapy homework with Eugene, said she wanted to accept Eugene—"as he is, with no expectations." (But, as Dad always pointed out, how can you not have expectations of a child? What is a child if not as-yet-unrealized potential personified?)

Our parents getting divorced was something I'd been scared of since I was thirteen and overheard Dad complain to Mom how preoccupied she was with Eugene and they hadn't had sex in more than a year. I don't have to tell you—the idea of your parents having sex is unbearably awful, especially since that would presumably be happening in our house, the space I share with them. Even so, I knew that wasn't good, that no sex for that long was a prelude to divorce, which is something we thought about incessantly because of the unreal statistic we'd heard that more than 80 percent of special-needs kids' parents get divorced. The ever-looming prospect of divorce was even more intolerable than the concept of parental sex, which is why, as disgusting as it was to talk (let alone think) about it, I told John what I heard and we came up with a plan involving frequent offers to babysit Eugene and gift certificates at romantic restaurants.

After the TFT fiasco, I got paranoid and upped my spying efforts. I didn't overhear any fights, which seemed a good sign until John pointed out that perhaps that was because they didn't appear to be speaking to each other at all. I checked our Wi-Fi router's browser history logs and saw *Northern Virginia marriage counseling, separation period Virginia, child custody stay-at-home mother,* and *special needs child Virginia custody arrangements,* although I couldn't figure out which parent was doing which Googling.

So against that backdrop, you can understand how divorce seemed inevitable when, about a month after TFT's visit, our parents sat us down to tell us "something important."

"We have an exciting announcement," Dad said. "I'm retiring, and Mom's going back to work, full time!" It was so unexpected that I remember thinking it must be part of the divorce arrangement, Mom needing money and Dad giving up his 24–7 job for a chance at some sort of custody. But Dad grinned and put his arm around Mom, kissed her temple, and it's not like Mom looked *overjoyed,* but she looked not unhappy. Dad said how Mom doing everything at home was exhausting and unfair, and besides, he wanted to spend time with us before we went off to college, so he'd be taking over everything—Eugene's therapies, cooking, grocery shopping, driving us around, the whole bit.

At one point, Dad said, "I couldn't be more proud to make this wonderful sacrifice for my wonderful family," and Mom did this thing with her face—a wince, then an immediate correction, like she hadn't meant to do that and caught herself. I remember thinking that not many dads I knew would give up a prestigious job so his wife could go back to *her* career, to *her* goals. I thought how proud of him I should be. And I was. But.

Here's the thing: I've always been more partial to Dad. I've heard people say that parents have their secret favorite child. I don't know about that for us—I think Eugene takes up so much bandwidth that it's hard to know how the miniscule amount left over for John and me gets divided. But I think kids have their secret favorite parent, and for me, it's always been Dad, which I think had to do with my seeing him as valuable to society, someone I wanted to emulate. But I thought how unfair that was, how that view of him came at the price of my seeing Mom as "merely" our caretaker. His noble generosity wasn't that—or maybe it was, but it's easy to be generous when you've taken so much.

Looking at Dad through this lens, at his grand gesture and grand speech announcing his grand sacrifice—a sliver of what Mom had done for sixteen years without once labeling it a "sacrifice"—it made me hate him. For just a microsecond.

There are moments when something we've idealized all our lives changes and becomes something less. Not by a noticeable amount, just an infinitesimal disappointment. But it's like going from 100 percent to 99.9 percent—imperceptible quantitatively, but dramatically different qualitatively, from flawless to flawed. After this point, I found myself questioning Dad's motives, doubting his perspectives, in a way I hadn't before.

Things settled down after that. Mom went to work, Dad quit and took over at home, and there was a lot of talk about truly accepting Eugene, helping him to be as fulfilled as possible, not trying to change him into something he's not. But I could never let go of that flash of resentment I saw in Mom, that momentary wince, and the way it seemed to return whenever Dad mentioned sacrificing his career for the good of the family. We heard through the grapevine that TFT got kicked out of the PSW training program for her unsanctioned hand-over-hand support method and her practice shut down, but friends would mention other therapists using new variants of text-based communication therapies from time to time, which Dad immediately shut down. It became an unwritten rule in our house: we were not to mention alternative writing therapies for nonspeakers in front of Mom.

———

SO YOU UNDERSTAND WHY JOHN and I wanted to run to the porch, get the CPS therapist out of there ASAP.

"Let's try this first," the therapist said. At first I couldn't see what she pulled out of her bag because of the camera angle, but she put it down on the table.

It was a letterboard. Not an electronic one on a tablet, like the one TFT used, but a plastic stencil letterboard a little bigger than regular printer paper.

Mom said, "I'm not sure why you brought this. I thought you talked to Eugene's speech therapist. He's not . . . he doesn't use this, and I don't know why—"

"Oh, I'm sorry," the therapist said. "I saw a stencil letterboard in the items recovered from Mr. Parson's backpack, so I assumed—"

"What are you talking about? I didn't see anything like that in the pictures from the police. He wouldn't have that, anyway, because Eugene doesn't use a letterboard."

Detective Janus said, "I think it was in a folder. Once it was dry, the lab opened it and there was an item just like this one in there."

"Well, why don't we just ask Eugene?" The therapist said to Eugene in a surprisingly normal, non-infantilizing voice, "Eugene, have you seen this before?"

Eugene had been focused on his iPad, but the therapist held up the stencil in front of him, waved it around to get his attention. Eugene put down his iPad, grabbed the stencil, and clutched it in both hands. Stared. It's funny—I know for most people, masks make it harder to read faces. But for Eugene, because of its ever-presence, his smile functions as a mask of sorts, and paradoxically, his wearing a Covid mask made it easier for me to read his emotions, to filter out the smile and focus in on his eyes, eyebrows, forehead. There was a faraway look in his eyes, an unfocused dilation of his pupils, and crinkling at the bridge of his nose. It looked like intimacy and longing, the way you might look at a photograph of someone you love and miss. Mom had said Eugene hadn't been enrolled in the gene-replacement study, but was it possible Dad had changed his mind about text-based therapies?

"Eugene, can I see that?" Mom sounded like she was trying hard not to lose her temper. She snatched the letterboard from him, a deep frown between her brows—a flash of impatience she usually didn't exhibit with Eugene—and I thought, Uh oh, Eugene will not like that.

What Eugene did next, we all misunderstood. It's a common logical error, the post hoc, ergo propter hoc fallacy—meaning that because $y$ happens after $x$, you assume $x$ caused $y$. But it wasn't just the sequential order of events that made us assume Eugene was reacting in anger. It seemed natural that a mother snatching something from a teenager would make him lash out against her.

Eugene grabbed a pen from the table, gripped it in his right fist like a dagger, and stabbed it toward Mom, at her face. Mom was holding the letterboard in front of her eyes—she seemed transfixed, like she was studying it for clues—and the pen's trajectory was right through the hollow space in the letter D, straight toward Mom's left eye. The strange thing was that Eugene didn't look mad or aggressive; he had a pleasant look on his face, which we might have taken as a clue to his actual intent and arrived at the answer more quickly. But since we'd seen him smile even when he was out-of-control furious, we couldn't discount the possibility that he'd lost his temper and was determined to hurt Mom. Detective Janus ran to Eugene and somehow managed to grab his wrist just as the tip of the pen went through the stencil, stopping it from reaching Mom.

Mom reacted instantly, standing to get around Detective Janus to get next to Eugene, but the detective yelled, "Ma'am, stay away!" putting out her arm and thumping Mom in the chest. Eugene screamed, and maybe it was the shock from that or maybe the awkward angle of grabbing Eugene's wrist, but Detective Janus lost her balance as Eugene swung his arm to get free, and she fell and hit her mouth on a sharp table corner, it looked like, and as she was raising her head, his elbow thwacked her jaw and cheek. She was still holding his right wrist and lunged to grab the other, and Eugene fought it, eyes closed and head shaking in a violent *no,* and clawed wildly, scratching her face and sending her staggering back.

"Holy fucking shit!" John and I said at the same time—I know, it's a very specific thing to say, but as I've said before, there's something to this twin synchrony thing—and started running to the porch, Eugene's squealing howls reverberating through the house. When we swung open the door, Detective Janus was twisting Eugene's arms behind his back, and Mom was on the other side of Eugene, shushing into his ear, trying to hug and rock him, despair and desperation all over her face.

Detective Janus's face was a mess: her mask torn off, her lower lip bleeding, a bright red line down her cheek—Eugene hates anyone cutting his nails, so they're long and sharp—and the other cheek pink from the elbow jab. But even with all that, she didn't look vulnerable. The opposite—she looked fierce and aggressive, and she said over Eugene's howls, "Dr. Park, you need to step back. Eugene, I need to place handcuffs on you. You need to stop fighting me."

"Handcuffs? It was an accident," Mom said. "He just got excited, and you startled him, you scared all of us, grabbing him like—"

"Ma'am, please step away if you don't want this to get worse." Detective Janus got handcuffs on his wrists, sending Eugene's screams up another half octave, an unbearable wail of suffering and confusion.

We pled with Detective Janus, said she was hurting him, couldn't she see he was just a boy, only fourteen? That he didn't understand? That he was scared? Mom said, "Please, I can calm him down if you just let him go." She turned to the therapist, who was cowering in the corner. "This is cruel. Aren't you supposed to be the child's advocate? Tell her!"

I saw the way Detective Janus and the therapist were looking at Eugene: not as a scared child deserving of protection and sympathy, but as a *thing,* like a wild animal, a threat to be neutralized. Detective Janus said, "I need to protect all of us—all of *you, and* Eugene as well. He was attacking you, and I intercepted him from hurting you, physically. I'm not going to put anyone at further risk. I need to take Eugene to headquarters."

"What?" "Why?" "Like an *arrest?*" Our questions bounced against each other.

"I need to file an APO incident report. It's mandatory anytime an officer receives injuries, and a juvenile intake officer will review. I can tell you from experience, the more you cooperate, the better off Eugene will be." She reached for her mask and used it like a tissue, wiping away the blood on her chin, taking a long time, almost theatrically.

Maybe the showiness combined with the threat was supposed to intimidate us. But for me, it did the opposite: it took my messy mix of emotions and strained off the fear, left me just pissed and determined. It seemed to do the same for Mom, because she gave her this long, cold stare that was kind of scary and pretty awesome. "Fine," Mom said. "But I am going with him and staying with him. The entire time. And you will not say a single thing to either of us until our lawyer arrives."

Detective Janus blinked, nodded. "Of course." She sneered. Tried to, anyway, but had to wince, her lower lip getting fat at an alarming rate. "I'll make an exception and allow you to accompany him. But I need him to get in my car. Now."

"You have Eugene in handcuffs. He's not going anywhere, and he's not going to hurt anyone. I personally find this completely outrageous, but we will cooperate fully. But I *respectfully* request five minutes to calm him down so that we can get him into the car peacefully. And I further request, again, *very* respectfully, that you refrain from laying one more finger on my son." Mom turned to John and me. "Mia, play the iPad. John, help me with the chair."

The iPad was paused on some superhero fight sequence, gunfire everywhere. No. I switched to the Manhwa video from yesterday and held up the screen to Eugene, at eye level. A simple tune in G major, the happiest key, the cartoon animals in primary colors, laughing in uniform glee, their mouths opening and closing in harmony.

Eugene's screaming turned to a quieter but more disturbing mix of high-pitched whimpering, moaning, and wailing. It sounded like a baby animal being tortured, and Mom whispered into his ear that she loved him, she was so sorry about his wrist and the handcuffs, it would all be over soon and everything would be fine. Over the loud singing of baby dinosaurs learning to share one sticky rice cake, Mom quietly told John and me what to do, where to go, who to call. I paid attention and told myself it was all going to be fine, the way Mom said. But I kept my eyes on Detective Janus and the therapist in the corner. I saw the way they were looking at each other, the way they were looking at Eugene and Mom, and I could tell: it wasn't going to be fine. Not even a little bit.

# THIRTEEN

## What We Talk About When We Talk About Dad

THE STREETS WERE DESERTED. WE WERE HEADED TO HENRY'S HOUSE, which is right off a major six-lane thoroughfare outside DC, and driving on this normally congested traffic artery with no other cars in broad daylight—the eerie apocalyptic vibe was not good for my psyche.

I'd been to Henry's House a lot over the years. Our parents had chosen our home for its location, only a few miles away. It was our family's hub—not only Eugene's school and therapy center and John's workplace for the summer, but the primary social community for all of us. It served kids with a wide range of diagnoses, many with multiple conditions, which made us feel a sense of belonging we hadn't felt in family support groups catering strictly to Angelman syndrome or autism. Not that they weren't welcoming, but it's like being biracial. In a group of all white people, I feel Asian; in a group of all Asians, I feel white. Our family life didn't fit the predominant experiences of either AS or autism families, and it was nice to be able to talk about it without wondering where that placed Eugene on the spectrum of either condition, or feeling the exhausting combination of thankfulness, guilt, worry, and jealousy about his particular constellation of symptoms.

Henry's House was usually peaceful and quiet, all activity contained inside the homey one-level building, but today, it was bustling, two dozen kids and therapists running around outside, which was even more unsettling than the empty streets. I knew from John how much they were doing outside, most of the parking lot having been turned into tented activity stations and small-group therapy zones, but it was a strange sight, like an oasis, the only concentrated parcel of human activity as far as I could see. Or maybe it was the disorientation of realizing that other people's lives, their regular routines, were continuing. When an emergency happens, you expect the whole world to shut down, or at least you wish it would, because, of course, your own world has. I'm sure this is a narcissism of some sort, an egocentric cognitive bias that assumes other people's reactions mirror your own. Whatever it was, I was feeling it acutely.

We were here to carry out the assignment from Mom: track down Shannon Haug, the go-to lawyer for Henry's House families. We couldn't reach her, and John thought the head of Henry's House (also unreachable by phone; she put away her phone when working with children) would know how to find her. As I turned in to the parking lot, John said, "You can't come in; no visitors allowed. Just wait in the car, okay?" and opened the car door, mid-turn.

"Try to get Shannon's home address, too," I yelled as he ran into the building. I was desperate to follow him to see what was happening, but I had to maneuver the car at zero to two miles per hour to avoid the kids. It was remarkable, how even though so many schools and camps had shut down, Henry's House had never been busier. I think it's all the emphasis on the importance of early diagnosis and therapy; there's an urgency element to special education, a deep fear that losing even a week of classes and therapy will result in a significant slide backward you can never make up. We siblings talk about it all the time, the way our parents treat it like a race, like there's a limited window of opportunity to "fix" them and at some point, the kids' brains will become inelastic. That's why the quarantine had been especially awful for families like ours, and why Henry's House fought so hard to stay open.

I had just parked by the entrance when John came out and got in the car. "The good news is we found Shannon," he said. "The bad news is she's not reachable."

"Why? Where is she?"

"They're trying to deport Young's family—remember, I told you? I can't believe I forgot, but today is the hearing, and of course Shannon's their lawyer. It's virtual, but she can't be disturbed." Young was the deputy head of Henry's House and a Korean immigrant the same age as Mom—the first time they met, they realized they'd graduated high school the same year in Seoul, though they didn't know each other—so John kept us updated on any news. "Anyway, Teresa said it should be ending soon. When they call, she'll come out and let us talk to her."

The news had disturbed me deeply when I'd first heard about it, thinking about this family who'd been in the US for more than ten years having to move back to Korea. But now, with Eugene in hand-cuffs and Dad who knew where, it seemed like a mere technicality where you live. Seoul, DC—who cares?

John said, "I texted Mom to let her know. I wonder how Eugene's doing. Should we call her?"

"Absolutely not," I said. "She needs to focus on Eugene right now. Don't distract her."

John nodded. Bit his nails. Closed his eyes, then opened them. Checked his phone. Sighed. Checked his phone again. It was kind of soothing, watching his jittery nerves—mirrored catharsis.

Two women came out of the building. They waved tentatively and started walking our way. "Oh God, Dad's GMs," John said, referring to the posse of moms of Eugene's therapymates, whom we secretly referred to as Groupie Moms. They'd always been a close bunch, starting back when Mom was in it, doing a lot together—field trips, playgroups, weekly coffees—but John swore the "girls' (plus one boy's) nights out" had gotten a lot more frequent since Dad took over. ("You're pretty cute; I'd better watch out—I bet they all have crushes on you," Mom teased Dad, winking and laughing. She'd just gone back to work, and I remember thinking how much I loved seeing Mom like that, frothing over with self-confidence.)[10]

The Groupie Moms came over to John's side of the car, and he lowered the window. "John, Mia. We are so sorry. How are you doing?" GM1 said, and GM2 said, "We're all just devastated and praying for you. We're about to head over to the park to join the search. I think Susan's already there."

I realized these moms must be in the same playgroup circle as Susan, the woman from the park this morning. Right after Detective Janus played the voicemail from that Anjeli woman, I had thought back to Susan's "horrible news from last week" comment, wondered if that could be related. Divorce, maybe, which Dad had announced to his friends prematurely—that he's in love with another woman and leaving Mom—and they thought it was a done deal and therefore "news" we already knew about? I'd been meaning to tell John we should call Susan and demand to know what she really meant, but looking at these women, their overeagerness, I had a better idea.

I leaned toward them and said, "Thank you. It really helps to know people care."

---

10 It's funny how being different from everyone else in a group can make you feel either isolated/insecure or special/important, depending on the social hierarchy of the trait in question. Take race: being white is considered "best" in the US and even in Korea, which is why Mom felt awkward and unwanted when she first moved to the US as a teenager, whereas Dad had no issues being the only white person visiting rural Korean villages, people gawking as if he were a celebrity. Same with gender. Mom says how hard it is to be taken seriously as the only woman at work, whereas Dad has essentially been anointed king of the stay-at-home parent circle.

"Oh, of *course*," and "It must be *so* hard," the women said.

I put my hand on John's arm and pinched ever so subtly, our old signal for *Just go with me here; play along.* I said, "It's a lot to deal with, especially on top of the horrible news from last week."

They both nodded, scrunched their faces into looks of agonized sympathy, but unfortunately, they didn't say anything.

"I'm sorry," I continued. "I assumed Dad told you what happened—the horrible news last week—because you're so close and I know he confides in you and . . ."

"He *did* tell us," GM1 said. "We were devastated."

GM2 said, "Wasn't the second opinion yesterday?"

Second opinion? What the fuck? I felt a sense of dread, like the gravitational pull of earth was increasing, making my body heavier and denser. "So Dad told you about the . . . first . . . I mean, the initial, um . . ."

Both women nodded. GM2—or maybe GM1, I'm not good with noticing parents' faces—said, "It's so awful. He's so young. He said there's family history—your grandfather, right?—but even so . . ."

At the word *grandfather,* I swallowed to keep from throwing up. John's hand was gripping the car's gear stick between us, the peaks of his knuckles white like a snowy mountain range. I told myself to say something, get them to say more, but I couldn't figure out what to say.

Because my grandfather, Dad's father, had died three months after being diagnosed with stage 4 prostate cancer.

———

DAD HAD BEEN KIND OF obsessed about cancer. I can't blame him, given that his father died in his fifties (which had sounded really old when we first heard about it when we were four), when Dad was still in college, before he even met Mom. Dad's an only child, and his father didn't want him to feel overburdened, so they didn't tell him until his father was on his deathbed. Dad vacillated between being infuriated about it—wishing he could have had more time to process it, spend more time with him—and being grateful to his parents for sparing him the monthslong agony of watching his father suffer. His mother died of breast cancer before we were born, and I remember Dad asking several of Eugene's doctors if his Angelman gene could be related to his parents' apparent predisposition to cancer. (The answer was always no.)

GM1 said, "I hope I'm not prying, but we were wondering—was the appointment in the morning, before . . . you know, the park? Because if it was bad news, we were wondering if . . . well, if that was something the police considered relevant . . ."

I cleared my throat and willed the words to come. "So you were thinking he got the second opinion yesterday morning, and it confirmed"—I forced myself to say it—"stage four prostate cancer, and he . . ." I swallowed, couldn't say *suicide.*

GM2 said, "Oh God, it's stage four? I knew it was prostate cancer, but I didn't realize . . . I'm so sorry, that's awful."

My stomach lurched. I tasted the vile coffee from this morning.

GM1 said, "We were wondering if it was something like that. He was so depressed and upset already, and then finding out it's stage four, I can't imagine what he . . . what that news must have . . ." She put her hands over her masked mouth, like it was just too awful to voice.

John said, "Depressed? He was depressed?" He was having trouble talking, his words hoarse and halting.

I looked at the women, their eyes wide, their heads craned toward us, arms on each other's shoulders, like spectators at a fatal accident, and I was furious with them all of a sudden, with their fucking *concern* and horror-filled pauses and *we*-were-wondering gossipy voyeurism.

Luckily for all of us, Teresa came out right then to tell us she'd talked to Shannon, who was on her way to the police station and would see us there in fifteen minutes.

I thanked Teresa, closed the windows, and backed out without saying anything to the GMs. John didn't say anything, didn't look at anyone; he looked shell-shocked.

"Which way am I going?" I said as we approached the exit. No response. "John! Hello! Focus! I need navigation. Which way to the police station?"

He didn't say anything, just plugged his phone into the car, letting the soothing nav-robot's voice guide me out and through the streets.

"Can you text Mom about the lawyer coming?" I said.

Again, no response. But I heard John write and send the text—the artificial typewriter clacks, then *swoosh*. I knew what it meant when he got like this, all moody and silent, and I couldn't deal with it just then. I had to focus on driving to the station. Make sure everything was squared away with the lawyer. Check in on the search in the park. There was too much going on, all urgent and dire. I couldn't fall apart, too. Someone had to get shit done.

But here's the thing about driving on a near-empty, straight road. It's so mindless that you can't keep from thinking. Don't think about it, don't think about it, don't think about it, I told myself, but it's like there were neon-lit balls spelling out *S-T-A-G-E-4-C-A-N-C-E-R-!-!-!-!* rolling through my brain. How could Dad have cancer? He would never keep something like that from us, and he certainly wouldn't tell some random "friends" before he told his family. Then again, just a few hours prior, I would have sworn that texting/calling a mystery woman behind Mom's back for months was definitely not Dad, only slightly less plausible than the idea of Dad carrying around a letterboard. Was it possible that I—we all—could have been so fundamentally wrong about who Dad was?

As unbelievable as it was that Dad had cancer, if we accepted that premise as true, that could explain Dad's disappearance. Yes, I hated the GMs for even attempting to voice the possibility, but someone goes missing right after finding out he has the same disease his father suffered a miserable death from—of course you think, Suicide. I could picture him at the edge of a precipice at the park, the foam of the whitewater below, wondering how he was going to tell Mom, tell us, wanting to bypass all that, escape the pain.

Or maybe the opposite. If the prognosis was bad, a few months to live, let's say, maybe that would make you go all carpe diem, leave your responsibilities behind—your marriage, mortgage, errands, kids—and run away with your newfound love, the hell with everything else. Empty out your IRA, max out your ATM and credit cards, max out on other things, too—fun, happiness, sex—and justify it all by telling yourself it's for your family's own good, to spare them the pain and trouble of taking care of you, to leave their memories of you untainted by sickness, by chemo, vomit, shit.

"Your destination is ahead on the right," the nav-robot said. The police station was just two blocks away. Mom was there. The lawyer would be there soon. I could tell them everything and trust them to figure it out and tell me what to do, what to think.

"We're almost there," I said to John. "Get it together. It's going to be hard enough, telling Mom about the cancer thing. You cannot fall apart, okay?"

"We can't tell Mom."

I whipped my head around. His eyes were slightly narrowed and his lips pressed together, which—dammit to hell—meant he was serious. "What? Why?"

"Watch out!" John yelled, pointed to a red light. I slammed on the brakes. No one was behind us, we were fine, but still, my heart raced and pounded; I could feel it all the way in my palms and fingers gripping the steering wheel.

He said, "It's too much. It's too hurtful. We need to focus on Eugene and finding Dad, and I don't think this has anything to do with Dad being missing."

"How can you say that? This is motive. It could mean he killed himself, or this could be why he decided to run away with that Anjeli woman. Or maybe she's his doctor. That could be what she was saying on the voicemail, about how Dad needs to come clean with

Mom. That was about the diagnosis. That's got to be it! That's why he took out the money back in October, for some experimental treatment, and he didn't want Mom to know about it."

He pointed. "The light's green."

"There's no one behind us."

He shook his head, like I was the one being irrational. "You can't just sit at a green light. It's highly illegal, and we're right next to a police station, for fuck's sake. Go. At least pull over so you're not blocking the road," he said, which was ridiculous, given that no one was around, but fine, I kept my mouth shut and pulled over. One of us had to be mature about this. I put the car in Park.

"Look," I said. "I'm just as upset as you are. But—"

"Tell me you actually think there's a chance in hell Dad killed himself or ran away with some woman because he has cancer."

I couldn't.

"See? You agree with me. It's not like Dad to do something like that. No way, even if he found out he had two days left to live."

"But that's not the point. Even if it's a coincidence and it has nothing to do with Dad being missing, it's a huge thing Mom needs to know. It's bad enough Dad was keeping this and four thousand other secrets from her. We can't do it, too. It's, like, compounding the problem, and so disrespectful to Mom. I mean, who are you to decide what she can and can't handle? She's the parent—*she* gets to make decisions like that about *us,* not the other way around. She's not some fragile, weak damsel in distress, and it really pisses me off that you're being all"— I wanted a fighting word—*"paternalistic."* [11]

"You're right," he said in a whisper. I was really worked up about this, the ridiculousness of keeping a secret about a secret, and I wanted to

---

11 I don't know if you have stuff like this with siblings, but the point is not the word itself, or even what it signifies—the origin was stupid; some girlfriend accused John of being "paternalistic" for always opening the door for her or whatever, and he was outraged because he thinks of himself as a feminist. The point is, he knows that I know he hates it, which means that he knows I'm saying it specifically to piss him off, which is what ultimately pisses him off the most.

keep venting, but damned if those long wet fluttering eyelashes didn't wear me down. "I'm sorry," he said, sounding all *wounded,* which made me feel even more guilty. "I just . . . none of this makes any sense. This isn't Dad. How can he be so different from who I thought he was?"

"I know, I keep thinking the same thing," I said. "It happens, though. I mean, there are men who lead double lives, who have two wives and two sets of kids in different towns, and they travel back and forth for years, and when they get found out, everyone says no, they have the wrong man, *their* husband or dad would never do anything like that."

John shook his head like I was crazy. "That's one of those things that only happens in soap operas, like identical twins that trade spouses every other day or whatever."

"What? Why would you trade . . . *what?*" I shook my head. "Okay, anyway, what *I'm* talking about is a real thing. I just read an article about it, like, last week, about how all the men with two families are getting found out because they can't travel anymore, you know, because of the quarantine." Even as I was saying it, though, I thought— was that a legit article? Maybe it was a fake news piece from *The Onion,* or a so-preposterous-it-seems-fake-but-is-actually-real piece in some humor blog? (This was one of the many problems with living in a world in flux; these categories were getting harder to tell apart.)

John said, "How could Dad possibly lead a double life, given that he's with us all the time?"

"I'm not saying Dad *is* one of those men, just that it's similar, conceptually. You know, because we were talking about how we could be so wrong about what Dad's like." I frowned. "But also, Dad isn't with us all the time. He's gone every day for at least like four hours, with Eugene to the park. He could do anything with anyone, and we would never know because Eugene can't say anything. It's actually a brilliant alibi, if you think about it."

"So now you think Dad was having sex with some woman in a public park? In front of Eugene?"

"Eww, no. But wait, maybe Eugene's met that Anjeli woman. Maybe he really likes her."

"What? What are you talking about? Why are we even discussing this?"

I had no idea. More importantly, why were we sitting a block away from the police station babbling on about nonsensical stuff instead of going to be with Mom and Eugene? "Our brains are fucked up because we both need sleep," I said and started driving again. It occurred to me that it was actually kind of hilarious in a deeply tragic way, the idea of Dad having a secret life and relying on Eugene not talking to get away with it. If this were a movie (but this would only work if we were really amazing actors, like Saoirse Ronan/Florence Pugh level), John and I would start laughing uncontrollably, one of those laughs that's so hard you start tearing up, and then you realize you're crying and that makes you laugh harder, and then you switch somewhere in the middle altogether and end up sobbing. But this was real life, not a movie, and I was too exhausted to laugh or cry, much less both at the same time. I really did not feel well.

Pulling into a parking spot, I thought how I could crash into the VISITOR PARKING sign pole in front of me, and maybe the cops would come out and arrest me. "Hey, do you think if I crashed into this pole, I'd be sent to jail and I could take care of Eugene?" I said, although it occurred to me I'd be sent to a different facility for adult women, so maybe that wasn't a good idea.

John's phone sounded. The *South Park* Kenny ringtone—*Oh my God! They killed Kenny! You bastards!*—which meant it was his friend Kenny texting. I really didn't want to laugh—it was highly inappropriate, not to mention stupid—but I was too tired to stop from chuckling despite myself and getting really mad about it when John said, "What the. . . ."

"What?"

The text on John's phone screen read: *Dude, isn't this your dad?*

Under the text was a picture, a zoomed-in screenshot of Dad's face, looking terrified and in pain, his glasses half-torn off his face, his jaw red, and a bright red line down his cheek. And in the bottom corner, a snippet of the person closest to him, the person who was presumably attacking him. You couldn't make out who it was, everything a blur, just a smidge of color: a bright, almost fluorescent yellow.

# FOURTEEN

# Pretty Fucking Far from Okay

HAVE YOU EVER HAD SO MANY THOUGHTS FLYING SO QUICKLY THROUGH your mind that you couldn't speak? Hyperspeed paralysis. Most of Eugene's doctors describe his condition in terms of deficits—an underdeveloped brain, the nerves not quite as thick, long, or numerous as they should be. But last year, I went to a TED Talk–style lecture by this philosopher-neurologist who posited that autism-related conditions might be disorders of too much rather than too little. Under this theory, Eugene not speaking might be a symptom of a hyper-verbal and hyper-cognitive mind rather than a hypo- one, the paradoxical consequence of an overabundance of thoughts fighting for processing bandwidth, clogging up the nerves like a traffic jam and causing a total breakdown. He likened it to a bunch of neurons telling the same part of your body what to do, and that part gets so confused, it gives up and takes a nap instead.

That's how I felt just then, seeing Kenny's text: my brain sent so many panicked commands to my body that everything shut down and went blank, the simultaneous commands being the following, in no particular order—

- Yell out, *What the fuck?!*
- Ask John, *Is that Eugene?!*
- Ask myself (but out loud, thereby also asking John), *Where is that picture from and when was it taken?*
- Ask the universe rhetorically, *Is that really Dad?*
- Tell John to enlarge the picture, to see if Dad's glasses were actually broken (in which case the picture had to be from yesterday, since his glasses were unbroken when we last saw him) or just knocked off (in which case this picture could be from earlier)
- Tell John to text Kenny and ask where he got that picture, or maybe just call instead, but on speaker
- Ask John, Is it just me, or is it really eerie how the red line down Dad's cheek looks almost exactly like the scratch mark on Detective Janus's cheek—a diagonal straight line from the left temple to the left upper lip?

—the outcome of this neuronal overload being my doing the one thing I did not will my body to do, which was to keep looking at John's phone screen, brain overheating, mouth ajar, saying nothing.

John seemed to suffer a similar reaction, saying, "What the . . . Where . . . Is that . . . ?"

I managed to tilt my head closer to John's phone—Dad's glasses were definitely broken, the nose bridge bent at an awkward angle—before John clicked to call Kenny and yanked it to his ear.

"Where'dyougetthatpicture?" John's words blurred together. My brain was still sluggish from the overload. I hit myself in the head, hoping for a brain reset (I'm a big believer in percussive maintenance, the act of hitting malfunctioning equipment to jolt it into working[12]), and scrubbed my face, and heard John say, "Yes, it's my dad, of course it is, you moron, why wouldn't you just—"

I opened my eyes at *moron*. It wasn't like John to use that word—to the contrary, he went out of his way to (usually over-tactfully) explain to others why language like that can be hurtful—or to be so short with his friends. Not that he never insulted them, but he did it the jokey way guys do with their buddies. The mean tone, laced with true irritation and annoyance, he usually saved for me, sometimes our parents. Kenny wasn't one of his closest friends, and there's an inverse correlation between how close you are to someone and secure in their love, on the one hand, and how nice you are to them, on the other.

John was yelling into the phone. "I haven't told *anyone*. Dude, my dad is missing, so we've been kind of busy dealing with the *police,* so no, I haven't said anything on Discord, I haven't even *been* on Discord, and I can't be*lieve* you're wasting time like this instead of asking your mom to send me the video. Go do that right! Fucking! Now! And call me right back and report back. Go!"

He threw his phone into his lap and put his head back. "Fucking Kenny says he's fucking *hurt* that I didn't fucking come to him with the fucking news of Dad being fucking missing," he said. It worried me, the number of *fucking*s in that sentence. John didn't believe in "cursing for cursing's sake," whatever that meant, had accused me of overusing fuck/fucking in a way he claimed was cliché for people our age (recent escapees of parental censorship). He said it was frankly a little embarrassing, which I didn't get before but was now beginning to.

---

12 I know people think it's stupid to hit electronic equipment, but there are valid reasons why this actually works: 1) electrical circuitry sometimes gets out of alignment, and jarring it may restore physical and electrical continuity; 2) vibration could dislodge gas bubbles around the batteries' contact points; and 3) a hard-enough hit could knock off a thin layer of oxidation (think: rusty film) preventing conductivity. Also, if all else fails, smacking something can make you just feel better.

"All right, but what did he say about the picture? Where did he get it?"

"His mom sent it because he looked familiar. She said it's from a video from their neighbor, related to"—he scoffed, but not in an angry, bitter way, more in an exhausted, I-can't-believe-this-could-possibly-be-happening way—"some incident nearby yesterday."

"*Incident?* He said that?"

"He said *she* said that. His mom. Anyway, I told him to find out everything and send me the full video. I can't believe him. I mean, how many times has Dad given him a ride from school, and he barely fucking *recognizes* him? Un-fucking-believable."

I thought how I didn't really look at my friends' parents, how they seemed more like blobs who perform functional roles rather than distinct people whose specific facial, vocal, and other features I actually process and retain, but I didn't say anything, just nodded like I agreed. He was scaring me a little.

John's phone sounded, and I swear he answered before the *God!* in *Oh my God! They killed Kenny!* traveled the two feet to my eardrum. "Where the fuck is the fucking video?" he said, his mean curtness making me wince.

He swallowed. "Sorry, Mrs. K. I didn't realize you were . . ." He breathed. "I really, really cannot say enough how much I need to see that video, and whatever information you have about—" A pause. "So you didn't see it? Do you know what's on it?" John glanced at me, shook his head in a *no*. "Well, thanks anyway. I appreciate anything you can do. And yeah, of course give her my number." He looked like he was about to hang up, but he said, "Hey, Mrs. K? One more thing. Do you know why she took that video? I mean, she obviously doesn't know my dad, and I guess I don't understand why she would record random strangers?" He frowned, bit down on his lower lip. "What kind of blog? What's it called?" He looked out the window, squinted like he was trying to see something in the distance, shook his head again. "No. Got it. Yeah, understood," he said, some of that meanness re-infusing his voice, and hung up without saying goodbye.

"Holy shit, a *blog*?" I said. This screenshot presented many problems, the most fundamental being its troubling implication for what happened to Dad, especially given the blood under Eugene's fingernails and on the yellow shirt. But it would add a whole incendiary layer if it got out in the world, seen by people, especially if those people included the police, one of whom had a bloody scratch with an uncanny resemblance to that in the picture.

"Yup, one of those mommy blogs," John said. Of course. I should have guessed. Parent shaming on mommy blogs had quadrupled since the pandemic. Shaming about over-parenting, under-parenting, helicopter-parenting, ghost-parenting, puppeteer-parenting, free-range parenting, overfeeding, underfeeding, over-disciplining, under-disciplining—we knew all the subcategories, this being a frequent topic of family-breakfast ranting by Dad. The most alarming escalation had been in the number of people seemingly going out of their way to record kids like Eugene mid-meltdown, then post analyses blaming bad parenting—lack of discipline, overindulgence, or maybe just not caring at all. And then the final kicker: an anonymous complaint to Child Protective Services, with the oh-so-helpful video evidence.

"So that means Eugene's definitely the one who . . ." I couldn't bring myself to say *injured Dad*. "I mean, why else would a mommy-blogger record that?"

"Kenny's mom hasn't seen it, but apparently, the blogger woman said the kid in the video's so out of control, he was actually causing injury to nearby people."

"*People*? As in multiple persons?"

"Who knows? But she apparently sent the screenshot around to see if anyone knows Dad because she wants to contact him and get his comment."

"Comment? Like she's an investigative reporter for *The Washington Post* or something?" I wanted to punch this woman. No, better—hack into her site and put something horrible on it. A superimposed watermark with that biblical verse about how it's a sin to judge others, lest ye be judged back or whatever. Or a huge-font warning that this blog is from a Russian bot that'll infect your computer with a virus. Or maybe porn. "What's her blog name?"

"She says she doesn't know—such bullshit. But she did say she'll try to get me the video."

"We have to stop her from posting it. The police cannot see it."

John nodded, rubbing his forehead like he was getting a migraine, but stopped mid-rub. "What if she's already posted it?"

"Send me the picture from Kenny. I'll search for it." Catfishing and revenge (semi-)porn posting were all the rage in my college, and I'd become an expert at using reverse image and video searches to find the originating website.

I initiated the search on four apps with different methodologies—redundancy was important given the difficulty of finding a screenshot from a video—and set up notification alerts for any hits. It would take a while, but hopefully, Kenny's mom would reach her before she finished the write-up and posted the video.

As I was finishing up, I got a text from Detective Janus's evidence team with instructions to access scanned pages from Dad's HQ notebook. Following the link to a secured site and entering the password, I saw this in Dad's handwriting:

Counterintuitive Case Study #1: The Curious Case of the (Essentially) Equally Happy Lottery Winners and Paraplegic Accident Victims:
A group of people win the lottery, and a second group get into accidents and become paraplegic or quadriplegic. Within a year of these life-changing events, they undergo surveys comparing their happiness level. The answer seems like a no-brainer: the lottery winners must be ecstatic, and the accident victims miserable.

Wrong. A 1970s study found that the lottery winners were no happier than controls, and the accident victims slightly less happy but still above average happiness levels despite having lifelong disabilities. What's more striking, the lottery-winner group had more trouble than the accident victims in finding joy in life's "mundane pleasures" (talking with friends, hearing a joke, getting a compliment), as well as lower "anticipated future happiness" ratings. In other words, the paraplegics had the brighter outlook and believed they'd become happier in future years.

Counterintuitive Case Study #2: The POW Paradox: US officers are prisoners of war in a horrific foreign camp for years. Who fares better and survives—optimistic or pessimistic POWs? Surprisingly, James Stockdale (vice admiral in the navy), POW for 7 years in N. Vietnam, wrote in his book that the most optimistic of his fellow POWs didn't survive. They kept saying they'd be rescued soon, by Xmas, Easter, etc., and eventually died of a broken heart.

Counterintuitive Case Study #3: Things or Experiences?: You have $1000. You can buy something to keep, or use it for an experience (trip, concert). Most assume the object will provide happiness for longer than a fleeting experience.

Again, wrong. A study found that the happiness levels are equal at first, but as time goes by, people's satisfaction with their material purchases decreased, whereas it increased for their experiences. In other words, people's memories of experiences made them happier longer than owning objects.

Preliminary Thoughts: I find fascinating what these phenomena share at their core: the concept of the relativity of happiness, that you can't judge the happiness level of an experience in a vacuum. In the examples, the objective markers of happiness—how a reasonable outsider would rate your happiness; that is, how happy you should be—don't match the subjective levels of your actual happiness. Why this misalignment between the predicted and the actual? Are there factors we can control to maximize our happiness levels?

I believe there are. I'm convinced that studying these variances will yield insights, and that I can mold them into a quantitative marker that can provide practical strategies to increase the happiness level of a given experience.

"Here, more pages from Dad's notebook," I said to John, who was rubbing his temples in small circles. He started reading, scrolling, as I thought about what Dad had written. I was especially fascinated by the POW thing that seemed to support what I'd thought all along, that optimism and blind faith were inane and, quite frankly, dangerous—but the thing that was looming in my mind was the lottery-winner-versus-paraplegic study. I'd heard about it, though not from Dad. As a prerequisite for his major, socio-psychology, Vic had to take a class on happiness (apparently based on Yale's happiness course, which Yale says is its most popular course in three hundred years), which he thought would be vapid but ended up getting *very* into. I remembered something he told me: how the professor who ran the study (which he called "the iconic study on happiness") died by suicide in his thirties, jumping from his university office building. That irony was compounded by something else Vic told me, that his so-called Happiness Professor was on leave due to stress.

John's phone was between us on the car console, still open to the picture of Dad. I reached for it and spread my fingers on the screen to zoom in on Dad's eyes. They were red, teary, it looked like, and I thought again about Dad and cancer, depression. Was it possible? Had he been obsessed with happiness because it was elusive for him, getting further and further away?

When John was done reading Dad's note, I told him about the lottery researcher's suicide, the Happiness Professor's leave. "It's one of these things that seems paradoxical but actually makes perfect sense. You don't become obsessed with happiness, trying to maximize it and experimenting to calibrate it, unless it's a mystery. If you're already happy, if it comes easily to you, you don't need to ponder it. It's only if you can't attain it that it consumes you."

"That's ridiculous. Dad did not kill himself and leave Eugene all alone, away from home. He wasn't obsessed with happiness because he was miserable. You saw the notes about the gene therapy study. He was trying to figure out what to do about Eugene. He has a son with a condition people call the happiness syndrome, and he's always been into philosophy. Of course he's into this stuff."

He had a point. Or did he? My brain was mush.

"We should go inside." He got out and slammed the car door shut.

———

I HAD NEVER BEEN INSIDE a police station, but I had a firm notion of what one should look like (Dad was a channel-surfing fan of all six *Law & Orders*). Our station looked more like regular corporate offices—although actually, I hadn't been inside regular offices, either, just seen them on TV—cubicles, gray filing cabinets, etc. I suppose what would have made it match the image in my mind was uniformed officers, which this space lacked. Another unforeseen byproduct of the quarantine—my first trip to the police station not meeting my expectations.

The receptionist looked like our high school librarian—short, flat all-white hair atop a long, narrow face with a pointy chin—so I unwittingly expected her to be curt, like her, but she turned out to be chatty, telling us all sorts of things like how lucky we were to have Detective Janus in charge of our dad's case, she was an extremely hard worker, was here all the time, especially lately since the adoption fell through because of Covid (a baby girl from China, or maybe it was Korea), burying herself in work, poor thing, and oh, by the way, she heard our lawyer was *Shannon Haug* (uttered in a scandalized whisper, like you would profanity in church), whom Detective Janus had had run-ins with and, just between us, seemed *very* unhappy to have to face again. She said this last part conspiratorially, like she was sharing delicious gossip with officemates, and it made me kind of sad how lonely she must be, not used to being alone in that big office, starved and grateful for an attentive audience. Her oversharing was kind of worrisome from a county-resident perspective—like, shouldn't people who work for the police department be more tight-lipped?—but very interesting from a sister-of-juvenile-detainee perspective, and I encouraged it by acting engrossed, which she seemed to crave.

After she got the go-ahead from Detective Janus to bring us back (not exactly kosher, but everyone tended to relax the rules when it came to juveniles, especially special-needs juveniles, double especially these days with the station being near empty, she said), she walked us to a small room where Mom and Eugene were waiting for our lawyer. It had been maybe an hour since we last saw her, but Mom hugged us tightly as if she hadn't seen us in weeks. I understood, of course—I felt the same way, especially since the last time we'd seen her, she and Eugene had been locked up in the back of a police car behind a steel-mesh barrier.

John and I did the same with Eugene as soon as Mom let us go, sandwich-hugging him from opposite sides like we used to when we were little. He seemed really freaked out, rocking in his chair even as he was watching his iPad with headphones. Thankfully, he wasn't handcuffed anymore, but his wrists were red, his skin raw and chafed.

Our lawyer arrived right behind us. It's hard to believe now, but my first impression of Shannon was: *This* is the brilliant, high-powered trial lawyer I've been hearing about? It's not that I expected her to be thin with sexy hair and dramatic eye makeup like female lawyers on TV, more that I expected her to look and, more importantly, sound like someone who fights people for a living, who *likes* it, lives for verbal sparring. Gruff and serious, a little scary and mean, with a permanent scowl, slightly annoyed at everything and everybody, speaks in dazzling paragraphs with rapid-fire speed.

Shannon had a veneer of old-fashioned domesticity: a loose, wrinkled skirt suit; her hair a poofy graying blob the shape of a bike helmet; doughy cheeks with dimples; pancake-syrupy smell. The thing that really worried me was how damn *nice* she sounded: "Mona, thank you so much for getting us water, so thoughtful," said to the receptionist; liberal sprinklings of heartfelt "I'm so sorry for everything y'all have gone through" and "Oh, that's awful," with sympathetic nods and shakes of the head throughout Mom's explanation of what happened. All spoken softly and evenly, with a slight Southern drawl.

How is this woman going to stand up to Detective Janus, handle someone as devious as her?, I was thinking, when Detective Janus knocked and stuck her head in to let us know the intake hearing would begin in ten minutes. Her face looked awful; she hadn't cleaned up at all, dried blood streaked her scratched cheek and mask, and her jaw and other cheek were starting to bruise and swell.

Shannon said in a warm tone, "Detective, it's been so long since I saw you—the Bellamy trial, I think; you look well," and I thought, What the fuck, this is not a cocktail party, but she continued, "Well, except your face. You should really get cleaned up and grab a new mask before the hearing. I wouldn't want to have to accuse you of looking bad on purpose, dredge up that old APO case."

Detective Janus didn't reply.

"Also," Shannon said, "your incident report references a witness statement by a CPS consultant who was present. I'll need a copy of that before the hearing."

"How did you get the incident report? I just filed that."

"I have my ways. You know that." Shannon smiled, her dimples deepening next to her mask. "Now, I'd like to confer with my client and his family in private. The door, please?"

Mom waited a few seconds after Detective Janus left to ask about the "old APO case." "Assault on Police Officer," Shannon explained. "There was an allegation she faked an injury, wore a brace to make it look more serious. She denied it, said it was for carpal tunnel, and there was no official finding, but it was embarrassing for her. She was probably going to get cleaned up anyway, but just in case . . ."

"I noticed it, too," I said. "It bothered me she wasn't icing her face."

"She's helping you with your dad's case, so I know you want to trust her and cooperate, but this APO charge with Eugene, her being so aggressive—she's up to something. I don't know what she's thinking, charging a nonverbal boy whose father is missing and who's

obviously overwhelmed by everything, not to mention the racial over-
tones with all the anti-Asian stuff these days."

This is when John and I should have spoken up, of course, shown
her the screenshot from Kenny. But in my mind—and John's, too, he
later said—that was wholly separate from the incident with Detective Janus, and I wanted to let our lawyer focus on the immediate
emergency at hand: the intake hearing.

Shannon explained that it wasn't a formal proceeding, not
"court," but an informal meeting where an "intake officer"—usually
a parole officer trained to work with minors—talks to the minor and
the arresting officer, collects information, and decides whether there's
sufficient cause for the case to proceed to juvenile court. Lawyers
usually didn't attend, she said, but she always did for cases involving special-needs children who can't advocate for themselves. She
said she had a lot of experience defending teens like Eugene under
similar circumstances, which happened more than you'd think—so
much so that Virginia enacted a special law making conditions like
Eugene's a defense to criminal charges.

The hearing room was across the hall. John and I couldn't go in
with them, but Shannon asked us to remain in the waiting room,
nearby in case we were needed, telling us to dial 0 for Mona if we
needed anything. We hugged Mom and Eugene, said goodbye standing at the door like they were going on a long trip. Mom lingered at
the hearing room doorway, turned to us. "Hopefully, it won't be too
long. Try not to worry," she said across the hall. Shannon, who had
been a few steps ahead of Mom, stepped back to check on her. "Are
you okay?"

I saw a hint of the tiniest sad smile on Mom's face and knew
she was thinking the same thing I was: "I'm pretty fucking far from
okay," a line from *Pulp Fiction,* Dad's favorite movie, which we had
just watched for Father's Day three days ago with all the scenes re-
arranged in chronological order by John and me as Dad's gift. We'd
started the project late Saturday night, thinking we could download
a chron-order compilation on YouTube, but they were all taken down

for piracy, so we had to edit it ourselves using Dad's DVD. It was slow, tedious work, so we started drinking, which made us silly and giggly, and around 1 A.M., when I was mid–laughing fit, literally rolling on the floor (I became convinced Dad named me after the Uma Thurman character, which made her heroin overdose scene seem particularly hilarious in my then-drunken-logic state), Mom came in to tell us to keep it down and asked, "Are you okay?," at which point John and I said, "I'm pretty fucking far from okay" in unison (we'd *just* recorded that scene) and guffawed, which made Mom laugh. (She thought John and I had grown apart and loved anything that brought us closer.) This went on throughout the night, with each of us prompting "Are you okay?" at random times. The next day at breakfast, when we were hungover and Dad asked if we were okay, John and I exchanged glances and chuckled, which Mom noticed and joined in.

Our exchange of sad smiles across the police station hallway was completely different, of course. It wasn't that the movie line was still funny. It was more an acknowledgment of the fucked-up-ness of our current situation in light of our giddy frivolity less than four days ago.

"Sorry, yes, I'm fine, they'll be okay," Mom said and followed Shannon in.

I almost believed it.

# FIFTEEN

# A Maze of Beige

THERE ARE MANY THINGS IN THIS WORLD I HATE, BUT NONE QUITE AS much as waiting for something really important with no idea what's happening and no way to influence the outcome. I tried to focus on the search for Dad, the screenshot. I checked on the reverse video screenshot search. All four apps were done with the initial search, and no hits. Finally, a bit of not-horrible news: there was a good chance Kenny's neighbor hadn't posted the video yet. There were so many things I needed to discuss with John—we hadn't even mentioned Eugene possibly reading or the letterboard in Dad's backpack—and things I should do, like run an old-fashioned Google search for local mommy blogs, research juvenile detention centers for our county, and on and on. But I was too nervous about the hearing. Mom would have to turn off the iPad when it started; would Eugene be okay?

"I'm trying to convince Kenny to break into the neighbor's house," John said, and I said I needed to go to the bathroom and left the room.

I went straight across the hall and put my ear to the door of the intake-hearing conference room, but it was so muffled I couldn't make anything out. It was probably good that our police station was well constructed, with their important rooms soundproofed properly, but it was frustrating as hell.

My phone buzzed. Another text from the evidence team. For this next set of scanned pages, Dad had clearly used pens that run—much of his writing had been blotted away or blurred—but red and green must have been more water-resistant, because they were much more legible:

> Happiness is not absolute. It's relative—your today compared to your yesterday (baseline) + your vision for tomorrow (expectations). Examples: C student who gets B probably happier than A student who gets same B on test; unranked player who gets bronze medal probably happier than #1 player who gets silver.
>
> The 3 case studies demonstrate the power of your mind in setting your baseline/expectations. What was intolerable (becoming paraplegic) or amazing (winning millions $) can quickly become your new normal. But this adaptation power is not uniform (per POWs). Can we focus to turn it on/off (or dial up/down) to our benefit?
>
> This is where HQ comes in. It's a useful shorthand—numeric representation of the relativity of happiness.

I wished he'd spelled out HQ, verified my assumption it stood for *happiness quotient*. I knew these were Dad's notes to himself, but couldn't he have been a bit more considerate of people trying to decipher them? I scrolled through to this next legible bit:

> Why use numbers to represent states of emotion? I believe that trying to create a quantification method for happiness is

Is what? That was the last page. Shit. Did HQ mean happiness quantification, not happiness quotient? I had no idea why this mattered so much to me. I texted back to the evidence lab, *Thanks! Could u send next page ASAP? V important!* but I just got one of those automated replies. *You have entered an invalid reply. Please text HELP for help or STOP to unsubscribe.*

God, this was infuriating. I'd have to wait who knew how long for the next pages to be dried, scanned, encoded, and sent via some government-security channel triple-routed around the world or whatever—all when the notebook was in this building.

Wait. The notebook was in this building. Was that true? Were evidence processing rooms inside the police station, or were they in some offsite lab somewhere? I remembered passing a directory, maybe by the elevator.

I walked to the end of the hallway where I thought the elevator was, but that just led to another hallway. I tried going down more hallways, but they all looked the same, mind-numbingly bland with closed door after closed door. Mona had said most people were working remotely, but still, the emptiness was unsettling. I tried going back, but maybe I'd gotten turned around because I had no idea where I was, plus I caught sight of a surveillance camera in the corner blinking and moving. Not only was I trapped in this hellish maze of beige corporate uniformity, but I'd been caught. Shit.

I faced the moving surveillance camera full on and waved my arms around like a castaway signaling to rescue planes overhead, mouthed *HELP, I'M LOST!* Better to act helpless and stupid than be arrested for snooping around the police department. I heard a far-away *ding* of an elevator followed by "Mia? What are you doing?" Oh, thank God—Mona. I walked toward the direction of her voice, and I almost hugged her, I was so relieved she was alone. I had planned to say I got lost looking for the bathroom, but seeing her friendly, amused smile, I had a better idea.

"I'm so happy to see you. I got lost trying to find you, actually. Shannon said I should ask you if I need help." I explained about

Dad's notebook, showed her the texts from the evidence team, and said, "I know they're super busy and I feel so bad they're having to scan and all that nonsense. I figured, I'm just sitting here, so maybe they could just let me see it, save them the hassle."

She said it sounded like a good idea. She made a quick call and said it was fine, the notebook was in the evidence overflow room, which, infuriatingly, was of course right around the corner from our waiting room.

The "evidence team" turned out to be one balding, bespectacled guy with a face shield and lab coat named Octavius and the "evidence overflow room" an empty room set up like a classroom with six rows of tables with long strips of translucent white wax paper on top, like tablecloth runners. I'd pictured Dad's notebook in some fancy high-tech drying machine, but no; Octavius was taking Dad's notebook and painstakingly peeling and cutting the pages from the bloated, waterlogged block by hand, placing each separated page on the wax paper to make sure it didn't stick to the table as it dried. Getting closer to the pages, seeing Dad's multicolored writing on the wavy, crinkled drying pages, I blinked, my eyelids heavy and hot with tears. Seeing this notebook in person was messing me up. Maybe it was simply grief at this dismemberment of Dad's notebook into *evidence*, the stark visual reminder that this was a criminal investigation. Maybe gratitude toward Octavius, this stranger's caring handling of what might well become a family keepsake. Or maybe my nearness to this repository of ideas I wished I'd allowed Dad to share with me, my regret over squandering my chance to ask the questions I may now never get to. All these things I'd already known, yes, but something about seeing it laid out, quite literally, in front of me—it shook me in a way I hadn't expected.

I reached out to touch a page—was it damp still?—when Octavius yelled, "Whoa, whoa, stop right there. Don't touch that. Don't touch anything." I jumped and turned to say I'm so sorry, but his face softened. "Sorry, but these are still wet and we have to be careful.

Here." He handed me latex gloves, which seemed inconsistent with the whole don't-touch thing, but I just tried to say sorry and thank you through my sobs. God, what was wrong with me? I'd cried more in the previous twenty-four hours than in the entirety of my life. Octavius was as uncomfortable with my emotions as I was; he muttered something about needing to get back to work and sat down in the corner and separated more pages.

I took in a deep breath. Okay, I needed to stop blubbering. Scanning the pages, I found it easily, the two lines of bright red from the last scan and the page that followed. Put together, it read:

Why use numbers to represent states of emotion? I believe that trying to create a quantification method for happiness is futile and meaningless bc ratings are inherently subjective and impossible to standardize. J's 8 might be M's 5, but does that mean J had happier day/life than M?

Quantifying happiness levels is useful only for quick, rough comparisons within one person (not J vs M, but J today vs J tomorrow).

This is why happiness quotient is THE key driver of ultimate happiness level. HQ = how does your actual experience (numerator) compare with your mindset (denominator)?

Similar to golf handicap. Gross score = number of strokes. Net score = adjusted for handicap, based on past performance (golf baseline).

(Consider using subtraction, not division? But quotient is a better expression of the extremes (going from extreme misery to extreme joy, or vice versa) per M's insight. Also, the semantics are better. "Happiness difference" sounds like a concept, whereas "happiness quotient" is clearly a number and also has the benefit of having a certain titular panache. On top of all that, I just looked it up online and saw that people have used that phrase, and it makes me happy (haha) to think I might be joining that discussion. Maybe contributing to it in some way.)

I cannot emphasize enough how excited seeing the phrase *happiness quotient* made me. It wasn't just discovering that I was right about HQ being *happiness quotient* (although I have to admit, I love being right). I'm not sure that I could have recognized it at the time, but I think it was the reprieve from the nonstop onslaught of awful news. Finally, one thing—even if it was a little thing whose origin I couldn't explain—that made me feel a connection to Dad, like we shared a foundational memory. And *titular panache*—that made me smile. That was my phrase; I'd used it when we were in high school during a family breakfast to describe some novel title. John rolled his eyes and said, "Why don't you just say the title is cool or lame, like a normal person?" but Dad took my side, said I should never apologize for being or trying to be different. On top of that, Dad crediting my "insight" and answering my question—why quotient rather than difference?—made me feel a deepening connection, like Dad and I were in conversation through these pages.

### HQ Applied to Counterintuitive Case #1 (Lottery/Accident):

— Assume 5 is average baseline before lottery/accident.

— Right after lottery/accident, lottery winner is on a high and happy (HQ of 7/5); victim is in pain and miserable (3/5).

— ONE YEAR after lottery/accident: they've adapted. Lottery winner's new baseline is 7, so average day in new life (objectively better than before) now feels neutral (HQ = 7/7 = 1.0). Same with accident victim, who has new adjusted lower baseline.

— Because lottery winner's baseline (denominator) is now higher, small moments of joy affect them less. Conversely, those small things make accident victims happier.

### HQ Applied to Counterintuitive Case #2 (POW):

— Let's say prison life is average happiness level of 2, pretty bleak.

— For realist/pessimist, the typical prison day becomes the new anchoring baseline. Since new baseline is 2, a small moment of non-misery of 2.5 (a warm cup of tea or being outside for 2 minutes on a sunny day) becomes a moment of relative happiness (2.5/2).

— Optimist's baseline is still 6, his old life in US with his family—he hasn't adjusted; he refuses to adjust, that's the optimism—it's all miserable and awful (2.5/6).

— When Xmas comes and still in prison, the optimist is devastated, experiencing a 2 instead of the 9 (being rescued/released) he was expecting.

### HQ Applied to Counterintuitive Case #3 (Object vs Experience):

— An object you buy and keep becomes part of your new normal, your baseline, so seeing it after a year no longer yields pleasure.

— But once a vacation or concert is over, you return home and your baseline life remains the same. So every time you remember the experience, you derive pleasure from it afresh.

— Article describing object vs experience study proclaimed: "adaptation a formidable enemy of happiness." But adaptation is also an enemy of misery. Adaptation moderates your happiness level, drives it toward neutrality, away from the extremes of joy and misery.

I'm a fan of counterintuitive anything, but reading these, I kept thinking, Okay, Dad, all interesting, but so what? If I knew Dad (which, admittedly, was in doubt), these were not theoretical musings. For our school essays and science fairs, Dad always pressed us for the real-world implications, saying ideas were useless without practical application.

I scanned the pages. More eye-glazing equations, studies, numbers, examples . . . and there! At the top of a page:

### SO WHAT?: Practical Application

Why does all this matter? After all, there are many ways to be happier, and the world is full of studies, books, and TED Talks on how to increase the gross happiness level—exercise more, leave toxic relationships, find better-fitting jobs, meditate—for a more satisfying life. So why focus on lowering the baseline/expectations? Is that as inane as preparing for a golf tournament by raising your handicap (play worse for a while to "game the system") instead of trying to improve your swing?

I suppose I'm fixated on HQ because I'm trying to prepare my family for the dramatic experiences in store for us. I can't change what's coming; the numerator is fixed. Many other variables that influence happiness are fixed (genetics), require long-term efforts (a lot of therapy), or are not workable for my family (I can just imagine trying to get Mia to do gratitude meditations!). But if I can do things from the sideline to lower my family's baseline/expectations and thereby heighten the positives (and, even more importantly, decrease the traumatic downside) of what's coming, that would be huge.

But how? It's easy to say "change your mindset"; actually doing it is the challenge.

That's why I need experiments. Figuring out: Is it possible to manipulate happiness levels, to change your (or your family's) mindset to maximize happiness and minimize sadness? What unforeseen consequences might result from this?

What was he preparing? Was he just thinking in generalities, like every family goes through ups and downs, or was he anticipating specific things he knew were coming, like cancer? For the first time reading Dad's notebook, I thought, Do I really want to keep reading?

### HQ Experiments Q1: Expectations vs Baseline

For a long time, I thought the key to maximizing happiness was lowering expectations as much as possible. But that can backfire. If you expect to lose, you'll lose, may not even try at all.

My hypothesis is that lowering the BASELINE can increase happiness without the potential downside of lowering EXPECTATIONS. Baseline and expectations are distinct. You can have a low baseline (you've always stayed in run-down motels) but high expectations (you booked a luxury hotel with amazing reviews), or vice versa.

The counterintuitive examples show that changing your baseline—your conception of yourself and your normal life—impacts happiness levels tremendously. When something good happens (promotion, engagement), don't get used to it too quickly; keep thinking of your old life, old job, old house, as the point of comparison for new experiences. Conversely, when something bad happens (disease, death in family), adjust your baseline downward as quickly as possible; don't get stuck clinging to your pre-tragedy life, like the optimistic POW.

That's easy to say, but is it doable? How? I've seen people do this—wedding/anniversary toasts ("I was alone, convinced I'd never find someone special before I met you"), award speeches ("five years ago, I had no agent, rejected left and right"), college essays, graduations, etc.—all invoking a low past baseline to compare how far they've come. Imagine if we could do this on normal days, for everyday life, instead of bringing that mindset out only for social media posts and milestone occasions.

So that's the key question, the goal of my HQ experiments. Can we manipulate the timing and levels of this normally subconscious baseline adaptation process? How? Is it as simple as being aware of it? Daily visualization of an anchoring memory to which you intentionally compare today's events? Will merely thinking of that low point 3x a day, like brushing your teeth, be enough to change your baseline?

## HQ Experiments Q2: MAXIMIZING HAPPINESS for Loved Ones

Here we come to the crux of this whole endeavor: using the HQ principle to prepare your loved ones for something great coming up.

Per HQ, the bigger the gap between actual experience and baseline/expectation, the more dramatic the resulting happiness (or sadness). Happiest = low baseline + expecting horrible situation, then get sudden amazing news (innocent death-row inmate gets last-minute reprieve; homeless, ill person wins lottery). Can/should we lower our loved ones' baselines to bestow the gift of that low-to-high thrill, a moment of intense joy that will resonate and reverberate throughout life?

### HQ Experiments Q3: MINIMIZING SUFFERING for Loved Ones

The worst in terms of happiness = huge sudden jump down with no warning (young, healthy person gets fatal disease diagnosis). This is my biggest goal: <u>avoiding the intense, shocking trauma</u>. For impending bad news, can I lower the baseline—little by little, like frog in boiling pot, get as close as possible to bad-news level before actually delivering the bad news, make the coming painful news easier to bear?

———

"EXCUSE ME, MR. OCTAVIUS, SIR? Sorry to bother you, but the rest of these pages are blank. Have you come across any more pages with writing on them?"

He didn't look up, just kept ever so slowly peeling one page off, careful not to tear it. "Yup, I just hit some writing." He placed the page on the wax paper. "Hmmm, the writing's upside down, on the bottom of the page. He must have used the flip side."

Octavius turned the notebook over and carefully opened the thick back cover. In the middle of the first/last page, in thick print, were the words HQ EXPERIMENT OVERVIEW. I did that, too, use one notebook for two things—front side for lecture notes, back for lab—and it occurred to me, I'd probably seen Dad do this when I was little, copied him without realizing.

The back page was still too wet for Octavius to separate. It was so wet, in fact, that you could see through to the writing on the other side, although you couldn't read it because the writing was backward. I took a picture with my phone and mirror-imaged it, increasing the contrast to darken the lettering from the other side.

There. On top, in red: EXPERIMENT #1: 4/19/2017. Wow, Dad had been doing this for three years? A few lines down, it read: (illegible) Mia and John (illegible) OCD outings (illegible) Q&D movie. The rest of the page was in the blue ink that bled more, forming a soft, diffuse cloud of light blue throughout, so it was difficult to figure out, but I got the gist. First, I need to explain about our Only Child Days. When Eugene got the autism diagnosis, the family therapists warned our parents against focusing all their attention on Eugene and breeding resentment, especially with us being twins and already not feeling special as individuals, blah blah. My parents are both only children, and that's where the idea of John and me being an only child once a month started. So let's say it was my turn to be the "only child." They would drop off Eugene at Henry's House for an all-day, overnight respite and John at a friend's for a sleepover. It wasn't all treats and outings. I also had to do all the chores and help with grocery shopping and cooking, but we did at least one fun outing.[13] It sounds stupid talking about it, but it really was kind of special. I looked forward to those days, even when I was a teenager and spent most of them with headphones on, playing video games.

This first experiment involved *The Queen & the Drone,* a campy, fun sequel film featuring two superheroes—one male, one female. Dad took me to see it on an OCD, saying how all his friends' kids said it was exponentially better than the first movie and sending me select reviews. On our way home, he asked for my rating. I remembered refusing to reduce an experience to a number but him insisting and me finally giving in. I gave it a 2, saying I was disappointed it didn't live up to the rave reviews. According to Dad's notes, he took John to the same movie, telling him to brace himself, it was awful (he sent him the pans), but he needed to see it because a college friend co-

---

13 The fucked-up-ness of experimenting on your children (!) aside (more on that in a minute), it occurred to me that this setup was perfect for experiments because John and I were never supposed to talk to each other about these days, to maintain the illusion of this being a separate sphere of existence. We ignored this, told each other everything when we were little, but we weren't exactly chatty by high school.

produced it. John apparently gave it a 7, saying he was surprised at how much better it was than he was expecting.

Reading through this, I thought, *Really?* What the fuck? Dad performed an experiment on us? Isn't it unethical to experiment on people without permission, especially on kids, double especially on your own kids?

I sat down on the cold, hard plastic chair and tried to think. I knew this was the least of my concerns, but I felt betrayed, that what I'd thought was a special father-daughter date—that's what he'd called it, and I'd sighed and acted like that was stupid but secretly liked it—was a ruse. If you'd asked for my fondest, most treasured memories of Dad, that would have been in the top ten. That whole day leading up to the movie, walking to the theater from the parking lot, I was giddy—we were going to see this great movie, the sun was shining, and we had just had sushi and ice cream. It didn't matter that the movie turned out to be blah because the happiness I felt anticipating it, looking forward to it, made up for it, as well as the fun afterward of debating its merits with Dad, who doesn't share my taste in movies but is really smart and entertaining to disagree with.

"Oh, look what I found. A loose sheet, folded in the middle. It's typed, too," Octavius said, placing it on the wax paper.

### HQ Experiments: Master List

CAVEATS: These are not true "experiments" (no controls, test subject size of 1–2 people), not reliable or generally applicable. I'm using only as sanity checks to help me refine my thinking. One major problem to consider is that my "test subjects" are M and J. Consider whether M is too cynical for results to be valid. Her sarcastic attitude and general disregard for others' feelings vs J being a joy to be around → query whether my own reactive mood around them influences and skews their ratings? How to control for this factor?

I leaned closer to the paper, reread the passage. It felt like someone was pressing a thumb into my neck, forcing me to take deep breaths to keep my lungs from shriveling. Was that really how Dad felt? That I didn't care about others'—about his—feelings? That I was cynical and sarcastic, whereas John was a joy? It wasn't untrue. I knew that. The gist was stuff my parents and teachers had told me—hell, I'd said it myself, and, truth be told, even prided myself on it—but with a different spin, that I was an independent thinker, that I cared more about authenticity and honesty than tact. Dad's assessment on paper stung, like hearing people whisper about you behind your back, and I wished Dad were here so I could rail against him, tell him that his "experiment" was banal and reductive and fundamentally flawed in numerous ways: first, John and I have totally different tastes in movies; second, I bet there are studies saying the opposite, that high expectation-setting actually leads to higher ratings because people are conformist sheep and believe what they're told to think, which is why influencers are paid a gazillion dollars to create hype, for God's sake; and third . . . I was so upset I couldn't think of what the third was, but I was sure there were countless obvious reasons why Dad's so-called Experiment #1 didn't prove anything except that he was an asshole.

I stood up. I wanted to run out of this room, to hell with Dad and his ridiculous theories and cruel experiments, and never see these pages again.

That's when I saw it, the last row on the typewritten page: EXPERIMENT #24: 6/23/2020. Yesterday. What was the experiment? When and where? Involving whom? Could Dad's whole disappearance be an *experiment*? It seemed so ridiculous just a few minutes ago, but discovering that his experiments were on us, the cruelty in his words about me . . . But John and I were one thing. Dad couldn't do that to Eugene, could he? I closed my eyes. I wanted to throw up. It would feel so good to throw up.

"I'm going to go, thank you so much, but please, if you could send more pages as soon as you can. . . ." I managed to say before running out.

John was around the corner, standing outside the women's bath-room, door ajar, peering in. "John? What the fuck?"

"Mia, where have you been?" he whisper-yelled. "I've been trying to find you. Why didn't you answer my texts?"

"Oh my God, I have so much to tell you. I found—"

"Okay, whatever. Listen—"

"No, *you* listen. This is really important. You need to—"

"Mia, will you shut up? I talked to her. The neighbor-blogger woman. The one with the video. She's had it since last night."

I thought, Okay, what am I missing? Of course she had the video last night; she took it yesterday morning, so . . . Wait, was "she" not the blogger? Was he talking about Kenny's mom?

John continued, "*Last night,* and she never said a fucking word about it, after going on about sharing information and telling us everything and—"

"Wait, what? Who are you talking about?"

His body slumped as if each of his cells had lost half its energy and he was too tired to say more.

"The police," he said. "Detective Janus."

# PART III

## THE NEW LOW BASELINE

# SIXTEEN

# The Needs of the Two

THE FIRST TIME EUGENE HAD A SCARY, PHYSICAL OUTBURST WAS ON John's and my thirteenth birthday, which happened to fall on a Friday the 13th, the inauspiciousness of which I blamed for what happened—not because I believed in the bad-luck superstitious nonsense, but because I didn't.

Let me explain. Birthdays are a big deal in our family; our parents make a fuss, Dad because he grew up with lavish birthdays (the only child thing) and Mom because she didn't (her parents were poor and unsentimental). Ever since Eugene's diagnosis, our parents have gone all out to demonstrate that we siblings Still Matter. With this being a milestone year—our becoming teenagers, or, as Mom likes to say, our biological age finally catching up to our attitudes—we imagined a laser-tag party in Gangnam, maybe our first-ever phones or sleepaway camps as presents.

But a month before our birthday, something strange started happening with Eugene, who was seven. One night, he woke up at 1 A.M.

with a high-pitched wail and started jumping with a ferocity we'd never seen, landing with thunderous booms that vibrated through the floor of our apartment (and presumably our neighbors' ceiling below us). Dad scooped him up and cradled him, which added a tortured quality to his already disturbing vocals. Mom fed him his favorite ice cream, which seemed like a good idea—he couldn't scream if he was eating—but he gagged and threw up, prompting Dad to let him go, at which point Eugene resumed jumping and wailing. This went on for hours. I remember at one point being awed by Eugene's stamina, his ability to sustain such amplitude for so long without getting hoarse; our choir teacher would go crazy for his vocal technique and the precision of his rhythm. He finally fell asleep around dawn, resuming when he woke up a few hours later and continuing throughout the day and into the night, when the cycle began again. No one could sleep, and Dad was sure we'd be evicted from the apartment. Eugene's neuropsychologist gave Mom a brochure of an institution in Seoul that accepted children.

It was during the second week of our crisis, late at night when I couldn't sleep, when I overheard our parents stressing about our birthday plans. (Okay, I confess: I was actively eavesdropping.) Mom said she hadn't done a thing to plan our party, and how were they going to host one anyway when they couldn't get a babysitter or take Eugene anywhere?, and Dad said the doctors' visits and tests were costing so much money, he didn't see how they could afford summer camps. "We can't do nothing," Mom said, the mix of exhausted and resolute in her voice making her sound weirdly unhinged. She said it again—"We can't do nothing"—but her voice broke on *can't*.

I went straight to John's room to tell him. I felt bad about waking him up—sleep was a precious commodity in our house those days—but this was an emergency. We took turns ranting and venting about a shitty birthday ahead, not to mention a shitty summer stuck at home playing assistant to therapists following Eugene around all day, holding out M&M's for treats, saying, "Eugene, let's say buh, buh. Lips together, then apart. Buh."

The shittiest part of all: there was nothing we could do about it. We definitely couldn't complain about it; Mom's near- (possibly actual?) crying made that clear. Of our parents, Dad was the crier; Mom did not cry. Obviously, we knew to blame her extreme fatigue, that she wouldn't have been all weepy if it hadn't been for her lack of sleep and her depression about Eugene. Still, the thing that broke her, that made her cry, was something to do with us, with our stupid birthday.

My last-ditch-effort idea was to come clean about overhearing them and volunteer to plan the party and pay for it and the camp ourselves—we both had chore money saved up, and we could tutor kids in English to make more—but John vetoed it, saying that would just make Mom feel worse.

We ended up telling our parents that for our birthday, what we really wanted was no party (they're for little kids, we said, acting like we were afraid of offending them) and no summer camp (we said we found out they take away all your electronics—true, which we'd known all along but hadn't cared about) and in light of our becoming thirteen, could we have as our present just the freedom of doing nothing that summer, with unlimited computer time?

If they were relieved, they did a good job not showing it. Mom said, "This is really what you want?" and we said yes, of *course,* but maybe too fervently. (We're not the best liars.) They studied us, Dad smiling this knowing smile and Mom doing the opposite, squinting and frowning a little as if seeing something alien. Dad said he appreciated how much thought we put into this decision together, so it was okay with him if it was okay with Mom. Mom said one word, a barely audible "Okay," tinged with something I couldn't figure out—not disappointment exactly, or at least not disappointment in us (a tone I knew well); maybe regret.

If I'm being honest, it kind of shocked me that they went along with it. When they said okay, they trust us, I wanted to say, *No, what are you doing? We're dumbasses; don't trust us,* and I could see that John felt the same way, even as we nodded and acted grateful. That was when I realized—a part of me had hoped they wouldn't take us seri-ously. Maybe I even expected it, counted on it, that they'd call us out on our façade and reward our noble generosity by refusing to go along, by throwing us an even more lavish party with undreamed-of presents. Wasn't that what always happened in the stories we read, in fables and myths? The best of both worlds: our acting mature, sac-rificing for the good of our family, but not having to actually live with the consequences. I think this is the first time I remember thinking, Maybe being an adult is not so great.

The one saving grace was the pair of cakes. We woke up on our birthday and found our parents in the kitchen, standing over two cakes they'd baked together, a first. (They both hated cooking.) They'd made one coconut cake with vanilla frosting (my favorite) and one banana cake with chocolate frosting (John's favorite), cut both in half, and assembled the semicircles into two half-and-half cakes, one for us to take to share with friends during recess, and the other for a special family dinner that night.

Eugene was already up and was licking a spoonful of the choco-late frosting. Eugene had been their special helper, Dad said with a wink, "taste-testing" different varieties of frosting all morning. John and I pretended to beg for a taste, and Dad said, "No cake for you!" in a strangely militaristic voice, which John and I didn't get (it was apparently an impersonation from some ancient TV show), but it made Mom laugh so we went along and laughed, too.

In one sense, what happened next was my fault, because if I hadn't brought up the whole Friday the 13th thing, none of the rest would have happened. Looking at the 1 and 3 candles next to the kitchen calendar, it dawned on me that it was Friday the 13th. I said, "Hey, look, our thirteenth birthday is on Friday the thirteenth! And it's April!" (Four is considered an unlucky number in Korea.) "Does that mean we'll get triple bad luck?" I made ghost noises at John and laughed. He's superstitious and gets spooked out easily, which I like to roast him for.

No one laughed, and I think Mom felt bad for me; she started

pontificating in an overly bright voice about the origin of these ridiculous superstitions, saying how at least the Korean bias against
the number four made sense, since the Chinese version (from which
Korean derived) sounded like *death*, whereas no one knew why Friday the 13th was supposed to be unlucky, at which point Dad started
debating Mom's point, saying being against a number because of
how it sounds in a foreign language was stupid, and at least Friday
the 13th arose out of an actual calamity. Dad didn't know what that
historical event was, so we all ran to the family computer to Google
the origin story, which turned out to be biblical—Jesus dying on a
Friday and Judas, the disciple who betrayed Jesus, being the thirteenth to join the Last Supper—when we heard a huge clang from
the kitchen and ran back.

It was our cakes. Both of them. Completely smashed up. Eugene
was destroying them, one hand *inside* each cake, squeezing, mauling,
smushing, clawing, and flinging all over. If he'd desperately wanted
the cake and lost control shoveling it into his mouth, I might have
understood. But it wasn't that. It was like he hated everything the
cakes stood for and wanted them gone from this world, like every
morsel was an enemy that needed to be vanquished. Or, no, like *we*
were the enemy, John and I, and he wanted to punish us. To destroy
everything good in our lives.

Standing across the kitchen, looking at Eugene, my first thought
was: Do you hate me as much as I hate you? I bet you don't because I
hate you so much. I wish you were gone, wish you'd never come into
our lives. Our lives would be so perfect without you.

Before, when I felt these shameful thoughts lurking in the background, I suppressed them, told them to go away like unwanted
guests or nightmares I didn't want bothering me. But this time, I
let myself think and feel them fully, allowed them to take over my
entire brain and infuse every cell, every neuron, while fully holding
Eugene's gaze. It's funny, Eugene usually had bad eye contact, but
now he was staring intently with a huge grin, as if taunting me, as if
daring me to just do and say what I'd been holding in.

I've thought about it a lot since then, and I think many people might say (although I don't know because I've never spoken it aloud) that this is a normal sibling emotion, that everyone hates their annoying little brother from time to time. If Eugene had been a "typical" kid, I think I would have felt fine thinking it, even saying it out loud. I'd heard friends tell their siblings, "I hate you; I hope you die!"—hell, John and I said it to each other all the time—but John and I have never said anything like that to or about Eugene. I think we were afraid to. Because it's too close to the truth. If an outsider heard me say that to John, they'd assume I don't mean it, that it's just sibling frustration and of course I love him. But if they heard me say it to Eugene, wouldn't they automatically wonder if that was really true, deep down? I guess I was afraid others saw Eugene as unlovable. Maybe that I did as well.

Anyway, it embarrasses me now, just thinking how it must sound—a rational person becoming so enraged over a pair of slightly crooked homemade cakes. I remember being embarrassed even at the time, turning away from everyone to hide how upset I was getting, chiding myself—why are you letting this tiny, insignificant thing get to you? I think more than anything, what upset me was Mom and Dad, just standing there. Their impotence. I could see their fear that no one do anything to set off Eugene, like nothing mattered except keeping Eugene calm. That was what our family had come to.

Eugene picked up the school cake platter and threw it into the trash can before picking up the other platter. It outraged me that I hadn't had even one bite of these cakes, my sole birthday present. A clump of cake remained on the platter, and it was like an Epiphany with a capital E with trumpets blaring: YOU MUST GET THE CAKE!

I ran across the kitchen and grabbed the platter. It seems important to point out that I didn't mean to touch Eugene, but he wouldn't let go of the platter. His stubbornness infuriated me. Really, how dare he? "Let go!" I yelled—it's strange to think these were the first words anyone had uttered, the rest of my family in some state of shell-shocked paralysis—but he didn't, just smiled bigger, and I yelled again, "I said, let go!" and I meant to tap his hand as a physical cue, or maybe I didn't, maybe that's an excuse, because what came out was not a gentle tap. It was a slap. I freaking slapped his hand away with a *thwack,* so hard that my palm tingled. And it worked, too, but he grabbed my fingers with both his hands to wrest them away from the cake. He was seven, half my size, but the surprise factor made me let go of the platter, which thunked onto our kitchen table, and still, he clung to my fingers, wouldn't let go, grabbing and pulling, bending my right index and middle fingers back at an awkward angle. It should have hurt like hell, but it was like what they say about adrenaline flooding your body in an accident and mothers lifting cars to save their babies or whatever. I was focused on one thing: that bite of cake on the platter. It was John's, the banana-chocolate, which I personally thought was disgusting, but I didn't care. Using my left hand, I clawed it into my mouth and chomped with relish, with a loud "Mmmmmm, delicious!" and swallowed.

Eugene freaked out. He clawed at my mouth and neck, as if to break through to my esophagus and gouge out the cake, and he picked up the platter and threw it. Later, it occurred to me that he was aiming for the trash can next to me, but the angle was off, so it seemed like he was throwing it at me, to hurt me. I managed to step out of the way, but just barely, and the platter hit the wall, the explosion of glass sending shards everywhere.

One of the bigger shards ricocheted off the wall and hit my right palm, sliced it. "Mia, your hand," John yelled, and I looked down at my palm, the thin crimson line of blood pooling and swelling.

"It's fine; it's nothing," I said, making a fist to stop the bleeding. I told myself that my casual tone was why neither of my parents checked on me. They focused wholly and exclusively on Eugene, who was in full outburst mode, jumping, screaming, and punching the air, head shaking violently. Every time Eugene's bare feet landed on the floor, the glittering shards of glass fluttered and trembled, the pieces closest to him leaping and twirling like ice dancers putting on a show. In my parents' defense, it was scary; I didn't blame them for panicking, oblivious to everything but Eugene's own obliviousness to the glass, both rushing over to stop his jumping, finally giving up and resorting to manhandling to get him out of the kitchen, Eugene's rhythmic screaming getting farther away like a siren passing by.

John and I looked at each other, and I could tell that he knew what I was thinking, I knew what he was thinking, and our thoughts were aligned: this is majorly fucked up, and we need to get the hell out. I stepped over the glass shards to get out of the kitchen, and we got our school bags and left. On the way out, John grabbed the stack of bright rainbow-colored Happy Birthday napkins meant for our school cake. He handed them to me one by one to press into my palm and soak up the blood.

———

THE PROBLEM WAS THE INJUSTICE. Yes, Eugene was "special needs," but he was still a human being who chose to act a certain way and, at seven years old, was old enough to be held accountable. But of course, he wasn't. Our parents did nothing. No stern talking-to, no time out, no punishment. They treated him like he lacked free will, which made me indignant on his behalf, but more than that, I have to admit, resentful and jealous. Our parents saw him the way Christians see newborns, as incapable of sin, his inherent virtue untainted by the evils of the world. It was infuriating.

What John and I did in the aftermath of the Cake Incident was not a true, literal silent treatment where you say nothing at all. We didn't even act moody, which I think would have been understandable given what happened, not to mention appropriate with this being our first week of officially being teenagers. We responded to direct questions and comments. Yes, please; Thank you, sir; No, ma'am; Would you mind passing the kimchi, please? Our excessive politeness was, of course, a withholding of intimacy, meant to wound. Speaking overly formally is a great way to punish your parents because it communicates distance and also has the benefit of making you feel grown-up, but it's not anything they can complain about. When they asked what was wrong (and they did, often), I said, "Wrong? What could be wrong? Everything's *great*. How are *you*?," making my tone bright and singsongy, which they hate, and which, more importantly, they know *I* hate. Our treatment of Eugene was even easier; because he didn't talk, you had to be proactive to interact with him, so all we had to do was stop trying.

Look, we were thirteen, so it's not like we weren't like this from time to time, but usually for brief hormonal periods, and not at the same time. Mom bore the brunt of it. Dad was working on some big, multicompany deal, so he left three days after our birthday for a weeklong trip to New York, leaving Mom to deal with it all. Mom relied on John and me to step up with extra chores and babysitting when Dad was away, but this time, I stayed in my room as much as possible and pretended not to hear when Mom called for help.

It was that Thursday—the seventh day of our (Not) Silent Treatment—when everything changed. Our principal pulled us out of exams (in itself unprecedented and alarming) and led us directly outside to a taxi. He said not to be worried, everything was fine, but our mother was at the hospital, and again, everything was fine, but our brother was going into emergency surgery—but a minor one, very safe; he was definitely, absolutely positive Eugene would be just fine—and our mother suggested, if we didn't mind too much, it might be good for us to come to the hospital right away.

I think you automatically assume there's a direct correlation between the amount of verbal padding and the level of worrisome news; the more cushioning, the worse the situation. Here, the number of insulation words to impact words was 5:1, which was all wrong.

John and I didn't say anything in the taxi. At the hospital, a kind nurse who spoke excellent English explained that Eugene had ulcerative colitis, which had been causing awful pain but, because he couldn't tell anyone, had gone undiagnosed and been getting worse until it caused a bowel obstruction, and yes, this was serious, but they caught it in time and the surgery was going very well, and Mom was giving blood in case he needed it but she would be here soon, and did we have any questions?

I had one: Would eating sugary things, like cake frosting, cause pain?

She said people were different—for example, some experience the most pain while eating, others in the middle of the night when their stomachs are most empty—but sugar was a common irritant, causing sharp pain, especially on an empty stomach.

"It's funny," she said as she got up to leave, "your mother had the same exact question."

———

BEFORE I GO ON, I have to explain about Mom's obsession (passion, she'd correct) for Star Trek. Our whole family loved it, but Mom's dedication went beyond fandom to bona fide expertise. It's a linguistics thing; she interned for the linguist who created the show's Klingon and Vulcan languages and, as one of the dozen or so advanced members of the Klingon Language Institute, she even helped edit the libretto for the Klingon opera 'u'.[14] She introduced John and

———

14 The world premiere of 'u' was at The Hague, and because Dad and John detest opera, she took me—our special girls' trip, she called it. I was ten, and everything about that trip was magical. Being in Amsterdam and the event itself, of course—I adore opera, and Klingon is surprisingly perfect for the form, the guttural language enhancing the gritty, raw power of the music—but more than anything, I loved being with Mom, just us. During intermission, I said how amazing it was that linguists like her turned an actor's random, alien-sounding gibberish into a working language, and could we maybe turn Eugene's splaughs into a language based on pitch and rhythm, like Morse code? Mom was vigorously swirling her Bloodwine, Klingon-style, and she guffawed and said, "bItaQ," which means *You are weird*, and I was feeling insulted, but then she hugged me, so tight it hurt, and said, "ach bIDun. 'ej bangwI' SoH," which means *But you are wonderful. And you are my loved one.*

me to the franchise early, and we both loved Vulcans, me for their anti-sentimentality and logic, and John for the mystical mind-meld, merging with others to access their thoughts and memories. We have videos of us at age six, John murmuring incantations with his fingers spread over our geriatric cat Spot's "temple," and me "speaking logically" by connecting every sentence with "which means, therefore." (Example: Mom: "Where are the cookies I just bought?" Me: "I was starving. Which means, therefore, I had to eat the first thing I saw." Mom: "And since I left the cookies out, you saw them first and had no choice but to eat them all?" Me: "That would be logical.")

That's when Mom came up with the Mind-Meld Logic-Chain Game. A verbal LEGOs in which we connected our minds and spoke as one, taking turns saying a sentence each to build a joint chain of thought. Consistent practice will dramatically improve your mind-meld *and* logical speaking skills, Mom guaranteed.

We played this game all the time. We were bored and lonely— Mom was pregnant, and we had just moved to Korea and hadn't made new friends yet—but even more, we loved how awesome we were at it, it being a twin coordination thing we were predisposed to. Also, it was very useful for getting out of trouble. During parental interrogations, we'd mind-meld and jointly deliver a co-confession, so they couldn't tell which one was actually at fault and couldn't fairly punish either of us. (After a while, they started punishing us both, saying the mind-meld confession made us accomplices in the cover-up.)

It changed as we got older, as everything does. We stopped touching each other's temples, stopped saying "which means, therefore" with every sentence. It became a way to think out loud together what was too painful to face alone—when we were afraid of the answer, when it was too hard for one brain, when we'd fucked up and wanted to split the responsibility, or, most often, all of the above. It's a powerful thing, an addictive thing, the turning of *I* into *we*, coupled with the logical tone, siphoning the emotion away.

So this is what we did after the nurse left, one thought block after another, like dominos. Tick, tick, tick:

- That's why he woke up every night. He was in agony, no idea why, screaming for help, and we got annoyed he wouldn't shut up.
- But he figured out the frosting made him sick.
- And he didn't want us in pain, too. That's why he ruined the cakes. To protect us.
- When we ate the cake, that's when he freaked out.
- Because he loves us, even though we're dumbasses.
- Hateful dumbasses.
- Hateful, awful, evil dumbasses.

Usually, I felt better after we did this. But this time, I just felt like a fraud. Because *we* didn't do anything. I alone acted despicably, yelled and taunted and slapped. I didn't deserve the comfort of sharing the blame. "This is bullshit," I said. "I'm the hateful dumbass, not you. You didn't yell or hit or do anything. And God, I've been such a bitch to Mom."

John shook his head, started saying that wasn't true and he had the same awful thoughts and feelings and blah blah, but I couldn't focus. Because behind him, in the doorway, appeared Mom, moving slowly into view. Our eyes locked, and she looked so sad that I thought for sure something had gone wrong with Eugene, and I wanted to demand to know, but something gooey like a wad of bubble gum was blocking my throat.

John turned around. "Mom, oh my God, Mom," he said, running to her. "How's Eugene?"

Mom smoothed his hair and said everything's fine, the surgery went great and we could see him soon. I closed my eyes, gulped in air.

I felt a hand clutch mine. Mom had taken the seat next to me, her face up close to mine. "You're not a bad sister. Or daughter. *I'm* the one who screwed up. I've been . . ." She bit her lip and stared out the window at the blue sky. "You know that institution the doctor recommended?"

I did. He gave our parents a brochure, which Mom tore into tiny pieces and threw into the trash can.

Mom said, "I took him there this morning."

I don't know why I gasped. I shouldn't have been surprised. Wasn't that what I'd been hoping all along, for Eugene to go away? Wasn't that why I was bitchy to Mom—to express just how much I resented Eugene, his very existence, for daring to *inconvenience* me?

"What?" John said, his voice all shock and outrage. "What about what you and Dad said? We're a family, and families stick together. The needs of the one outweigh the needs of the many. How could you forget all that?"

Mom took in a deep, audible breath through her nose and spoke in clipped facts. She'd thought about it. Decided she needed to find out more. Truly consider it. Made an appointment. Took Eugene for a visit this morning—here, her voice, which had been even, shook, and she paused before continuing—where the head administrator said Eugene's middle-of-the-night jumping and wailing sounded like a textbook response to gastrointestinal pain, which he'd seen in numerous autistic patients, and called the hospital, which confirmed the suspicion and operated, and the problem was fixed. Our family crisis was over, just like that.

"So you see," Mom said, "if I hadn't brought Eugene to the institution, we might never have discovered his condition."

It clicked into place, why she told us about the institution. She thought that would make me feel better, convince me that my being an awful sister had been a good thing. But it didn't. Selfish was selfish. An accidental, convolutedly indirect byproduct couldn't change that in hindsight, no matter how beneficial it wound up being.

She was tracing with one finger the lines meandering through my palm, winced when she got to the faint glass cut you could barely see. "I know you feel guilty, but you shouldn't. You have a right to be mad—at me, Dad, Eugene, the whole situation. Both of you. You're very smart and capable, so I sometimes forget. But you're still children. And I've been doing a pretty bad job of being your mom."

John and I protested, said she was a great mom, but she shushed us. "I really screwed up your birthday. Yeah, I knew what you were doing. I shouldn't have gone along with it, but I did because I was exhausted. And I think it's human, very understandable, that you were hurt and fed up and wanted to remind me that you have needs, too. And sometimes . . ." Her face twitched, I couldn't tell whether in amusement or pain, or a little of both. "Sometimes the needs of the two outweigh the needs of the one."

"Does this mean we get iPhones?" John said, clearly trying to hide how emotional he was getting, and Mom played along, said, "Definitely not," in a fake-serious voice, and laughed, not boisterous or anything like that but almost under her breath, her eyes glassy.

Here's the thing. To this day, I don't like remembering that time—the middle-of-the-night mayhem, the cake debacle, the institution, the hospital. I felt guilty for a long time after that. And I'm not saying this ten-minute talk with Mom made everything okay and turned that awful day into a good one. But it was a good moment. It felt like forgiveness. It didn't occur to me until later that she might have been asking for ours.

# SEVENTEEN

# Logic Chains Gone Wrong

THAT DAY AT THE HOSPITAL MARKED THE END OF OUR MIND-MELD-talking era. The next morning, Mom said to us, almost a throwaway, "I didn't realize you guys still did that mind-meld game thing," and it was like when I was in kindergarten and she said, "I didn't realize you still sleep with your baby blankie; it's so adorable," and I gave it up that day.

But sometimes, in moments of great distress, we revert to childhood habits. That's what happened in the police station, next to the women's bathroom, after John told me about Kenny's mommy-blogger neighbor—how she saw the dashcam recording from a car accident on a neighborhood app and recognized the boy she'd videotaped in the park; how she got concerned the boy seemed to be alone and called the police; and how a Detective Janus came to her house around 7:30 P.M., took a copy of the video, and instructed her not to post it "because it's evidence" (though for what, the detective didn't say).

"Seven-thirty," I started slowly, trying to process the timeline. "So *after* we reported Dad missing to those cops asking about the car accident—"

"—but *before* Janus came to our house," John continued my sentence, muscle memory kicking in and restoring our old back-and-forth rhythm, "which means the entire time she was talking to us, she had the video but said nothing."

"Because she was testing us. She wanted to see if we'd come clean about Eugene having scratches and blood and stuff when he came home."

"She wanted to keep us clueless, so we'd think she's on our side and give her stuff she wanted, like an interview with Eugene with no lawyer around. But it's clear that Eugene's a suspect—"

"—and *that's* the real reason she arrested him—"

"—and she's probably trying to convince a judge he's violent and needs to be locked up, and our lawyer's going to be blindsided—"

"—because we didn't tell her about the screenshot when we saw her—"

"—because we were too busy crying and whining." (And thinking about fucking *Pulp Fiction,* I thought but didn't say.)

Our verbal volleying had been crescendoing, our words faster and overlapping, but everything came to a halt right then.

"We fucked up," I said. "We have to fix this."

We had no idea how. But this is the benefit of a coordinated effort. It's easy to goad each other on, the fusion of energy taking on a self-sustaining momentum as you both tell yourselves the other will take care of the hard part you have no clue how to tackle, even as you both (rightly) suspect the other is thinking the same thing.

We ran to the hearing room—in retrospect, a bad idea given how it exacerbated my ankle injury and made my limping more noticeable. Thinking back to that moment, my hand on the doorknob of the hearing room, I wish I could yell at myself to stop. That if Shannon knew what we were up to, she would've told us to leave the building, stat.

We barged in. I turned the knob as John pushed the door, and we stumbled inside. The "hearing room" looked like a regular conference room, similar to the evidence overflow room I had been in, with a large conference table where everyone sat: Shannon, Mom, and Eugene on the left end and Detective Janus on the right. An oversized screen hung on the wall in the front of the room.

Shannon had explained earlier that the intake officer wasn't a judge, so it's not like I was expecting a crusty, white-bearded man in a robe, but I did not expect the figure on the screen. He was young, like college-TA young, and casually dressed in a noticeably form-fitting short-sleeved shirt that did nothing to hide the extremely well-defined muscles in his arms and chest, with tattoos down his arms and wavy coal-black hair that hung below his shoulder blades. Frankly, he was hot.

The hot quasi-judge dude (there really was no other word for the guy) said, "Ah, this must be Mia and"—he looked down at his notes—"John?" (A little thrill, at realizing he knew my name but had to check for John's—I know, this was hardly the time; I'm annoyed at my vapid, ridiculous self, too.) "We were just talking about you. Why don't you come in and sit? I'd like to hear from you."

This was not what we planned. Not that we actually planned anything, but I had a vague notion of our disruption actually disrupting things, creating chaos, the judge-type person having to bang the gavel and call a recess to restore order, like in *Law & Order*. But what could we do but obey? John and I walked to the table in front, my ankle sending flashes of pain every time I stepped, making me limp and wince.

"I heard you hurt your ankle yesterday," said the judicial dude—getting closer, I could see his name on the Zoom screen on the bottom: Officer Higashida. "Looks like it's really bothering you. What happened?"

What should I say? What could I say? My cheeks burned and I repositioned my mask as I took my seat, murmured something about my mask falling. How did he hear about my ankle? Why were they discussing it? Had some neighbor recorded Eugene pushing me, and Detective Janus managed to find it? "So, my ankle," I said. "When Eugene got home yesterday, he was running really well, which is something he works on, so I got excited and I was jumping up and down. And I fell." I really wanted to avoid lying to government officials, so I phrased it so all my sentences were true.

He didn't fall for it. "Between your jumping up and down and your falling, did Eugene push you or hit you or do anything that caused or contributed to your falling?"

There was no room for evasion. I looked into his eyes—God, they were *smoldering,* staring straight at me, slightly squinted, as if he could see through my clothes, like an X-ray—and said, "No, Eugene would never do that; he's very gentle. I just lost my footing and fell. I can be really clumsy sometimes."

Detective Janus interrupted. "John, is that true?"

This really pissed me off, a female detective pulling that sexist crap. "Why are you asking *him*? He wasn't even there."

"My colleagues who came to your house yesterday asked John about your limping. John said Eugene was very agitated when he came home and pushed you so hard that you fell."

Instant fire on my cheeks. This is why I hate lying, because I find it humiliating to be caught in a lie and my red-cheeks gene goes into overdrive, which makes it impossible to hide the humiliation and thus confirms the lie. Luckily, my mask was covering my cheeks. "John must have misunderstood me, or the police misunderstood him." I looked at John, a you'd-better-fix-this-right-fucking-now glare. I mean, really—what was he thinking, mentioning this to the *police*?

John said words, but each syllable was separated by so much stammering and spluttering it was hard to figure out what, precisely, he was saying. If you transcribed what he said, removed all the *um*s, and spliced the remaining syllables into words and ultimately into sentences, I believe it might have read: "I don't know. Why would I say that? That's wrong. I don't remember. I was confused. Very upset."

"We were all extremely worried and upset about my husband being missing," said Mom, "so I hope you can understand how we didn't take the time to get clear on the details around Mia's boo-boo." (God, I loved Mom's caustic sarcasm when it wasn't directed at me.[15]) "But like I was saying before, Eugene did not cause Mia's injury. He would never hurt his own sister." I had told this same lie a minute prior, but it impressed me how convinced—and, therefore, convincing—Mom sounded and looked, something that would loom larger in my mind in the days that followed.

Detective Janus said, "Officer, I suggest that we move on. Mia's ankle is a minor side issue—"

"—which *you* brought up," Shannon said.

"I brought it up because it helps to demonstrate that what happened with me this morning is not an anomaly, that Eugene was and continues to be dangerous to others. I have evidence that Eugene Parkson was violent at the park yesterday morning, when and where his father disappeared. Notwithstanding his family's denials, I believe he was violent toward his sister later that same morning, and today, he continued to lash out at others, first attempting to stab his mother in the face with a pen and then attacking me."

"What is this evidence, Detective?" Officer Higashida said.

"I obtained a video recording of Eugene and his father taken by a witness yesterday morning at the park. It's unclear if or how this is connected to Mr. Parson's disappearance—that's why I haven't shared this with the family yet, because I wanted more time to investigate and figure out the context. I was still considering whether to bring it up at this hearing. But with his family's insistence that

---

15 I think Mom's sarcasm is particularly effective because of her accent. An accent can make you assume the speaker doesn't *quite* have the language down. You expect them to get by, but not to use the nuances of language/syntax/diction/ etc. to be particularly witty or quick. I think that's what makes Mom's sardonic comments in English so delightful: Mom defying our ingrained expectations enhances the perceived cleverness of the comment itself by a factor of at least two, applying a variation of Dad's HQ formula.

Eugene has never harmed them, I believe it's relevant to counter that claim, and I'd like to play it for you."

A bunch of things happened at this point: Shannon objecting, Detective Janus accusing Shannon of overstepping, Officer Higashida reminding everyone this was an open discussion, not a trial, everyone interjecting over each other, and Eugene rocking in his seat, his hands over his ears. I wanted to yell that I objected to people going around recording and judging the worst moments of other people's lives, how it was a betrayal for Detective Janus to act like she was on our side, working for us to help find Dad, while keeping things from us.

It was all noise. Officer Higashida shut everything down by saying he was going to watch the video, and we were welcome to stay or leave.

It opened mid-scene, Dad struggling with Eugene. I'd seen Eugene out of control before, but this felt different—more aggressive, more hysterical, the jerky video giving it an unsettling documentary feel. The worst of all was the sound; I was used to hearing Eugene's high-pitched screams, but amplified and fed from the big speakers, each squeal jabbed through my eardrums.

Dad was yelling Eugene's name, screaming it over and over to get through to him. Dad was behind him, hugging him to stop his arms from flailing out, Eugene squeezing his eyes shut and open repetitively like something was wrong with them, kicking to get free, but then Dad let go for some reason and howled, like he was hurt, and Eugene turned around, eyes still shut, and half-clawed, half-hit in Dad's direction, and it was hard to tell because Eugene was between Dad and the camera, but it looked like Eugene must have injured Dad's eyes, because Dad yelped and put his hands over his eyes, his eyeglasses half-dangling off his face. "Oh my God, are you okay?" the woman holding the camera said, even as she kept the camera focused on Dad and Eugene while walking toward them. It wasn't until Eugene turned back to face her—his eyes still squeezed tight, as if he couldn't stand to let in any light—and started clawing in her direction that she jumped and backed away from the scene, Dad's screaming for Eugene and Eugene's pained screeching getting fainter until the screen finally cut to black.

―――――

WHAT YOU HAVE TO UNDERSTAND is that Eugene reacted pretty much the same to all videos, from cartoons and musicals to subtitled foreign horror films, even our family's own videos: eyes fixed on the screen and smile on his face, and at the video's end, a high-pitched humming while rocking, which we took as an impatient but playful request for another video. But this video was different. After the screen went blank, Eugene stayed still, his face blanched and eyes wide, as if in shock, with no smile under the mask I could make out. You might think, Well, of course he's going to be traumatized seeing himself behaving in such a scary way, realizing for the first time how it looks to others. But his therapists had tried showing him pictures of himself to develop a stronger sense of the self, and they'd always reported that Eugene didn't seem to recognize his own image.

About a minute after Shannon started making points about the video being taken out of context and not knowing what preceded and provoked this scene, Eugene rubbed his fists into his eyes, grinding them so hard I was afraid he'd gouge them out. Before any of us could react, he stopped abruptly and popped his eyes open, put his fists in front of his face and stared, as if he was unsure what they were, and started squeezing his eyes and fists in unison—shut and open, shut and open. Was this some kind of new motor loop? A precursor to another meltdown? The hand-fist thing was something we hadn't seen, but what he was doing with his eyes was unnervingly familiar, from the video scene we'd just watched.

"Is he okay?" Detective Janus said.

"It's been a long and stressful day. Could we maybe just start a video for him?" Mom tried to put his iPad in his hands, but Eugene refused it, using both hands to push Mom's hands while turning his head the opposite way. It was a peculiar-looking movement, which I recognized: it was my thing, what I did when my parents interrupted something important, a nonverbal *Leave me alone and let me focus!* After Mom put the iPad down, Eugene put his hands together on the table, fingers laced tightly as if in desperate, fervent prayer—the position his behavioral therapists called *calm hands.* As if Eugene knew this was an important meeting and was determined to hold things together.

Officer Higashida smiled at Eugene. John later said he thought for sure he'd rule all charges should be dismissed, but I knew. The smile was one of pity—a pre-apology: *I really wish I could, but . . .*

"This video has made me realize," he said, "what happened this morning with Detective Janus was not an isolated, onetime incident. Whatever provoked Eugene's aggression in the park yesterday was obviously an ongoing factor that continues to pose a risk of danger to himself and others. Given these potentially grave matters, I feel I have no choice but to allow the petition to be filed and refer the matter for hearings. In the meantime, I'd like to go ahead with secure placement."

This eased my mind. Maybe because I knew just enough about criminal proceedings from movies and the news to be on the lookout for words like *indictment, arraignment, pretrial detention,* and *bail,* not realizing that the juvenile justice system has its own linguistic system with euphemistic parallels like *petition* (warrant), *refer* (indict), *disposition* (sentencing), and *secure placement* (jail). I know this is meant to comfort kids and their families, but I think the softened language can actually do a disservice, lull you into a false sense of security that doesn't match reality. You can call it whatever you want—*secure placement* or *detention* or even *luxury villa*—but as long as you're 1) locked up, 2) away from your family and the rest of society, 3) as a consequence of committing (or being accused of) a crime, you're being sent to jail. Which is what this officer was talking about without my realizing it.

Mom did, though, and she flipped out at *secure placement*. She stood up and half-yelled, half-cried in this hysterical tone of despair and outrage I'd never heard from Mom, even through the craziness of the last twenty-four hours, "Are you insane? He won't survive. He's a *kid* with sensory issues who can't talk and obviously went through something traumatic yesterday and got scared by an over-zealous police officer grabbing him way too hard. I told you at the beginning, he didn't get really upset and out of control until he saw me get smacked in the chest, because he was trying to protect me. Locking him up in a prison, during a pandemic, when his father is missing, after God knows what awful thing he went through yesterday? I am telling you, he will *not survive*."

Later, Mom said it was too much, and maybe that's right. God knows I understood her hysteria—as soon as Mom said *prison* and I understood what was happening.

Officer Higashida clenched his jaw and said this wasn't a *prison*, not even a jail, but a recently renovated and very safe, caring detention facility with a division specifically designed for accommodating juveniles with disabilities. "Believe me; I understand. I *really do* understand," he said, "but with all respect, as a reminder, Eugene did assault and cause injuries to a police officer." He motioned to Detective Janus. "I have a duty to consider and protect the safety of everyone involved—not just you or the other officers but the juvenile himself, his family, and his community."

Shannon had been whispering to my mom, trying to calm her down and stop her from interrupting. Once the officer stopped talking, she squeezed Mom's hand and stood up. "Officer Higashida," she said, "I respect that you have wide latitude to do what you believe to be in Eugene's and the public's best interest. But I also know you specialize in juvenile cases, and how knowledgeable and thoughtful you are about the law. Which is why I'm asking you to consider some of the special circumstances here." And this is when she made the arguments that still trouble me to this day.

First, she said Eugene is not competent to stand trial because he can't talk and therefore can't provide meaningful assistance to his counsel. Second, she said the Virginia legislature enacted a law only two months ago that provides a new defense based on autism or intellectual disability. Shannon put up a copy of the statute on the shared screen, explaining it was similar to an insanity defense; even if you committed a criminal act, you're "not guilty" if that act is related to the disability. She said, "Eugene clearly falls under the legal incapacity *and* intellectual disability protection of our laws. In other words, he is not responsible for his actions because he didn't know what he was doing. No matter what he did, given these threshold issues, it would be in violation of his rights to have to go through a trial and end up in detention. No judge would do that. I'm asking you to respect your role within these laws, and not subvert them by ordering Eugene to be imprisoned."

I know Shannon meant well. I know that from her perspective, from the perspective of protecting Eugene and keeping him safe at home with us, these laws were a godsend. And more than just the utilitarian aspect, I told myself it was morally right that our society was recognizing this important point that Eugene couldn't help but act like that, that he shouldn't be punished for things he couldn't control and didn't mean to do.

But here's the thing: no matter how beneficial it was from a logical and practical perspective, Shannon's words—*clearly intellectually disabled; clearly incompetent*—were devastating. It hurt to read the clinical words on the screen, this special law for those with "significant subaverage intellectual functioning" using a "standardized measure"—IQ tests, which of course required the ability to point to the correct answer, which Eugene lacked. An official codified declaration that this person you love is incompetent, not a full citizen, not a moral being capable of telling right from wrong. Like one of my little-kid logic chains gone wrong: you can't speak or point; which means, therefore, you get a low score on an IQ test; which means, therefore, you're less intelligent; which means, therefore, you're less worthy; which means, therefore, you're less human. In the eyes of everyone in that room, those words destroyed his humanity.

Maybe I was just projecting, but I could swear Eugene was reading the screen and getting upset. Not angry upset, but sad and resigned, his face going saggy, shoulders drooping, as if each cell in his body had grown heavier and harder to hold in place. Shriveling in shame.

"Thank you, Ms. Haug," Officer Higashida said. "These are worthwhile, undoubtedly valid points to raise—and you can, on Friday afternoon at the detention hearing with a judge. My previous decision with respect to Mr. Parkson stands." He sounded cold and impersonal, calling Eugene "Mr. Parkson" for the first time—had the words on the screen done their damage?—and said, "He is to be transferred to temporary secure placement until the hearing."

His video feed ended and a screensaver came up, an American flag waving against a cloudless blue sky. There was something cruel about its beauty, the majestic patriotism of it, and Mom, John, and I hugged each other and Eugene and cried.

Eugene didn't react. He'd stayed calm the whole time, which I'd taken as a sign he was understanding and reading, trying hard to stay focused. But as we hugged him, I noticed him continuing to peer at the screen, seemingly mesmerized by the flag, the repetitive waving and flapping, and it occurred to me he might have been focused because the officer was on a screen, the whole thing a video, and he'd understood nothing at all.

Which was better: to know something awful was coming, to have time to prepare for the fear and panic of being torn from your home, your family; or to have no idea and just be thrust in, preserving the relative comfort of the status quo for as long as possible?

I'd never been one to advocate for the ignorance-is-bliss side, but looking at Eugene's face, his eyes wide with the innocent, simple pleasure of being lost in a beautiful image, encircled by those who love you . . . I've always thought I never wanted kids, that I wasn't capable of the all-encompassing love and the desire for self-sacrifice mothers are supposed to feel. But I understood for the first time. Because in this moment, I would have done anything to exchange places with Eugene, to feel the turmoil and excruciating terror I feared awaited him, if he could stay in this moment just a bit longer.

# EIGHTEEN

# What Happened to Adam Parson?

THE DETENTION CENTER DIDN'T LOOK LIKE A PRISON. MORE LIKE A suburban elementary school, with that simultaneously bland yet distinctive combination of gray concrete and red brick, blue-and-yellow cafeteria-style picnic tables outside, even an outdoor basketball court painted in different primary colors. Or maybe not; elementary schools didn't usually put barbed-wire fencing around basketball courts and thick iron bars and grates outside all the windows.

It was 0.2 miles from the police department, an easy five-minute walk down a path through the government complex. The temporary detention order was immediate, meaning Eugene had to go straight to the detention center, no stopping at home to get his special blanket, favorite shirt, or electronics. Shannon convinced Detective Janus to let all of us walk with him, uncuffed, to give us these last few minutes together, with the detective following behind.

As we walked, Shannon explained to Eugene (and us) in simple terms what to expect: We're going to that building, a place for teenagers.

Detective Janus will go in and bring out forms to sign. We'll say good-bye outside, and a detention officer will take you inside. You'll stay on a floor just for boys with special needs, with counselors and guards who'll keep you safe—give you food, clothes to wear, take you to the bathroom, showers. Because of Covid, visitors aren't allowed, but we'll see you in two days, on Friday, at the juvenile court building right next door.

Did he understand any of this? And if he didn't, how would he feel when a stranger took his arm and forced him inside a strange place, his mother, brother, and sister remaining outside, not following him, not protecting him?

―――――

"READY?" DETECTIVE JANUS SAID TO US, finger on the security entrance intercom at the outer gate to the detention center—a rhetorical question, surely, since how could any family ever be ready for something like this? Mom said yes, even as she was shivering, the word catching in her throat, barely audible.

We waited inside the locked gates while Detective Janus walked to the building. She would go into the building, get the paperwork, Mom would sign, and that would be it. I paced. The walkway inside the gates was lined with four display cases. Whoever designed them had gone for a friendly, whimsical look, with each display case's title—OUR MISSION & VISION, OUR HISTORY, OUR PROMISE, AND OUR POLICIES—in colorful letter cutouts in Comic Sans font. But as with the detention center itself, look for more than two seconds and you saw the incongruence with the actual substance: phrases like *troubled youth, long-term rehabilitation, safe return to society, suicide prevention,* and (my personal favorite) *implementation of PREA,* which, according to the tiny-font full description, stood for Prison Rape Elimination Act. I wanted to break through the glass and rip these up.

John saw me staring at the PREA notice and came over, read it himself, sighed. I said, "I'm sorry, but I don't care how much you love fun fonts—you cannot talk about prison rape in Comic Sans. I mean, who runs this place?"

John said, "Eugene can't stay here. He just can't."

Detective Janus returned to where we were waiting and said no one was answering the door buzzer, it must be a temporary glitch, and why didn't we go sit at a picnic table nearby while she tried to figure out what was going on? Shannon went with her. Given how much I was dreading our separation, maybe this delay should have made me grateful, but if anything, it made me more despondent, more sure this center must be a run-down, shoddy facility and the people running it incompetent, sure to emotionally scar Eugene for life.

The picnic tables were in the shade of a weeping willow, with one slash of sunlight through the curtain of leaves. I led Eugene to a sunny spot at a yellow table. He'd been watching his iPad on mute, just following the bright colors of the animals in the old comforting Manhwa video, but I turned the volume back on. I wanted Eugene to soak up all the brightness, all the music and silliness and joy possible while he still could, store them away for later like a camel with water before a long, hot journey across the desert.

I sat across the table from Eugene, with Mom and John on either side of Eugene. Looking at this tableau—Eugene enveloped in the bright spotlight sunbeam, tiny sparkling strings of light piercing through the green veil of willow branches undulating back and forth in the summer breeze, cascading all around him as if dancing to the music from the iPad, Mom hugging Eugene, her arms tight around his body, her fingers combing his hair, smoothing it—if you were an outsider, you would think this was a carefree picnic of a beautiful, happy family.

Except for John. He was looking up at something behind me and frowning, clearly upset. I turned to look.

Through the strands of willows, I saw someone inside the detention center, a face in a window behind thick rusted iron bars. An older boy of sixteen or seventeen, his whole face eerily devoid of emotion. Just empty. How long had he been here?

———

WE HAD BEEN UNDER THE willow tree for a long time, long enough for the Manhwa video to loop back to the beginning, when Shannon strode over to us. "We may have caught a break of sorts. There's a Covid outbreak in the juvenile detention center."

I realize how despicable this must seem, but fuck it, I'm going to say it—it was great news, a goddamned *miracle*! A Covid outbreak! "Does that mean . . . ?"

"Total lockdown, strict, no ins or outs except if you're being hospitalized. The quarantine order went into effect a few minutes ago. Eugene can't be admitted."

"Oh, thank God," Mom said, but Shannon put her hand up. "It's possible Eugene will be sent to another facility in a different county, although that seems drastic for a two-day detention. Detective Janus and I are going to call Officer Higashida right now to see what he wants to do, so say a little prayer."

I'm guessing she didn't mean that literally, and it feels hypocritical to say this because I'm not religious—my whole family is agnostic—but I did. Mom and John did, too, all of us silent, our heads bowed. I prayed to God, Jesus, the Holy Spirit, and the Virgin Mary, plus a host of other deities I remembered. I justified it as a practical thing, akin to insurance—can't hurt, so why not try, just in case?—but the lockdown order really did feel miraculous, because if it had come even an hour later, Eugene would have been admitted and locked inside for who knew how long. Not to get all theological about it, but I felt like I owed God, the universe, whom- or what-ever, for granting my wish. Now, to be clear, it's not like I'd made an actual bargain, Faustian style; I'd thought (to no one in particular) I'd do a vague, general "anything" to keep Eugene out of jail. But if anyone had offered a specific deal— Eugene's freedom for my own, money, torture, whatever—I would have taken it. That no one did seemed like a technicality. That the Covid outbreak had already occurred before I made my wish, likewise an irrelevant detail. I had to keep my end of the hypothetical bargain because there was still the transfer possibility, not to mention the Friday hearing. I couldn't screw this up. I had to supplicate, and I did.

When Shannon came back and said, "It's official; Eugene's going home"—our elation at that moment . . . I can't do justice to it. Like we'd been collectively holding our breaths, then a sudden intake, the rapturous influx of air, revival. All through Shannon's explanation—all intercounty transfers were on hold, so Officer Higashida ordered a house arrest—we sobbed.

Our walk back was so different. Just fifteen minutes prior, during our walk to the detention center, the perfect cloudless sky had seemed ominous, the austere beauty staged by the universe to mock us, a cruel confirmation of our irrelevance. Now, it looked graceful, an enhancement to this celebratory moment with my family. And yes, I knew Shannon said there was danger ahead on Friday, but that seemed distant. I think we can get myopic sometimes, especially when we're in the midst of something intense, good or bad, in the immediate here and now. Plus, there was something of an invincibility I was feeling: We'd received one miracle, our prayer answered, so why not more?

I think Shannon wanted to let us enjoy the unexpected freedom of being outside together, because she waited until we were back in a drab windowless conference room at the police station before she said anything else. "We got some news on the investigation. They got another hit on Adam's ATM card. Same area, but this store had security cameras that actually work. They're trying to get the video now."

A shock of shame. Dad. How could we have been elated, relieved, celebratory, feeling anything other than gnawing worry and grief? How could we have *forgotten* about Dad? And once I thought, Dad, I remembered his words about the relativity of happiness, the Graveyard Incident, how our being missing overnight had changed the baseline of his life so drastically. What would he say about what happened today? It was kind of amazing, how this brief period of believing Eugene was being sent away changed everything. How until this morning, the state of Eugene remaining at home had been the unremarkable, expected baseline of our lives, but because of this short-lived detention order, returning to that previous baseline became this extraordinary thing, creating so much happiness that it canceled our torment over Dad.

I wished Dad were here, so I could tell him I understood now—not just intellectually, but experientially. A real-life example that illustrated the very concept Dad had been trying to prove and refine through his experiments. And then, at *experiments,* the nausea returned as I remembered the experiment dated yesterday, the fear in the back of my mind—was that what he'd wanted? For us to experience what he had?

I remembered with a jolt that no one else knew about the HQ experiments, not even John. And we hadn't told Mom about the cancer thing, either. This whole previous twenty-four hours had been a series of urgent, awful emergencies getting interrupted and displaced by more urgent, more awful emergencies. No more. This had to stop right now.

"I have to tell you guys something," I said. "Actually, many, many things. John, too. Not that . . . I mean, we both—" It wasn't like me to be tongue-tied, but John was distracting me, kicking me under the table and glaring at me, until I couldn't stand it anymore—I had to turn and shout, "What?"

John shifted in his seat, his eyes darting between Mom and Shannon uncomfortably. "I think maybe we should talk about that when we get home. Right now, we should focus on listening to Shannon and preparing for Friday."

I understood his impulse. It might have been more prudent to talk it over first, plan what to say, in what order and how, to tell Mom privately and then download to Shannon together as a family. But hadn't we learned our lesson, already suffered one disastrous consequence from not telling Shannon about the mommy-blogger video when we had the chance? Thinking and planning were luxuries we couldn't afford. Who knew when the next uber-urgent disaster would strike and put everything else on hold again? (Answer based on the trajectory of the day: in less than fifteen minutes.) No withholding anything from anyone: that was my new mantra.

I told them everything. I was desperate to unload about Dad's cancer, but it's like in confessions (which, admittedly, I've never done, but I've watched many on TV): you have to save the highest-penalty sin for last; you can't start with committing murder and then go on to coveting your best friend's earrings. I built up slowly, starting with the most innocuous, least surprising stuff given the video—the blood under Eugene's nails and on the shirt I washed, the insurance policy file, the screenshot from Kenny, Detective Janus's visit to his mommy-blogger neighbor—before moving to Dad's notebook and experiments, particularly the last, dated yesterday. I was beginning to understand the appeal of confessions, the references to "cleansing" your mind, "clearing" your conscience—it was as if the previous day's revelations were cluttering up my psyche like debris from a fast-moving summer storm, and with each admission, I was blowing it away.

I saved Dad's cancer for last. I'd been hogging the mic for a while, and more importantly, John is way better at tact, so I said, "Okay, so the final thing . . ." and raised my eyebrows at John. He took over, but again, as with the hearing, he didn't talk so much as vocalize sounds, the excessive hemming and hawing rendering his words in-decipherable. I tried to be patient, I really did, but Mom was looking confused, and I just couldn't stand it anymore. "Dad has stage four prostate cancer."

Mom said, "What?" and John immediately stepped in. "No, we don't know that. Those women *said* Dad had appointments for can-cer. And also, Mia, *you* said it was stage four because of Grandpa. I've been thinking and—"

"Wait, slow down," Mom said. "Start from the beginning. What happened?"

We explained everything. Strangely, it was easier to tell Mom with Shannon in the room. A stranger's presence is like a dam. It slows things down, stops the unrestrained flow of words and emotions.

When we finished, Mom said, "Why wouldn't you call and tell me the minute you found this out?"

Shannon had been taking notes the whole time, brows furrowed in focused contemplation, but at this, she broke in. "Whoa, whoa, whoa, let's stop right there. We need to focus on the hearing and our goal: to convince the judge to dismiss the charges or at least defer and let Eugene be treated at home, *not* to be sent to a state facility.

"From that perspective, what Mia and John have told us is very important. Because the biggest factor will be what charges the government ends up filing on Friday. If the only charge is an accidental bruising of an overzealous police officer, I can't believe any judge would send Eugene away. That would be too extreme for a nonverbal special-needs child, especially given the climate right now, in the wake of George Floyd. But if Eugene is the prime suspect in Adam's disappearance as of Friday, and the prosecutor is talking manslaughter?"

We all gasped. *Manslaughter.* Such an ugly word, the implications not only of death and blame but of butchery, of carnage. Of course that's what we'd been dancing around all afternoon, but this was the first time anyone had said it out loud.

"How could anyone possibly think that a boy like Eugene could do something like that to his own father?" Mom said. "They don't even know if he's dead, there's no proof."

Shannon explained that a body was not a prerequisite to a manslaughter charge, and neither was intent; killing someone in the heat of the moment or even accidentally could fall under voluntary or involuntary manslaughter. "That's just a worst-case scenario. And we have strong arguments that we don't even reach that issue because one, Eugene is incompetent to stand trial, and two, the new Virginia defense for intellectual disability applies here. But even if the judge rules our way on those issues, you don't just get to go home like nothing ever happened. You have to go through remediation, and if the judge thinks an inpatient facility is the best option, Eugene might be sent away to a rehabilitation center or a psychiatric institution."

She paused for a moment to let us process this. She wasn't unkind, but it was also clear she wasn't going to go out of her way to soften it. She wasn't our friend. She was our lawyer, focused first and foremost on her duty—to keep Eugene safe—and we had to do likewise, push everything else to the back.

Mom said, "Okay, so if Eugene is charged with . . ." She swallowed. "With manslaughter," she said, her voice getting louder at that word, as if she were forcing herself to say it, to get used to saying it, "then even if the judge says Eugene is incompetent or not responsible under this defense, he can be sent away?"

"That's much more likely with a manslaughter charge than an APO with minor injuries. That's why I'm going to focus on the missing-person investigation. Based on what I've learned in the last few hours, here's how I see that. I need to warn you: I'm going to be blunt. I'm not trying to hurt you, and I wish this weren't happening to you. But our best chance to get through this is by being straightforward."

With that, she tore out the notepad paper she'd been writing on and laid it on the table in front of us:

Attorney-Client Privileged<br>Attorney Work Product

## <u>WHAT HAPPENED TO ADAM PARSON?</u>

### A. ALIVE

 1. Miscommunication

 2. Ran away (Anjeli Rapari?)

 3. Hiding for experiment

 4. Lost or injured incl. amnesia

 5. Kidnapped

### B. DEAD

 6. Suicide (cancer?)

 7. Murder by anyone other than EP (Anjeli Rapari?)

 8. Accidental death (fall, drowning) <u>without</u> EP involvement

 9. Accidental death <u>with</u> EP involvement

I like to think that I have a logical, organized mind, but I had struggled to make sense of the vast amounts of confusing and sometimes-contradictory information over the past twenty-four hours. And in comes this clearheaded, non-sleep-deprived professional who takes all that jumbled nonsense and reduces it to one sheet—an enumer-ated, categorized list with no emotion, no judgment, no bullshit. As hard as it was to read without flinching, it was what we needed.

"It's important to keep in mind that my goal is not to find out what happened to Adam, per se. The fact is, we may never find out con-clusively what happened. Missing-person cases are often the most frustrating, deepest mysteries because we don't know anything—even the most basic thing of what happened, let alone how or why or who caused it. It can exasperate families like nothing else, and I know you want resolution, and the police do, too. But from my perspective, de-fending my client, Eugene, I don't care if we ever find out what hap-pened; having no answer at all is better than having an answer that implicates Eugene, that comes anywhere near number nine." She pointed to 9. *Accidental death* <u>*with*</u> *EP involvement* on her chart.

"That's why I made this chart, why I'm going to ask you to think through all these options carefully, even the unlikely or unsavory ones. Because from a practical perspective, the best way to exonerate Eugene is to show that one of these other scenarios is more likely."

Shannon took us through the chart, marking it up as she went along. She said she felt comfortable crossing off (in pencil) *Miscom-munication, Lost or injured,* and *Kidnapped;* she really doubted he went away with friends and forgot to call, and the police hadn't found him after infrared and thermal searches. "Running away with this woman is something the police are actively investigating, so that's great, and it would be nice to confirm the cancer diagnosis because that gives us a very helpful suicide motive. And accidental drowning is, of course, always a possibility given this park's history." She starred those items.

When she said, "This entry Mia found about the experiment is very promising," putting a star by *Hiding for experiment,* I have to admit: that really shook me. When I told everyone about the HQ notebook, I stuck solely to the facts, didn't speculate what the last experiment could be. Partly, I was worried I was being ridiculous, but more than that, I wanted to see if others would come to the same conclusion on their own. That she listed it as a plausible explanation without any prompting from me, so matter-of-factly—it made me realize: that was what I'd been afraid of all along, that I might be right, that others might agree with me.

"I'm sorry, but can I say something?" John said. "I know you don't know our dad, but stuff like suicide and this experiment, it's just not possible. That's not our dad. I mean, Eugene almost got hit by a car on the way home from the park. No matter what, he wouldn't just leave Eugene alone. At the very least, he'd bring him home first. I can't believe we're even talking about this."

"It's my understanding that the near-accident occurred in your neighborhood, on a normally safe street where Eugene runs daily."

"Even so. He just wouldn't do that."

"I know it seems unlikely. But let's say your dad found out he doesn't have long to live and is worried about the pain and the financial impact on y'all, especially given the enormous costs of Eugene's care. His life insurance policy is . . . what?" Shannon flipped through her notes. "Three million dollars. I skimmed it on my phone, but it looks like there's an exclusion for suicide and double payout for accidental death." Was that the policy I found in the backup drive? If so, did that mean Dad had looked at it recently?

Shannon continued. "Okay, so if he disappears when Eugene's home and everyone's safe, the insurer might think: this man was just diagnosed, about to die, classic suicide. Adam's smart, knows that, so he sets it up to make people think it *must* be an accident, something no father would do intentionally. He gets Eugene near home, thinking he'll be safe running the rest of the way, and then carries on with it. Makes sure his family gets the double payout, six million dollars, enough money to protect them when he's gone, better than having them watch him die and nearly bankrupt them in the process. The only thing he doesn't anticipate is an overzealous detective who would actually go after kids like Eugene."

It scared me how plausible that sounded. I could see Dad making a spreadsheet, calculating the pain level multiplied by duration of suffering for cancer treatments versus accidental death. From the way John's face paled, I knew he thought the same thing. But he swallowed. Shook his head. "That's not Dad. I don't believe it."

Shannon's face softened. "No. Of course you don't; that's not my goal. But the more we can get outsiders—police, judges, people who don't know your dad—to believe any of these things, even awful things you'd hate anyone to think about your dad, the safer Eugene will be. This is what I'm going to focus on. I'm going to ask you to as well, even though I know it's unfair and you shouldn't have to; investigating is the police's job, not yours. But the police have one goal, to find Adam safely, and of course you want that, too, and you'll aid in that effort as much as possible. But we have another goal the police don't share, that they may, in fact, actively oppose: to defend Eugene and keep him safe at home. Which means, as unseemly as it may feel sometimes, we have to hope and try to prove that one of these other reasons is why Adam is missing." With that, Shannon flipped the chart so we could read it clearly:

## WHAT HAPPENED TO ADAM PARSON?

### A. ALIVE

~~1. Miscommunication~~

★ 2. Ran away (Anjeli Rapari?)

★ 3. Hiding for experiment

~~4. Lost or injured incl. amnesia~~

~~5. Kidnapped~~

### B. DEAD

★ 6. Suicide (cancer?)

7. Murder by anyone other than EP (Anjeli Rapari?)

★ 8. Accidental death (fall, drowning) <u>without</u> EP involvement

9. Accidental death <u>with</u> EP involvement

Need to rule out!!!

I felt a surge of anger mixed with confusion and shame and impotence. As much as we loved Eugene and wanted above all else for him to be safe, were we really supposed to celebrate if we found out that Dad ran away with a woman or was playing a cruel trick on us or, hooray, he died by suicide by jumping into a raging river while his fourteen-year-old special-needs child was alone, getting nearly hit by a car and traumatized in the process?

Shannon was right. It really was unfair. She was asking us to make an impossible choice. Dad or Eugene? Because—as unfathomable as it was, as disloyal as I knew it was merely to consider the possibility—what if finding out what happened to Dad and saving Eugene were incompatible? What if we couldn't do both?

I saw it then, the answer to the Dad versus Eugene dilemma. It was obvious, right there on Shannon's chart, easy to see. If Dad was alive, that meant he had run away or was experimenting, and he didn't deserve our sympathy or loyalty. If Dad was not alive, Shannon was right; as much as we craved resolution, to know what happened to him, it was far more important to keep Eugene safe, no matter what he may have done.

But this was no time for angsting over maybes. Shannon was rattling off tasks: contact the oncologist, interview Dad's friends, get her firm's private investigator to track down that Anjeli woman and break into Dad's computer and phone, interview the mommy-blogger, get Eugene evaluated, and on and on. She was like a general planning for war: delegating, assigning, and strategizing.

"We have two days and"—a glance at her watch—"two hours, give or take a few minutes, to prepare for this hearing."

This was our new goal. We had fifty hours to prove that Eugene had nothing to do with Dad's disappearance, and we would get it done. No matter what it took.

# PART IV

## THE MYTH OF THE HAPPY NONVERBAL BAH-BO

# NINETEEN

# Another Family, Another Home

MY FIRST TASK WAS TO MAKE AN APPOINTMENT WITH A COMMUNI-
cation therapist for Eugene's prehearing speech evaluation. Shannon managed to get me the juvenile court's list of ten prequalified
businesses, complete with cell as well as office phone numbers and
emails. How hard could it be?

Extremely.

The problem: these therapists worked regularly for the juvenile
justice system and were in and out of the detention center, which
meant they were affected by the Covid outbreak. The kids were apparently all fine so far (asymptomatic or with mild symptoms), but
the adult therapists and staff were hard-hit. Those who weren't sick
were in the midst of getting notified of the outbreak, getting tested,
preparing for quarantine, and canceling everything in their lives—
too busy and freaked out to answer a random, potentially spam, call.
The fifth therapist on my list (the first to answer, who apparently

picked up by accident) told me all this very quickly to explain why he couldn't take on any new cases. He warned that "evaluating non-verbal juveniles" was an intensive process, one he doubted anyone on that list could do this week.

John was mid–call of his own, leaving what sounded like an aggressively polite voicemail. ("*Please* call me back as *soon* as you get this. I *really very* much hope I'll hear from you within the *hour*.") He was trying to find a neuropsychologist for the intellectual-disability evaluation, the other side of Shannon's two-pronged attack for Friday. As soon as he put down the phone, I said how worried I was that we couldn't get the prehearing evaluations done due to the Covid outbreak, which would mean that—ugh, the irony of this!—the very thing responsible for our miraculous two-day reprieve might leave us worse off. "Oh my God," I said, "it's like that monkey's paw story. Remember? Where someone makes a wish for, like, *x* dollars and he gets it because his son dies and the insurance payout is exactly *x* dollars?"

John put this very Boy-Scout-ish we-can-never-give-up look of determination on his face and said, "You need to stop being so pessimistic. Something's going to come through, for sure. I can feel it!"

It was funny, because I'd also felt that sense of invincibility only fifteen minutes prior, but hearing the same thought come out of his mouth, I immediately thought, Wow, is that stupid.[16] Because if one miracle has been granted, doesn't that lessen the likelihood of an-

---

16 Have you noticed how different things sound out loud versus inside your head? Sometimes you think something and it makes so much sense, seems brilliant, even, but once you speak or write it, the eloquence disappears. I used to blame it on things getting lost in verbalization, the inadequacy of words to fully capture abstract ideas, but I think it's also that seeing/hearing the words triggers you to evaluate them, exposing flaws that the initial excitement blocked. It's like when your friends say something judgmental about a new boyfriend, and in order to respond, you have to process and evaluate what they said, which often starts that painful process of removing the infatuation filter that previously blocked all his flaws from view.

other miracle, statistically speaking, especially for the same family on the same day?

I was really tempted to point out the faulty logic of his assumptions, but I didn't. I even managed not to roll my eyes. I was too tired to pick a fight. Besides, maybe miracles didn't follow statistical probabilities. Miracles defied logic—that's what made them miracles, wasn't it?—and what did I know about any of this anyway? Truth be told, I was jealous; I wished I could return to that earlier moment when we were walking back in the bright, sunlit day, aglow with the possibility of magic, the miracle of a reprieve. Why take that away from him?

I continued with the list of therapists—calling and leaving multiple voicemails on both office and mobile numbers, not bothering to hide my panic, which kept growing with each unanswered call, and then copying, pasting, and sending the same URGENT: IMMEDIATE RESPONSE NEEDED emails and texts. Within ten minutes, John and I had contacted everyone on both the speech-therapy and neuropsychology lists, and the results were bleak: one firm no; nineteen unreachable; and zero returned messages, emails, or texts.

I thought our incontrovertible uber-failure would inject a dollop of realism into John, but it was the opposite, his rah-rah optimism ballooning into stubborn irrationality. "This just means we'll do it the old-fashioned way and drive around to their offices, like we did for Shannon."

I'd already scanned the addresses, seen that many were nearby or on our way home. It was most certainly a waste of time—no one was actually going into work these days—but it was the only option we had left.

I drove and John navigated (or rather, input the next address into his phone), Mom saying she needed to call Dad's doctors to figure out this cancer thing, but I think it was more that she wanted to sit with Eugene; the detention scare had upset us all, of course, and Mom's always babied him, but now she seemed downright paranoid, staying as physically close to him as possible, using her left hand to work her phone, her right clutching his elbow as if afraid he might run off.

The driving tour was turning out to be futile but quick—all office buildings closed, parking lots deserted, and lobby entrances locked—exactly how we expected. Rather, how *I* expected, since John bounded out of the car every time I pulled up to a building, clearly hopeful as he loped to the entrance, then seemingly shocked when the door wouldn't budge, lumbering back to the car crestfallen, shoulders slumped. After a while, it was getting seriously sad, and I was thinking of ways to discourage him, like when we were a block from the next building saying, "Oh, no, it looks totally dark," but then I hated myself for trying to manipulate his emotions—worse, using Dad's banal "theory"—and I shut my mouth and just let John be.

I don't know how many offices we'd visited—seven? Ten? I was losing count, just mindlessly obeying the nav-robot—when we drove into a residential area not too far from ours, about five miles away. One of those planned neighborhoods with ticky-tacky split-level houses in various shades of ecru—not too big, not too small, just the right size for families with 2.3 children—separated by narrow strips of grass.

"A home office," Mom said as I pulled into the short driveway and stopped outside the garage on the right side of the house. "I'm not sure about barging in like this."

"It's an emergency. I'm sure they'll understand," John said, opening the car door.

"Wait, let me at least come with you. Mia, you stay here with Eugene. Eugene-ah, Mommy will be right back, okay?" She kissed his cheek and said, "Sa-rang-hae," Korean for *I love you*. Eugene was clearly in the zone of whatever was on his iPad.

When Mom shut the car door, Eugene startled and looked up from his screen. He scanned our surroundings to orient himself, seemingly dazed, then stared at a wind chime above the garage, directly in front of us. "Eugene, you must be hungry," I said. "We'll be home soon and—"

Eugene threw his iPad, reached for the door handle, got out of the car, and *ran*. Fast, with purpose, on the grass yard—away from the front door, where Mom and John were—to the back of the house.

"Eugene, stop," I shouted and ran after him. Mom and John realized what was happening and yelled his name and joined in the chase. I was slower than Eugene—because of my ankle, I was going to say, but honestly, he was pretty fast—and by the time I caught up to him, Eugene was by the walk-out basement door.

"Eugene, stop," I yelled again, ready to grab him, but he reached down to a box garden next to the door and lifted a small ceramic turtle. "Eugene, what are you doing? Don't!" I screamed, sure he was going to throw it, but then I saw—a key underneath, which he picked up carefully, almost lovingly, before returning the turtle next to a ceramic rabbit. I was transfixed, vaguely aware of Mom and John next to me, a hypnotic mix of confusion, fear, and curiosity rooting all of us in place, silent and still, as Eugene put the key in the key slot, turned, and opened the door.

Let me stop right here. Putting aside how Eugene somehow managed to find a hidden key, what he did was not something he could have done without practicing at this very door, over and over. It was too smooth, too routinized, the way he stepped inside the basement and turned, knew exactly where to go, with no hesitation. We followed him inside, completely befuddled, as Eugene walked down a hallway into an open area, like a rec room. He went straight to a spongy orange ball lying on the floor and threw it underhand, granny free-throw style, to a jumbo basket half the height of a normal one, a copy of our own basketball toy set. He hopped over to the two-person trampoline—again, exactly like the one in our basement—and stepped up and started jumping.

What. The. Actual. Fuck? I remember thinking that, but I must have said it out loud, too, because Eugene laughed while continuing to jump. What was this place? Whose was it? I tried to remember the therapist listing from the court—no specific name, but something about unlocking speech? It was both astonishing and appalling, seeing Eugene so comfortable, behaving with so much competence and confidence, but in a way that clearly proved how hidden this part of his life had been. It was like he had another family, another home. The absolute discombobulation on Mom's face scared me, as if she had no idea what to think.

Mom started moving toward Eugene. Slowly, using small, careful steps, the way you do when you happen upon a bear in the woods or someone about to jump off a bridge. It was in the air, an ominous tension with a heaviness I could feel deep in my ears like when a plane is landing, the *creak-creak* of the trampoline springs like the soundtrack for a horror-movie scene where an innocent family is wandering around a haunted house, unaware of the axe-wielding serial-killer zombie ghosts approaching to slaughter them.

A door screeched open to my left, and I jumped, almost screamed. It was John, standing at the doorway of a room—an office? Was that a desk inside?—kitty-corner from the trampoline. Staring inside. He looked like he was surprised but also not at all. More than anything, he looked like he wanted to cry.

I wanted to rush over, but my legs were cold and stiff, as if I hadn't moved them in hours, and I shuffled over at the pace of Eugene's jump, the *squeaks* of the trampoline.

I was right. It was an office. A messy one, the desk cluttered with loose papers. No one in the chair. No one on the floor. No person, alive or dead. No Dad.

I grabbed the doorframe. Breathed. What was wrong with me? I'd actually expected to see Dad in some form—sitting behind the desk, grinning madly like a cartoon villain while manipulating pretend-death-experiment spreadsheets, or dead on the ground, blood already congealing. It was hard to say which was more terrifying.

But that begged the question: What was John so freaked out about? He nodded toward the side wall next to the desk, to a bulletin board full of yellow sticky notes. I don't see anything, I was starting to say, which is, of course, when I saw it: a big yellow paper heart with a smaller heart cut out in the middle with a picture of Dad and Eugene, smiling. And on the bottom, in Dad's slanted print writing: *We love you, Anjeli!*

# TWENTY

# S-O-L-A-R

YOU KNOW HOW THEY SAY THAT IF YOU HEAR HOOFBEATS, YOU SHOULD think horses, not zebras? When we first heard Anjeli's voicemail, I knew what it seemed like. Let's face it—a man has numerous secret calls with a mysterious woman who's upset he's not telling his wife about her, chances are it's an affair, but there was still a chance of an innocent explanation that would make us feel horrible once the mis-understanding cleared up. This was a long shot, closer to a unicorn than a zebra, but maybe Anjeli was a travel agent helping Dad plan a surprise getaway for Mom's fiftieth birthday—Mom had "kidnapped" Dad to Banff for his thirtieth birthday, which Dad said was the best present he'd ever gotten—and with Covid travel restrictions and the sneaking around, it was taking too much work and upsetting her. Or she could be a caterer helping Dad plan a surprise party, and our county's recent crowd-gathering restrictions were making her un-comfortable. Even my desperate idea of Anjeli being his oncologist was way better than an affair.

With the *We love you, Anjeli!* sign, that 1 percent chance was gone. This was Anjeli's house. Of course it was. Hadn't I known it, hadn't we all, the moment Eugene put the key in the door? We'd been caught off guard because we'd been focused on our search for a professional expert for Eugene, not at all expecting that to lead to Dad's mystery woman, but now that the shock was subsiding, it seemed inevitable. Anjeli was not some random project assistant, but someone with whom Dad shared an intimate relationship, close enough that he clearly brought Eugene here often. Of course she was related in some way to the special-needs world. That was 99 percent of Dad's world; how would anyone not in it even meet Dad in the first place, much less build a trusting, comfortable relationship with Eugene?

Pinned up near the yellow heart was a picture of a woman across the table from a boy Eugene's age. The woman—presumably Anjeli—was clearly delighted, her mouth open in a broad smile and her eyebrows lifted so high, her forehead looked corrugated. She was around Dad's age—glints of silver in her black hair and lines around her eyes and lips—but her face was so animated, radiated so much energy, that she seemed much younger. It was easy to imagine Dad meeting her somewhere, a seminar at Henry's House, maybe, and liking her, befriending her. But infatuation? Love? It had seemed unfathomable, the idea of Dad with anyone other than Mom. But honestly, when was the last time I'd seen them lovey-dovey with each other? They were both affectionate, but so much of that was saved for Eugene, especially for Mom. She always sat next to Eugene during movies, holding his hand and stroking his hair. She'd done that with John and me when we were little, but that had faded as we got older. Would that ever fade with Eugene? And if the answer was no, would Dad seek that elsewhere, maybe with this pretty woman with her carefree smile? Where could this woman be right now, if not with Dad? Was Dad looking into these eyes, kissing these lips, somewhere far away?

"Guys, have you found something?" Mom yelled.

Shit. Mom. I peeked out, and she was stretching her body to peer inside the office without letting go of Eugene's hand on the trampoline handlebar. I rushed to stand in front of the yellow heart to block her view. I know I'd vowed to never again hide anything from Mom, but there are times when it's impossible to be honest without being cruel, and this was one of them. The yellow paper heart wasn't just any "love" card, which was bad enough; it was identical to the yellow paper heart stuck on our refrigerator, except ours contained a picture of John, Eugene, and me, with a note reading *We love you, Mom! Happy Mother's Day!* That's right—fucking Mother's Day! Which meant that this would forever ruin all Mother's Days from here on out. I mean, what in hell was Dad thinking? You do not give the same exact thing to two women—didn't all hetero men know that? Could anyone get over something like that? No way I was going to let her see this.

"Guys, what's going on? What's in that room?" Mom let go of Eugene's hand to step over for a clear view into the office. At the doorway, she stopped and flinched—an extra eyeblink, a slightly sharper intake of breath. I thought for sure she'd seen the yellow heart. But no—she was looking in a different direction. I followed her stare. A framed diploma, hanging on the wall. *Anjeli Rapari* in fancy calligraphy.

Okay, I thought. Mom knows now, but she was going to have to find out this was Anjeli's house sooner or later, if she hadn't guessed already, and a diploma was way better than the heart. (Again, Dad and his stupid expectations theory.)

It took Mom a few deep breaths to recover. "What are you hiding?" Mom said, but to John, who was standing in front of shelves with storage bins, each labeled with two letters. "I can see it behind you. What is it?"

John looked like he was about to deny it, but he sighed and stepped aside. The bin labeled EP was open, a yellow stencil letterboard on top. "We started using a similar system at Henry's House, to make it easier to disinfect," John said, moving the bin to the desk and taking out the items inside. "Everyone has their own box, with their own materials, workbooks, therapy notes, everything you need for your session." He took out a white binder and handed it to Mom.

She opened it and began to read. "But this log says . . ."

"I know," John said.

"What? What does it say?" I said, but Mom didn't answer, just kept reading and turning the pages, deep frown lines traveling up her forehead like train tracks.

"Can someone please tell me what's going on?"

"She's a speech therapist, specializing in a type of text-based communication for people who can't talk, a new spelling method," John said. "Eugene's been coming here since October. Three times a week for eight months."

But Eugene already had a speech therapist at Henry's House he saw five times a week. Why would Dad bring Eugene to another one? Dad hated spelling therapy, didn't believe in it at all. Should I be happy because this might mean they weren't having an affair and the $20,000 was for therapy? Or was it proof of Dad's infatuation, that he'd let this woman talk him into trying this type of therapy again, maybe believing in it, something Mom couldn't do? I looked at the grief etched in the lines on Mom's forehead, around her mouth, as she kept turning the pages. Given their history, was this even more of a betrayal for Mom than a duplicate homemade Mother's Day card?

The trampoline had been squeaking with every jump this entire time, its constant, consistent rhythm turning it into background noise we stopped noticing, but Eugene started vocalizing on the offbeat like he sometimes does when he gets really into the jumping. It was nothing we hadn't heard—the trampoline spring's *squeak,* then Eugene's high *heee* in F—but the change in rhythm was alarming, especially in this strange, new setting. Mom pulled out of focus, said, "Eugene-ah, you okay?" She went to him, taking the therapy box with her. "You keep jumping. Mommy's going to read this book, right here, okay?"

As soon as I heard that, I made sure Mom wasn't looking my way and took the yellow heart off the bulletin board. As much as I wanted to tear it up and throw it away, I couldn't bring myself to. What if this was *evidence* in some way, and tampering with it a crime? We had enough legal trouble, and the way things were going today, I really didn't want to risk another kid being thrown in jail.

"Hey, help me hide this," I whispered to John, but he was opening the door to what looked like a walk-in closet for the office. It had a strange setup. Tiny, with no windows. Just a plain, square table in the middle with two chairs on adjoining sides, and an iPad on a tripod in the opposite corner facing the chairs. I put the yellow heart under some paper in a desk drawer and followed him in. "You think she videotapes her therapy sessions?" I asked.

John was studying a poster on the wall, the only decoration (if you could call it that) of any kind in the room. It was titled THE PPT PROCESS with three columns—STAGE 1: POKE; STAGE 2: POINT; STAGE 3: TYPE—each with smaller writing underneath. I rushed over to read it, but I noticed John looked more freaked out than I'd seen him all day, slack-jawed and upset.

"What is it?" I said. "What's wrong?"

"I know this. It's the latest thing. I heard about it from one of the parents at Henry's House. Dad and I actually had a fight about it on Monday night."

"You and Dad never fight. Why?" As I said this, I thought of the way John and Dad were being so sickeningly sweet to each other the following day. "Is that why you guys were being so weird at breakfast yesterday?"

"I said some stuff I really . . ." He bit his lip. "I got an email last week about a study one of my professors just published about a method just like this, so I told Dad, and he acted like he'd never heard of it. Anyway, I asked Dad again on Monday if he read the study, and he was really dismissive. He said he was too busy to chase every fad, and I got mad and accused him of being selfish. I said he was a bad father."

Shit. "John, I'm sure he knew—"

He shook his head. "It doesn't matter. The point is, if he knows her, if Eugene's been doing this with her for months, then why—"

I heard a woman's voice. John and I looked at each other. The police had said Anjeli's house was empty, but had she returned?

We ran out of the office. Eugene was still jumping on the trampoline and Mom was sitting on the floor next to the open binder, watching something on her phone. That's where the woman's voice was coming from. It was a YouTube video. Anjeli, with the same slight Indian accent I'd heard on the voicemail, giving a lecture at some conference. "What is that? How'd you find it?" John asked.

"A link on her website," Mom said, pressing the Back button. A logo uploaded. *Unlock Your Voice,* with the initials in oversized, overlapping letters. "The binder says all therapy sessions are recorded and uploaded to a client portal, but I can't find the password."

UYV.

"I think I know it," I said. "Here, go to the portal login." I took Mom's phone and put in Dad's email address for the username as I explained about the login code written on the manila folder I'd found in Dad's desk. "It was U-Y-V, the at sign, then four numbers. I think one-zero, or maybe zero-one." I put in 10, and Mom said, "Was it one-zero-one-four? The first session was October fourteenth. Try that."

Nope. Mom took her phone back. "Let's try month, year." She put in *UYV@1019.* Hit Enter.

It worked. The portal welcome page loaded, and Mom clicked on Recorded Sessions. There were so many, listed by date. "They had almost a hundred sessions," John said. Mom clicked on the top one, the latest, dated June 12, 2020. Twelve days ago.

The video opened to Anjeli sitting next to Eugene in the video room we'd just come out of. "Okay, let's start with a science lesson today." Anjeli lectured about energy generation and the ozone layer for several minutes, then said, "Eugene, you ready? Let's focus. Can you tell me one of the five types of alternative energy?," which I remembered being one of the questions in the manila folder. She handed Eugene a pencil and held up a yellow stencil letterboard directly in front of his face. He held the pencil in his fist like a knife and made an overhand stabbing motion toward the letterboard, but very slow and awkward-looking, not a trace of violence or aggression.

"That's it, Eugene. Go ahead. Find the letter and poke it through. Take your time." Eugene moved his shoulder and whole arm until the pencil got to the letter S and poked the tip through its hollow outline.

"S, that's great. What's the next letter?"

Hands still shaking, his eyes jerking all around, Eugene brought his arm back and then jabbed forward again, this time poking the letter O.

"O. What's next? I know it's tiring. Keep going."

Eugene poked through L, then A, then R, Anjeli cheering him on the entire time. "What's next?" she asked, and Eugene poked a rectangle on the bottom row. "End of word. Great," she said. "S-O-L-A-R. Solar." She put the letterboard down and wrote on a piece of paper, 5 *types alt. energy? SOLAR.*

"Um, *what?*" I said. John and Mom both looked stunned. Eugene was next to us, jumping and squealing like a happy toddler with not a thought in his head. How could this be the same person as the one in the video, who had just answered a science question, who was communicating?

Anjeli was saying, "What else? Keep going." It seemed interminable, each letter taking I'd estimate about ten seconds for Eugene to poke through, with a lot of cheering by Anjeli, but he spelled out W-I-N-D (end of word) and N-U-C-U-L-A-R (end of word). Misspelled, but how was he doing this? He had never had a remotely academic lesson, his "classes" kindergarten level—arts and crafts, ABCs, counting to ten, songs. Learning the colors of the rainbow was the most rigorous "lesson" he'd had.

Mom's and John's faces were full of questions, too. Not just questions of doubt, like mine, but of hope: Is this really possible? Can Eugene really communicate? Can he read, spell, learn?

I thought back to That Summer, TFT, and I couldn't stand it, couldn't bear the thought of Mom being hurt like that again. I reached over to pause Mom's phone screen. "Okay, this can't be real, right? I mean, the video has to be doctored, or maybe she's manipulating him in some way."

"But she wasn't touching him," John said, "and she wasn't moving the board in any way." He sounded unsure, though, not entirely convinced of his own objections to mine.

"But why was she holding up the stencil in front of him in such a specific way?" I said. "Why not let him do it all by himself? It has to be a trick, like when magicians use illusions and special equipment to make something appear to be happening when, of course, it's not. I mean, maybe the stencil's rigged and she's activating a color around each letter we can't see on the video, or maybe it's magnetic." I reached for the yellow letterboard in Eugene's box, held it up to the light. It looked like plain plastic, like something you could get from Target.

"It's a scaffolding thing, I think," John said. *Scaffolding* is a big thing in the developmental-therapy world. Providing temporary support to help kids learn a new skill, like bicycle training wheels or swimming wings. "That's what that PPT poster was saying. For kids with motor issues, you hold up stencils with big letters right in front of them to make it easier—using their entire arms, *gross* motor—and then you move on to *fine* motor, having them point to letters, and the final step, having them type completely on their own. Eugene's obviously still in the Poke stage and needs that support."

That made sense. I knew that many kids who have trouble speaking, a fine motor skill, have trouble with alternatives like letter-pointing or typing, also fine motor skills. But instead of scaffolding through physical support, like TFT did, why not turn it into a gross motor skill, which is easier for kids like Eugene? So smart. Oh my God—it occurred to me right then—was this why Dad had been doing so much physical therapy homework with Eugene? Was there a connection between what we were seeing on the video and Eugene's beautiful, fast run?

"Let's watch it again," Mom said and restarted the video. This time, I focused on Anjeli rather than Eugene, looking carefully at her hands, her eyes, ready to catch any type of subtle cue, thinking of my phenomenology class about Clever Hans, a German horse that astounded the world a hundred years ago by spelling and doing basic algebra—*The New York Times* had even written a fact-checked article about Hans's amazing feats—but was shown to be responding to his trainer's subconscious cues. I could see both of Anjeli's hands, and she was keeping remarkably still. No blinks, no looking at the next anticipated letter, nothing.

We went past where I'd stopped the video, and Anjeli chuckled and said, "I'm guessing you meant *nuclear,* Eugene, N-U-C-L-E-A-R." She looked offscreen and said teasingly, "I'm blaming *you* for this. Because you don't say it properly, your poor son can't spell it," laughing, the camera clearly picking up her warmth and genuine affection for the person in the corner. I knew it was coming, of course, but when Dad's offscreen laughter joined in with hers and Eugene's, I winced. Dad saying "nu-cu-lar" was something Mom and I liked to tease Dad about, but he was super-sensitive about it. The last time we teased him, Dad got annoyed and definitely did not laugh. So to see this woman knowing that Dad says "nucular" and joke about it with him so easily, almost flirtatiously . . . Mom looked hurt. Betrayed. Or maybe I'm just reading into it because that's how I felt.

On the video, Anjeli was saying, "Let's keep going. Another alternative energy source?" Eugene spelled out I-T-S (end of word) M-I-A-S (end of word) M-O-U-T-H (end of word), put down his pencil, and a bark of laughter came from offscreen. Anjeli seemed puzzled. "I'm not sure what—"

Dad stepped into the video. He was still laughing, looking delighted but also kind of stunned. "Mia's mouth. As an alternative source of energy, because Mia talks so fast and so much." I felt that familiar emotion of amusement combined with embarrassment and irritation when your sibling gets you good, but I'd never felt it with Eugene before. Dad was saying, "It's a joke. He's poking fun at his sister. Eugene, you made a joke. Anjeli, you said this was going to happen. This is a huge step. He's not just repeating back words from the lesson. He's communicating his own thoughts. That's what you're doing. Right, Eugene?"

Eugene picked up the pencil, and Anjeli picked up the letter-board again. R-I-G-H-T. "Right," Anjeli said, and Dad said, "This is amazing, a miracle. Eugene, I can't believe we're getting to hear what you think. Oh my God," hugging Eugene and laughing and crying, and Anjeli joined in, saying, "I told you this would happen. I told you we had to be patient," and the three of them were hugging, Dad holding both of Anjeli's hands with his and saying, "Anjeli, I can't thank you enough. When I think of how much patience you've given me and how much courage and love . . ." He got choked up, and she was all teary-eyed, and I swear they looked like they were going to lean in and kiss each other when Eugene, clearly overexcited, got up and started jumping, and Anjeli and Dad looked at the camera as if they'd just remembered this was being recorded and were embarrassed and pulled apart, and Anjeli pressed a button and the video ended, the screen going black except for the date that remained frozen on the bottom right corner.

You may think *devastation* a strange word to describe our feelings at this time, when we'd just witnessed video evidence—maybe? probably?—that Eugene could communicate. We should have been elated, or at least hopeful. And there was an undercurrent of that, of course. The wonder of this unbelievable discovery.

So why the gloom? Two things. The first was Anjeli. The way she'd looked at Dad—teasing him, with what looked like longing and such heightened happiness when Eugene made that joke about my mouth. The partnership of two people working closely together, and when that succeeds in such an emotional moment, the inevitable intimacy and shared passion—weren't books and movies full of stories of collaborators falling in love precisely because of these factors? And if they fell in love, wouldn't that be the perfect reason why Dad wouldn't tell us immediately about this miracle of Eugene communicating, why he'd keep it a secret from his own wife, Eugene's mother, who'd worked tirelessly for more than a decade to help him to communicate?

And second, Eugene. Looking at him now, jumping up and down mindlessly, making silly noises like a preverbal kid, it didn't seem possible that this was the same person. But he had appeared to be communicating. It was painfully slow and limited, but he did it, spelling words by poking letter after letter. No one was holding up his arm or touching him in any way. His eyes were unsteady but definitely on the board. And Anjeli didn't seem to be doing anything but holding the letterboard in front of him, still and unmoving—a human easel. Cheering him on, giving him energy through her confidence, the way a great rehabilitation therapist does when people are learning to walk again after a horrible accident and the like.

But this made no sense. Not only because it seemed impossible. Not only because it was incomprehensible why, if Dad knew this twelve days ago, he never told us. But because of the questions that kept swirling around and clouding over my eyes as I looked at my little brother, jumping happily next to me.

Eugene was the only one who knew what happened to Dad, the only eyewitness. If he could communicate, what the hell was he doing, remaining silent? Why wasn't he signaling to us that he could communicate, trying whatever method he could? Why wasn't he getting off the trampoline to grab his yellow letterboard and pencil and tell us everything he knew?

Was it possible, could it be, that he didn't want to?

# TWENTY-ONE

# Jumping for Joy

WHEN WE FIRST MOVED TO KOREA, BECAUSE I LOOKED KOREAN, EVERY-
one expected me to be fluent in Korean. When they found out I
wasn't—I couldn't understand or speak Korean at all—they assumed
something was wrong with me and called me a bah-bo. *Idiot.* Harmonee's friends—the middle-aged ajummas who lived up to the stereotype for being aggressively and proudly frank and nosy—said it
often while looking my way, not particularly quietly. It was especially
upsetting for me because being told I was smart was the one thing
I'd had before then: I wasn't great at making friends; I was awful at
sports, always the last to be picked for teams; and I understood from
an early age that I was not pretty, with *not* meaning *opposite of* rather
than mere *absence of*. It's remarkable how when your twin has desirable attributes you lack, people feel compelled to comment on them,
usually to your parents within (your) earshot. Being stripped of this
one thing I'd clung to—that hurled me into a deep well of insecurity,
self-doubt, and shame.

Because John looked "American" (meaning, white), everyone in Korea expected him to speak English, not Korean. The ajummas even tried to speak English to him, laughed at themselves, and apologized for not speaking English well. Once we both started picking up on Korean (but still not speaking it well), they treated him like he was a genius or something, whereas me, they continued to pity for being "slow," despite Harmonee telling them that we were twins, in exactly the same situation. I tried to talk to John about it, but he didn't get it, and neither did Dad.

Mom did, though. She said how she felt the same way when she moved to America as a teenager, how she went from being a smart girl with friends in Korea to feeling lost and frustrated because she couldn't understand or say anything. "I know you guys sometimes feel that, too, that frustration when people don't understand you or you don't understand them," she told Dad and John, "but that's no-where close to when people judge you, when you know people think you're stupid. I remember yelling at myself for feeling this way, tell-ing myself it's in my head, no one actually thinks I'm stupid. But when I learned enough English that I could understand it, I found out I wasn't paranoid, after all; people really did look down on me. Because when you can't talk, people assume you can't understand and talk about you in front of you. It's humiliating. Just thinking about it today, twenty years later, it really just . . . It's still hard to talk about."

I hope it doesn't make me sound like a selfish brat to admit this, but it was amazing how much better I felt, knowing Mom went through the same painful experience. Partly, it was the validation—I knew Dad and John were trying to make me feel better by saying I shouldn't let others' opinions affect me, but it just made me doubt myself more, like my reaction was unnatural and wrong—but more, it made me feel less alone. "Do you think that's why you went into linguistics?" I asked Mom.

Mom looked at me the way she does sometimes, her head cocked and eyes slightly narrowed like she's trying to peer into me, to study me, and then after a few seconds, breaking into a slowly unfolding smile that makes me think she's proud to be my mom. "I think you're right," she said to me. "I find it really fascinating how deeply ingrained it is in our society—not just the US, but human society in general—how we equate verbal skills, especially oral fluency, with intelligence. And when you lose that, even when it's for an obvious reason, like being from a different country, it changes you. Because I'm human, too, I operate under that same assumption, so when I had trouble expressing myself, I felt like a bah-bo. Even today, I'm a different person in English than in Korean." Mom said how it still happened, the presumption that she was not American, must not be all that smart or well-educated, hadn't quite mastered the nuances of language and culture—all because she had an accent.[17]

Watching Eugene's video, this is what I thought back to. That frustration, the insecurity, the self-doubt. We talked about it later, Mom and me—why we didn't try to communicate with Eugene immediately upon watching that first solar/Mia's mouth video. "If this

---

17 Dad kept unusually quiet throughout most of this discussion, but at one point, he confessed he was having trouble understanding Mom's feelings because he'd never felt stupid for not speaking Korean even though he lived in Korea. "I don't think anyone expects me to speak Korean fluently, and if they did, I'd think they're being unreasonable and I wouldn't let it get to me," he said. "Maybe you're just more confident in yourself than I am," Mom said, "but I wonder if it has anything to do with your being a white American guy, which is considered to be at the top of the social hierarchy even here in Korea." I've thought about it a lot, and I think Mom's right: assumptions about racial superiority are built into the whole linguistic-fluency-as-intelligence thing. It's not just the juxtaposition of Mom's and my experiences with Dad's and John's that makes me suspect that. After we moved back to the US, two non-English-speakers started at our high school around the same time. One was French, the other Chinese. I don't know why, but for some reason, the French kid speaking subpar English with his heavy accent sounded chichi and astute, like he was too brilliant for us to understand, whereas the Chinese kid seemed pathetic, speaking "broken" English. (Even our word choice—do we say of European white people that they speak "broken" English? I've only heard it with respect to Asians.)

is real," Mom said, "if Eugene can really read and spell and communicate, that would mean he's been trapped in there all along, just suffering. No one believing in him, treating him like a . . ."

"Bah-bo," I said. I hated that word, hated the memory of the time I associated with that word, and saying it out loud, it actually hurt, physically—a zap behind my eyeballs like the beginnings of a migraine—and the room seemed to tilt.

And just think, Mom's and my situations had been limited and temporary—nothing, one-millionth of nothing, compared to what Eugene would have felt, what he was feeling now, if he could think, understand, read, and have fully formed words he wanted to say, just no way to say them. That's what made the letterboard video so scary and painful to think about, why I knew it wrecked Mom to wonder if it was real. Back in Korea, I *knew* I would learn Korean eventually, and I didn't even really need to—I had no trouble communicating with my family, I was about to attend an English-based school for expats, and I knew we would eventually move back to the US. So if it was this painful for Mom and me, what was it like for those who have beautifully formed thoughts they can't express their entire lives?

I've heard people call Angelman syndrome the happiness syndrome. But if we've been wrong all this time, if the video was real, that would mean he's been suffering—his smile masking the trauma of being belittled, of having no outlet, of being thought of as a bah-bo.

Given all that, can you blame me for that tiny part of myself that wished, just for a moment, that the video was fake—that Eugene hadn't had all his thoughts trapped in his mind for fourteen years?

———

I'VE BEEN THINKING A LOT about expectations, about what someone hearing this story for the first time might expect us to do or say at any given moment. Part of that, of course, is driven by my spending time with Dad's happiness quotient notes. But even more, I think it's the process I've been going through—trying to recall and make sense of those anxiety-filled forty-eight hours after Dad's disappearance and putting them into words. It makes me see it as an outsider might, to analyze everything we did and felt.

As soon as we saw the video of Eugene communicating, we wanted to immediately force Eugene off the trampoline and into a chair, thrust a letterboard into his face, and pelt him with the questions we'd been dying to ask: "Where is Dad, Eugene? Is he dead or alive? How can we save him?" But we were afraid—of this being real, of it being a sham, of the answers that might come—the different strains of fear weaving through and around one another tightly, forming a collective noose. Not enough to stop us from trying, but to make us pause, long enough to remember the last time we jumped into a new skill without preparation (a particularly painful bout with tandem-bicycling) and what Eugene's therapists had drilled into our heads: that paradoxically, to get the quickest results, we had to wait—to take a breath, not rush things, learn the basics before the all-important first attempt.

We couldn't take hours, of course. Mom suggested fifteen minutes to get ready. Just long enough to scan through the brochures and website FAQs and the video from Eugene's intro mini-session with Anjeli back in October 2019, which said under the title, "A great video to share with family and friends to explain the basics of the program." (This stung—there went my fantasy Dad was desperate to tell us but couldn't due to some cultlike gag rule of Anjeli's program.)

This one opened with Dad sitting next to Eugene. From the start, even through the perfunctory basics with Anjeli introducing herself and her business, I noticed that she addressed and talked to Eugene directly, not to/through Dad.

"Eugene," she said, "I know you've seen dozens of therapists, and I'm guessing you're just waiting to get this over with because in your experience, speech therapy is a complete waste of time. Well, you know what? I agree with you. I have no interest in getting you to copy me saying *dada* and *mama*. So let's forget about *speech* altogether. Let's focus instead on *encoding*.

"Encoding is the process of turning thought into any kind of communication. Texting, phone calls, magazine articles, cartoons, emails—it's all encoding, but of course the most common form is direct face-to-face conversation,[18] like we're doing right now, which is why some people think *encoding* is just a fancy, technical-sounding way of saying *talking*. But here's why I like using it. Because using this unfamiliar word helps us to think about talking differently than we're used to, as a multistep system with separate parts." Here, she held up a chart:

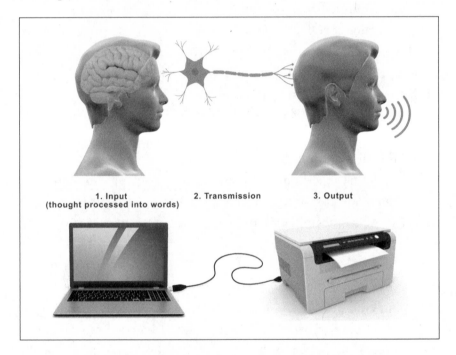

1. Input
(thought processed into words)                2. Transmission                3. Output

"You start with the cognitive part: thought processed into words. Then your brain sends out orders to your body, and hopefully, you say those words out loud. It's similar to words on a computer being sent

---

18 It's funny how dramatically things have changed since this recording less than a year ago. During lockdown, I bet texting/messaging overtook face-to-face conversations (even including Zoom in that category) as the most prevalent encoding form, especially for us Gen Zers. That may be the one upside of the pandemic: it's made our society more accommodating for non-oral-encoders who can't speak but can type.

to a printer. I like breaking it down like this because it makes it clear that not being able to talk might have nothing to do with your thinking, just like a printer not printing might have nothing to do with the computer. You could be intelligent—brilliant, even—but your body won't do what your brain is telling it to because there's a breakdown further down the system. Also, just because you can't talk doesn't mean you're *nonverbal*—you have words, meaning, you are *verbal*, but you just can't communicate them orally.[19]

"Now, in the olden days—before we knew about different parts of the brain and neurons and all that—we considered a person's speech and intelligence to be directly related; in fact, the word *dumb* in Old English means *mute* or *without speech*. We now know that's not true, but it seems to be a deep prejudice that won't go away. Even to this day, if you can't talk, people automatically jump to the assumption that it's a cognitive problem: you're 'dumb' in every sense of the word," Anjeli said, using air quotes, her voice taking on a passionate, almost evangelistic tone. "It's incomprehensible, the complete opposite of what we should do, but we presume incompetence unless proven otherwise, unless you're someone like Stephen Hawking who lost his ability to speak *after* the world already knew he was brilliant.[20]

---

19 It's a common mistake, saying *verbal* to refer to oral speech. It's a pet peeve of mine when people say "verbal, not written," because written *is* verbal. So why do we call nonspeakers "nonverbal," use the label "nonverbal autism"? It leads to the unwarranted assumption that those people are wholly without words. I've brought this up to people, and they dismiss it as "just semantics." But sometimes semantics matter. Words matter. They influence our thinking.

20 This reminded me of when Eugene first received the "cognitive deficit" label and I asked Dad—but what about Stephen Hawking? (I've idolized him ever since his cameo on *Star Trek: TNG* playing poker with Data.) How about the boy at my school who's in the highest-level classes but hardly says anything because he stutters? It wasn't until Dad told me that Eugene scored a 62 on a nonverbal IQ test that I stopped questioning. I think a lot of people are like this; we believe numbers, something about the quantification making it seem objective and verified. It wasn't until recently that I looked into it and realized: even a nonverbal IQ test relies on your ability to consistently make your finger point to what you want it to, a fine motor skill at the heart of Eugene's challenges.

"Well, I think that's total BS and tremendously unfair to you. As long as we don't know for sure and we're just guessing, I'd rather give you the benefit of the doubt. Our society has the presumption of innocence to prevent innocent people from being physically imprisoned. I want the same for you: this basic emotional, mental equivalent, the presumption of intelligence, competence, to prevent an internal imprisonment—of your mind, your *soul*.[21] And I'm not doing that just to be nice, because I feel sorry for you, but because it makes sense, especially for people like you with motor dysfunction. You've had issues your entire life trying to get all these different parts of your body to do what you want, so why wouldn't you have the same motor-planning issues with speech, which is one of the most complex motor skills, and with pointing to pictures or YES-NO cards, which is fine motor combined with ocular motor, coordinating what you're seeing with moving your finger to that exact spot? Why wouldn't we say, 'There's obviously a general problem with step two, the transmission through the nervous system, so let's work on *that* and see if that helps'?

"So that's what I'd like to do. I want to start with encoding using your arm, moving your shoulders—*gross* motor, which I know is easier for you than using your fingers or your mouth. Your dad says you tried using letterboards, which is great because that means you've been exposed to the whole concept of communicating through spelling, but he also said your old therapist physically supported your arm. My method is different. I'm not going to touch you at all, anywhere."

Anjeli held up a stencil with three letters—X, Y, and Z. "But I *am* going to make it easier for you by using big letterboards with only a few letters each. And based on your vision therapist's report, I think holding it a bit below your head makes it easiest for your eyes to

---

21 It occurred to me how, on top of our systematic presumption of incompetence, Eugene was almost imprisoned earlier that day despite the supposed safeguard of the presumption of innocence. The system has failed my brother in so many ways.

focus, so let's try this." She adjusted the stencil and held up a thick pencil with her other hand. "Now, I'm not going to lie. It's going to be hard, a ton of really slow, frustrating work. So you need to really *want* to do this. And you're old enough that you need to decide. So if you want to give this a try, I want you to tell me yourself. I want you to take this pencil and spell *yes*. If you don't, you can just put the pencil down."

This entire time, Eugene had been looking away. If you didn't know him, you would have thought he wasn't paying attention at all. But we knew—if he wasn't interested, he would have gotten up and started jumping long ago. The way he was sitting still, his fingers laced in the *calm hands* position—he was riveted. He grabbed the pencil and struggled to place it in a tripod grip like his occupational therapists were always trying to get him to, but Anjeli said, "It doesn't matter how you hold it. And you can move your arm any way you want. Whatever's easiest."

Eugene gripped the pencil with all five fingers, held it up by his head, and ever so slowly—I swear it took a full minute, and it was so nerve-racking that I wanted to reach through the screen and grab and move it myself—he moved his hand in a super-slo-mo stab toward the stencil, stopping when the pencil tip was right by Y.

"Keep going," Anjeli said. "Poke the tip all the way *through*. That makes it easier for me to tell which letter you want. Plus, your brain will get the sensory feedback from how it feels." Eugene's smile stayed the same, but his eyes widened and bulged out with a mischievous gleam, and he stabbed the pencil into the space right in the middle, at the intersection of the three lines of Y. "Bull's-eye! That's it!"

Anjeli put the X-Y-Z board down and held up a different one with D, E, and F on it. "Okay, what's the next letter?" It seemed to take Eugene even longer this time, but Anjeli kept smiling and encouraging him to keep focusing with not a hint of frustration or impatience (wow, would I be horrible at this job!) until he finally stabbed E, and she switched to the S-T-U board. "One more. Final letter." Eugene began rocking back and forth in the chair, and when he got his hand in front of the stencil, his hand shook like he couldn't stand it anymore. He jabbed, a deliberate, hard thrust into the middle of S with a high, delighted laugh.

"Y-E-S—*yes*," Anjeli said. "Congratulations, Eugene—your first word! It feels great, right?" The way he was laughing, bouncing in his seat, it looked like he wanted to jump up and hug her.

Was that right? Was that really the first word he himself had communicated in his life? Dad looked stunned, looking back and forth at the pencil, Eugene, and Anjeli over and over again as if this were a magic trick he couldn't figure out. "I, um," he said. "How is . . . Were you signaling with your eyes? I mean, he's never learned to spell."

Anjeli laughed. "Oh, come on, Adam. You think after watching *Sesame Street* nonstop for fourteen years, he wouldn't know how to spell *yes*?" She turned to Eugene. "What you just did—spelling out Y-E-S like that—that was amazing. You had a lot of help from me, of course. It was a simple word, easy to spell, and you just had to pick between three letters." True, I thought, but it wasn't a coincidence. The chance that Eugene happened to poke Y, E, *and* S randomly was—quick calculation in my head; 1/3 times 1/3 times 1/3—less than 4 percent.

"But it's enough to tell me what I already suspected," Anjeli continued. "You've been learning and absorbing all along from the sidelines, from TV, family dinner conversations, books read to you, your siblings doing homework, all that. But you didn't look the way you're supposed to when you're paying attention—again, because of your motor dysfunction—so everyone thought you were just in your own world. And I'm sure you were sometimes. It's too painful not to escape. But I know you know a lot more than anyone's given you credit for." She turned to Dad and asked, "Have you noticed if Eugene likes watching videos with closed-captioning?"

I went cold, a tingle spreading down my shoulders like a shawl. This explained our huge fight at Christmas. I'd always assumed

Eugene loved Japanese anime purely for the sensory input—the bright colors, music, and exaggerated facial features—since he couldn't understand the story line at all because he couldn't read the English subtitles. Last Christmas, I'd been so proud of myself because I got Eugene bootleg subtitle-free versions of his favorites. But when I showed him my present, explaining how he could now fully enjoy the animation without the meaningless, annoying letters on the screen, Eugene took the flash drive out of his iPad and threw it against the wall. I'd interpreted it as entitlement, total disrespect, and I scolded him and handed it back, but he held it in both hands to bend it, snap it in two. I screamed no and tried to pry it out of his hands, which was when all hell broke loose, with him thrashing, clawing, and kicking. I'd assumed then that the whole thing was due to Eugene's out-of-control brattiness, but it was occurring to me it was frustration and indignation, the only way he'd had to protest.

Dad was saying in the video that he hadn't really thought about it, but yeah, the closed-captioning was on, but he thought that was just because that was the default, because Mom likes that, and Anjeli was saying no, she bet he figured out how to turn it on, to learn and challenge his mind. She said to Dad, "Your reaction is really common. I don't know if it's because they've had to wait to use words to express themselves for so long, thinking and practicing in their minds, but my students who start when they're older, like Eugene, tend to write really well, with great spelling and vocabulary right out of the gate. It's fascinating, and a lot of parents are mystified by it."

She turned back to Eugene. "Okay, so given all that, here's the plan. We're going to start with these three-letter stencils until you get good and fast. I don't know how many months of repetition it'll take to build up those neural pathways, so to make sure you're not bored out of your mind, I'll give you lessons—real science, literature, history I think you'll be interested in—and ask you questions. And at home, I want you to really work on motor coordination with your dad. Once you master three letters, we'll move to boards with eight letters each, then thirteen letters, then a full letterboard, then point-ing using your fingers, and finally, typing all by yourself."

Anjeli paused, then said it again, slower, in full evangelistic mode. "Typing. All by yourself. With no one around you. *That* is the ultimate goal, Eugene, and I think it's possible for you, the same way it took months for you to learn to jump, your dad says, but it's part of you now, as easy and natural as breathing. It's going to take a long time—many years, probably—but what a goal to work toward, right? I believe you can do it. Just think—you'll be able to text and email people, whatever you want, whenever you want, on your own time. Tell people what you think. Study what you want, maybe even go to college."

At *college,* Eugene's body stilled. It's funny because this was one of the rare times his lips were not curled up in a smile, but I could swear he'd never been as overcome with joy and hope as he was at that moment. One of Anjeli's hands was resting on the table close to him. He reached and grabbed it with both his hands and squeezed.

———

I USED TO JUMP WITH Eugene in Korea. I'd forgotten about it until Anjeli mentioned it, but we actually started because Eugene couldn't jump and the therapists needed someone to bounce with him on the trampoline, get him acclimated to the motion. Our parents first enlisted John's help because he's athletic, but it turns out the key to coordinated jumping is not athleticism, but rhythm—being in sync, like playing a duet. And that, I'm good at.

Our therapy trampoline in Seoul had a bar in the middle, so you could both hold on, facing each other. I'd start bouncing, the move-ment would start *his* bouncing, and I'd jump higher, smile bigger, lifting my eyebrows to get him to look at my eyes. Once Eugene mastered mirrored jumping, I had the idea to try seesaw jumping, Korean style—instead of sitting, you stand, jumping onto the seesaw plank to propel your partner into the air, and when they land, you fly up.[22] It's tricky because you can't rely on your partner to do all the work; you have to match your tempo to your partner's jumping arc, the precise timing of its apex, which requires concentration at first. After a while, though, the rhythm becomes natural, and this—when I stopped thinking and intuition took over—was when the magic happened, when my primal connection with Eugene became palpable and I understood what Harmonee was going on about when she invoked jeong, the Korean sense of belonging to a whole. I felt that linking so powerfully when we jumped, the tranquility of the constant, rhythmic motion displacing all the noise in my head. Our parents joked they didn't know for whom this was better therapy, because it was the only time I'd stop jabbering for so long. We quit when Eugene's social therapist decided that (irony of ironies) Eugene was jumping too much and labeled his jumping a "stim" (short for self-stimulatory behavior) we were instructed to ignore and limit. I was nine, and I hadn't jumped on a trampoline since, hadn't even been tempted.

Eugene had been jumping the whole time we were in Anjeli's basement. But after his first YES on the video, I turned to him and watched him jump, really took it in. I wanted to jump like that, stop the thoughts swirling in my head—the questions and analyses and worries about letterboards and bah-bos and systemic biases and cancer and bodies in rivers and affairs and prison rape prevention programs and detectives who lie to you—and just feel that weightlessness

---

22 It's a game Korean women apparently made up to play during village festivals like Chuseok (similar to Thanksgiving) and Lunar New Year, while men were drinking. I thought it was really fun and got John to play it with me during recess, but his friends made fun of him, saying it was only for girls, and he stopped. Mom had warned us about the blatant sexism rampant in Korea, so maybe it's appropriate that my first year in Korea is when/where I learned the lesson that labeling something as "girls-only" can too often transform it into something undesirable.

when you're at the top of the jump, your hair flying into your eyes, and the wonder of all your body parts obeying your commands, moving together in one flow.

I got up, stepped up onto the bright blue trampoline mat, put my hands on Eugene's on the handlebar, and started jumping. It was awkward at first, getting used to the jiggly canvas, figuring out how to land on my sore ankle, and coordinating with a jumping partner who barely registered my presence. We hadn't jumped together in ten years, since he was four; I doubted he even remembered. But once we got in sync, Eugene noticed. He looked me straight in the eyes, and immediately, the zap of our linking and the rush of adrenaline dampened my aches, from my head down to my ankles, and I thought, I know, Eugene. I know why you jump. The freedom of flight, the affirmation of competence and the ensuing confidence—all that displacing the shame and outrage of being perpetually underestimated and misunderstood, dislodging them from your core. I felt it myself: we were, quite literally, jumping for joy, to attain it, or at least the absence of pain. If his need to jump was in any way correlated to the level of his pain, what did it mean that Eugene jumped yesterday for four hours straight after he got back from the park?

Later, looking back to this moment, I would think, What a comical sight. Here we were, a family with a missing father and a child under suspicion, with two people watching videos sprawled out on the basement floor of the also-missing (possible) mistress of the father, while two others seesaw jumped, Korean style, on a trampoline. It's as silly and ridiculous an image as I can think of. Maybe that's why I treasure it and hold it close to my heart. Because it was our one period of respite—not exactly pleasure, but giving in to and letting ourselves get lost in what we wanted, just for us.

We had been jumping in fully synchronized mode for only a few minutes when Mom yelled out a one-minute warning. I heard her tell John to get the letterboard and a pencil out from the therapy box, it was time to ask Eugene about Dad. I squeezed Eugene's hands to follow me, and we slowed down together, our jumps getting lower until we were just bouncing, our feet no longer leaving the blue mat.

A phone rang—Mom's default ringtone. I could tell from Mom's side of the conversation it was Shannon, looking for us, something was happening and Detective Janus was on her way to our house. Mom apologized to Shannon, said something huge had happened and we weren't home yet, but yes, of course we knew how serious the home arrest order was, and we would get home right now. She told John to pack up everything in the box, we needed to borrow it to ask Eugene about Dad as soon as we got home.

Eugene and I jiggled across the canvas and stepped down together, hand in hand. We walked out of the house and got into our car, calmly, almost casually, as if we were any other family out on a fun outing, as if we weren't afraid of what awaited us at home.

# TWENTY-TWO

# Please Please PLEASE Stop

WE WERE ALMOST HOME WHEN WE FOUND OUT WHAT WAS HAPPENING. It was Dad's ATM card. Another hit, this time in a store in Charlottes-ville, two hours from us. "Detective Janus said we got lucky this time," Mom said, the briefest pause before *lucky.* "A security guard man-aged to stop them—"

"*Them?*" I asked.

"A couple trying to use the card. A woman and a man matching the descriptions for Anjeli Rapari and your father." (A jolt: Had Mom ever referred to Dad as "your father" before, instead of "your dad"?) "Anyway, the police are on their way, and hopefully . . ."

Mom's voice trailed off, and I was trying really hard not to think of what was in that silence—what should Mom, what should we all, be hoping for?—when Eugene snatched his hand from me and howled, high-pitched and plaintive, rocking in his seat the way he does when he needs to jump but can't. I thought again about his grief-stricken wail that morning, his freaking out at the texts from Dad's phone, all the things I'd interpreted as signs that Eugene believed Dad to be dead, because what else could upset Eugene that much? But the videos from Anjeli's house changed everything. Because I could very well imagine—if the only two people in the world who knew about the thoughts trapped in your mind ran away without telling anyone, wouldn't that be as tragic, as intolerable, as your father's death?

Mom seemed to be thinking the same thing. She said to Eugene—not in singsong baby talk but a serious, regular tone—"I know, Eugene. I can't imagine how infuriating this must be for you. But the police will intercept them soon, and we'll get some answers." Eugene stopped rocking, but I couldn't tell if it was from being comforted by Mom's reassurance or from the shock of Mom talking to him like a regular fourteen-year-old for the first time I could recall.

Or maybe it was the word *intercept*—jarring not only for the vocabulary level it presumed for Eugene, but for the images it evoked for me, and maybe for him, too: the police approaching the store, then a standoff, like in the movies. Dad and Anjeli refusing to give themselves up. A high-speed car chase, the winding country roads of the Shenandoah Valley. A cliff, a car crash. Not death, but maybe severe maiming. Dismemberment. And as soon as I pictured that, I thought—it's funny, the things that go through your mind at times like these—if that happened, maybe we wouldn't get in trouble for keeping Eugene out for so long. Maybe the entire house arrest order would be nullified and the dreaded Friday hearing canceled because they'd realize that Eugene obviously didn't harm anyone. Or if not canceled entirely (there was still the remaining matter of Detective Janus's facial injuries), then at least postponed until after Dad was out of the hospital, by which time Detective Janus's face would be fine and the judge would get annoyed at her for wasting the court's time with such trivial matters and dismiss the case with apologies.

I was going back and forth between Googling how to listen in on police radio communications in Charlottesville and imagining Detective Janus's reaction—the look of humbled contrition on her face, the wording of her apology to Eugene; how satisfying that would be, to hear her plead for forgiveness—when I saw Shannon waiting for us at the end of our driveway, between her car and Detective Janus's now-familiar sedan. John and I both ran out of the car, simultaneously yelling "Have you heard anything?" and "Did they catch them?"

Shannon's face was infuriatingly neutral, nothing signaling good news versus bad news. (Correction: bad news versus terrible news, because there was no possibility of good news in this scenario. What would that even be at this point? "Hooray! We caught your dad who faked his death, abandoned his family, and ran away for either 1) a carefree life with another woman or 2) a sadistic experiment designed to (another irony or ironies here) increase people's happiness levels"?) She waited until Mom and Eugene got out of the car before saying, "They're in custody. That's all I know so far. Detective Janus just got here, and she went out back to take a call from the Charlottesville police."

We went straight through our yard to our back deck, where Detective Janus was on the phone. Her face was even worse than when we last saw her—lips swollen, cheek purple. I caught a snippet of what she was saying—something about beavers and foxes?—and getting closer, I saw what looked like two mugshots, side by side, on the tablet in front of her, but the sunlight was making it hard to see the faces. Mom strode past me, picked it up. "What is this? Who are these people?"

I looked over her shoulder. One man and one woman who were most definitely *not* Dad and Anjeli.

Detective Janus said a quick goodbye and put down her phone, put on her mask. "These are the people who've been using Mr. Parson's debit card. My colleagues in Charlottesville are still questioning them, but I asked them to expedite the photos. Obviously, we knew it was highly unlikely, but we wanted to confirm ASAP that it wasn't Mr. Parson."

*Obviously?* Later, thinking back to this moment, it would dawn on me: of course the police thought it wasn't Dad. I should have realized at "they're in custody"; because yes, it's a shitty thing to do, but was running away from your family and using your own ATM card a crime, one that got you arrested? We'd all concluded as much this morning—if Dad had concocted some elaborate runaway plan, why would he use his own, traceable cards?—but I'd let those ridiculous happiness quotient experiments screw with my head, inject doubt, thinking it must be a clue.

But at the moment, *obviously* did not sit well with me. "But they said the descriptions matched," I said to Detective Janus. The rage welled within me, looking at the pictures of these people who looked *nothing* like Dad or Anjeli. I hated the security guard who said they matched, hated Detective Janus who repeated it without taking the tiniest micro-glimpse to verify. "What was their description? Human male and human female? They're, like, *young*. And this woman is *white*. I mean, doesn't this security guard know people are *depending* on them? How hard is it just to say, 'I don't remember what they look like,' and not raise our hopes?"

I hadn't realized I was shouting until I stopped. Detective Janus said, "I know it's frustrating, but sometimes people are trying so hard to be helpful, they make mistakes."

Mom put her hand on my arm and said to Detective Janus, "So what does this mean? How did they even get Adam's card?"

Detective Janus didn't answer. She picked up her tablet and asked us all to sit, she had something to show us.

I didn't recognize the object in the picture, it was so mangled, until John said, "Is that Dad's wallet?"

"It appears to be, but we were hoping you could verify that." Detective Janus swiped to the next picture, then the next, then the next. Different angles on what I could finally make out as Dad's plain, indistinct black leather wallet, but torn apart nearly in two, with jagged edges, like a wad of too-tough, charred steak someone tried to eat and finally spit out.

It was obviously Dad's wallet—the last few images showed his driver's license and credit cards, his library card, car insurance cards, all mangled and torn up. Who, *what*, had done that? If this happened to his wallet, what could have happened to him? Images of violent whitewater pummeling jagged rocks, animal claws mauling soft flesh, Dad's clothes torn, body mutilated—they gushed in and churned through my brain.

Detective Janus explained that the man in custody claimed he found the wallet the previous night with his friends at a "bonfire" in the woods (said with air quotes, which I didn't understand until Shannon later explained this was a popular hangout spot for drug deals). He said the wallet wasn't wet, which the initial inspection seemed to confirm—a little damp but definitely not soaked the way you'd expect if the wallet fell into the river. Also, the spot where he allegedly found the wallet was in an undeveloped riverside forest several miles *upstream* from the park.

"He's clearly lying, then," Mom said. "He must have stolen it from Adam."

"It's possible," Detective Janus said. "He says he worked from nine A.M. to six P.M. yesterday. We'll verify that, of course, and the same with the woman, who lives and works in Charlottesville. But based on the condition of the wallet, it's also possible it fell out near the river and animals got to it and carried it to a different location."

"But that doesn't preclude the possibility that someone robbed Mr. Parson, took the wallet, and discarded it elsewhere, where the animals found it," Shannon said.

"Or," I said, "maybe Dad got separated from Eugene"—God, it felt awful talking about Eugene as if he wasn't sitting right next to me, and I glanced at Eugene to signal an apology but his eyes were fixed on the wallet-carcass picture—"and Dad got lost searching for him in the woods and went the wrong direction and ended up outside the park in that upstream forest and he's there now, hurt and lost . . . Oh my God, there aren't bears there, are there? Or foxes—do they attack humans? Because that wallet—"

"Mia, that's very unlikely," Detective Janus said, explaining that the upstream forest was separated from the park by a deep, wide tributary difficult for people to cross. "That's why we didn't search that area last night, because it's considered inaccessible on foot. But given this new information, we're broadening the search. We're sending out alerts and calls for more volunteers, announcements through TV, radio, and social media, posters, everything."

"We should go out there," Mom said. "We should be looking for Adam, all of us, right now."

It struck me: I really hadn't searched for Dad, like, at *all*. John and Mom went to the park by themselves yesterday, looked around, but aside from the parking lot this morning to find Dad's dot, I'd done nothing.

"No," Shannon said. "I know you want to help, but other people can do that. There's a lot we still need to tackle that only you can do."

"I agree," Detective Janus said. "Actually, the thing that would be most helpful is if you could reach out to friends, neighbors, social media, and ask them to volunteer. Would you be willing to do that?" Detective Janus looked at each of us in turn, waited for a nod or "yes" before moving to the next person. Except for Eugene. She skipped right over him, as if he wasn't a person, wasn't even there. Everyone had been doing this all day with no objections from us, so maybe I was being unreasonable—honestly, we'd been doing it ourselves all his life, and it wasn't like Eugene was on social media—but I still felt awful, a sickening mix of offended and depressed. I reached for Eugene's hand and raised our joined fist in solidarity as if I was speaking for both of us. "Yes, of course we'll do that."

No one seemed to notice or care, even Eugene, who took back his hand as soon as I let go. Mom and John were already on their phones, asking Detective Janus for the details on the search party, and Shannon suggested a fifteen-minute break for emails/texts/social media. Mom said the news was starting to spread, how many emails she had saying so sorry, they'd heard about Dad, how were we coping, anything they can do? "I'm writing an email we can just copy and paste for everyone: *Actually, there* is *something you can do—you can join our search party,*" Mom was saying into her phone, her fingers furiously typing.

I unlocked my phone and saw notifications on every app—double digits in red throughout my screen. Dozens of texts, direct messages, and snaps, many from local friends from high school and Angelman/Henry's House sibling groups who'd heard from their parents. I hadn't been great about keeping in touch, especially during the pandemic—there was something kind of comforting about having to isolate, the forced pause in normal life relieving me of the burdens of civility, legitimizing my occasional need for self-indulgent loafing, to just *be* and do nothing and see no one—but I have to admit, their concern really touched me. Also, the last twenty-four hours with my family and the police, the bombardment of disaster after disaster—it had been *intense,* claustrophobic and suffocating, and interacting with people outside that bubble felt like a depressurization, a hiss of steam venting and dissipating into the air. So many sentiments of sympathy and compassion that warmed me like (I had to smile at what popped into my head, wished Dad were here so I could tell him I had secretly agreed with his happiness example) sitting by a roaring fire after hours stuck outside in a blizzard.

Even social media, which I generally find stressful, was easy—easi*er,* anyway—thanks to John. By the time I opened Instagram, he'd already tagged me in a perfect, guilt-inducing plea about the search party, "confiding" in his 900-plus followers (I'd roll my eyes, but that's how John genuinely thinks, which is scary but comes in handy at times like these) how afraid we were of a low turnout because of the lockdown. Another tagged post by a high school classmate, Brittany, featured a selfie at the park by Dad's MISSING flyer, asking people to join the search for *my dear friend @miaparkson2000's awesome dad* and to stay tuned for a virtual vigil. I didn't think we were close, didn't even think she liked me much, if at all—our "friendship" the byproduct of repeated school-mandated proximity (similar class schedules), formed out of habit rather than by choice—but at this display of caring, I felt a ballooning affection, a sheepishness for having misjudged her, our relationship.

On the other side of this social media mismatch of expectations were those I thought I'd hear from but didn't, chief among them Vic, whom (yes, we'd just broken up and he couldn't text or call because I'd blocked him, but) I'd expected to put the pettiness aside and reach me some other way, at least comment or send a quick obligatory private message saying he's sorry, am I okay?, etc., once he heard about Dad, which he absolutely had to have, given how many of our mutual friends had reached out. I looked, and nothing. No post, no comment, no story, no snap, no Discord mention. I knew this was no time to wallow in post-breakup disappointment, but seriously?

"Everyone, five more minutes," Shannon said. I stopped hate-scrolling and went to do what I came to Instagram to do, which was not to browse or even post—I hated Instagram and had, like, sixty followers, mostly nonlocal—but to go to my high school orchestra's private group, where everyone was local and knew my dad, so I figured this was the highest-impact thing I could do. Brittany was the group's organizer, and several other members had commented heartfelt messages, which made me feel less awkward about popping in for the first time in who knew how long and asking for help.

Creatively named RHSConcertOrchStateChamp2018, the chat group opened to a bunch of pictures and videos of people celebrating with balloons and cake, interlaced with fireworks GIFs and serial hearts. What in hell? I scrolled back and saw Brittany's announcement a half hour ago welcoming everyone to . . . oh God, I remembered her spam-text about June 24, which was—I checked—yup, today: Virtual Celebration of the Second Anniversary of RHSCO's State Championship '18!!!!!!!!!!!!!!!! (I'm assuming there were eighteen exclamation points, although I didn't count.) I should have closed it right then, but I couldn't help scanning the messages—*Happy Anniv best group ever!; Love U all!; Simply the best; Thx 4 organizing, Brittany!; RHS18 RULES!!!!* No mention of my dad, me, maybe postponing the anniversary celebration in light of the heavy hearts several of them had written about.

I had to laugh—at myself, my inane naivete. I should have known—I *did* know—that their declarations of devastation for their *dear* friend, the planning of virtual vigils, etc., were performative, like so much else on social media (like everything on social media). Of course their day wouldn't actually be consumed with prayers for me, of course they weren't literally crying for me, walking around with heavy hearts. But the time stamps proved it with such crushing clarity. They commented publicly on John's post, and less than a minute later, in this private forum, they posted selfies with huge smiles, confetti, party hats framing looks of orgasmic joy plastered on their faces—it seemed lewd, like I should avert my eyes, the incontrovertible evidence punching me in the gut.

It was anger and betrayal, but more than that, it was envy. For my family, the grief was ever-present and all-encompassing, whereas for everyone else, it was a choice. A choice to reach out, to comment, to think about it or not, to feel bad for a minute before turning to the silly, the trite and trivial. I wanted that. A fucking break is what I wanted, and I hated that these so-called friends of mine had it and I didn't. I left. Not just closed the app but found the button to leave the group. Would they notice? Would they chat amongst themselves, feel guilty for a minute before they forgot about that, too? Or maybe their guilt would lead to some good, with them trying to show they really did care by joining the search and posting about it, tagging me for proof.

*Are you sure? You will no longer be able to access the group's messages,* the app warned. I pressed the red Confirm button—thwacked the screen so hard my finger hurt—and the group disappeared, bringing me back to the app's inbox. I saw a smattering of unread messages, but I was done. I was closing out the app when I saw *Adam Parson* in bold. An unread message from Dad. But how? When?

I clicked. A picture of him with us kids, my forced smile making me look awkward and slightly annoyed as usual, the three of them beautiful and happy. Dad's Father's Day post three days ago, which he sent me with the message, *I didn't tag you!,* and his standard trifecta of emojis—heart, wink, laugh-cry. I scrolled through the earlier unread messages, dozens of his posts with me in the picture, all with the same I-didn't-tag-you message with three emojis, no replies on my side until two years ago. The day of my high school graduation, he'd tagged me in multiple posts, and I'd replied *I beg you to please please PLEASE stop,* to which he'd sent a laugh-cry emoji. I'd been tempted to reply *I'M NOT JOKING!* but I thought, No, that won't work, Dad's incorrigible, so I muted him instead, resulting in this long, sad chain of post after post, message after message, all ignored and neglected.

I was looking through the thread, the pictures of us he'd posted, when Mom said, "Oh my God." On her phone screen was an email from our phone company with a voicemail sound file, dated today at 12:32 P.M. I started asking why this was a big deal—all our landline voicemails get emailed to her, so she gets dozens every day, most of them robocalls—but then I saw: VADOH COVID TEAM. She clicked on the file.

A bright, boyish voice sounded, obscenely cheerful as if he were calling about an exciting car refinancing offer: "Hi, this is the Covid Contact Tracing Team from the Virginia Department of Health trying to reach the legal guardian of Eugene Parkson. We have reason to believe that he is a close contact of someone who has Covid-19, with an exposure date of Saturday, June twentieth, four days ago. Please call me back as soon as you can for testing and quarantine instructions."

# TWENTY-THREE

# A Very Pessimistic Kind of Optimism

WHEN WE LIVED IN KOREA, FOR A HISTORY ASSIGNMENT IN FOURTH grade, I interviewed Harmonee about the Korean War, which she had lived through as a teenager. I still remember her shaking voice, the deep crimson of her cheeks, as she told me how terrified she and her sisters had been at the prospect of foreign soldiers breaking in to rape them. (She actually said "attack," but I'd watched enough Korean War documentaries and *Law & Order: SVU* to figure out that was a euphemism.) I asked why she felt this way since, statistically speaking, this was unlikely; I'd read that despite the record number of civilian killings in bombings and massacres, home invasions were relatively rare.

Harmonee's eyes went round, the edges crinkling, like a dumpling. "Is that what your history books say? 'Rare'?"

I showed her my book, the numbers and percentages I'd highlighted in yellow.

She stared at the page. When she spoke, her voice was quiet but with a hard, bitter edge. "It did not feel 'rare' living through it. It happened to us. In our village. Everyone thought they were next." She closed her eyes, a pained frown on her face.

Mom had been videotaping our interview, but she stopped and said that was enough for now, it was time for bed. I wrote up my interview notes and put down as "Lesson Learned" something about different villages having different experiences. (Later, when I was studying the Korean War for AP World History, I rewatched the video and wrote about how history blends individual experiences into smooth, homogenized narratives of "average" experiences, but of course there is no "average" (or "best" or "worst") until you've reached the end.)

It wasn't until much later, after Harmonee died and we were back in America, that Mom told us the real story. It was Harmonee's birthday, so we did a memorial dinner in her honor, sharing funny stories and memories. Harmonee had this bizarre look-on-the-bright-side thing, which Mom called a "very pessimistic kind of optimism": whenever anything bad happened, she said you have to be thankful something worse didn't happen, and proceeded to imagine and list multiple worse-case scenarios. I told the story of when I spilled milk all over Dad's suit at breakfast, making him late for an important meeting and he lost the deal. Harmonee said not to feel bad, think of what could've happened if he'd left the house earlier: crossing the street in his dark suit in the still-darkish morning, he could've been hit by a car; or he could've gotten the deal, had to travel to Jeju Island, and died in a ferry accident. "She was the best at thinking of agonizing, unexpected ways to die," John said, laughing, and joked that if he died in a horrific accident, she'd say it could've been worse, the whole family could've died, not just him.

Mom went all quiet at that, looked down, traced with one finger the blue-green veins in the back of her other hand, something she does when she's upset. We asked what was wrong.

Mom said we'd been too young before, and besides, Harmonee never talked about it, she was ashamed, but when Harmonee was sixteen, a few months into the war, soldiers attacked her home. Her whole family had been outside, burying kimchi jars in the yard. Harmonee threw broken jar pieces at the soldiers and told her younger sister next to her—Aunt Chesuk, whom we'd met—to grab the shovel and swing. The soldiers took the two girls inside to punish them. Harmonee blamed herself for getting her baby sister involved, thinking, If only I'd grabbed the shovel myself, if only I hadn't started throwing things. While they were inside, a bomb went off outside, and her family was killed—everyone except for Harmonee and Chesuk, who were saved because they were being raped, side by side.

―――――

I'VE BEEN THINKING ABOUT THIS a lot. It's inevitable, I suppose, with how functionally similar Harmonee's version of optimism is to Dad saying we should adopt a low baseline to be happier. They're conceptual cousins.

But I think it's also remembering Mom's phone conversation with the Virginia health department. I wonder what the history books will say about 2020, what the retrospective "average" will turn out to be after this is done and over, how kids fifty years from now will judge what happened. Memories are short, I guess is what I'm trying to say, and even now, only three months since that day, it already seems strange to me how we were outside with masks on, all relatively healthy, and yet, as soon as the Virginia Covid Team's voicemail message played, Shannon and Detective Janus (who, it turned out, both had family who'd been hospitalized from Covid) packed up and got the hell out, grabbing antiseptic sprays from their respective bags and spraying their faces, hair, hands, clothes, bags, phones, etc., as they jog-walked to their cars and yelled they were sure everything would be fine but good luck with testing and please call as soon as we got the results.

Mom was on the phone with the health department for more than five minutes (ten, if you include the hold wait time). Here's what she found out about Eugene's exposure: nothing. No name of the person who was sick (due to HIPAA medical privacy laws), no time when the exposure might have occurred (because disclosure of that information might enable us to figure out the Covid-positive person's identity), no location (same), not even this person's current condition, whether it was asymptomatic or dead or something in between.

Look, I realize the state health department's goal wasn't to help us figure out our dad's whereabouts ("Matters of safety in terms of crime as opposed to medical well-being are outside our jurisdiction," the guy said), but it was like they didn't care. Even after Mom explained the situation about Dad, how Dad could be an unidentified Covid patient in an ICU (we'd asked only about people brought in from the park with injuries), the guy merely repeated that they couldn't reveal any information unless they had a death certificate, citing some legal presumption of being alive unless proven otherwise.

"What good is this presumption?" Mom yelled into the phone. "It's not like presumed-innocent-until-proven-guilty, which keeps people out of jail. How does being presumed alive when you might be dead help anyone?"

It wasn't like Mom to lose her calm, but you have to remember—she'd been running up against the medical-privacy barrier all afternoon, trying to get information about Dad's cancer from doctor's offices, laboratories, and insurance companies. It was Kafkaesque, how we were stuck in this circular dilemma in which we couldn't get access to information needed to figure out whether Dad was dead unless we could first prove he was dead.

The only useful thing that came out of that call was when he informed us that Eugene had to isolate for a minimum of fourteen days, the only exceptions being for testing, doctor visits, and hospitalizations. For anything else, including mandatory court appearances (Mom specifically asked), Eugene was excused from attendance by law.

There was something ominous about all this, the eerie coincidence of the Covid outbreak at the detention center saving Eugene temporarily until Friday, and then, a few hours later, getting a further reprieve by yet another Covid emergency, closer to home: Eugene's Covid exposure. As we hurried to drive to the testing center, I couldn't stop thinking of the monkey's paw story, the temporary, short-term wish granted due to a tragedy, leading to a bigger tragedy, then another, until the things most dear to the wish-maker were all gone. What would the analogue be in our case? If we all got sick and died, and it turned out that Dad was the transmitter, the close contact with Covid? But that made no sense—it had to be like we thought, one of the many therapists Eugene saw on Saturday, which . . .

"Wait a minute. John, didn't you work at Henry's House on Saturday?" I asked.

He looked at me. "Oh my God," he and Mom both said, one right after the other.

Mom said, "John, check and see if you've gotten any messages from the Covid tracing people. They would have contacted you directly; you're not a minor."

John unlocked his phone even as he was saying he'd already gone through all his messages and there was nothing like that. He checked again but no, nothing.

I was driving but I pulled over, didn't trust myself to keep driving just then.

Because if I was right about who the close contact was, that changed everything we'd been thinking about Dad and where he might be, with whom, and why.

# TWENTY-FOUR

# Shitty in Real Life

MOM, LIKE MANY WHO GREW UP IN THE PRE-WI-FI ERA, LOVES TO rhapsodize about the simplicity of Life Back Then, the dangers of machines and algorithms taking over our lives and changing the fabric of society and the fundamental nature of humanity itself, blah blah, but let me tell you—our phones are extremely useful for re-creating the minute-by-minute details of a particular day to figure out who exposed your little brother to a deadly virus, even as you're sitting in a car in the parking lot of the county health department, waiting your turn for an emergency test. We were able to easily deduce the following about Eugene's whereabouts on Saturday, the day of Eugene's exposure, three days before Dad's disappearance:

- Morning: Home (per alarm system, which was on all night and morning until John disarmed it at 9:43 A.M.);

- 9:43–9:55 A.M.: Driven by John to Henry's House (per John's text to Mom reporting safe arrival);
- 9:55–4:02 P.M.: Physical therapy, occupational therapy, vision therapy, speech therapy, and group socialization therapy sessions at Henry's House (per attendance/billing log in HH client portal), no other attendees or therapists of which had Covid or had been contacted by the Covid tracing team (per HH staff group-text chain);
- 4:02 P.M.: Picked up by Dad (per HH client portal);
- 5:27 P.M.: Brought home by Dad (per garage door notification history on Mom's phone, plus Dad's family group text saying he's home, about to start cooking, please vote for grilled salmon or veggie burgers for dinner (I didn't want either so I replied Dad shouldn't cook on Father's Day Eve and we should order pizza, Mom and John concurred, and Dad replied with an eye-roll emoji, which we interpreted as acquiescence));
- Rest of night: Home (per alarm system, which recorded no door openings after John got home at 6:14 P.M. with pizza he picked up at 6:08 P.M., per pizzeria email receipt).

This meant the exposure had to have occurred between 4:02 and 5:27, the only time window unaccounted for. We hadn't seen video recordings of any sessions after the solar/Mia's mouth one twelve days ago, but John checked Eugene's lesson progression log in the box we'd borrowed from Anjeli's office, and sure enough, they'd had a session on Saturday at 4:15 P.M. That settled it: the person with Covid who prompted the contact-tracing protocols for Eugene had to be Anjeli. (But questions in the back of my mind: Where was the video of this session? Was it simply a matter of Anjeli not having had a chance to upload it?)

We immediately called and relayed this information to Shannon, who seemed as excited as we were, saying she'd coordinate with her private investigator to follow up on our lead. "Before you go," she said, "I just heard: the evidence team is done drying the notebook, and they think they found a list of Adam's phone passcodes. I guess he changed it from time to time."

"I told him to do that," Mom said. "Jot them down somewhere to keep track. I've been looking for it everywhere. So the phone's unlocked?"

"They're still trying to decipher it. They're not numbers, more like clues. I have the list here, and some are easy, like *SSN backward first four,* or *mom bday,* but the last one says *add all H and add all Q.*"

"What in hell does that mean?"

"Exactly. Mia, you've looked through all the HQ notes and files. Any ideas?"

"No," I said. "Maybe adding the happiness level numbers in the experiments? But I don't have those pages yet."

"They said they sent you the final batch an hour ago. I know a lot's happening, but why don't you take some time to look through and see what you can come up with?"

"Makes sense," Mom said. "And John's trying to find another PPT therapist. We have to figure out how to get Eugene to spell with us."

I unlocked my phone as soon as the call ended. I'd missed a bunch of notifications while I was driving, including a message from Octavius: *Uploaded remaining pages from notebook's back section. Many pages illegible except top line (number, date).*

Shit. I hoped the experiment dated yesterday wasn't one of the illegible ones. I put in the password and scanned. Halfway through, I saw it: Experiment #24, dated yesterday. No text underneath, not even blurred and splotched. I figured there wouldn't be notes on the results yet, but I thought he'd have written what he was planning— the goal or setup, *something.*

Okay, I had to focus on the passcode. I found Dad's list in the back and studied the wording: *add all H & add all Q.* Ampersand, not a plus sign—Dad's passcode was 4 digits, so a 2-digit sum of all happiness levels and another 2-digit sum of all quotients from the experiments?

I went back and read from the beginning. From what I could make out, the experiments involved taking John and me on fun outings like movies, restaurants, and museums. For some, he gave us the same experience after setting opposite expectations (like he did with the first movie experiment). For others, he tried to establish opposite baselines by giving us different experiences; for example, he told me he got a one-year pass to this budget second-run cinema and took me there several times to lower my baseline for cinemas before taking John and me to the super-fancy IMAX restaurant-cinema. (I was kind of annoyed I got stuck with the crappy theater, but Dad switched it up for different categories, specifically noting "sibling parity and fairness issues"; I got the amazing restaurants and John the blah ones, for example.)

The strange thing was that even though John and I appeared to be the only subjects of the experiments, abbreviated J and M, there were several references to E written with a thicker-point pen, starting with Experiment #1:

#1: Lower expectation = happier experience? Yes BUT**.
— M high expectations (sent rave reviews)
— J low expectations (sent pans)
— Take to Q&D movie. Movie ratings: M = 2, J = 7, E: M2 = J5, J7 = M4
**BUT rating of whole day: M loved. J bummed anticipating bad movie
**Key lesson: Lowering expectations can ruin the experience. If you spend today telling yourself/family tomorrow will be bad, tomorrow may be happier, but boy, is today going to suck.
**E: Don't go into storm and be miserable all day just to be happier when you read by a nice fire.

Was E Eugene? But that didn't make sense. E could stand for experiment, equation, maybe some constant or variable I hadn't focused on. I looked for more Es and found two more, both in thicker strokes:

#6: Lower baseline, equal expectation = happier experience?
Yes.
— Gave M low baseline (take to budget run-down theater 3x)
— J kept regular baseline (keep taking to our regular AMC)
— Take both to fancy IMAX dinner cinema with heated reclining
    seats. M = 9, J = 8 (*E = 10)

#11: Possible to keep low baseline despite later "better"
experience? Yes.
— Kept reminding M new fancy cinema is once-only special treat,
    need to go back to budget theater
— Said nothing to J (his new baseline becomes fancy cinema?)
— After 1 month, took both to regular AMC. M said it's better than
    she remembered (compared to budget cinema), J complained
    about seats (compared to IMAX theater)
— M = 6, J = 5 (*E = 4 because fancy cinema is impossible to forget)

M, J, E, each with a rating. E had to be Eugene. Which meant . . .
what? That Dad had been reenacting his experiments with Eugene?
Could Experiment #24 have involved Eugene in the park, and it
went wrong?

Even more disturbing were two of his most recent entries, which
confirmed that he was expanding the scope of his experiments beyond John and me, beyond movies and restaurants. The first involved
the family vacation this summer our parents had been planning.

#23: Reminder of older, worse experience = lower baseline? TBD
(trip postponed).
— Family's starting baseline: no trips possible bc Eugene needed
    home routine
— 5 years ago: I went all out on luxury trip, used all my miles/points
    from business trips → became new baseline for whole family
— All trips since then have been so-so, compared to the luxury trip =
    whole family disappointed

— I need to lower the family baseline. Is this possible? Talk about
the years when we couldn't take vacation at all, how a "regular"
Parkson vacation = staycation

** 6/2020: Trip being postponed due to pandemic adds interesting
wrinkle. On the one hand, the pandemic lowers family's (and
society's) baseline such that we should get more pleasure out
of travel (and restaurants, plays, etc.). On the other hand, because
those outings are more rare, we might place unrealistically
high expectations on them. <u>Will the lower baseline and higher
expectations cancel each other out?</u>

Then, after the near-blank Experiment #24 and several blank
pages, this note:

<u>APPLYING PRELIMINARY FINDINGS TO FAMILY</u>: It's one thing
to play around with movies and restaurants, another to apply it
to more important decisions about the kids' futures and how we
handle (and how we teach the kids to handle) life-altering choices
and tragedies. *But in starting this new phase, I have to be wary of
unintended consequences. It goes without saying—you can't put your
loved ones through suffering to produce this dramatic differential.
Example: don't break up with someone to maximize their happiness
at the moment of marriage proposal—that would be cruel. A doctor
shouldn't tell a patient they're going to die just so they'll be happier
when it's revealed they're cured. (Also, this will piss off the lover/
patient so much they won't want to have anything to do with you
anymore. And rightly so!)

Dad's recognition of the cruelty and futility in intentionally making someone miserable in order to make them happier later seemed
promising, as was his writing the note this month about future trips,
but the reference to broadening his experiments to more important family matters was unnerving. The more I read, the more I sus-

pected he tried something with Eugene he thought was innocuous—beneficial, even—and then, something unplanned. Catastrophic.

Mom's phone rang. Mom was in the middle of sealing Eugene's vial of spit, so I answered on speaker. "We found her," Shannon said. "Tim, tell them. This is Tim, my most trusted PI guy."

A deep voice: "Hi. So yes, I found Ms. Rapari. Well, 'found' is kind of a stretch; all I did was leave a message on her office phone, and this woman calls back, says she's Anjeli's partner—girlfriend-partner, not business-partner, I asked; actually, she said 'fiancée but not official,' which I don't really know what that means—but the point is, you were right about her having Covid. Anjeli Rapari, I mean. She's apparently part of the whole detention center outbreak, which makes sense, given that she was on their list of recommended therapists."

My heart, which hadn't been feeling great anyway, felt like someone was grinding it in their fist. I took deep breaths while Tim continued to explain that Anjeli was currently in a hospital we'd passed twice that day and could probably see if I moved the car a few spaces over. She was apparently doing much better, which was why her fiancée was taking a break and finally returning calls.

"What about Adam?" Mom asked. "Does this fiancée know where he might be? Could he be at the same hospital?"

"No," Tim said, "I'm still checking the other area hospitals, but I confirmed that Mr. Parson is not at that particular facility. I have an inside source, a nurse who . . . never mind. Anyway, the fiancée said she's been with Ms. Rapari since Saturday night—even in the hospital; she's been camping out in her car in the parking lot, she said she's still there—and she hasn't seen your husband at all. She said she told the police this already, but Ms. Rapari was supposed to meet your husband and son at the park yesterday morning to help them resolve some conflict, but she got sick and she has asthma, so they rushed her to the hospital and she never made it to the park."

"I need to talk to her right now," Mom said. "What's her phone number?"

"She called back from a private number. In any case, she flat-out said she doesn't, quote, 'feel comfortable saying anything more.' She said the only reason she returned my call is because the police told her to, about the Covid close contact thing, for public safety."

For a good five seconds after the call ended, Mom didn't say anything. But I saw what lay in the direction of her gaze.

It was a nonsensical, ridiculous plan. We didn't know this person's name, didn't know what she looked like, didn't know what her car looked like, didn't have her phone number. Not to mention, it was borderline stalkery to go to a hospital parking lot to track down the loved one of a possibly dying patient, especially since she and we were both under quarantine orders due to exposure (although by the same person—did that cancel each other out?). Even if we could somehow miraculously find this woman, what useful information were we hoping to get from her? And yet, we all felt it. This inexplicable need to find her.

———

I READ A STORY IN high school English class about someone who goes to strangers' funerals because they crave the comfort it brings them to see others in pain, the concentration of grief in one room easing their own. I remember thinking what a stupid story about a crazy character and why didn't they just go get some therapy, which they clearly needed? I didn't know back then that there are some things you can't say out loud.

I thought of that story while driving through the hospital parking lot. I'd been to this hospital lots of times for Eugene's tests and appointments, but I'd never seen the parking lot so full. Mom had had the idea to make a sign saying DO YOU KNOW ANJELI RAPARI? and hold it up if we passed a car with a person sitting inside, which seemed like a good idea, but being here, we realized the sheer scope of this task given that most of the cars were occupied with people holding vigil for their loved ones inside the building, the Covid policy having turned the parking lot into one giant waiting area, all the usual intensity and anxiety of the inside space spread out, given room to breathe.

Still, we tried. While John held up the sign, I coasted up and down each row slowly and methodically, looking into the cars of the people talking on their phones, praying, eating, staring at the building, crying. A lot of crying. Is it weird that I felt a tinge of envy? Because yes, they were in this purgatory state of waiting, maybe some of them were even mourning their loved ones' deaths, but at least they had an anchor to ground their grief—they knew where their loved one was, had an idea of what was happening. Such an elemental thing we take for granted, like air, that once it's gone, you'd give anything to have it back.

We didn't find Anjeli's fiancée. No one responded to our sign. Still, I'm glad we went. Driving around in circles helped, similar to pacing when a family member is in emergency surgery—as a way to process the un-processable, to let the vibrations of the movement begin to shed off the shock.

Anjeli was engaged to a woman. Anjeli wasn't missing. The voice-mail wasn't The Other Woman pushing to confess their affair, but a therapist asking to tell a child's mother about his miraculous communication abilities. Anjeli's basketball and trampoline weren't copycat props for a secret second home but standard sensory equipment for a therapy waiting room. Even the yellow heart. For Therapist Appreciation Day last month, John had come home with a huge cookie saying *We love you! You're the best.* I could see Dad forgetting to get gifts for Eugene's therapists and making last-minute cards with the leftover paper and template from Mother's Day.

I'm a sucker for twist endings; I love to turn back immediately to the beginning and rewatch/reread, marvel at the impact of one assumption being upended, how the scenes are the same but their

meanings changed, things you didn't notice before popping out—
a great illustration of the selective perception and anchoring biases at
work. As fun as it is in fiction, though, it's shitty in real life, which is
probably true of most things. It was all I could do not to bonk myself
on the head while driving around the hospital parking lot, thinking
all this—heuristic bias or not, how could I have clung for so long to
the ridiculous notion of Dad running away for a clichéd midlife-crisis
affair and jeopardizing Eugene's life, even after I found out Anjeli
was Eugene's therapist? John kept insisting that wasn't Dad, but I
let my petty jealousies and hurt over Dad's frank assessments of me
(which, let's face it, were true) distort my view of him. What a hypo-
crite I was, going on about people making unfounded assumptions
about Eugene's intelligence level and people matching descriptions,
when I'd done worse, about someone I'm supposed to love.

It wasn't until later that night, when we put up Shannon's *What
Happened to Adam Parson?* chart and crossed off *Ran away (Anjeli
Rapari?)* that the answer came to me: not that I'd fallen into yet another heuristics trap I couldn't get out of, but that I chose to believe
in this idea at some level, magnified its plausibility on purpose. That,
as ludicrous as it sounds to say I liked the idea of my father having
an affair, that was in fact a fantasy I clung to because if you knocked
down this secret-lover premise, what did that mean? A domino effect: *Dad crazy with love* knocked down, leading to *Dad running
away* knocked down, leading to *Dad being safe (albeit being a despicable pig who deserves to die)* knocked down, and so on and so forth.
How many more knockdowns left until there remained no standing
blocks, even faltering or teetering, in which Dad was, or could be,
alive?

This wasn't some new revelation that hadn't occurred to me before. Ever since Detective Janus told us about Dad's backpack in the
water, I knew Dad might not be alive. But my belief in the possibility of Dad being alive, as tenuous as it was, had sustained me. Just
one not-impossible alternative that gave me an out, that lungful of

oxygen I'd needed to keep me from giving up on treading water and surrendering. Or maybe it was how mad it was making me at Dad, which, strangely, enlivened me. Does that sound absurd? But here's the thing—being furious at your dad feels so much better than grieving for him, being scared to death you'll never see him again.

# TWENTY-FIVE

# A *No* to the NO

YOU KNOW HOW SOMETIMES WHEN YOU FIRST GET BACK HOME AFTER a long trip, it seems a little different from how you left it? As if during that time away, the air inside your home has congealed into this unfamiliarity filter that warps your senses and things seem *just* askew enough to be noticeable—the faint smell of old paint dust in the air, the tilt of the waning sunlight as it beams in through the kitchen windows, the faded comforter on your bed; even the dimensions seem off, the rooms smaller, the ceilings lower.

That's how it felt returning home after our detour to the hospital parking lot. Home didn't feel like home. Walking into our house, wondering if we were now a family of four, felt both momentous and disorienting. Not just smaller in number, but unbonded and chemically re-formed into a different thing altogether, like $O_2$ versus $O_3$: oxygen, healing and necessary to life, versus ozone, dangerous pollutant. And yet, once we went inside, we had to carry on with the typical everyday stuff that seemed too insignificant to continue—think about dinner, drink water, use the bathroom, take out contact lenses. That's the thing about biology; it doesn't give a shit about outside emergencies.

This was especially true for Eugene. Eugene thrives on routine, and on a bewildering day like today, he needed a return to basics before he could handle anything else. Mom took him upstairs for his favorite predinner treat: a long, hot shower with no time limit. Not only because he deserved a little pampering—he'd been through hell several times that day—but because it allowed us to prepare for the thing we'd been waiting to do until we were finally settled at home: try to communicate with Eugene using Anjeli's stencil letterboard.

I know to some people, all our angsting and preparing might seem baffling. All Anjeli did was hold the board at an angle and height we can replicate and say, "I know you can do it!" If Eugene can do it with one person, why not with everyone else?

One thing we've learned through Eugene's many therapies is that it's not that simple. Many things in this world look easy, physically speaking. Take a conductor. The first orchestra concert I attended, I remember thinking, Why are people clapping for the conductor? Playing these instruments—*that's* hard. Whereas standing there and moving a baton around like a human metronome in a tuxedo—what's so hard about that? Why is he (and it's always a he; there are zero—I'm not exaggerating, *zero*—female conductors of elite orchestras in the world as of 2020, since Marin Alsop left Baltimore) the one getting the accolades, the highest salary? And then I tried conducting.

Lion tamers, skating coaches, all these people ordering the actual performers around—it seems like anyone could substitute in, but an untrained person copying a lion tamer's exact physical movements and sounds would get their head bitten off. It's not the external aspect, is my point, not just the person flicking their wrist a certain way that makes the lion not eat them, or that brings the instruments together and inspires the group as a whole to feel and transmit longing, joy, vivacity, etc. It's an ineffable talent, like leadership, that depends on a person's interpersonal connection and influence, which cannot be faked; the conductor has to know the music cold, the same way the lion tamer can't feel fear, because the lion knows. The conductor has to intentionally and confidently embody a certain emotion and let the baton embody it, too, zap that through the air, let it course through the musicians and *their* instruments, and will it to envelop the audience.

Just as important as the leader's talent is the relationship built with the performers through hours of practice and repetition. A genius maestro can't step in five minutes before a performance to conduct an orchestra they've never met, just like the world's best lion tamer can't step into the limelight with an uncaged lion they've never worked with.

John, whom Mom had tasked with going through Anjeli's notes and therapy materials, reported that it took 91 hours of Eugene giving one-word or -phrase answers based on short lessons before he made the milestone breakthrough of answering open-ended questions. Those hours consisted of:

- 32 hours practicing on the easiest stencils with 3 letters each;
- 18 hours on 8-letter stencils;
- 12 hours on 13-letter stencils; and
- 29 hours on a custom-made stencil for Anjeli's students, with all 26 letters plus numbers, "end of word," period, and common symbols. It's important to note that Eugene couldn't communicate openly before moving to a full letterboard, as he was dependent on Anjeli to anticipate which letter he needed and hold up the correct letterboard. It took him 29 hours of practice giving short close-ended answers on the full letterboard before he started freely expressing his own thoughts and "conversing" in an open way.

Just think: If it took Anjeli—an expert with years of experience working with dozens of nonspeakers with a variety of conditions, someone described on chat boards as The Nonspeaker Whisperer—that long to get Eugene to open up, how were we, who'd never even heard of this technique let alone ever attempted it, going to ask him traumatizing questions about something that freaked him out so badly he came home and didn't eat, didn't go to the bathroom, didn't do anything but jump and scream for hours, and expect him to answer?

A second factor uncovered by John's research: being family was a liability, with many nonspeakers unable to spell with family members even after reaching open fluency with therapists. This made sense because have you ever had your parents teach/tutor you (or, if you're a parent, tried to teach/tutor your own child)? In my family's experience, it's torture, ending in raised voices and tears for everyone involved. I don't know what it is, but everything my parents said, even (maybe especially) if delivered gently and lovingly, I couldn't help but take personally—as an expression of disappointment, a buried wish they had a different child. It made me vacillate between trying too hard, desperate to impress, and refusing to cooperate and giving up, both to cope with the anxiety overload and to punish them for putting me into that state to begin with. If getting better at math or baseball was this fraught, I couldn't imagine practicing communication with a nonspeaking child—the expectations, the fears, the anxiety magnified ten thousandfold.

But I didn't truly get it until I read a blog post explaining it as a chronic form of complex PTSD. Eugene and others like him had been suffering trauma their entire lives in which they'd been trapped, with no one realizing their bodies had been betraying them and locking in their thoughts. The absolute and final totality of this entrapment was devastating to ponder: not just challenged in one language for a few years like for Mom and me, not just in one mode of communication like for people who stutter or lisp, but shut down in *all* languages in *all* forms, including written and sign language, due to their motor issues, for all their lives. (It made me ashamed that I'd tried to compare Eugene's experience with my Korean bah-bo experience.) This psychological trauma added an extra burden that compounded the motor difficulties, made them exponentially harder to overcome. The consensus seemed to be that because family mem-

bers are the people with the longest history of loving but also not believing in you, around whom you've wrapped years of frustration and
maybe even betrayal and resentment, communication attempts with
them often activated and intensified this barrier of trauma. So even if
you had learned to communicate with someone who believed in you
fully from the outset, like Anjeli, you couldn't replicate that with just
anybody, most of all the very people who reminded you most acutely
of that debilitating history of doubt and shame.

This family-trauma barrier was not merely theoretical for Eugene. We saw it for ourselves. John found a video of Dad working
with Eugene during a session Anjeli labeled as "Parent coaching for
homework." I couldn't bear to watch more than a few minutes—it
was too painful, too awkward to linger on—but the snippets I saw
were of Dad seemingly doing all the things Anjeli had, using the
easiest three-letter stencils. The reason I say "seemingly" is because
of how differently Dad's imitated words and actions came across.
Anjeli's "Come on, Eugene" was an I-can't-stand-how-excited-I-am-
oh-my-God-I'm-on-the-verge-of-watching-a-fucking-miracle cheer,
like someone applauding a team crushing the other side. Dad's
"Come on, Eugene" sounded like a fan for the team getting crushed,
less I-believe-in-you encouragement and more what's-taking-so-long
complaint. Dad's smile was the kind the *Star Trek: TNG* android
Data puts on after analyzing pictures of human joy and replicating
their facial muscles. Maybe a robotic side-by-side comparison of Dad
versus Anjeli would have been fooled, but I knew. And you could
tell, Eugene absolutely knew. The look on Eugene's face—it was the
same expression from earlier when I'd been talking to him normally
(for once) about Dad's HQ notebook but stopped to test him. Every
part of his face drooping almost imperceptibly, by a millimeter—
disappointed, but at himself, like he should have expected that he'd
be condescended to like he'd been his entire life. Eugene wanted
nothing to do with Dad's questions. He stabbed the table with his
pencil, grinding it so hard into the wood that the lead broke.

I'm tempted to stop right here and skip over this next part because I don't like remembering it. Maybe that's why I'm fixating on theoretical justifications about families and Dad's shortcomings—as a preemptive defense, to put off for as long as possible the transcription we found in Eugene's therapy box.

It was hidden in the back pocket of a binder. God, listen to me— I say *hidden* like it's some nefarious thing but it wasn't like that, not hidden on purpose (although maybe it was, given the content). We'd seen in videos that Anjeli used loose sheets of plain paper to record their exchanges, hurriedly scrawling her questions, like 5 *types alt. energy?* but writing Eugene's responses letter by letter, in real time. She dated and kept them in a manila folder in the box. Anjeli's therapy binder had general notes for Saturday, June 20, their last session, but the transcription for that session wasn't in the manila folder with the others. John finally found it folded in half and tucked in the binder's back pocket.

It started out like the others, with Anjeli's questions from a lesson titled "Helen Keller Biography." But after a few short answers, the session shifted to a real back-and-forth exchange, Eugene replying with more than just a few words.

How does HK story make you feel?
  LUCKY I CAN SEE AND HEAR. BUT JEALOUS SHE GOT HER
  TEACHER AT AGE 7 AND HER FAMILY BELIEVED.
Your dad believes.
  THEN WHY DOES HE NOT TELL MY FAMILY?
He will soon. As soon as you can spell with him. You can do it if you try.
  I CANT BECAUSE HE DOESNT BELIEVE. AND HE DOESNT BELIEVE
  BECAUSE I CANT.

There it was. Such simple words encapsulating the central dilemma of their relationship. A vicious circle of doubt and trauma. It astonished me, made me feel a deep pride in Eugene, his ability to see his own situation so clearly and cut through to the essence of the stalemate he was caught in. It wasn't just that Dad was

untalented and awkward at being Eugene's communication partner.
It was more that he didn't fully believe. Dad was one of those naturally hyper-skeptical people. You know the type, who equate cynicism
with depth and intellect, who go around saying "anecdotal proof" is
oxymoronic, who demand objective evidence, by which they mean
quantifiable and replicable data from double-blind placebo-controlled
tests. (I know, because I used to be one of those people.) Based on
his excitement on the solar/Mia's mouth video, I think he'd started
to let that go, to truly believe in Eugene. But there remained a trace
of skepticism he couldn't fully hide, not without Eugene communicating directly with him, and Eugene couldn't do that at this early
stage of his learning process with someone he knew was faking it. It
was an impasse they couldn't break through, and it was hard not to
blame Dad for it. It takes time to build confidence and motor skills
to reach full fluency and independence. That's what Dad wanted,
needed, to let go of his residual skepticism, and that was unfair to
Eugene. Eugene deserved better from us. He was doing more than his
part, doing the impossible to overcome a lifetime of trauma and inborn
neural anomalies. Was it too much to ask that Dad overcome his inborn skepticism and just believe? Shouldn't the burden have been on
Dad?

But here I go again. Focusing on Dad to deflect the spotlight and
the ensuing blame. Because the next bit is what devastated me, what
I'm trying to avoid:

Let's show this to your dad, tell him how much it hurts to keep this from
your family.
    MAYBE.
It might be easier to spell with mom or sibs?
    MOM TREATS ME LIKE A BABY WITH NO BRAIN.
You're the youngest. My mom does that and I'm 48. How about J? He
has training, HH work.
    JOHNS TOO NICE. HE SAYS NOT TALKING DOESNT MATTER BUT
    THATS STUPID. HES A BIT TOO MUCH.

I almost laughed out loud because this was a parroting of something I thought all the time and said on occasion, especially the "bit too much" part. John was as nice and understanding as humanly possible, but it was like he was overcompensating. He went around saying how disabilities shouldn't and didn't matter, it's what's inside that matters, which was ridiculous because of *course* it matters whether you can talk or not, we live in the real world, and you'd better believe it mattered to Eugene. Still, Eugene's cynicism was disturbing; it's like when you see yourself through someone else's eyes and you cringe, and it made me want to defend John. Yes, John's hyper-optimism is annoyingly naive but it's because he loves you, and what's more, he's right. Not that it doesn't matter, but that it *shouldn't* matter.

But then Eugene continued: AT LEAST MIA DOESNT HIDE. SHE THINKS BEING SMART IS WHAT MATTERS AND IM STUPID AND WORTHLESS.

Reading this, I felt small. Literally, as in, I felt myself shrinking, the space between the atoms in my body narrowing, shortening, producing heat that encircled me. The searing honesty of those words, which I couldn't deny. Was I that transparent? I wanted to yell out that wasn't true, I didn't judge people in that way. But didn't I? It wasn't that I didn't love Eugene, or believe he was a worthwhile human being. But if I was being honest, truly and painfully honest, I was impressed by a person's verbal talents more than anything else. That's why the whole bah-bo thing with the Korean ajummas had been particularly painful for me. Math, I dismissed as something akin to manual labor, merely indicative of one's ability to contribute to society in a menial way, like a worker bee to a hive.[23] But verbal

---

23 I also think I dismissed the whole math thing because of the racial element. I remember once our high school AP math teacher making some joke about how even though we're twins, it's "uncanny" how I'm so much better at math than John is, given that I obviously have more of the Asian gene than John does (because I look more Asian, presumably?). When you're told there's an explanation for something you're good at, and that explanation is something no one particularly wants to be, it no longer seems desirable, especially to a kid. I think that's why the whole all-Asians-are-good-at-math thing is offensive to many Asians I

acuity, that was what I myself admired and equated with intelligence. Didn't everyone? Wasn't that why everyone loved those fast-talking (and therefore smart) characters in *The West Wing*?

I don't think any of us was eager to sit down with Eugene and a letterboard after this. We all felt horrible and inadequate in our own way. I thought Eugene's critique of me was the most disqualifying, although John disagreed, saying at least Eugene appeared to respect my position. No matter how you spun it, though, you couldn't get around the bottom line: Mom's and John's faults were of loving him too much, whereas mine was of arrogance, plain and simple. Being an asshole.

———

HERE'S HOW MOM DEALT WITH our dilemma: she apologized to Eugene. Not just with words, by saying it, but by truly showing it, acting like it, by talking to him about—God, I can't believe what I'm about to say—Noam Chomsky. Specifically, Chomsky's psycholinguistic nativism theory that humans have an innate ability to learn language, something that separates us from animals. I thought this theory was offensive because it made so-called "nonverbal" people *less than,* but I realized that she saw it differently, as validation of her belief that language, the ability, was there, an innate part of Eugene—in other words, that Eugene was not *nonverbal* but merely *nonspeaking*—and we needed to find the trigger to unlock and access it, activate that group of neurons or whatever.[24] In other words, she'd viewed Eugene with more generosity, less cynicism, than I had. "So you see, Eu-

———

know. It feels like an attempt to downplay something good and turn it into something bad. So if you're Asian and good at math, it's no big deal, just something that comes with your genes—a dismissal of a genuine talent. And if you're Asian and *not* good at math, you're a disappointment to your race, an anomaly. Can you blame Asians for being offended and annoyed by this stereotype? (Also, Mom thinks it has to do with the idea of math being robotic, to perpetuate the myth of Asians being cold and stoic, to which she says: Have you seen K-dramas?)

24 I have no idea if Chomsky interprets his own theory in this way, just that Mom does.

gene," she said, "I always believed you had words. You just couldn't express them because we failed you. *I* failed you. And I let guilt get in the way and tried to make up for it by treating you like a baby, doing everything for you, instead of respecting you.

"Well, that stops now. I don't know why your father didn't tell us, but I'm grateful he found Anjeli and opened this door for us. Her materials say we need to spend a lot of time building trust before we can expect you to spell openly with us, and I know she'd say it's unfair to ask you about Dad this early, on our first try. But given the situation with Dad, we can't ignore it. We have to try. So let me ask you, are you ready for that? Can we ask you about Dad and what happened in the park yesterday? It's okay if the answer is no, or nothing at all. I believe in you no matter what your response is. So knowing that, can we try? If you feel ready, I want you to answer YES."

Mom picked up the three-letter stencil board from Eugene's therapy box with X, Y, and Z, and she handed the yellow pencil to Eugene. He grabbed it tight in his hand the same way he had in the video with Anjeli, and he bent his arm into the ready-to-stab position. I felt the same sense of anticipation, the *whoosh* of blood in my eardrums, all of us moving forward a tenth of an inch, our breaths held. I zoomed in on the tip of the pencil gripped in his fist, moving so slowly toward the Y, time itself seemed to have slowed, the *thrum* of my heartbeat a rhythmic soundtrack to this unbearable scene, and in that moment, our collective hope became this palpable *thing* I swear Eugene could see and feel, enough to make up for Anjeli's absence, the very air itself brightening, and I heard it in my head, this anthem in G major, could already feel the tears of joy and relief, of sadness, too, for Dad. You could see the tension in Eugene's arms, his muscles bulging, his hands gripped so tight around the yellow pencil that it shook. Closer, closer, toward the right top of Y, and he slanted his wrist like the pencil was fighting him, trying to control it like an arm wrestling opponent, get it to bend to his will, and just as the pencil touched the top right of the Y, tip to tip, Eugene's wrist bent back, sending the pencil sliding across the slick plastic and through the Z.

My disappointment was nothing compared to Eugene's. He retracted the pencil back through the Z, his fingers gripped so tightly around the pencil that veins popped on the back of his hand and wrist. His lips remained upturned, but his jaw was tense, and he stared at his hand the way parents do at disobedient children—trying to be patient, chiding them while smiling through gritted teeth—as if asking his arm why it kept refusing to obey.

Eugene tried again, but faster this time, less intention, less expectation, less effort, and the pencil tip missed all the letters, ended up below X, nowhere near Y. On the third try, he bent his elbow but his wrist remained floppy and he dropped the pencil, not deliberately but more as if his fingers lacked the muscle tone to hold on. The pencil hit the table with a hollow *thwack.*

I wanted to scream and cry out, I was so frustrated. No wonder Eugene squeals and screeches and makes whatever piercing, loud noise he can. Try it yourself. I have, and even more than a garden-variety scream, a continuous screech at the highest possible pitch will grate your throat and create sharp vibrations in your sinuses that mix and bounce all around the hollow spaces inside your head, making it *hurt,* slicing straight through your deeper, chronic pain, eviscerating it. All afternoon, I'd been condemning Dad for keeping this whole PPT therapy from us, but it occurred to me just then: maybe we should be thanking him for sparing us months of this seesaw between elation and pain, belief and doubt, gratitude and guilt.

The one person who didn't seem frustrated was Mom. She handed the pencil back to Eugene with a patient smile. I wanted to kick her, say, *Can't you tell he's exhausted and demoralized?* But instead of holding up the XYZ board again, she picked up the MNO board, said, "Let's try something different. Same question—do you want to try to communicate with us?—but this time, spell out NO if you don't want to. It's okay if you don't."

Eugene took the pencil. He held it up and gripped it, squeezing as if to say, *Look at me. Look at my fingers. Look at me move my arm.* Slowly, he cocked his elbow back, that same ready-to-stab motion.

Very slowly, very deliberately, he turned his arm away from the board, and again slowly and deliberately, he brought the pencil down to the table, his eyes tracking the pencil so you couldn't mistake his intentionality, and only when the pencil thudded on the table, he let go and placed his hands together in the *calm hands* position, a quiet dignity in the firm grip of his interlaced fingers.

Look, I know that objectively, what happened was a failure. We got no information. No word. No progress. And yet, the energy that zapped through us at that moment—was I delusional? Were we all? Because why did it feel like success? Eugene looked triumphant. I felt it, could see it in Mom's face, John's. It was as unmistakable as if Eugene had uttered the word out loud. A *no* to the NO. Just because I couldn't quite say YES doesn't mean NO, doesn't mean I don't want to or can't communicate. Believe me. I am in here. I have things to say.

When Mom's phone rang, I wished she wouldn't get it. But of course she did. She had to. And maybe it was good that we were forced to move on. Because this confirmed Anjeli's warning that it would take a while to reach the point of useful communication, a real long-term effort, which wasn't appropriate for the acute-emergency situation we were in. It's like signing up for CPR classes when someone's drowning.

It was Shannon, calling with two pieces of not-great news. First, Tim's search of the hospitals in the area yielded no Covid patient matching Dad's description. (No one reacted; it's not like we seriously thought that was a possibility.) Second, she managed to get Anjeli's partner to call her by leaving a vaguely threatening message about a subpoena on Anjeli's office voicemail. "Worked like a charm, took less than ten minutes to call me back," Shannon said. "Like Tim said, she was pretty close-lipped. But she did let something slip that was, quite frankly, troubling."

God, what now? No one said anything, just stared at the phone as Shannon continued. "This woman—Zoe, her name is—said the reason Anjeli wanted to go to the park was to help resolve some conflict between Eugene and Adam. She refused to elaborate, but her reason for not saying more is that this 'conflict' involved some evidence she gave the police, and she didn't feel right helping a, quote, 'murder suspect.'"

Murder? What the fuck? We didn't even have a chance to react out loud because right as Shannon was telling us not to overreact— she said many laypeople used *murder* for any homicide including involuntary manslaughter, which was a far cry from murder—our doorbell rang, followed by a quick knock.

I automatically thought: police. I knew the whole police-always-tell-the-family-bad-news-in-person thing hadn't exactly borne itself out, but instead of making me discount it as a myth, it made me positive the next time, the next ring, would be *it;* it was inevitable and we couldn't escape it forever. Mom asked Shannon to hold on and went to answer the door, but a few steps toward it, she said, "Oh my God," her head turned toward the window to our driveway, her body going still, mid-step, mouth open, like one of those petrified corpses from Pompeii. I stood up to look out the window. A police car.

I ran straight to the door, overpassing Mom, the opposite of the previous day when I stood paralyzed at the door for a full minute. I opened the door without putting on a mask, looking through the peephole, anything, just flinging it wide open, and I screamed. Not a little yelp of surprise or even a regular one-second scream, but a piercing, sustained, hands-to-my-mouth, bloodcurdling horror-movie *scream*.

Between two uniformed officers, the same ones from yesterday, stood the last person I expected to see.

It was Vic.

# TWENTY-SIX

# The Bright Cerulean Sky

VIC HAS GIVEN ME A LOT OF GRIEF ABOUT THAT SCREAM. THIS EXACT progression of words and facial movements at least ten times, easy, since that moment: "You scared the shit out of me," said with a slow shake of the head, followed by, "Not cool, Mia. Really not cool."

Admittedly, it was not good, the effect of that scream on the police officers and my family. Vic wasn't handcuffed, but one of the officers grabbed his arm as if to stop him from attacking me, and the female officer put her hand on what appeared to be a gun, frightening me into stopping. But in my defense, I recovered really well, especially given the ensuing chaos and cacophony—Mom and John yelling variations of "Oh my God, what's wrong? Who is that?," Eugene jumping and squealing, and Vic yelling, "For God's sake, Mia, tell them you know me." I could have really screwed him by saying, "Do I really though?" the way I was thinking, but I just said, "Sorry, Officers, I don't know why I did that just now."

"So you know this young man?" one officer said while the other said, "There was a complaint against him at the park, and he said you could vouch for him. He said he's your boyfriend."

There was a tiny part of me, the part still pissed and bitter about the whole semi-ghosting thing, that wanted to say, "Oh really? That's interesting because he's not," but I noticed the officer's hand still on the gun-shaped object, so I forced myself to take the high road and say, "Yes, he's my boyfriend," without adding *former* the way I was thinking, which might have done the trick of getting the police to relax, except for Mom saying, "*Boyfriend?*," and John saying, "What? Since when do you have a boyfriend?," which made the officers frown at Vic suspiciously, making me realize they thought something very strange might be going on here, like maybe this big Black dude had kidnapped Dad and was forcing me to say I was his girlfriend, but then Vic looked at me, all wounded, and said, "You didn't tell your family about me? Not even John?"

"Can we please discuss the nature of our relationship later?" I said (thinking, Hopefully never? I really did not want to have to deal with further recriminations from Mom about not sharing details of my love life with the family). "And could someone explain to me what's going on? What complaint? What happened?"

"I heard about your dad," Vic said. "I'm so sorry." He looked at Mom, John, and Eugene. "I can't imagine what you all must be going through. Once I heard, I couldn't stay away and do nothing. I told my parents I wanted to help search, and they said okay, so I got in the car and started driving."

"You *drove*? From *Ohio*?"

"It's only eight hours. I started at six and got here around two and went straight to the park. I just wanted to help. I wasn't going to bother you, that's the last thing I wanted to do, but . . ." Vic looked down and bit his lip, like he was trying to figure out how to say something. "Once I was here, I just really wanted to see you, see if I could help in any other way. But I didn't have your address, so I couldn't just come over. So I was trying to figure out how to get in touch with you because . . ."

"Because I blocked you." I looked over to the others to explain. "We had a fight yesterday morning and kind of broke up."

"I asked this woman if I could use her phone to text you, but she was all suspicious, and her hat blew off so I got it for her, and she went crazy and told me to get away. I tried to explain I already had Covid so I'm immune—"

"You had Covid? Are you okay?" Mom said.

I intervened. "Don't worry, Mom, it was months ago. I told you some of my friends got it right before everything shut down, remember? That's why I had to quarantine before coming home."

"Yes, I'm fine now. Anyway, this woman seemed to think I was saying I had Covid *now,* and she got all paranoid and she pepper-sprayed me—"

"What? She actually sprayed it?" I turned to the officers. "Is that legal?" I asked Vic, "Are you okay?"

"Yeah, no, I'm fine. I started running as soon as she reached into her purse. I thought for sure she was grabbing a gun, and . . ." Vic's jaw tensed up. "Anyway, I screamed at her that that was uncalled for and I may have accused her of racism and hating Black people—"

"For good reason," I said. I was livid.

"—and she got offended and said she's making a citizen's arrest and all this crazy nonsense. Anyway, she called 911 and these officers were nearby."

The female police officer said, "We know this woman. She makes a lot of complaints, especially about teenage boys, and we've gotten complaints about her using pepper spray at that park. We'll definitely follow up with her, but given the situation with your father and this young man claiming to be your boyfriend but not knowing your address or being able to call or text you, all that, we thought we should escort him and make sure everything checked out."

"I really appreciate you officers doing that. It was really considerate of you to take the time to go out of your way to make sure I was okay," Vic said in this awkwardly serious voice I wasn't used to.

"Did you, um, leave your car at the park?" I asked, and Vic nodded.

"These officers thought it made sense for me to ride with them."

I reached for his hand. It was trembling a little and cold, even though it was a hot day. Clammy. I stepped closer and looked up into his eyes, and it was like all the pent-up sadness and fear and anger and frustration hit me at once, seeing Vic looking so vulnerable and scared and also thinking about him just getting in the car even though I'd blocked him, even though he didn't know our address, even though I'd been an insensitive coward afraid to talk to him about hard and uncomfortable things, and after that long drive, trying to call me and thinking he might be shot by a shrill woman and again by two cops who put him in the back of their car like he was a criminal, and him then having to be overly polite to them the way I knew his parents had made him practice, and I couldn't help it, I kind of forgot myself, forgot about our breakup and the semi-ghosting and his infuriating sanctimony from yesterday morning and just threw my arms around him and buried my face into his chest and he put his arms around me and we kind of rocked back and forth and cried together. God, we were a mess.

I heard Mom tell the police officers that everything was okay and we would take care of Vic, and their reply that they were going back to the park, no news on Dad yet. They left, and Mom hem-hawed an "Um, so we'll go inside and . . . just come in whenever you'd like." As the door closed, I heard John say, "I guess they're back together?"

After I stopped crying and unburied my head and we went inside, but before I had a chance to do the awkward family introductions, Vic said to everyone, "I didn't want to say this in front of the police. And I am so sorry again for just barging in like this at this horrible time, but the reason I had to try to contact you is that I found something I have to show you."

He explained that after arriving at the park and searching for Dad for an hour or so, he realized the flyers posted around the park didn't have the special hotline number (888-FIND-ADAM) and email address (findadam@gmail.com) he'd seen online, offering reward money for information. He decided this was a better way to help and created a flyer on his phone (including a more recent picture of Dad from Instagram) and sent it to a print shop nearby, picked up 250 copies, and spent the rest of the afternoon putting them on car windshields, posting them, and handing them out to people around the park. Most people said they already knew about Dad and sorry but they didn't know anything, but some said they saw him and no, nothing huge to report, but they'd contact the police anyway and took the flyer.

After a few hours of this, he came across a woman who said she might have something. She'd spent the previous morning at a park on the Maryland side of the river, and while videotaping birds from an island in the middle of the river, she had heard screaming. She hadn't heard about Dad—she was an out-of-towner on some bird-watching trip down the East Coast and had just gotten to Virginia that afternoon—and showed him her video. Vic realized immediately it was Dad and said so, at which point she tried to email the video to the police but it wouldn't send because the file was too large. Vic offered to help (she was older and apparently not tech-savvy) and, while pretending to edit it down in size, surreptitiously AirDropped himself the video. The most important part: having seen the video, he thought it imperative that the police not see it (or at least that we see it first) so he said he couldn't reduce the file size enough to send. She said she didn't have time to bring her phone to the police station due to her tight travel schedule, so hopefully, that would be that, and the police would never get this video.

Thankfully, Vic didn't tell us this whole saga before showing us the video, except for the last part about there being a good chance the police didn't have this video and hopefully they never would. After seeing the video, I understood why Vic took the extra seconds to say this prior to playing it, but at the time, it freaked me out—not only the torture of waiting but wondering: What was so horrible on the video that it was important the police didn't see it? "Vic, what is on this video? Can you just play it?" I managed to say.

Vic held up his phone and clicked on a video marked June 23

11:09 A.M. It opened on a super-zoomed close-up of a red bird chirping, the volume turned all the way up, then an abrupt stop as Vic skipped forward to the eight-minute mark. "It starts around here." 11:17 A.M. More than an hour after the mommy-blogger video. Around twenty minutes before Eugene's near-run-in with the car right outside the park. I got a sick feeling in my stomach, like my heart had dropped into my stomach and my stomach had further dropped into my intestines and I could feel my heartbeat there, pulsating behind my belly button.

Finger still on the screen, the image frozen on a bird in flight in the cloudless blue sky, the glare of the sun just above the frame, Vic looked up. "Eugene, this might be really upsetting. You sure you want to see?" Vic said, looking behind me, his speaking normally to Eugene making me fall a little more for him. I think it had the same effect on Eugene. Normally, the sudden appearance and presence of a stranger like Vic would freak him out even more, but Eugene was calm, taking a large step toward Vic and his phone—right foot forward and then left foot joining it precisely, deliberately, like a drum major in a marching band. A nonverbal *Yes, I'm sure. I want to listen.* Vic looked at Mom, and she nodded.

For six long seconds, there was nothing. Just the bird in the sky, the roar of the water in the distance. And then, a voice. Yelling. Almost inaudible because of the way it blended with the water's roar, so you had to pluck it out and focus on it to make out the words: *Hey, no! What are you doing? No, Eugene, don't do that.* Nothing but birds and water for a few seconds. *Stop. Stop fighting me. Help. Someone help me.* The camera was jerking all around, the bird-watcher clearly putting the phone down and moving her body, and then Dad's voice again, a long *Eugene, nooooo.*

The woman said, *Oh my God, what is that?*, which I'd thought was in response to the screams, but right then, a huge flock of black birds flew up from the jagged cliffs and tree branches, making this beautiful fluttering, as if you were looking at a painting and a whole swath of trees you assumed were in the shade because of their dark leaves all shook and the darkness lifted like a pointillist special effect, the shadow rising into the air like smoke and ash, the chorus of caws and wing flaps drowning out Dad's scream. Before the recording stopped and the video ended, a blur of images flashed by: the jagged cliffs in the distance, the churning water below, then a flip to the bright cerulean sky above, the black birds rising up and up and up.

# PART V

## THIS IS NOT A
## MISSING-PERSON STORY

# TWENTY-SEVEN

# The Veil of the Waterfall

A PAUSE TO PONDER A QUESTION (*THE* QUESTION, ACCORDING TO SHANnon): What do you think the series of screams in the bird-watcher's video meant?

Could the answer be *nothing*? What if I told you I fervently believed those screams had nothing to do with Dad being missing *and* were unrelated to Eugene's earlier meltdown in the mommy-blogger video? Would you be incredulous, the way Shannon was? Laugh nervously as if I were becoming delusional, the way John did? Or guess that I was overcompensating for what I was really thinking, the way Mom did?

Before I explain, let me tell you something else first. (And if you're thinking this is a preemptive justification for what I was really thinking, you're probably right.) There's a concept in cognitive psychology based on Type I errors—false positives, which is when we believe in connections that don't, in fact, exist. We humans are bred for them. Back in the hunter-gatherer days, if you saw the tall grass move, it could be the lion you heard roaring in the distance yesterday, or it could be nothing, just the wind. Those who assumed it was the lion—who superimposed a causation-dependent narrative around the rustling grass—survived, whereas if you assumed it was nothing, being wrong could cost you your life. Over time, the theory goes, our urgent need to expect the worst or get eaten got passed down at a genetic level; our brains got hardwired to connect the dots and see patterns and associations. We invent causation. Which is to say, we invent narrative.[25]

When I first heard that *Nooooo* scream and every time I've re-listened to it (and I have, many times), there's a pause, like a power surge has blown out all circuitry in my brain, and it takes a good ten seconds for everything to reset. When my brain started back up the first time, what came to me was this: an instant replay of the terrifying audio, but accompanied by a movie in my mind, my brain filling in what might be happening offstage. A continuation of the previous mommy-blogger video, with Dad's broken glasses still hanging off his face, Dad frustrated with Eugene—saying, *Come on, Eugene, I know you're upset but you've got to learn to control yourself, you* will *do what I say, stop fighting me*—and Eugene also frustrated, his anger at Dad intensifying into fury, eyes squeezed shut, just wanting Dad to get away and shut up, a push, his arms snapping the way he did with me, Dad caught off guard, falling back, his arms flailing, screaming out, *Eugene, nooooo,* down and down and down.

This, or something like this, is of course how the police saw it, probably how most people would see it, not surprising given our innate bias for causation-driven narrative—needing to connect Eu-

---

25 Some people think dreams are nothing more than random images generated by our brains, but our need for causation and narrative is so strong that we layer stories upon them, which make sense in the moment, but after a while, that fades, leaving us with only the images, and we realize our superimposed story made zero sense. This theory also explains why people see Jesus's face in trees and animal shapes in clouds.

gene's earlier meltdown to this later scream, and to further connect the scream to Dad going missing.

But sometimes the rustling of the grass really is just the wind. Or a frog. Or the ground shaking from an earthquake miles away.

Just like here. The scream could be completely unrelated to Dad's disappearance. It might have been the tail end of Eugene's earlier meltdown, and by screaming at him to stop, Dad might have shocked Eugene out of the meltdown, and then ten minutes later, while standing at the edge of a cliff, pointing out the birds to Eugene, Dad had a sudden stroke or heart attack. A freak accident. Or Eugene rebelled against hard therapy exercises and ran away, prompting Dad to call out for help, and later, while searching for Eugene in the woods, Dad tripped and fell. Or maybe the scream *was* related, but the causal chain reversed—that is, Dad really did want to run away or kill himself and staged the yelling, knowing someone was within earshot, to make it look like an accidental death for insurance purposes.

Are you convinced?

Neither was Shannon. "This isn't a movie. This is real life, and we have to be realistic, no matter how painful," she said.

"That's my point exactly," I said. "This *is* real life, and in reality, weirdly coincidental, unconnected things happen all the time. It's only in made-up stories that things have to be related to everything that came before, or we call them deus ex machina and dismiss them as 'unrealistic.' But this is not a movie, it's not a novel, and in real life, 'the scream means nothing' is just as likely as anything else."

"That may well be, but the problem is that the police and prosecutors and judges have the same evolutionary programming we all do, so they won't buy it. And when the prosecution says there's enough evidence to go forward on a manslaughter charge, I need to be able to say no, that's ridiculous, because what happened is obviously *this*. And the *this* needs to be a story that does two things: one, explains all the evidence and ties it up in a neat little bow; and two, exonerates

Eugene. So we *do* need to come up with a story. A plausible one that they, with their genetically preprogrammed ideas of what's 'realistic' and 'believable,' will not laugh at."

I didn't say anything. Couldn't.

"What," Shannon said, "is that story?"

———

TALKING TO SHANNON, A HORRIBLE idea occurred to me. What if we never find the answer? I hate leaving puzzles incomplete, cannot stand equations I can't solve, get infuriated by those giving-audience-agency stories without definitive answers—*The Little Prince* (Dad's favorite book and thus the first of these types of books I ever read), Dad's old Choose Your Own Adventure books, the *Black Mirror* episode "Bandersnatch" with its over one million variations, *Life of Pi*, *Inception, The Sopranos*'s ending. There's this mathematician philosopher who, story has it, spent more than ten years trying to prove an equation and another twenty years trying to prove the equation wrong. He died without ever solving it, either way, his whole life a morass of ambiguity.

The thing about the mystery of Dad's disappearance is that there *is* an answer. Something happened to Dad. The problem is that Dad might be the only person who knows the answer. That's what makes true missing-person cases the ultimate mystery, the broadest and deepest: when you hear someone's vanished, you not only don't know the who-/how-/why-dunit (like in other crimes), but you also don't know what in hell *it* could even be. You don't know anything; all possibilities are open. When you find something, anything definitive, it becomes a different type of case—murder, suicide, kidnapping, amnesia, runaway, lost in the woods. Until then, as long as it remains a missing-person case, there's no body to test, open, or study. No murderers and kidnappers to try to catch and interrogate.

I think this is why missing-person mysteries are so popular in TV, movies, novels.[26] Why strangers are coming out to the park to look for Dad, clicking on the "Local Man Missing" article. Our brains are hardwired to want resolution, to want the answer. The bigger and broader the mystery, the deeper the satisfaction when it's resolved (a variation on Dad's low baseline theory). They turn the pages and join the search party, to accelerate the process of solving the puzzle, of turning it into a different kind of story.

Here was my fear: that Dad's story was a missing-person story and would remain one. Another thing that's fun for some in fiction but horrible in real life.

From Shannon's perspective, though, this wasn't something to fear, but to hope for: having Dad's case stay a missing-person case—that is, an unsolved, unsolvable case—was the safest thing for Eugene, unless we could explain the damning recordings in a way that exonerated him.

———

IT CAME TO US LATER that night. I don't even know how late it was, but we had all been doing different things—Mom going through Dad's insurance policies and financial accounts, John going through Anjeli's therapy videos, Vic and me getting his car from the park and then working to find the password to Dad's HQ files, which was surprisingly easy now that I knew what Q stood for (the 8-letter password was Quotient)[27]—while Eugene streamed videos on the family room TV.

———

26 There are so many of them. I've read/seen a lot of them this summer, I suppose hoping for insights, a new avenue of inquiry we hadn't thought of. Based on my perusal of the genre, most of the missing are girls/women (87.9 percent), with the missing-men stories all being espionage- or mafia-related. (Also, I've only read one genuine missing-person story that remained a missing-person story, which is to say, it remained unsolved: Tim O'Brien's *In the Lake of the Woods*, which Mom and Dad loved because, among other reasons, they happened to both be reading it when they met and had a heated discussion about it on their first date.)

27 You know when you're trying to open a jar that's stuck for like a full minute, and someone comes along and easily opens it? There's a logical answer to this,

At some point, John, Vic, and I came downstairs for snacks and ended up watching TV with Eugene for a break. I sat next to Eugene on the couch, and he seemed more comfortable with me, and me with him, than we'd been in a long time. He put his head on my shoulder, the oversized six-button remote in his hand, and fell asleep. John dimmed the lights and lowered the TV volume. We sat like that for a while, silently staring at the strangely hypnotic cartoon superheroes.

I don't remember falling asleep, but I must have dozed off, because at some point the TV had switched to an anime. I looked around and Vic was asleep, stretched out on the other sofa. Eugene was fully prone, too, his head on my lap for a pillow, feet on John's lap. Both of them were snoring, the syncopation off by a bit—Eugene's loud snores in 5/6 time, Vic's soft ones in 4/6.

John was awake. Fully awake, not a trace of sleep on his face, sipping water. He saw me stir, gave me a smile, a tiny one that looked sad. "I like him," he whispered, pointing his chin at Vic.

"Me, too," I whispered back, "except when he's being infuriating," which wasn't true. I liked him even—maybe especially—when he was being infuriating. The glow from the TV screen was casting light on Shannon's chart. "I hope Dad can meet him. He's a psych major. They'd have so much fun pontificating about repressed happiness or whatever."

"So you're back together?"

Were we? "I don't know. We haven't really discussed it. Doesn't seem like the right time."

---

which is that yes, you really did loosen it, and in the meantime, your hands have gotten cramped and sweaty, and someone else with non-sweaty, non-tired hands tries a slightly different angle. Fresh hands, fresh fingers, fresh approach. (Note: I may or may not have made this whole thing up. I know I've read about this before but I couldn't find any evidence to back it up, even on Reddit. (But it sounds true, doesn't it?)) Anyway, this is definitely what happened with the password. After I showed Vic the (I swear I'm not exaggerating) 467 variations and combinations of family birthdays, anniversaries, initials, etc. that I'd tried, explaining how none of them worked, he asked, did you try variations on *happiness quotient*?

"Why didn't you ever tell us?"

I'd been thinking about it. Vic, the major, all that. "College seems like a very different world than home and you guys, you know? When I'm there, everything here seems really distant, not really relevant to that world, and when I'm here, vice versa. I don't know."

We stared at the TV for a while. When whatever that show was ended, while credits played, John said, "You remember the thing with the bike in Seoul?"

We had been eleven or twelve. I'd been teasing John about something trivial, I don't remember what, and John got mad and pushed me, not even hard, and I stumbled, just enough so one foot went off the sidewalk onto the street, into the path of a bike. The bicyclist veered in time, barely grazed me, but he screamed Korean curses at me, and Mom went berserk, going on about how that could have been a car or a bus, just dumb luck I wasn't killed. I thought she was being hyperbolic and tuned it out, but John had been traumatized, apologized to me in tears, and took over my chores for a month as self-punishment.

"When Vic played that video," John said, "that's what I thought of. How it can happen so quickly. Being mad, then just, snap. Wanting to hurt someone, just for a second, and not even thinking about the consequences. And if you're unlucky, then . . ."

He looked down at Eugene, his sleeping face. Such an innocent smile, his long lashes casting shadows on his puffy cheeks. "Is it bad that I think . . . maybe that's what happened?"

I wanted to confess that I'd had the same thought, and worse, I kept seeing the clip of an angry Eugene pushing Dad off a cliff like a meme in a repeat loop, but I couldn't say it. I swallowed, managed to say, "No. I don't think that's bad. I think that's understandable."

"If you could choose, like if this was like those Choose Your Own Adventure books, what would you say happened to Dad? What would you hope for?"

John knows I hate those stories. Besides, whatever happened had already happened. Indulging in optimistic fantasies was not only a pointless waste of time but dangerous, leading to a subconscious raising of our baseline that might tee us up for an even more traumatic disappointment when we found out what actually happened to Dad. On the other hand, wouldn't it be a relief to displace the awful, disloyal video in my head with a new one? Not a fairy tale but not the worst-case scenario, either—something realistic that, if we never found the answer, we could tell ourselves may well be the truth, to bring us comfort. What would that be?

"Maybe they were at the waterfall," I said, thinking of Dad's and Eugene's favorite place.

"The overlook. That's what I thought of, too."

I pictured it in my mind. What would they be doing? "Maybe they were having lunch," I was saying, when a near-simultaneous flash of lightning and thunder jolted me. Strange—I couldn't even see any rain outside.

Eugene stirred, his eyelids fluttering, and I patted his chest and whispered "shhhhh" into his ear to calm him the way Harmonee taught me when he was a baby. John gently placed his hands on Eugene's legs, pressing down to let the weight soothe him. Eugene settled back into the deep breaths of sleep, and I stroked his hair, his breaths warming my hand. As my fingers grazed his forehead, I felt a tingling zap, a mild static electricity. Eugene's legs twitched, and John felt it, too, sat up a little.

The zap, the late hour, the darkness, the occasional flashes of lightning and thunder, the jibber-jabber of Japanese from the TV— these all fed an eeriness in the air. I'd later come to regard it with suspicion, wonder, and everything in between, depending on the day, but at that moment, it felt almost magical—John's and my hands touching Eugene, the three of us connected skin to skin, bonded into one unit. And maybe it was the sound of the rain that started falling just then, but I could see it in my mind—the misty veil of the waterfall, Dad and Eugene at the picnic table at the overlook, red birds in the tree nearby.

I linked eyes with John, and we continued our story, letting the rhythm of our old logic-chain game take over, our words in whispers, softer than the sound from the TV:

- They're having lunch at the picnic table. Dad points to a tree. Look!
- They stand up, go look. Birds, flying away.
- Eugene claps, jumps up and down. Laughs.
- They play a game. Eugene wins. They're celebrating. High fives.
- Dad heads back to the picnic table. Time to pack up, Eugene! But wait, people are there, going through Dad's backpack. Teenage boys.
- Dad yells, Hey, don't touch that, leave that alone. Starts chasing them.
- The boys take the wallet and throw the backpack—too hard, it misses Dad and it's going to go over the cliff . . .
- And Eugene's trying to catch it and Dad's screaming at him to leave it alone, but he keeps reaching, his back is to the cliff and he's backing up, getting nearer to the edge . . .
- His feet are on the edge, half-off, and he's losing his balance and falling backward, he's going to fall . . .
- But Dad gets him, he grips his arm, but Eugene's freaking out . . .
- Dad's yelling for him to calm down, stop fighting him, stop pushing him away, stay still, and Dad's desperate, panicked, yelling for help, screaming . . .
- And then . . .
- And then . . .

We didn't need to say the rest. It was easy to deduce from everything that came before and after, easy to see—in ourselves, in each other. Dad's fingers tightly gripping Eugene's arm, pulling, pulling, the gravel sliding his feet closer and closer to the unstable edge, and then the final effort, a last act of courage to save his son. An attempt at an even exchange, a body for a body: a huge tug hurling Eugene up and over onto safe ground, but the force required for the effort sliding Dad's feet off and beyond the cliff's edge, the two bodies crossing mid-air to change places, the terror of the fall overcome, overtaken, by the comforting knowledge that cushions him: Eugene is safe. He will live.

Hot tears filled my eyes, and I closed them, overwhelmed by my relief at these new images. The relief that what I saw exonerated Eugene *and* gave meaning to Dad's death, restored him in our eyes as the loving, self-sacrificing father he'd been.

"I've been thinking something similar," Vic whispered, rousing me from the semi-haze of the world in my mind. When did he wake up? It made me nervous, how I hadn't even noticed when his snoring stopped, and I looked at Eugene: Had he also—? No, he was still asleep, still snoring, though faster, louder, than before.

"Eugene's in danger," Vic continued, "and your dad falls trying to save him. That explains everything he yelled, and the boys stealing the wallet explains why it wasn't in the river with the backpack. It's perfect, does everything Shannon said."

It hadn't occurred to me until he said it, that this was the story our lawyer asked us to brainstorm: a story that incorporated the existing evidence *and* exonerated Eugene. Had our brains been whirring away in the background as we were watching TV, dozing, dreaming, and at a particularly vulnerable moment of peak fatigue, jolted awake by static electricity, we played our old twin mind-meld game to come up with our best joint answer?

It made perfect sense. At the time, I was even grateful to Vic for the reminder of our assignment, the confirmation we'd found the solution. But one thing I'm sure of now, because of the doubts it raised, because of everything that came after—I wish Vic hadn't said anything. I wish he had stayed asleep. Most of all, I wish John and I hadn't spoken it out loud, this beautiful, terrible scene in our minds, wanting to confirm it with each other, with spoken words, wanting to make it real.

# TWENTY-EIGHT

# Whispered Screaming Practice

WHEN EUGENE WAS BORN, BEFORE OUR PARENTS BROUGHT HIM HOME from the hospital, Harmonee made us practice being as quiet as possible. A newborn needs uninterrupted sleep and startles easily, she said, so we had to tiptoe and whisper, no sudden movements. What if something scary makes us scream? I asked. Or a funny joke makes us laugh out loud?

That's when she made us practice whispered screaming and laughing, something she said she and her siblings mastered during the Korean War. (Just the screaming, she clarified; she didn't remember uncontrollable outbursts of laughter being a problem.) Her family had slept in the same room—when you're under attack, she said, you don't want to be alone; you crave closeness with your loved ones, the comfort of facing terror and death together—and before going to bed every night, they'd practice whispered screaming to train themselves to remain quiet no matter what. She modeled for us, and we copied: a deep breath in, eyes and mouth open wide, then a high-pitched but barely audible *AHHHH*. We weren't very good at it—we kept giggling—until Harmonee made it a contest. The prize: our favorite ramen, the cheap kind with MSG Mom forbade.

All of us kids falling asleep in one room must have triggered this memory, because I dreamed about it. Harmonee was telling a toddler-aged Eugene he could beat John and me by making no sounds at all, all the time. And then fast-forward to a present-day Eugene in bed, waking up—a deep breath in, mouth open wide to release a scream, jubilant and utterly silent. He closed his mouth and said in an unremarkable teenage-boy voice, "I won! Who's making me my ramen?" A semi-corporeal Harmonee materialized, beaming in, à la Star Trek, and was telling him how proud she was of his unmatched mastery of the game when a phone rang and woke me.

It was storming, the heavy streams of rain pelting the window so hard I was amazed I'd slept through the noise. Eugene's head was still on my long-asleep right thigh, but his eyes were open, looking out the window. He noticed I was awake and raised his head and sat up, smiled at me. No high-pitched vocals, no jumping upon waking for the first time I could remember. It made me wonder again about the disconnect between your real self and the way everyone else sees you. I'd always assumed his morning wailing was due to his joy over a new day, an alarm to get the rest of us to wake up and join him. It hadn't occurred to me that it might be a cry of frustration—at leaving the dream world where his inner and outer selves finally matched, returning to this cruel one where he was a bah-bo.

"You're up," Mom said, walking in from the kitchen as John and Vic stirred awake. "Shannon called. Detective Janus is demanding to talk to us. We're getting on Zoom with them both in fifteen minutes. Shannon thinks the police may have gotten the recording."

To tell or not to tell Detective Janus about the bird-watcher recording was an issue we'd dissected with Shannon last night. On the one hand, the police seeing it wouldn't help in the search for Dad, as the area in the video had been searched many times over, but on the other, in terms of providing ammunition against Eugene, it was potentially catastrophic. We had to keep it locked away and hope the police never got ahold of it. It was a flimsy hope, we knew. The bird-watcher said she didn't have time to follow up, but she could've easily changed her mind—what was a little inconvenience, given the $1,000 reward (which, of course, my family was providing)?— or the police could get the same clip from others in the park at the same time, maybe closer, with visuals to match. But there's no harm in hoping, so let's do nothing, Shannon and Mom decided.

I wish I'd said something about the dangers of unwarranted optimism; it might have saved us from the consequences of what would prove to be a clear tactical error.

————

SHANNON'S FACE FILLED OUR SIXTY-INCH high-def TV, and my heart jolted. It had seemed a good idea to use our biggest screen—Dad had used it for Eugene's occasional virtual therapies to mimic the experience of having the therapist in the room—but seeing our lawyer's five-times-bigger-than-life-sized face was too much to handle first thing in the morning. I think I'll probably always have this visceral reaction to her, to any lawyer, really. You only need them if you're in trouble, so you don't want to have anything to do with them.

"Detective Janus is joining in a few minutes," Shannon said. "I don't know what this is about. Under normal circumstances, I wouldn't allow her to talk to y'all without giving me a heads-up first, but she claimed there's no time to wait, and given the urgency of the search for Adam, I agreed. But I don't like it. I'm guessing whatever she has to say, she knows I'm not going to like, so she wants to say it directly and play on your emotions. So I want you to be on guard. Don't say or commit to anything unless I say it's okay. At any point, if I'm not comfortable with how things are going, I'm ending the Zoom."

She paused for Mom's okay, then said, "Vic, I'm sorry to have to do this, but I need you to keep out of sight. This might involve the recording you uncovered yesterday, and I'd like to keep them from finding out we have it." I knew what she was thinking: the bird-watcher might have told the police about the big Black dude who took a copy, and if Janus saw Vic, she might put two and two together. "No, of course," Vic said and left, muttering something about needing coffee.

I felt horrible. I couldn't help but think—if he'd been some indistinct white dude, would Shannon have asked him to leave? Would it have occurred to her that he'd stand out, raise some subconscious alert in Detective Janus's mind? I ran after him. "Hey, I'm sorry," I said.

"It's fine. Really," he said, pouring me a mug of coffee.

When I came back to the room, Detective Janus was just coming onscreen. She looked hideous. Her right eye was swollen, halfway shut, her cheek mottled green and purple. I wondered if she was using some filter to highlight bruises and shadows, if her video camera had some weird color-tinting overlay or a fun-house mirror effect that made her look garish, all to gain the judge's sympathies. I made a mental note to ask Shannon about this.

"Good morning," said Detective Janus, "and thank you, Dr. Park, for sending the Covid test results. It's a load off my mind, especially given that I was unmasked for some time around Eugene and all of you yesterday."

"Yes, we're all relieved about that," Shannon said, "but let's keep in mind, despite testing negative, Eugene is still under quarantine. I filed a motion to delay the hearing."

"That's not necessary. The juvenile court allows virtual hearings."

"Makes it awfully hard to represent my client when I can't even stand next to him. Add on that I can't communicate with him, it's almost like some fundamental right of his might be being violated, like maybe the right to counsel, which I'm pretty sure is in the Constitution."

"Well, I'm sure you'll argue that to the judge tomorrow."

"Yes, I'm sure I will."

It was a little strange watching this, what, in person, I might have called a verbal volley. But on Zoom, with both of them looking straight forward, side by side, it felt surreal. Staged. Neither of them blinking, but instead of it looking like a staring contest, a power play, I wondered if their screens were frozen.

"Anything new on the search?" Mom asked.

"I'm sorry; nothing yet," Detective Janus said. "But we're still working, even with this weather. We've had tremendous response on the hotline and email, with some promising leads we're following up on."

I was glad for my coffee mug, a prop I could bring to my lips and blow on, sip, wince at the hot liquid—all these things I could use to hide my nervousness. Shannon was sipping her coffee, too, her eyes peeking out over the top, and I could swear she was looking straight at me, telling me: *Brace yourself. Janus is going to play the video with the* Eugene, *nooooo scream.* I wished we could ask Shannon—how should we react? Like we're surprised? Break down and cry?

"The biggest lead we have," Detective Janus said, and I gulped, relishing the burn of the hot liquid on my tongue. Here we go. Get ready. "I think you already know about it, from what the woman we talked to told us," she said, and I thought, of course, they put it together already.

"We found Anjeli Rapari."

I swallowed the coffee the wrong way, coughed so hard the coffee spilled onto my hand, but no one reacted. "We heard," Shannon said, calm and smooth as if this was exactly what she'd been expecting. "You talked to her fiancée last night and told her not to talk to us."

"I said no such thing," Janus said, and Shannon rolled her eyes exquisitely, expertly. "Look, here's the important thing, why I asked for this meeting. Anjeli Rapari is doing well. She's out of isolation, and I was able to interview her this morning on the phone."

"And? What did she say?"

"She has no information about Mr. Parson's whereabouts, but she agreed to help us interview Eugene using a letterboard. The logistics are complicated, though." She explained that even with the exigent circumstances, the hospital wouldn't allow visitors, and certainly not one in quarantine due to exposure to Covid (I just had to shake my head at the irony, given that Anjeli herself was the close contact), on top of which, Eugene was under house arrest anyway. "My team's getting everything set up for a virtual session with all of us, getting all the hospital authorizations and the equipment and supplies Ms. Rapari needs. She said she's never tried her method virtually and it might not work, but she's willing to give—"

"No," Shannon said. "I am not allowing my client to be interrogated, and that's exactly what you're proposing. A police interrogation, using Anjeli Rapari as an interpreter."

"Eugene has information critical to our search for his missing father. I'm merely attempting to continue yesterday's interview—"

"An interview I would never have allowed if I'd been present."

"Shannon, be reasonable," Detective Janus said, the first time I'd heard her use her first name. "Hannah, talk to your lawyer. We need this to find your husband. You need to get your priorities straight."

"Shannon, I—" Mom was saying, and I'm positive she was about to say she agreed with Detective Janus, let's get on a Zoom with Anjeli right now, but Shannon cut her off.

"I agree," Shannon said. "I agree that we all need to get our priorities straight and get Eugene communicating ASAP, no posturing, focusing solely on the lives at stake here. Finding Adam Parson and protecting Eugene Parkson are the top priorities. So here's what we're going to do. We're going to do what you suggest, have Anjeli attempt to communicate with Eugene virtually. Given the logistics, not to mention the subject matter, this is going to be extremely difficult for Eugene. To have any chance at making this work, we have to do what makes Eugene most comfortable, and I'm sure we can all agree that having a detective present, the one who arrested and handcuffed him for hours yesterday, will not make it easier for him. So it will be just us and the family, those of us Eugene *knows* are on his side and feels comfortable with. I will record it and immediately share anything pertinent to the search for Adam. Anything else, we can fight about later."

"I could subpoena him and force this," Detective Janus said.

"And I could instruct my client not to move a finger based on his constitutional right not to incriminate himself. Or I could contact Anjeli Rapari and her doctors directly, explain the situation, ask for her help as a therapist who cares about Eugene, and not bother to record it. You know I'd be perfectly well within my rights to do that. So why don't we cut the bullshit? You've already gotten everyone's permission. Help me to help you do your job and find Adam. Help me get this interview set up as soon as we can."

Detective Janus smiled, the forced, closed-lip kind like when you're trying to hide your distaste. "Fine. It's set for nine A.M.," was all she said before leaving the Zoom.

———

WE RUSHED THROUGH BREAKFAST IN silence. We'd been unusually quiet—not just that morning, but since leaving Anjeli's house the previous day, not speaking unless necessary to exchange information. I think it's how awkward it felt to talk in front of Eugene. Before watching Anjeli's videos, we had simply gone about as if he weren't there, conversation-wise. But having heard Anjeli say he'd been paying attention all along, that was impossible.

It seems silly to say that brushing my teeth made me think of Dad because we were doing that all the time—the rare moments *not* thinking about Dad were the remarkable ones—but this felt different. Thinking of *him*, rather than his absence. And then the thought—how long would I feel this way? When I'm ninety years old, will I finish breakfast, go into the bathroom, pick up my toothbrush, and think, Ready, set, BRUSH? Because presumably, this Toothbrush → Dad association will continue for some time, so would the remembering and wondering how long I'll continue to remember eventually become a self-reinforcing part of my toothbrushing routine, and even if I have dementia and can no longer remember Dad, I'd still get a melancholy vibe and spend the next hour trying to remember why picking up a toothbrush makes my heart ache?

I was stalling. The fact is, I was scared. The build-up of anxiety as we waited, anticipated, wondered what our first meeting with Anjeli would yield. Most families never experience this level of tension, even those who go through something as traumatic as a father gone missing. Without the communication gap, we'd have asked Eugene right away what happened to Dad and gotten some sort of answer. A starting point, a baseline. We got nothing. I said before how a true missing-person story—not a murder/kidnapping story in disguise—is the purest mystery because the only person who knows what happened is the missing person. But it clicked into place right then, the fact that we'd been living with another pure mystery our entire lives: the only person who knows what a nonspeaking person unable to communicate is thinking is that person himself.

This was why it had taken us hours yesterday to even work up the nerve to try to communicate with Eugene. Our first chance to break through that lifelong wall of mystery was intimidating enough, but there was a second wall, too—two mysteries we were trying to solve: 1) What happened to Dad? and 2) What was Eugene thinking? It didn't occur to me until much later—when the police accused us, Eugene, of fabricating evidence—that those were questions with two separate answers. That there might be a disconnect between them.

# TWENTY-NINE

# Connecting ... Connecting ...

THERE'S A *TWILIGHT ZONE* EPISODE, "TIME ENOUGH AT LAST," ABOUT A book-lover desperate for more time so he can do nothing but read. He gets his wish; he's the lone survivor of a global nuclear holocaust and ends up at a library with a lifetime's worth of intact books. He's excitedly sorting through them when his glasses fall off and shatter, leaving him unable to read.

Dad *loved* this story, thought it deeply ironic and tragic, which I didn't get—why not go to the ruins of an optical store and find shards of some other glasses? Or find super-large-font books? In any case, he would likely soon die from radiation poisoning and lack of potable water. Of course, now I realize it fits his theory about the dangers of raising your baseline too quickly.

I thought of that story watching Eugene wait for Anjeli to log on—literally at the edge of his seat, sitting on his hands, staring fixedly at the screen. Here was his conduit to the world, the only person with and through whom he could express the thoughts trapped in his mind. How afraid he must have been that he'd lost that right when he'd found it, his lifelong wish granted and then snatched away. Was it back? Would this new setup work?

A notification popped up—*Anjeli R connecting . . . connecting . . .* —and Eugene started bouncing up and down in his seat. Mom got closer and hugged him, a long and tight hug that felt like a goodbye, the wordless kind she gave me dropping me off at college for the first time. When Anjeli appeared onscreen, sitting up in her hospital bed, Eugene ran to the TV and put his palm on the screen. Anjeli reached her hand out, too, closing her eyes as if she could feel the warmth of his hand. She was close enough to the camera that we could see tears pooling in the corners of her eyes. "Eugene, I'm so sorry," she said. "I can't believe what's happened. I can't imagine what you're going through. And Hannah, Mia, John, I've been wanting to meet you for so long. Shannon, thank you so much for making this possible."

Mom said how much she appreciated her going to such extraordinary lengths for us when she's so sick. "I'm fine," Anjeli said. "It was a precaution because of my asthma. I got nebulizer treatments, and I feel much better now. I only wish I'd known sooner. I wish I could be there in person. Eugene, I know we've never tried spelling over Zoom, but I'm hoping the stand will help."

Eugene backed away from the TV and sat on a chair we'd put in the middle of the room. In front of him was something Shannon had picked up from Anjeli's house on the way to ours: a stand with an oversized stencil letterboard attached on top. "Adam made it out of Mia's old music stand, I believe," Anjeli explained. "It was his idea, to use it to hold the letterboard the same way I do, even when I'm there, to give Eugene more independence. This is a really advanced skill that requires a lot of self-regulation, something most students can't do without a lot more practice, but I agreed to try it because Eugene had such strong skills and I thought he might be ready for this next step." She talked Mom through making adjustments so the stencil would hang at a slant, just below eye level, the way we'd seen in the video. Mom handed Eugene a pencil and joined the rest of us off to the side where Anjeli asked us to stay to avoid distracting Eugene.

"Eugene, I know how worried and upset and frustrated you must be," Anjeli began. "But I need you to put that aside as much as you can and just be open with me. I've explained to everyone here how important it is for you to tell us your story your own way, in your own time. So I want you to relax, don't rush. No pressure, okay? But first I need your permission. Are you okay with communicating like this, with your lawyer and your family watching us?"

Eugene brought the pencil up in an overhand stabbing motion and slowly, as slowly as in the video of his first session with Anjeli, brought it to the letterboard. The tip of the pencil appeared to be headed for Z, to the right of Y, and he stopped, gripped the pencil harder, his arm shaking.

"I know it's strange, your depth perception's off with the screen in front, and I'm not there to reposition the board if you move your body, but you can do it. Remember to visualize the tip going through the letter you want. See it, then do it."

Eugene moved his arm, redirecting the pencil tip left toward Y, brought it an inch closer to the letterboard, a little more left, and then closer. It reminded me of the game Operation, using tweezers to pick up a tiny plastic bone inside a small opening without touching the edges. The pencil didn't go through the Y, landing instead between its diagonal lines.

"Close enough. That's amazing you got that on your first try. The first is always the hardest, right? Okay, let's take a deep breath and rest a minute. Before we go on, there's something I need to confess to you first. It has to do with when you were really upset with your dad on Saturday. I wrote down what you spelled like I always do, and my note . . ." Anjeli bit her lip, frowned as if in pain. "I'm so sorry, Eugene, I never meant to violate your confidence, I didn't even upload the video or show the note to your dad, but my partner, Zoe, you've met her a few times . . . anyway, she saw the note when she was gathering my things for the hospital, and last night, when the police tracked me down and I couldn't talk to them, they talked to her, and she . . ." She gritted her teeth, her look of guilt morphing into one of anger. "She showed them the note."

"What note?" Shannon sat up. "What did it say? If the police have it, I need to know what I'm dealing with."

"Eugene," said Anjeli. "It's important for your family and lawyer to understand what happened. Can I tell them about it and show them the note?"

Eugene turned to glance at Mom and, at her smile and nod, turned back to the screen. His movement still slow and careful, his arm still shaking, he brought the pencil tip to the edge of Y.

"Thank you, Eugene," Anjeli said and shifted her gaze to us. "Some context first: Adam told me from the beginning about your first spelling experience and how skeptical that made him and all of you. I'm so sorry you went through that. I've heard about her; I don't know that much about physically supported writing therapy, but I heard she wasn't properly trained and basically went rogue, which did such a disservice to that field in our area. In any event, Adam said he didn't want to put the whole family through another experience like that again and build false hope, so he decided not to tell you about our therapy unless and until there was definitive proof."

"But Eugene's spelling out words on his own," John said. "What more proof did Dad need?"

"It's not just your dad. There's so much skepticism out there. People say I must be cuing somehow with my eyes, maybe subconsciously, or subtly moving the board as a signal." She scoffed, shook her head, clearly angry. "It's ridiculous—as if these kids who are supposedly cognitively impaired, according to these same people, are managing to somehow see and figure out near-invisible secret signals to perfectly spell long answers.

"Anyway, I'm not saying Adam accused me of anything like that. But he wanted to wait to tell you until Eugene could spell with him directly. I gave them homework and they worked really hard, but it wasn't working. So we tried setting up a test for proof, like Adam showing him something I can't see and asking questions—"

"That's what he did with that first therapist, he set up this test," Mom said.

"I heard. Well, we tried it several times. It never worked. Eugene froze up. I've tried this with other clients, and sometimes it worked, but often, it didn't. I've asked them, and they don't know why they can't answer, either. Of course, they don't know why their bodies don't do what they want them to half the time; that's why they can't talk to begin with. My best guess is it's the anxiety of being tested. Anxiety is huge in the autism and Angelman communities to begin with, and testing triggers the old trauma of not being believed and aggravates the motor dysfunction. Because when things come up organically during our regular sessions, Eugene tells me stuff I don't know all the time, stuff Adam doesn't even know."

Something clicked right then. Eugene telling TFT about my stash of candy in the violin case, which Mom couldn't have told her about because she didn't know herself.[28]

Eugene jostled the letterboard stand, and Anjeli said, "Right, that's when we started practicing with the stand. We started last week and it worked, so we decided it was time to tell you all, on

---

28 Language is a funny thing. We've evolved to use it in context to communicate with others. It makes perfect sense to me that Eugene can't answer test questions. This happens to me all the time, especially during word games. There'll be some word I know how to use in context, but if someone challenges me to define it, I can't, so I start doubting myself, questioning if I actually know this word. When I look it up, I realize I *did* know and have been using it correctly all along. This happens to me with Korean, too. I can follow a K-drama or movie and know what they're saying even without subtitles. But if I heard a specific word or phrase out of context, I couldn't tell you what it means. Someone testing my Korean formally would likely conclude I have almost no receptive language skills, but I can listen to a question from Mom in Korean and know how to respond (although in English because that's easier for me). Whether it's from a testing-anxiety psychological barrier or a need for conversational context to trigger a particular linguistic knowledge, I think that's what's happened to Eugene.

Father's Day. We were going to spend Saturday planning some fun way to show you, and Eugene was so excited, he was giddy, but then on Saturday, Adam said we had to wait. Apparently, a professor used eye-tracking equipment to prove that nonspeaking autistic children who use letterboards are choosing the letters themselves."

"That's the study I told Dad about," John said. "He completely dismissed it."

"Apparently, he didn't," Anjeli said. "He actually read the study and was very impressed, and he wanted to ask this professor about using the eye-tracking device for Eugene to prove once and for all that it's really Eugene himself doing the communicating. Adam said he wanted to wait for him to call him back, to try and set this up. He thought it was worth the wait because it was scientific proof and after this, there would be no doubt."

She paused here and reached for a piece of paper on the bed-stand and unfolded it. "You have to understand the context. Eugene had been so happy, anticipating and planning, and then the abrupt change in plans. Adam not consulting us about it. Eugene was blindsided and beyond disappointed. He'd had a bad day anyway—he said he was frustrated doing kindergarten stuff at Henry's House all day, colors and ABCs, pointing to pictures of toys he wants to play with, and he just couldn't *wait* to show everyone. And then Adam just announces this delay and gets some call and has to leave without even discussing it. It seemed cruel. Eugene blew up. That's when he said this. Just one big stream of letters."

She held up the paper:

Just tell me how you're feeling.
    IHATEDADHESRUININGMYLIFEHATEHIMSOMUCHNEEDTORUN
AWAYWANTHIMGONEOUTOFLIFEFOREVERJUSTDIE

It took me a second to figure out how to separate this block of letters into words: I hate Dad / he's ruining my life / hate him so much / need to run away / want him gone / out of life forever / just die.

I told myself this was nothing, that I should laugh it off and say, *Oh, come on*, this *is what we're worried about? Let's get real, what fourteen-year-old hasn't felt utter hatred and rage toward their parents?* I had, and had said out loud plenty of hurtful screeds I later regretted about wishing I'd never been born, I couldn't *wait* to move out and never see them again, and once—to a friend, not to my parents directly, but still—that Mom was a c _ _ _ (God, I hate that word and I remember how icky but also secretly badass I felt saying it out loud, the hard *c* and *t* sounds rolling over my tongue) and if she died, I would be fucking happy about it. But the thing about off-the-cuff things said in heated moments is that they're transitory, not recorded and codified for future perusal. Think of how many things you say that you're glad can disappear into a memory and dissipate with time. But Eugene didn't have that freedom; by virtue of having to spell everything out, his words—no matter how embarrassing or stupid or meaningless—were recorded on paper, to be passed around and scrutinized. Such an unfair byproduct.

Besides, Eugene wasn't any fourteen-year-old kid, this wasn't a silly spat, and no one (least of all the police or our lawyer) was going to laugh this off. Shannon told us later that if she had to pick the lowest moment of the hearing preparation, this one was a top contender. She said, "The mommy-blogger video, the bird-watcher audio—through all that, we had the nonspeaking, innocent simpleton trope thing going for us. He had meltdowns, so maybe something bad happened, but an *accidental* something, nothing remotely intentional. What this note did was huge: it changed how we saw Eugene. It introduced motive. For the first time, the police had evidence of Eugene as someone who can snap, like any typical hormonal teenage boy. Someone who can get pissed off at his father and, even if just for a moment, want him dead. And who's to say Eugene didn't feel that for two seconds on Tuesday morning between eleven-fifteen and eleven-thirty A.M., and during those seconds, wasn't next to his father on a high cliff above the raging waters of the Potomac River?"

When Anjeli put down the note, Shannon said in a remarkably calm voice, "So the issue is, what happened between Eugene spelling this on Saturday and Tuesday morning? Did he cool off? Or did this anger carry over and explode on Tuesday in the park and—"

"No, of course not." Anjeli looked shocked. "There is no way, *no way* Eugene would do anything, no matter how upset he was, and to suggest anything else is plain absurd." She shifted her gaze to Eugene. "Eugene, I know you, I know your dad, I know your relationship, and there is no way you would do anything like that. You were just venting. You would *never* do anything to hurt your dad." Her words were declarative, a statement, but I could hear the silent question at the end—*You wouldn't, couldn't, didn't; right?* It was the fervor in her voice—a little too forceful, as if needing to convince herself—and the look in her eyes, searching, searing into Eugene's for reassurance she was right. Maybe if Anjeli's look of absolute belief in Eugene from her videos hadn't been imprinted in my mind as the baseline against which all her expressions should be measured, I would have been convinced.

"Did you see Eugene after Saturday?" Shannon said. "It would be great if we could present something concrete showing that Eugene had, in fact, cooled down."

"I didn't see him after that session," Anjeli said, "but once Eugene finished venting, I put everything down and just talked to him. I told him it's only a week, and this eye-tracking study could be huge, shut down all the doubters and haters. Eugene still wasn't happy, but he calmed down quite a bit. I thought it would be fine, just a few days to wait, but on Monday, Adam emailed that the professor was out of town and it might take a few weeks to talk to him, and I thought, No, this isn't fair to Eugene. He's had to accommodate the world his whole life, and this time, Adam is going to have to bend, the world is going to have to accommodate *him* for once. So I called Adam that night—"

"That's the voicemail we heard," Shannon said.

Anjeli nodded. "He called back, and we had a long talk." She shifted her gaze to Eugene. "Like I said, Eugene, I didn't tell your dad what you said. But I told him I thought he was hurting you, that waiting to tell your family was a signal he doesn't fully believe in you, like he was prioritizing your mom and siblings over you. He was really shaken up. He had no idea you felt this way. He wanted my help talking to you about it at the park the next day, but I got sick and went to the hospital so I couldn't, and I regret that so much. I wish so much that you could have talked and truly made up—"

It took me a second to figure out why she stopped talking so abruptly. I'd been too focused on the screen to notice Eugene. His arm was overhead, pencil firmly in hand, moving toward the letterboard. His movement was slow but confident. Purposeful.

My heartbeat, our collective breaths, the particles of air in the room, the faint *phwats* of the rain hitting the windows—everything slowed to match Eugene's arm, the distance between the pencil tip and the letterboard narrowing inch by inch, second by second, as we waited to see what Eugene wanted to tell us.

# THIRTY

# Because of Rock That's Broken

W
E
End of word

Anjeli: "W-E, we." (We who? Eugene and Dad? All of us?)

M (M for Mom?)
A
D (Mad? Eugene and Dad were mad at each
    other?)
E
End of word

Anjeli: "M-A-D-E, made." (Made what? Dad and Eugene made something?)

U

P

End of word

Anjeli: "U-P, up." (They made up a story?)

Period

*We made up.* Eugene's first sentence that day. Three simple words that would take a speaking person one to two seconds and almost no effort to say out loud. It took Eugene five minutes of focused concentration and holding up his arm, gripping the pencil, willing his nerves and muscles to cooperate, forcing himself to fight fatigue, frustration, distraction. And for the rest of us, our impatience with the letter-by-letter communication process increased exponentially by the life-and-death stakes of what he was telling us, the suspense of trying to figure out what the next letter was, what it could mean. How many more letters, words, sentences in how many minutes and hours would it take for us to learn what happened to Dad, if Eugene even knew what happened to Dad?

"You're getting the hang of this, Eugene. Great job," Anjeli said. "Okay. *We made up.* What do you mean by that? How? When?"

DAD TALKED TO ME AFTER YOUR PHONE CALL. HE TOLD ME WHAT YOU SAID. HE APOLOGIZED TO ME.

I timed myself saying this out loud—slowly, word by word. Ten seconds. It took Eugene ten minutes. He dropped the pencil after the last word and rocked in his seat, kicking the letterboard stand a little in the process.

Anjeli said, "I'm so glad your dad talked to you. I told him he should. And I want to hear all about it, but let's take another rest first. Hannah, see how the letterboard stand has gotten out of position? Would you adjust it so it's centered around Eugene's right hand?"

As Mom repositioned the letterboard, Anjeli said to Eugene, "I know it's going to get easier as you get used to this setup, but still, this is going to be a very long and tiring day. I know how careful and precise you are about spelling words correctly and using complete sentences, but given how much you have to tell us, how about if you give yourself a little leeway, just for today?"

Anjeli said to the rest of us, "I don't know if Eugene's like this with other things, but with spelling, he can be a *bit* of a perfectionist." She chuckled affectionately, and Eugene looked back at us and smiled, shy and a little proud. "Eugene has a reverence for language, which the teacher in me loves. But I've been trying to convince him he can use shortcuts in certain settings, like we all do in texts. We've even had a few lessons about it." She smiled at Eugene and said, "So if the spelling snob in you can stand it"—Eugene let out a huge laugh—"use abbreviations. Numbers and symbols. Leave out articles. Don't worry about spelling mistakes. Do whatever makes it easiest for you. If I don't understand something, I'll ask."

Mom hugged Eugene and kissed the top of his head and returned to her seat. Anjeli said, "Okay, so you were telling us your dad talked to you. Was this at the park?"

N. AT HOME. MON NIGHT.

Monday night, when I had my fight with Mom about my major, graduating early. Was that why Dad hadn't talked to me that night? Not because he was avoiding me, too hurt or disappointed in me to face me, the way I'd feared, but because he'd simply been busy talking to Eugene?

D TOLD ME ABOUT PETER.

Anjeli shook her head, a pained frown overtaking her face. "He told me about that, too, and it explained a lot."

"Who's Peter?" Mom asked.

Peter was another of Anjeli's clients. Older—nineteen—diagnosed with "so-called low-functioning nonverbal autism," Anjeli said, clearly angered by the designation. Dad had met his mom in the waiting area; Peter's sessions were right before Eugene's. He'd been making great progress, had even started spelling with his mom in a limited way.

During Christmas break, his older brother came home for a visit. His mom had told him about Peter's progress, sending him videos, but the brother had been skeptical, replying with articles he'd found claiming Anjeli was a fraud. When Peter wasn't able to spell with him on demand, the brother said outright that he didn't believe any of this was real. "Peter shut down, even with me," Anjeli said. "It took several months to get back to where we'd been before Christmas. To this day, Peter freezes up with his family. Hearing all that really upset Adam. He got kind of obsessive about making sure nothing like that happens with Eugene."

A tingle of guilt. Was I the reason Dad wanted to make sure Eugene's ability was beyond doubt? Because he thought I would challenge it without incontrovertible proof?

"Even more than that," Anjeli continued, "Adam wanted the moment of you all finding out about Eugene to be the happiest possible for Eugene. He had some theory about not wanting to get Eugene's expectations up too much, reminding him his family might be skeptical. I wasn't entirely convinced, but I thought his heart was in the right place."

PETER SCARED D. TAUGHT D TELLING FAM HAS 2 B PERFECT. NO DOUBT. BUT U MADE HIM SEE. MY FAM NOT KNOWING = WAITING = SUFFERING 4 ME.

"That's exactly what I told him," Anjeli said.

D SAID SORRY. DIDNT KNOW. LETS TELL FAM TOMORROW. WE CAN PLAN W U IN PARK. GET SHAMPAIN. I CAN HAVE SOME. I HUGD HIM 2 SAY OK. I WAS SO HAPPY.

This made sense. Because the thing I didn't get was how, if Eugene was so angry at Dad, they were managing to be all chummy-chummy at breakfast on Tuesday. Dad's water goblet rainbows, Eugene's giggly eye rolls—those were not signs of a son on the verge of boiling over with rage at his father, but a pair giddy with anticipation, holding in a delicious surprise.

"But I couldn't come," Anjeli said. "I had Zoe call your dad to explain but she said the connection was bad and she didn't know if he could hear."

D HEARD COVID & HOSPITAL.

"Is that what upset you? The police showed me a video of your dad trying to calm you down. They said you saw it at your hearing yesterday."

Eugene stayed still for a long while before raising his arm. He had been poking through the letters smoothly, gaining speed and momentum, but the first few words of his response took longer than even his earliest videos, his fingers gripped around the pencil in a tight fist, his hand shaking.

N. VIDEO BC PEPPER SPRAY.

Mom gasped, and Anjeli said, "Someone pepper-sprayed you? Who? Why?"

D HELD UP LETTER BOARD 4 POKING PRACTICE. SO BORING. COULDNT FOCUS. 2 EXCITED HAPPY LAUGH JUMP. BIG BOYS PASSED BY. CALLED ME

Eugene brought the pencil to the letter R, but just as the tip was at the edge, he paused, his hand trembling slightly as if something invisible was blocking it. Just as Anjeli started saying it was okay, he didn't have to spell that word, he resumed. His hand steady, he poked R, and then E, T, A, R, D, his arm movement getting smoother and faster with each letter. Anjeli said the individual letters out loud, but at the end of the word, she said, "I'm sorry, Eugene, but I refuse to say that despicable word." Eugene smiled, a silent *Thank you,* and continued.

BOYS LAUGHED. SAID BABY LERNING ABC. D YELLED HEY WE CAN HEAR U & U R BEING REALLY RUDE. THEY CALLED D FREAK WITH WEIRDO SON. RAN AWAY LAUGHING. I WAS SO MAD. SCREAMED JUMPED & KICKED ROCKS. WOMAN YELLED AT ME 4 DISTURBING PEACE. PEOPLE DO THAT SOMETIMES. D ALWAYS SAYS SORRY. MY SONS DISABLED DOESNT KNOW WHAT HES DOING DOESNT UNDERSTAND. BUT THIS TIME D SAID DIDNT U SEE WHAT HAPPENED? DONT U THINK HE HAS RIGHT 2 B MAD KICK & SCREAM? I DO & IF U CANT HANDLE IT U SHOULD LEAVE. SHE SAID SORRY BUT WHAT DO U EXPECT F TEENAGERS? IF HE

CANT HANDLE THAT & U CANT HANDLE HIM U SHOULDNT BRING HIM IN PUBLIC. D WAS SO GREAT. SAID WELL IF U CANT HANDLE NOT BEING HEARTLESS IGNORANT BULLY U SHOULDNT BRING URSELF IN PUBLIC.

Eugene spelled these words as fast as I'd ever seen him, the whole thing taking about twenty minutes, with Anjeli repeating the letters and words softly, careful not to interrupt his flow. After he finished spelling out *public,* he let out a huge laugh and put his arm down to rest.

"Well, good," Anjeli said. "She clearly deserved it. What a jerk. And those boys. You must have been very mad."

SOOO MAD.

"So then what?"

SHE KEPT YELLING & FOLLOWED US. SO MEAN 2 D. SAID HES A BAD FATHER. I KICKED ROCKS 2 MAKE HER GO AWAY. SHE SCREAMED STAY BACK & SPRAYED SOMETHING. SHE WAS FAR AWAY BUT SPRAY STILL REALLY HURT. BURNT EYES. I COULDNT SEE. I TRIED GETTING OUT OF EYES BUT D GRABBED MY ARMS. I GUESS I HURT D TRYING 2 GET FREE? I DONT REMEMBER DOING BUT SAW VID.

I remembered the scene, both Eugene and Dad with their eyes shut, really hard, Eugene screaming and completely out of control, Dad trying to hold his arms down. It must have been agonizing. I wanted to kill this woman.

"Oh, Eugene," Anjeli said. "I'm sorry. I wish that hadn't happened."

ME 2 EXCEPT

"Except what?"

IT HELPED ME

"Helped you? How?"

THATS WHEN I STARTED SPELLING W D

"What? How?"

AFTER WE CALMED DOWN & CLEANED UP WE SAT UNDER TREE 2 REST. D KEPT SAYING SORRY HE SHOULDVE KEPT QUIET &

JUST WALKED AWAY BUT COULDNT HELP IT & I GOT HURT. I
REALLY WANTED 2 SAY NO IM GLAD. THANK U 4 STANDING UP
4 ME. HIS FACE WAS HURT. BLOODY & GLASSES BROKEN. IT
SCARED ME. DID I DO THAT? I DIDNT MEAN 2.

"Your dad knew that. I'm sure of it."

I KNOW BUT I WANTED 2 SAY IT. SO I PICKED UP BOARD & GAVE
2 D 2 HOLD UP.

"Oh my God, and you did it?"

Eugene paused, as if he was trying to figure out how to word this
next part.

N I TRIED BUT COULDNT W D HOLDING BOARD. D MADE FUN OF
SELF 4 BEING BAD PARTNER. HE SAID HE WILL KEEP TRYING &
B PATIENT. HE SET UP BOARD LEANING ON ROCK PILE. HE SAID
I DONT HAVE 2 USE BUT ITS HERE IF I WANT. BC WHAT JUST
HAPPENED WAS INTENSE CANT BELEIVE SPRAY FAR AWAY HURT
SO MUCH. I LIKED HAVING IT NEAR BUT ITS MY CHOICE. THEN HE
TALKED 2 ME ABOUT SO MANY THINGS BUT NO QS. SHOWED ME
HQ NOTEBOOK.

Anjeli said, "HQ notebook?"

Eugene looked back at us, at me. Smiled in an inviting, almost conspiratorial way. I explained what HQ stood for. "It's a theory Dad had
about happiness being relative, keeping expectations low, stuff like that."

ITS ALOT MORE COMPLICATED THAN THAT. HE EXPLAINED ALL
2 ME.

I chuckled at the pride in those words as he glanced back at me
again, his smile seeming to say, *No offense or anything!*

I DIDNT GET ALL OF IT. SOME OF HQ SEEMED

After *seemed,* he paused, then finally poked H-M-M-M. Anjeli
laughed, said, "I have to admit, he told me some of the ideas and I
felt the same way. Hmmm."

Eugene laughed. BUT I LIKED D TALKING 2 ME ABOUT SERIOUS
THINGS. D TRUSTED ME 2 UNDERSTAND. HE KEPT SAYING SORRY 4
NOT TELLING FAM SOONER. I REEEEALLY WANTED 2 TELL HIM ITS
OK. SO I DID IT. GRABBED PEN & SPELLED I 4GIVE U.

"Oh my God, Eugene, that's incredible. So this was with the stencil leaning against the rock?"

Y

"That's amazing. Your dad must have been so happy."

Eugene smiled. I WAS SOOOO SLOW. MESSED UP ALOT. BUT D SAID LETTERS REALLY SOFT. MADE EASIER 2 FOCUS. I SAID SORRY 4 HURTING UR FACE DIDNT MEAN 2 HURT U. HE SAID ITS FINE BUT GLASSES BROKE & WORLD = HALF BLURRY LIKE WINKING. WE LAUGHED. HAD CHIPS & GATORAID. D LET ME READ HQ BOOK & ASK QS. HE ASKED WHAT I THINK & WROTE WHAT I SAID IN NOTEBK. MADE ME FEEL GOOD LIKE D CARED ABOUT MY OPINION. LIKE MY IDEAS R IMPORTANT.

"I'm sure he felt the same way, you being interested in what he was working on and being able to discuss it with you in a meaning-ful way," Anjeli said, and it hit me: this wave of grief and envy and shame, mixed in with admiration and pride for Eugene—that Dad trusted him with his ideas, shared them with him, and Eugene was generous enough to let him.

Eugene smiled. BEST TALK I EVER HAD W ANYBODY EVER. He started to put his pencil down but then he added: NO OFFENSE.

"None taken," Anjeli said.

———

IT'S NOT LIKE ANY OF us had forgotten about the urgency of getting some answers, *the* answer. Shannon had been patient, giving Anjeli leeway and trusting that Eugene needed time to acclimate. But by this point, three hours into Eugene telling us what happened that day, I realized that saving Dad was a lost cause. That if there was any chance of Dad being found alive, Eugene would have told us how to find him earlier. That he was stretching out the earlier parts of his story because he couldn't bring himself to verbalize what hap-pened to Dad. I couldn't blame him. I was grateful for his lingering on this beautiful memory. A father and a son bonding by fighting bul-lies, laughing together, planning how they would give their family the most wondrous news of their lives and toast with champagne. How I wished the story could end there.

Maybe Anjeli had the same instinct. Instead of asking what happened next, she fixated on their first conversation, saying, "That is hands down the best first-talk story I've ever heard. I mean, you went from not being able to spell out single-word answers to having a full, rich, meaningful exchange. It's just unheard of. Completely unbelievable."

She would come to regret those words, of course. We all would. But at that moment, we savored them. Just as her words began to sink in and it dawned on me what they might convey to others—how, say, the police might interpret her comment about how "unbelievable" this was—Anjeli said, "I can't wait to see the video of it. I know they're working on unlocking your dad's phone."

Eugene responded: D DIDNT RECORD.

"Really?" Anjeli said—her tone, for the first time, laced with doubt, just a trace but unmistakable. She must have realized how that might sound to the police, because she recovered quickly. "That makes sense. After all, this wasn't a homework session; it was a private conversation, just you guys, so of course he wouldn't want to record it for me."

N WE WANTED 2 SHOW U. D JUST FORGOT. BUT HE WROTE WORDS LIKE U DO. TOOK PIC OF ME W 2 PAGES 2 SHOW U LATER.

"Oh, that's great. I can't wait to see it," she said, the lines in her face relaxing in enormous relief.

Shannon cleared her throat—not impatient or obvious, but her meaning was clear: let's get a move on. Eugene raised his arm, his hand shaking slightly as he spelled: I DONT LIKE THIS NEXT PART.

Out of the corners of my eyes, I saw Mom edging forward on her seat, barely sitting. Eugene wrote IM SCARED, and I wanted to run to him, too, do anything I could to make him feel better.

Anjeli said, "I know. Me, too. Take all the time you need. And remember, we're all here for you. We love you. We'll understand. No matter what you tell us."

Anjeli asked Mom to adjust the letterboard stand again—I'm not sure it needed repositioning; she may have just wanted to give Eugene time to rest—and after Mom finished, Eugene wrote out the rest of the story without interruption. It took about an hour. He paused from time to time to rest his arm, but Anjeli didn't goad or encourage, didn't respond, didn't ask, "What next?," just waited and simply said the letters and words softly, almost in a whisper. Her eyes were droopy like she was drowsy, and maybe it's because of that that it had the lulling feel of a bedtime story, or a fairy tale.

D ASKED DO U WANT 2 GO HOME? I SAID LETS STAY. CANT LET SPRAY WOMAN RUIN OUR DAY. I PICKED GREEN TRAIL. MY FAVE. SHORT & PICNIC TABLE BY WATERFALL BUT NOT LOUD BC REALLY HIGH ABOVE WATER. ATE LUNCH. D SAW RED BIRDS IN TREES. WE WENT 2 LOOK.

It's hard to pinpoint when I became uneasy, what started my questions. The picnic at the waterfall overlook made me think about John and me whispering the same thing the previous night, but it wasn't a big deal, as Dad had talked about them doing that often enough. The red birds gave me a bit more pause—John hadn't said the birds' color, but I'd seen them in my mind: red. That made sense, though, given the red birds in the bird-watcher's video. Still, the location, the lunch, Dad spotting the red birds in the trees—the matching order and little details combined. Did that mean anything? I thought of Anjeli telling Dad how Eugene heard everything, even—especially—when you thought he wasn't paying attention. Could he have heard us? But it wasn't like he'd been preoccupied with something else; he'd been asleep.

I WALKED TO EDGE TO LOOK AT WATERFALL. MAKES ME FEEL BETTER ABOUT MYSELF. WATER FALLS BC OF ROCK THATS BROKEN. SOMETHING NOT PERFECT JUST LIKE ME.

DID JUMPING JACK CONTEST. I WON. HIGH 5.

As soon as Eugene spelled *jumping jack,* I turned to John. What was happening? Because I remembered John saying they played a game, but he didn't say which game. It could have been anything—throwing rocks, skipping, staring contest. But again, I'd seen it in my mind: Dad and Eugene doing a jumping jack contest. I would verify with John later, of course, but even before that, I knew, could see from the bewildered blinking of his eyes: the game John had visualized in his mind last night was a jumping jack contest, too.

D WENT 2 GET OUR STUFF. SAID HEY THATS OUR STUFF LEAVE THAT ALONE. I TURNED & SAW 3 BOYS GOING THRU OUR STUFF.

This was when my unease surpassed bafflement and grew into full-on freak-out mode. Because *I* had said the part last night about the teenage boys. I'd seen three boys in my mind and stopped myself from saying the number, thinking it would be a bit much to include those types of (what I'd thought of as) made-up details, as if they were real. How many coincidences in a row did it take to no longer be believable as mere coincidence? What did it mean that Eugene's account matched not only the outlines of what John and I had whispered last night with Eugene between us, but the unspoken images in my mind?

BOYS SAID OH ITS THE R WORD. TOOK D WALLET & RAN. D CHASED YELLED HEY STOP DONT U DARE DO THAT. HE REALLY SCREAMED STOOOOOP.

BOY THREW DADS BACKPACK. TOO HARD TOO HIGH ITS GOING 2 FALL OVER CLIFF. I TRIED 2 CATCH. D SCREAMED LEAVE IT JUST STOP DONT DO IT E BUT I TOUCHED IT BUT D KEPT SCREAMING E NO BUT I HAD IT BUT GOT DIZZY. I DONT KNOW WHAT HAPPENED BUT GROUND WAS GONE. NOT TOTALLY GONE. UNEVEN. I WAS FALLING BACKWARDS. SO SCARED. JUST SHUT EYES & DIZZY & D GRABBED MY ARM & IT HURT & SO SCARED THERES NOTHING UNDER 1 FOOT LIKE IN POOL DEEP END.

This was where we'd stopped last night, where John and I couldn't voice any more. And like last night, I didn't care where these images were coming from, if they were real, what the implications were—all that, I would ponder and discuss with John later. For now, I only cared about what was to come, what the next words were, Eugene's shaking arm, the quiet sobs from Mom, my having to blink away my own tears to focus on the trajectory of Eugene's pencil.

I JUST WANTED D 2 LET GO OF MY ARM HIS HAND HURT SO MUCH HIS SCREAM SO LOUD CANT STAND IT. I WISHED SO MUCH I COULD TALK SO I CAN YELL AT D 2 JUST LET ME GO IT HURTS I CANT BREATH I CANT SEE I CANT HEAR I CANT CALM DOWN EVERYTHING SO LOUD & ALL WHITE & BLUE & IM SO SCARED I JUST SCREAMED SO I WONT HEAR ANYTHING ELSE.

I FELL UP LIKE WHEN D THROWS ME IN AIR BUT MY FACE LANDED ON GROUND. I TRIED 2 OPEN EYES BUT SO MUCH DIRT. WAITED 4 D 2 HELP ME UP DONT KNOW HOW LONG. I THOUGHT D HAND WAS AROUND MY ARM BUT I OPENED MY EYES & D WASNT THERE. HAND WAS GONE.

As Anjeli said, G-O-N-E, gone, I felt this unbearable sense of finality. There it was, the answer to the question we'd been desperate to ask him for the last forty-eight hours. Eugene dropped his arm, his whole body slumped, and the pencil fell from his hand onto the floor, like he was too exhausted to keep his fingers curled. He had done this for us, for Dad, and he had nothing left in him, like one of those soldiers you see in movies pushing himself on a long odyssey home, and as soon as he steps into his house, falls to the floor.

Mom was the first to go to Eugene. I wanted to go to him, too, but I didn't know how to make my body obey, what to do or think to make my legs move the right way. When Mom touched him, crying and kneeling beside him, he started, like he was shocked, but he didn't move as she wrapped her arms around him. Didn't hug her back or lean into her or anything. "Oh, Eugene," Mom said, "I'm so sorry. This has been so awful for you." He tried to move away from her, not bratty, like a teenager trying to avoid his mom's overbearing hug, but gently, slowly, with dignity, the way a family member might at a funeral to signal they need space to grieve. He stood and walked out of the room, his steps quickening as if he'd been holding it together really hard but could no longer bear it. He ran up the stairs and into his room. Then the rhythmic *heee-boom*. Jumping to forget. To restore his senses. To cope with the pain he'd had to endure.

# THIRTY-ONE

# Relatively Happy for the Rest of My Life

IT FELT LIKE THE END. IT SHOULD HAVE BEEN THE END. WE HAD OUR answer. We knew what happened to Dad. The only thing we wanted to do was grieve and begin to learn to live with this new reality— children without a father, a wife without a husband.

Unfortunately, it wasn't quite that simple. We still had the hearing to prepare for and go through, which seemed impossible given our exhaustion. It had taken Eugene more than four hours to tell us his story: 255 minutes of painstakingly poking a pencil through 5,056 letters comprising 1,084 words, all for a boy with low muscle tone and motor difficulties. The unfathomable physical, emotional, and mental toll it must have taken. Anjeli later likened it to the phenomenon of mothers who lift cars to save their babies, and said she wouldn't have believed it if she hadn't witnessed it firsthand, that she sometimes wondered if she'd dreamed it all up.

The rest of us were merely sitting and listening, but everything about it hurt. The gut punch of finally finding out what happened to

Dad, the intensity stretched out over four hours, heightened tenfold by the stress and suspense (and yes, I'm ashamed to admit, also by the impatience and frustration) of the letter-by-letter spelling process. With each new letter, a quickening of my heartbeat, clenching of fists, holding of breath, rushing of panicked thoughts as to what this word could be, whether it would reveal yet another detail that inexplicably matched the previous night's images in my head, John's and my whispered words. By the end, I felt light-headed and achy, and all I wanted was to be alone with my family, to cry and curse fate and bullies and birds and gravity, scream and drink, jump with Eugene, think about nothing and no one except each other.

Ten minutes. That's how long we got to fall apart. Mom, John, and I followed Eugene upstairs and sat on the floor in his doorway, wanting to give him space to jump but needing to be with him, to let him know we were with him. We didn't say anything, to him or to each other. We wept, but silently, careful not to call attention to ourselves and burden Eugene. Mom held our hands, John's in her right, mine in her left, so we could squeeze her hand when it hurt too much, the way she used to do when we were little, getting shots or our blood drawn.

When Mom's phone buzzed in her pocket, she squeezed our hands gently for several seconds before letting go to check it. "Shannon," she whispered. "She's leaving."

By the time we got downstairs, Shannon was on her way out. "I'm sorry we ran off like that," Mom said. "Anjeli left Zoom, I take it? I wanted to thank her, we owe her so much. And you, too—coming here like this."

"Don't worry about any of that," Shannon said. "I know you must be devastated. I'm so sorry. But I hope you can find some comfort in finally knowing, and also in finally being able to communicate with Eugene. What he accomplished today, his strength—it's remarkable. I'm so proud of him. I know you are, too."

Mom asked about the hearing, and Shannon said she had just

sent a recording of the relevant portions of Eugene's interview, along with the corresponding transcription she'd typed up, to Detective Janus and Officer Higashida, asking them to drop the case and rescind the referral.

"The hearing, the detention," Mom said, "all that would go away?"

"That's the hope. What Eugene told us explains everything—the blogger video, the wallet, the backpack in the water—and all in a way that clearly shows he's not to blame for any of this. If you have half a heart, you can't hear that story and not immediately think, This poor kid has gone through enough and we need to leave him alone. Of course, when a suspect tells a story that exonerates himself, the authorities tend to be skeptical. So they'll probably need more from Eugene, get his help identifying those three boys, some sort of corroboration. But I'll try my best to keep that to a minimum."

I'd been in a fog of grief, but *corroboration* pierced right through and blew it away, isolating the question I'd been trying to suppress. The waterfall overlook picnic. The stolen wallet. Backpack thrown too hard. What explained the presence of these specific details in John's and my shared story and, now, Eugene's as well? Eugene could have heard, of course, just as Vic had. But jumping jack contest. Red birds. Three boys. The details I'd distinctly seen in my mind but that neither John nor I had spoken out loud. I thought back to when I touched Eugene's forehead, with John touching Eugene's leg—had that not been static electricity, but the zap of our collective connection in some mystical familial Bluetooth neuro-network, Eugene's memories flying up our arms and into our brains, and John and I translated his visual transmission into spoken words as co-interpreters in a true three-way mind-meld? Or was it what I'd initially thought, that given what we knew of Dad and Eugene, as well as the constraints from the bird-watcher video, we came up with the truth, what really happened, and we happened to get a few extraneous details right, by chance?

Mom walked Shannon out through the garage. The door between the kitchen and garage was ajar, and I overheard something that I wish I hadn't, given what happened later that day. It might have stopped the suspicions that still, even now, keep me up at night.

They were discussing the potential need for corroboration. Mom was saying she doubted they could find the boys, much less get them to confess what they'd done, and Shannon said how another key element was Eugene's first communication with Dad because that showed Eugene had calmed down after the meltdown in the mommy-blogger video and was no longer upset with Dad. Shannon said she would push the police to focus on unlocking Dad's phone to get the picture he took of Eugene with the two pages of notes from their first conversation. "It's too bad the two pages weren't in Adam's backpack," Shannon said. "If we had that, I don't see how they justify continuing their case."

———

VIC LEFT, TOO. HE SAID he'd taken the liberty of making us salad and mac and cheese for lunch (the only two things he can make, I knew), he hoped that was okay, he figured we'd all be famished after that marathon session—this of course further endeared him to Mom, how sweet he was, thoughtful and considerate, etc.—and he didn't want to leave so soon, but he wanted to give us time to be together, just the family. It's a mark of how bereft Anjeli's session had left us that no one protested him leaving, or maybe it was the closeness we felt toward him after the near-all-nighter; we were beyond politeness for politeness's sake.

As I walked him out to the car, it occurred to me how you could hear everything going on in the TV room from the kitchen. He had most likely heard Eugene's story, at least the part toward the end about what happened to Dad. I wanted to ask what he thought. Was I right to be quietly freaking out about the matching details between Eugene's story and John's and my whispered conversation? Because any way you looked at it, that was weird, right? Eerie if you thought we got the images zapped from Eugene's brain, obviously, but troubling in a different way if you thought Eugene heard and repeated our whispers, our words having seeped into his dreams, causing him to conflate those images with his own traumatized and discombobulated memories. But—and here was the thing I was most unnerved by, the thing I needed to talk out—what if Eugene repeated our words intentionally? What if he took the core of our spoken story and embellished it, adding in details he'd heard earlier like the pepper spray from Vic, maybe even making up the whole miraculous last conversation with Dad, something he wished had taken place, to give us a last story about Dad to treasure? (Or, to be more cynical about it, to take care of Detective Janus's whole angry-kid-kills-Dad theory?) As someone who heard our middle-of-the-night whispers, Vic could provide an objective assessment of these questions.

At that thought—Vic was a witness, the only witness—I felt a new fear sprout in my chest. I wrapped my arms around him, burrowed my face against his shoulder. Seen through the lens of last night's whispers, it seemed dangerous, him being here. I wanted him gone, far away. Having him around me, or rather, around other people, especially the police, scared me. I couldn't say any of this out loud. I couldn't involve him any more than he already was. I told him to drive safely, to not stop anywhere until he was out of the state. He said okay, didn't ask why.

He said goodbye, and with his lips to my ear, he whispered, "I left you something. On your desk."

———

ON MY DESK WAS A handwritten note from Vic, with a flash drive.

> Used image enhancement apps on HQ notebook pages. You can read much better now. All saved here. Also, finished cataloging all HQ files on backup drive and found/printed file from your dad I think you should read. I think you'll see why.—V

Under his note were typewritten pages titled *Notes for Mia—Fall 2020.* I knew what this was. For the last two years, at college drop-off in the fall, Dad had left me a letter on my dorm room desk saying how much he was going to miss me, giving me advice for the year, reminding me to call home every week, blah blah. They tended to be on the long side, and I told him how sweet it was but wow, it must have taken a long time to write, what with the footnotes with annotations and recommended reading lists and all. Dad laughed and said nah, it's easy because he keeps a file, like a journal, where he jots down stuff he wants to tell me, stuff that reminds him of me, and by August, he has a book's worth of stuff to copy and paste from.

I took the pages to my bed, leaned back against my pillow, and read:

Monday, June 22—Hannah found out Mia changed her majors and is planning to graduate a year early. We're not sure, Mia's being evasive, but it sounds like this happened months ago, and she never told us. Hannah's upset about Mia not being close with us, not sharing anything, but I don't know about that. I remember not telling my parents when I decided to shift away from premed and go into business, mostly because I didn't want to disappoint them. Hannah is a linguistics PhD, so I can see Mia not wanting to disappoint her, no longer following in her footsteps, all that.

The substance of her decision is what upsets me—her dropping philosophy as a major and graduating early. We're talking to her tomorrow, but I've been trying to figure out why this upsets me.

They say we always want more for our children than we have for ourselves, and what I want for her is a better perspective on life than I have. Balance and happiness have been more elusive for me than objective success, and I'm afraid she's like me. I wish I could get it through to her—it's great to achieve and strive, but if you immediately raise the bar, what is the point of the achievement? Why is she in such a hurry to graduate? Why not do a semester abroad, enjoy college friends? And it bothers me that she's going into what sounds like software engineering. I hope she's doing this because she loves computer music. Because I know she loves philosophy. I want to tell her how important it is to choose something you love, not something you think will get you a prestigious, well-paying job.

And music, too. I know she was never going to perform professionally, but I loved hearing her humming around the house, working out her latest compositions, figuring out some strange-sounding chord progression on her keyboard. Will she still do that?

\* \* \*

Found early HQ notes related to this I was thinking about for an essay on crazy college admissions culture:

## Mia and the Dalai Lama: How to Be Ambitious *and* Happy: Jan 2018

Mia got this fortune cookie last night: "The Dalai Lama says to be truly happy in life, you should learn to stop wanting what you don't have." It's a pet peeve of hers to get this type of "non-fortune"—"fortune-cookie philosophizing," she calls it—but she was especially vexed about this one. She went on for quite some length about how "idiotic, reductive, and banal" (her favorite phrase these days) this was because 1) it's very difficult (maybe impossible) to simply want less, from a psychological perspective, and 2) it's not good for you personally or the human race as a whole because it encourages complacency and stagnation; we would never learn, grow, expand, if we didn't yearn and strive for that which we don't already have. She said, "I think happiness is overrated, anyway; if I had to choose between that and achieving things I want, I'd happily give up happiness."

I laughed and told her it's not an all-or-nothing thing, that the message is one for perspective, for balance, but I've been thinking about that ever since. Is happiness truly incompatible with ambition?

The happiness industry does seem to assume an inverse correlation between happiness and ambition; there are countless articles about how you can become happier by moderating your ambition.

But Mia's right. There are people like her who can't or don't want to compromise their ambitions. Hannah and I have often said to each other how it's a gift, John having more modest ambitions that are easier for him to reach, but given that Mia is not naturally like that, I don't want to force or trick her into striving for less. Is Mia doomed to a life of disappointments, or can she have both?

May 2018: I think you can reconcile ambition and happiness by lowering the baseline while keeping expectations high. Many of us have a tendency to subconsciously define the baseline as the most/best we've experienced, especially those ingrained in the American culture of always wanting more, seeking "the best," and when bad things happen, needing to remain "hopeful" and "optimistic," keep your "chin up," this is just a temporary setback, and so on. Mia does this a lot, an achievement immediately becoming the new baseline and needing the next new thing. I used to be the same way, especially within the up-or-out corporate culture; you get promoted and you're happy for a week until you adapt and your baseline moves up, then you want the next promotion, higher and higher.

Is this an inborn, immutable trait? Or is it possible to teach Mia to keep striving upward and achieving more, but to keep the baseline at the bottom position? Make a point to interact with the people at that baseline position, remember yourself in that position. As you make an upward jump, work hard to maintain your baseline at the original level, which will help you to revel in each achievement for longer.

I looked up the Dalai Lama's quote (mostly to win a bet with John, who was convinced the fortune-cookie printer confused the Dalai Lama with Dumbledore, who told Harry Potter that in the Mirror of Erised (desire), the world's happiest person would see himself exactly as he is). The real quote is: "We need to learn how to want what we have NOT to have what we want in order to get steady and stable Happiness." Here's how I interpret it: Of course you will and can want more. You *should* want more. But you should also <u>spend time trying to want what you already have</u>. It's slightly different from "practicing gratitude" or appreciating or thanking a higher force or God for what you have. (Mia would never do those things.) It means: Don't let what you already have be the baseline. Think of yourself before you gained what you have, and remind yourself how much you want that, what you already have—your spouse/partner, your family, your house, your job. Imagine you in an alternate universe where you don't have your family, can't have your kids or your partner, how desperate that alternate-you would be to get what you have. Or if you don't believe in the multiverse, the you from five years ago.

Would this work? Mia loves multiverse/time-travel anything. A one-month challenge to do this once a day while brushing your teeth in the morning?

That was the end. I read it again, and again. Closed my eyes. Wondered what Dad would say if he knew I'd give up college, grades, honors, everything he thought was so important to me, if I could talk to him about it for five minutes, if I could read the letter he would have written me.

I pulled Dad's note to my chest and put my head on my pillow. I pictured the tomorrow me, the next-week me, brushing my teeth, actively remembering the present-day me who desperately wanted Eugene safe, all charges dismissed, all of us here at home, together. I would keep this moment—today, right now, with Dad gone and Eugene in jeopardy of being thrown behind bars—as the baseline, ensuring that I'd be relatively happy for the rest of my life. Because this had to be my family's bottom point. Things couldn't possibly get worse.

# THIRTY-TWO

# The Beginning of the End (?)

IN MUSIC, THE LONGER A DISSONANT CHORD IS SUSTAINED, THE GREATER the emotional satisfaction when it resolves. When the discordant sound stretches, going on a little too long—it sounds wrong, and you know it will resolve soon, it has to, but impatience and anticipation build, and while those notes are still sustained in the vibrations of your eardrums, the consonant chord plays. The promise of that liminal state when both things exist, the dissonance and consonance colliding into an exquisite messiness until the dissonant notes fully dissipate into harmony.

This is one of the elements I've been trying to capture in my algorithmic programming work—trying to figure out if there is a limit to the period of dissonance. At what point would the listener get frustrated and give up on the promise of resolution?

————

AFTER EUGENE'S ZOOM SESSION WITH Anjeli, we were in a strange purgatory, transitioning from Dad being missing to Dad being dead. We knew he was, but the world at large didn't. The police search was still ongoing. People were still emailing and calling with tips about having seen him. Local media were still carrying updates, although thankfully juvenile proceedings were confidential so no one had picked up that the missing father's son was scheduled for an appearance in court. It seemed premature to tell them to stop, especially since there was a chance, however miniscule, that Dad had somehow survived the fall and been carried by the river's currents somewhere inaccessible, injured but managing to survive by drinking rainwater and eating plants. No one said anything about notifying friends or making funeral arrangements or anything of the sort. Everything, including mourning, had to wait.

We ate. Showered. Cried in the shower. Joined and browsed area blogs for women who like to pepper-spray teenage boys. Googled *what's the highest fall someone has ever survived* and scanned local newspaper articles of hikers and kayakers involved in near-drownings in and around our park. Made a list of the names and dates. Paid $50 to an online directory to get their phone numbers and addresses. I knew it was all pointless and I was torturing myself, but anything was better than the stasis of waiting.

It got worse after Shannon called to let us know that based on the notes and recording of Eugene's account, Officer Higashida had scheduled a virtual meeting at eight that night to discuss the possibility of nullifying his order for the arraignment hearing. By the time she came over and the Zoom hearing started, we had surpassed excruciating to hyper-calm.

"Eugene," Officer Higashida said, "I'd like to start by apologizing for everything you've had to go through. I know it's been a long day, so I'll try to keep this as short as possible. First, I'd like to dispense with the matter of Detective Janus yesterday. Your attorney has argued that this was a simple misunderstanding. You moved your arm toward the letterboard, which Detective Janus mistook as a stabbing gesture toward your mother. Detective?"

"I'm fine with dropping this matter. For the record, the reason I brought Eugene to the station was to follow protocol about logging injuries. Eugene, I'm truly sorry for grabbing your arm like that. I can understand how alarming that must have been. I hope you understand that I was trying to protect your mother."

There was something unnerving about Detective Janus's oversolicitous apology. She seemed to be going out of her way to prove her fairness, the way you might to build up credit for something you were planning for later. Or maybe I was being paranoid, letting my hatred of this woman color my perception, and I should just savor her apology the way Shannon and the rest of my family appeared to be doing.

"That leaves the matter of Mr. Parson," Officer Higashida said. "Ms. Haug has argued that Eugene's statement makes clear that this was a tragedy that came about through no fault of Eugene's. Detective Janus, you agree?"

She sidestepped the question. "I realize this is an informal hearing, but even so, my colleagues at the Commonwealth's Attorney's Office were pointing out that they don't believe they've ever seen this type of communication method used in legal proceedings."

"This specific method, spelling using this particular stencil letterboard, may not have been used in court," Shannon said. "But it's no different from using an interpreter for a foreign-language speaker or a typing pad or sign-language specialist for a hearing-impaired witness. Eugene Parkson is like any other person who needs an extra step to help their thoughts be understood by others. And you can see from the video—the words I transcribed were *his* words, chosen by him. You can call it poking or encoding, but all he was doing was spelling and writing on his own, using a slightly different tool than I might, say, in typing a memo."

"That makes a lot of sense to me," Officer Higashida said, and Detective Janus smiled stiffly, like she reluctantly agreed. "So, treating Eugene's statement like any other statement by any other juvenile, what are your thoughts, Detective?"

Detective Janus said despite their "reservations" about the format of "Eugene's story," they'd worked hard to follow up on the leads from

"Eugene's story." (She repeated *Eugene's story* fourteen times during the course of this exchange. I kept count.) She said the woman known for pepper-spraying young men had admitted to being at the park on Tuesday morning but had firmly denied seeing, much less pepper-spraying, Dad or Eugene. The mommy-blogger said she did not see anyone else near Eugene and Dad. Also, Detective Janus's team had not been able to track down the boys "alleged by Eugene Parkson to have instigated the difficulties resulting in Mr. Parson's disappearance."

Look, I know about legal parlance. I know the police and lawyers have to use words like *allege* and *instigate,* the legal presumptions and blah blah. But there was an edge to the legalese being uttered by Detective Janus, an emphasis that made it clear this wasn't a formality.

Shannon said, "These objections are irrelevant. It doesn't surprise me that someone who used pepper spray to attack people, a felony, would deny having committed that crime. The blogger videographer not seeing the pepper-sprayer near Eugene and his father also proves nothing; Eugene made it clear he was in distress for a long time, so she could easily have encountered them several minutes after the pepper-sprayer had left the scene. I suspect there's a larger point here, something Detective Janus is trying to insinuate. I would appreciate it if she could stop playing games and say what she means."

"I have to agree, Detective," Officer Higashida said. "What are you trying to say?"

Detective Janus narrowed her eyes. "Look, I wish I didn't have to say this." (Then don't say it, I thought.) "But we're having trouble corroborating Eugene's statement. We procured new evidence this morning, a very disturbing recording made by a bird-watcher from an island in the river around the time Adam Parson went missing. It raises a lot of questions, and I'd like you to review it."

As Shannon objected and the officer said this isn't a formal proceeding and told Detective Janus to go ahead and play it, I saw on my family's faces the same confusion I was feeling. Was this a different recording made by a different person? How many bird-watchers on an island in the river could there be?

The video played. It was the same video, the same segment Vic had gotten for us—nothing before the red bird in the sky, nothing after Dad's *Eugene, nooooo*—with nothing that contradicted Eugene's explanation.

"I don't understand," Officer Higashida said. "This recording is perfectly in alignment with everything in Eugene's statement. It corroborates it perfectly."

"That's what I thought at first," Janus said. "But then we found out that Eugene, his family, and his lawyer actually got this recording yesterday, before we obtained it. The woman who provided this recording told us that an African American young man surreptitiously copied this recording onto his phone without her permission somehow, she thought perhaps to collect the reward money. Anyway, officers on my team recognized this young man's description as similar to Mia's boyfriend, whom they escorted to the Parksons' home yesterday, which makes sense—that's why he snuck a copy, to show the family—the fair inference being that they all saw the video last night. *Before* Eugene gave his statement."

Shit. This was exactly what Shannon had warned about. I wished Vic hadn't brought it, that none of us had seen it. The ideal scenario was if this recording had turned up *after* Eugene's statement, serving as independent proof verifying Eugene's account—end of story. What happened was the worst possible scenario. Detective Janus saw the recording, which confirmed her existing assumption that Eugene harmed Dad. When she heard Eugene's account, she probably started wondering if she'd jumped too quickly to form an unfair assumption, maybe scolded herself. *Then* she discovered we had the recording all along. On top of all the doubts, she now felt hoodwinked.

"Okay, let's ask them," Officer Higashida said. "Did you see this recording? If so, when?"

"Yes, we did," Shannon said. "Last night. So what? What exactly are you accusing us of, Detective?"

"I'm not *accusing*. But as I'm sure Officer Higashida will agree, it's very rare to get an explanation that so perfectly matches all evidence uncovered up to that point. Very convenient and lucky how Eugene's story happens to neatly address the most incriminating details from the blogger video *and* the bird-watcher audio." This was, in essence, exactly what Shannon had said to praise Eugene's statement—how it perfectly explained everything—but in Detective Janus's words, it sounded sinister. It was then that Janus uttered for the first (though definitely not the last) time that oxymoronic phrase I've come to despise: the "ideal realistic story," as in, "You couldn't design a more ideal realistic story if you tried."

Shannon was livid. "I am outraged by this. Are you accusing me and my clients of *concocting* the story here? Perhaps Eugene's explanation perfectly matches the evidence because it's the truth!"

Officer Higashida said, "Detective Janus, I understand what you're saying in theory, but I'm confused why you sound so sure something's awry. Do you have specific reasons to doubt Eugene's statement? Evidence that calls it into question?"

Vic. Oh my God, had she followed him out of my house, arrested him, threatened him? Or maybe he had an attack of conscience, went straight to the police from our house? My judgment was all off and I was having trouble figuring out whether this was the most ludicrous idea ever or completely and totally plausible. Thank God, Detective Janus said, "No, no evidence, but—"

"Are you suggesting," he said, "that a fourteen-year-old boy with significant communication and cognitive impairments took the evidence before us and managed to synthesize it into a complicated story that explains all facets of it?" I knew his point was in our favor, but it was hard not to feel offended on behalf of Eugene. Was he still doubting Eugene's intelligence? Eugene smiled, and he looked for all the world to be proving Officer Higashida's point—a happy simpleton, a bah-bo incapable of strategizing, synthesizing, manipulating. But sometimes we smile to cover up deep shame, and that's what I suspected it was.

"Let's not forget," Detective Janus said, "Eugene had at his disposal family members who are all very invested, and—"

"Well, let's ask them. Dr. Park, Mia, John, did you make up this story and repeat it to Eugene and have him memorize it and then somehow will him to repeat it letter by letter, word by word, over the course of four hours this morning?" The way Officer Higashida said this, it was clear: he was offended on our behalf and having none of it.

Mom said, "No, of course not. That's ridiculous. It's insulting."

Detective Janus wasn't cowed by Officer Higashida's contemptuous tone. She said, "John, Mia, is that true?"

John started hemming and stuttering and I thought, Oh my God, no. I said, "No, I didn't make up this story for Eugene as some sort of alibi," reminding John, I hoped, that whatever we may have done last night, it was not some conspiratorial attempt to subvert the truth or whatever.

John got it, said, "No. I would never do that."

"I'm sorry I had to ask," Detective Janus said. "But an unsubstantiated statement by the accused is not enough to just—"

"What about Adam's phone?" Shannon said. "Any progress in finding the picture of the two pages Eugene told us about?"

Detective Janus said no, they'd tried getting pictures off the phone without the passcode but couldn't. "Actually, it's those two pages that led us to question Eugene's story to begin with. We found it strange that the pages weren't in the backpack, especially since we found that notebook and the letterboard there. Add to that how skeptical Ms. Rapari seemed about them being able to communicate all of a sudden, I felt it was my duty to bring this up."

Officer Higashida seemed more convinced by this line of logic, asking if any of the backpack's compartments were open (answer: no), when Shannon said, "What if the pages weren't in the backpack? What if Mr. Parson put them in his pocket?" Detective Janus said they considered that, but that Mom had told her Dad was wearing gym shorts with no pockets.

"Maybe it was in Eugene's pocket," Mom said. "He was wearing those black shorts he loves—they have pockets. We should check."

I really didn't want to go down this road. Not because I doubted the existence of those two pages—I didn't at that point; not yet— but because I remembered where the shorts were: in the washing machine where I'd put Eugene's stained clothes, right before telling him to scrub off the blood under his nails. Had I, in my attempt to protect my little brother, inadvertently destroyed the one piece of evidence we desperately needed to prove his innocence? I was about to confess when John cut in, said he knew where they were, and ran upstairs.

He came down within a minute, couldn't have done it faster if he'd grabbed the first thing he came across without even look- ing. I thought for sure he'd come back empty-handed and say no, they weren't where he thought they'd be (behind the bathroom door where Eugene puts all his dirty clothes). But instead, John held up Eugene's dry, dirt-covered shorts. He handed them to Shannon, say- ing, "I feel something in this pocket."

Shannon, who already had on latex gloves as part of her Covid- protective gear, asked Detective Janus and Officer Higashida for per- mission before checking. As she took out and unfolded some paper from the pocket, I tried to think. Had the shorts fallen out of the pile of laundry I compiled and carried to the washer, and in my rush, I'd missed them, the same way socks get flung and lost? Or had I been so focused on the blood-blotted shirt that I'd left the shorts behind? Maybe when I was talking to the police, Eugene stopped the wash, remembering about the pages and wanting to save them? But why hadn't he mentioned that while telling us about the pages? And how did John find them so easily and quickly?

Shannon scanned the pages before holding them out to the cam- era for everyone to see. The letters were reversed on the screen and hard to make out, but I saw immediately that it was the same paper and style of writing as on the pages in the manila folder I'd found that first night, the pages I'd mistaken for code. It was the block print Dad used for important points in his HQ notebook, the grocery list he kept on the refrigerator, the silly notes he'd put in my lunch bag during high school. (I'd thrown them away, and now I wished I'd saved them. Just one.)

Shannon said, "You can see random letters on top—Eugene said they were practicing poking letters earlier—and the first real sentence halfway down, I FORGIVE YOU. The image is reversed, so I'll read the whole thing."

John said, "Actually, just ours is mirrored. Here, I'll fix it," and adjusted the settings. As the image flipped, Dad's writing snapped into focus:

I FNORGIBVE U

SORRY I HWURT UR EFACE

I DIDMNT MEAN 2

LOL

HUNGRY

CHIP

M MAD SHE GOT BAD MOVIE?

M6 = J9 LOL

IM 7

IF IN STORM HAPPY LATER BUT AWFUL NOW

WHY R U INTO THIS?

LETS TELL FAM ABOUT U 2

HQ

TODAY

PROMISE?

Something seemed wrong about the note. I scanned the words on the screen, Eugene's comments and questions in Dad's block print, line by line, letter by letter. What was bothering me?

As I kept studying the words—something about the abbreviations, maybe the numbers?—Officer Higashida flipped through a document in front of him. "I don't know about you, Detective Janus, but this is pretty convincing to me. I'm looking through Eugene's statement and this is consistent with that. Eugene apologized, they joked, the LOL, asking for chips, the rest must be questions and comments on his father's notebook. Even if you don't find anything else, this ought to be enough to convince any reasonable person that things happened the way Eugene said they happened. I can't think of anything that makes me question his account in any way."

That was the beginning of the end. Detective Janus didn't say she agreed but she didn't say she disagreed—just vague generalities about how they were still following up on (unspecified) leads, maybe they could polygraph the pepper-spray woman and try to identify the three boys—and I let myself think what I'd been afraid to think, that the threat of Eugene's detention was maybe, quite possibly (although not definitely, I had to warn myself) over. There would be more investigation in the days to come—identification of other pepper-spray women, as it turned out that there were several, the result of a semiviral post in our area about women and Asians being attacked in the park; Eugene having to look through pictures of boys known to frequent the wallet-drug area; verification from forgery experts about Dad's writing. But that would all be later, in the period we'd come to file away in our memories and conversations as Afterward.

Officer Higashida said, "Detective Janus, I realize the investigation isn't over. But I'm not going to keep this case open on the offhand chance you find something in the future. If you do, you can come back. As of now, there's nothing that makes me suspect Eugene is anything but a tragic victim and someone we should be taking care of, not accusing. So can we agree that we should leave this poor family alone?"

Detective Janus didn't say anything, and Officer Higashida said, "Great. I'll go ahead and nullify my previous temporary detention recommendation and house arrest and have this expunged from the juvenile detention court's records."

The rest of the hearing went by in a blur. What I remember most is how Officer Higashida scribbled something on his legal pad and put the cap back on his pen slowly and carefully with a loud *click* and then, just as slowly and carefully, put the pen down in precisely the middle of the pad. As he gave his final remarks, I stared at the pen on the screen, kept thinking of that boy's face in the detention center window behind the bars.

Yesterday, we'd been jubilant at the announcement of a temporary reprieve. And yet, when the Zoom ended and the screen went blank, none of us celebrated—no hugs, no thank-Gods, no smiles. The removal of the threat against Eugene—that was huge, something we'd been desperate for, and I expected it to ease the pressure squeezing my lungs and heart, for the aches around my body to lessen. But if anything, the pain intensified and deepened, as if my worry about Eugene had been covering up something else, like a bandage, and now that it was ripped away, I was having to face the permanent hurt beneath.

Shannon said, "Listen, I know you're devastated about Adam, of course you are. But what happened just now, it's a good thing, it's something you can and should be grateful for and even feel happy about. I think maybe you're feeling guilty because it feels unseemly to be celebrating at a time like this. But it's a triumph. Not just the hearing, but Eugene finally getting to communicate his ideas and advocate for himself. I'm so proud of you, Eugene. I'm so happy and relieved for you, for all of you. So take the time to process everything, and make sure to enjoy those moments when you do feel glad and relieved. I'm sure that's what your father would want. What he did for Eugene, that was heroic, and you should celebrate that, too. He deserves that."

She was right, of course, and her words seemed to wake up Mom, who thanked her for everything—for putting her life on hold to focus on Eugene's case so wholly, for putting her health at risk to be in the same room with us, for so expertly handling us and the authorities to get us the best possible result.

Shannon packed up her notes, put the two pages into a Ziploc bag to drop off at the police station, and walked to the door. Mom followed from a distance to say goodbye. When we heard the door close, John, Eugene, and I looked at each other. I half-expected Eugene to run upstairs again and jump, but I could see exhaustion over-take him, his slumped body and huge eyes making him look more like a vulnerable little kid than ever. We were all sitting on the sofa, Eugene between John and me, and we collapsed into each other, our heads touching.

Mom walked back into the room. She stopped next to the stencil-letterboard stand, head slightly cocked, and studied us the way you might a painting you loved but had never before seen in person—with new appreciation, a cataloging of the facets you're noticing for the first time, a deeper love than you realized. Or maybe it was me seeing her that way.

Mom stepped toward us, and Eugene bolted up and ran to her, into her open arms. John and I reached for each other's hand and squeezed hard.

We stayed that way for a long time. John and me, our eyes blurred with tears but open to take in the image before us. Mom and Eugene in a tight hug, tears coming together where their cheeks touched. Beside them, the letterboard stand, Eugene's lifeline, and on the wall in front of us, Shannon's chart.

*What happened to Adam Parson?*

Finally answered. *Accidental death <u>with</u> EP involvement* ruled out.

Later that night, when Shannon sent the notice of cancellation of Eugene's juvenile court hearing, we would put a thick marker line across the final bullet-point item on the chart and rip it off the wall.

In the days and weeks to come, we would place the letterboard stand in front of Eugene and cheer and hope and wait for him to communicate with us without Anjeli for the first time; we would try multiple times a day, for as many times and as many days as needed. And when that finally happened, we would put into words all that we had felt during these sixty hours—the panic and complacency and self-blame and doubt and even the moments of fury and hatred toward Dad—and begin to process what we had gone through and learn to accept our family with Dad only in our memories. All that, we knew was to come.

For now, the beginning. Tomorrow, or next week, or next month, we would begin anew, find a new baseline from which to rebuild, new bonds to form a new family unit, smaller than before. But that would wait. John and I stood up. Hand in hand, we walked to join Mom and Eugene. We stepped into their waiting embrace.

# PART VI

## A HUNDRED DAYS

October 1, 2020
*Thursday*

# THIRTY-THREE

# Zebras, Unicorns, and Occam's Razor

WE END WHERE WE STARTED. A MAN DOESN'T COME HOME FROM THE park. The boy he was with, his youngest son, runs home by himself, scraped up, blood under his nails, traumatized. He jumps and screams for hours, trying to calm down in vain. He doesn't. He can't. The park is a place with high cliffs, raging waters that churn, where it's easy to slip and fall and never be seen again.

The English philosopher William of Ockham, who advocated a problem-solving principle of thrift and parsimony that became Occam's razor, would say: when choosing between hypotheses, the simplest answer requiring the fewest assumptions is most likely correct. In other words, don't overthink it. The obvious answer is that this missing man fell into the water by accident and died. So why did we spend so much time looking for zebras and unicorns?

Same with Eugene. A boy with motor-planning difficulties evident in every aspect of his life, especially fine motor capabilities, can't talk. Isn't the obvious answer that it's a motor issue? Why is the first assumption that it's a cognitive issue, a behavioral issue? Why not the thing consistent with everything we can see? And if that boy finds someone who makes communication possible by holding a letterboard at an angle easiest for him to spell out words, why the unicorn answer that the supposedly cognitively deficient kid is somehow managing to detect and decode some near-invisible signal to perfectly spell long answers? Why do we avoid the obvious?

We spent a lot of the summer and fall working with Eugene on spelling and moving to typing on a portable tablet. As we've been telling people about Eugene's work with Anjeli, we've encountered a shocking number of people who flat-out refuse to believe. I'm not talking about people with questions, unwilling to believe without proof. I'm talking about outright deniers who reject proof, claiming it's all an elaborate hoax. Videos of nonspeakers typing independently—must be doctored. Nonspeakers typing responses to audience questions at conferences—preprogrammed tablets, or maybe their parents typing responses from backstage. One of Anjeli's earliest clients is a nonspeaking autistic boy whose frequent repetitive behaviors include arm-flapping and head-banging. To enter college, he had to take an exam in an empty room by himself with the university's own computer equipment. The deniers wrote long analyses, like they were dissecting magic tricks: hidden camera in hair plus covert earpiece, the mom outside by the building whispering letters, one by one, or typing them in directly using a Bluetooth keyboard. It's depressing, infuriating, and fascinating all at once—the herculean efforts people will exert to not believe what they're seeing, to reject anything that doesn't fit into the narrative they've been given about how the world works. Like a particularly stubborn anchoring bias at the collective level. It's exhausting to deal with, and when we say no, that's enough, they'll say, *See? They're hiding something.*

If you set the epistemological bar high enough, there are things that can never be proven; extreme skepticism leads to nihilism, the erasure of all meaning. What I don't understand is why. And then I think of Mom saying she was terrified to believe that Eugene had been locked in his whole life, the guilt she bore for causing her son's agony. If believing your eyes and accepting proof might mean you were wrong, you've unwittingly been responsible for condemning a whole group of people to internal imprisonment—it might be easier to deny. But I can't ever forgive them for it.

I'm not saying all nonspeakers are like Eugene, can benefit from methods like Anjeli's, their issues motor rather than cognitive. I'm just saying, please don't make assumptions before you know, based on the incorrect "nonverbal" label, based on how someone looks and acts. Take the time to find out. Which brings us back to Occam's razor. Because it's a heuristic rule of thumb, a mental shortcut designed for efficiency, and if this whole experience has taught me anything, it's the fallacies inherent to heuristics. Shortcuts, cheats, cognitive biases, things we do and assume for efficiency, based on probabilities and statistics, instead of taking the time to figure it out. Being Asian as a proxy for being a math-loving, un-American foreigner, being a Black man as a proxy for having criminal intent, being nonspeaking as a proxy for being nonverbal, being unable to point to the right answers on IQ tests as a proxy for being stupid (further a proxy for being less than human), smiling as a proxy for being happy, and on and on.

Dad would say we need to keep the baseline low, anchor it to when we thought Eugene was truly nonverbal, to keep the world's inexplicable doubts and downright hostility from disappointing us. But I haven't been doing that. We discussed it, and the thing is, I'd rather keep the baseline as what it should be, what it needs to be: people presuming and accepting intelligence and competence and worth. To do anything less would be like saying, let's keep as the baseline when women couldn't vote, when Black people were slaves, when American citizens were imprisoned for being Japanese, and let our hearts soar and sing Kumbaya that's not happening today. Fuck that. That's the fundamental thing I'm not sure Dad and other happiness-maximization proponents out there get: for some of us, the premise that happiness is the end-all and be-all of life is flat-out wrong.

Eugene has a different take. Not on the societal baseline and the presumption of competence—we agree on that—but that even though Dad didn't mean for everything that happened to be an experiment, that's what it became, in effect, for our family. Our baseline became one in which not only was Dad dead, but Eugene himself was lost to a prison. We are devastated by Dad's loss, but comparing our situation with that baseline—what could have happened, what almost happened—makes us feel a little bit better. In that sense, Dad has proven his point, and Harmonee has as well.

Eugene extends his generosity even to the deniers. Not that he's not infuriated by them, but he refocuses that anger on work, to fuel his motivation to fully transition to independent typing and connect with other nonspeakers. Anjeli hosts weekly hangouts in her backyard. Eugene's been observing only, intimidated by the pace of the discussion, but he loves going, seeing this community of nonspeakers communicating with each other—joking, sharing, connecting, like any other group of teenage friends.

There are two other observers like him, both autistic boys around Eugene's age who are relatively new to using the letterboard. The three of them have been doing group therapy sessions, taking turns answering Anjeli's questions about history, science, literature, similar to a small homeschool group. As they've grown more comfortable with one another and with using letterboards, Anjeli's been encouraging them to work on collaborative poems. She says it must be their lifelong deprivation of verbal output, or maybe autistic people's natural inclination for patterns and the intensity of their sensory processing, but her clients have a natural affinity for poetry. I've asked if I can use my composition program to set this one to music, as part of my thesis.

> Remembering the anger and trembling fear
> grimly weary, ghastly teary.
> New voices in my ears.
> Now the end of isolation nears.
>
> I am happy to be here
> where I have no fear.
> I bereave your fear.
> I am here, I am here.

It's a refrain you see a lot in the poetry and essays of nonspeakers. *I am here.* Such a simple declaration of existence that shouldn't be necessary for any human being, so what does it mean that this whole group of people feels the need to say it so often? It's the repetition that breaks my heart. The insistence, the touch of defiance. It makes me want to grab every one of their deniers by the shoulders and shake them, scream in their faces, *Do you see? They are here. They're fucking here, same as you.* They have words, thoughts, opinions. I want to show these people the video of Eugene, the ferocity in his clenched hands as he spelled I A-M H-E-R-E, then the comma, not a period, then another I A-M, then him pausing, arms still in the air, turning to his friends, one by one, an unspoken understanding passing between them, and all three of them spelling out together, in unison, H-E-R-E.

———

TODAY IS THE HUNDREDTH DAY of Dad being gone, although because there's no body, he hasn't been legally declared dead yet. Shannon's filing a petition for the death certificate, which is necessary for things like the life insurance payment and release of medical records. A few months ago, Detective Janus closed Dad's case and returned his things to us, which we took as a conclusive end, but Shannon warned it can be reopened at any time. Dad's case is still considered an unresolved missing-person case.

In the Korean-Buddhist tradition Mom grew up with, the hundredth day of a person's death is considered the official close of the mourning period. It seems appropriate, somehow, that Dad's case is still considered unresolved. Because here's the thing. Just as the first hundred days are supposed to be for mourning, for all the questioning, denying, being angry, and whatever the steps of grief are, we've spent a lot of time going around and around on the still-unresolved questions about Dad those first sixty hours uncovered. Some, we've resolved (or decided to leave alone) more than others, one being the whole cancer experiment thing. By talking to Dad's doctor (who talked to Mom after local news coverage of Dad's presumed death) and friends, as well as scrutinizing the HQ files, here's what we've pieced together: Dad had been waking up frequently to pee, a sign of getting older or prostate cancer, so given his family history, he had his annual blood screening test early. It came back positive, but—and this is a ridiculously huge *but*—the test has a false-positive rate of 15 to 75 percent (!!!!), and he was torn about scaring us needlessly. While waiting for the biopsy, he did two things: 1) scheduled a second screening test for June 23, the day he went missing, and 2) told three of his six core Henry's House friends about the positive test (although not the high false-positive rate) and the second scheduled test. He didn't tell Mom about the initial positive test.

This leaves two mysteries I don't think we'll ever solve. One is whether the last HQ experiment dated June 23 involves this repeat screening test. I say yes, that Dad must have told half the mom group about the test (asking them to tell no one, not even the others in the group, the way he did with John and me in the earlier HQ experiments) and left the other three as the control group. Given Dad's notes about protecting his family from traumatic news, I think it makes sense he'd experiment on friends; would learning about the positive screening test earlier lessen the pain if the later test confirms cancer? Would it intensify the relief in the case of good news? John counters that Dad's own notes said he wouldn't do anything cruel, and experimenting about cancer would definitely qualify as cruel, even for casual friends. He thinks Dad vented to the first friends he saw after getting the screening test results but, once he calmed down, decided the test was too inaccurate to tell us or anyone else about until the repeat test. Mom and Eugene vacillate, depending on the day. Vic has no idea, won't even venture a guess, but he thinks I'm eager to pin this down as the June 23 experiment because I need to cross it off and move on. Because if this isn't the experiment, that opens up a whole new area of inquiry as to what in hell it could be—it could be *anything,* and that much uncertainty, I'm apparently uncomfortable with and would not be able to stand. He's probably not wrong, although I would never tell him that.

Of course, the mystery remains: Did Dad actually have cancer? We will never know; no one knew, including Dad or his doctors. Dad would say we should assume yes, because then the baseline from which we measure the tragedy of his early death will be lower. But when your happiness level is 0.00000001, does it matter if you divide it by a baseline of 10 or 1? It's still fucking horrible. Like that point about nuclear bombs and the Cold War—it doesn't matter if you could kill everyone in the world ten times over or one hundred times over; dead is dead.

The greater mystery stems from Eugene's statement and the two-page note found in his shorts. I'd estimate that in the last ninety-seven days, I've thought about these things approximately 70 percent of my waking hours, or 1,630 hours. There are so many questions and sub-questions, so many possibilities, I had to make a chart:

| Question | Best Case | Middle | Worst Case |
|---|---|---|---|
| 1. Is Eugene's story true? | Yes | Partly | No |
| 1a. Dad's apology the night before | Yes | Partly | No |
| 1b. Pepper spray leading to scene in video | Yes | Partly | No |
| 1c. First open communication with Dad | Yes | Partly | No |
| 1d. Dad's fall | Yes | Partly | No |
| 2. Was John's/my vision real? | Yes | No | No |
| 3. Did Eugene hear and use John's/my story? | No | Kind of (subconsciously) | Yes (intentionally) |
| 4. Is the 2-page note in Eugene's pocket the real note written by Dad? | Yes | | No |
| IF NO: <br> 4a. Created/planted by Mom, John, or both? | | One | Both |
| 4b. Why created/planted? | | Just in case (insurance) | Don't believe note existed (don't believe Eugene's story) |
| 4c. Does Eugene think it's fake? | No (very similar to real note) | Not sure (knows note exists but thought it looked different or it wasn't in shorts pocket) | Yes |

I highlighted what I believe at least 80 percent of the time, which is (ironic and surprising, given my usual anti-optimism stance) the ideal, best-case scenario: everything happened exactly the way Eugene said it did; he was asleep the whole time and didn't hear anything John and I whispered; I screwed up somehow and didn't wash Eugene's shorts, and the note in his shorts was genuine. Simple, in line with Occam's razor. The only thing I waver on is the co-vision I had with John; I'm fifty-fifty on whether it's from an inexplicable telepathic link with Eugene akin to Blue Brain, or whether it's the subconscious byproduct of our years of mind-meld chain-talking practice.

The chart's right-hand column is the worst-case scenario: that

John and I made up the whole story; Eugene heard our whispers (which is why his snore got louder—he was pretending to be asleep) and embellished it to make up a fake story; and when Shannon fretted about needing corroboration, Mom and/or John used the time between our Zoom with Shannon and the nullification hearing—six hours, with me out of the way upstairs for enough time to pull it off—to forge a fake note, put it in Eugene's clean shorts, and rub in dirt and grass from the backyard to make the shorts look unwashed; and in actuality, what really happened was that Eugene and Dad never made up, and in a moment of frustration and fury, Eugene pushed Dad off the cliff. I don't believe this version one iota, not even 0.001% of the time.[29] For one thing, that last breakfast, with

---

29 I did consider it for about thirty minutes (0.0006% of the last hundred days) and even said it out loud, though only to John. It was in July, after we'd spent all day rewatching Dad's favorite movies in honor of his birthday, what would have been his fifty-first. Mom let Eugene watch most of them, even *Pulp Fiction* (a censored version that bleeped out all the *fuck*s, which—given the 255 instances in this 150-minute movie, or once every 35.3 seconds, on average—was annoying as fuck). She saved *Primal Fear* for after Eugene's bedtime, and watching it, I noticed something I couldn't believe I hadn't before: it (SPOILER ALERT!) features a twist in which the seemingly innocent simpleton (a stutterer, of course, with, yes, a simpleton-like ever-present smile) turns out to be a brilliant, sneering, fast-talking criminal mastermind. I said to John (Mom had fallen asleep), "Okay, you know how he got away with everything because he seems 'slow,' he can't talk fast, and he smiles? Are we doing the same thing? Like, we *say* we know Eugene's smart, but the other day when he solved that quadratic equation, I tried to hide it, but I was really surprised, you know? Like, why don't we believe he could've made up this whole story? Does that show we're secretly still biased?"
John looked at me like I was crazy. "No, it's because we don't think Eugene's an evil, psychopathic liar and murderer. The same way I never considered that you might have killed Dad and gotten rid of his body and blamed the whole thing on Eugene even though if anyone in this family has the brains for it, it's definitely you." He said this last part in a way that made me think it wasn't a compliment, but I chose to let it go. Turning off the TV, I said, "If this were a movie, you know who the mastermind-killer would turn out to be? You, the lovable, charming, wonderful son." John looked annoyed instead of laughing it off as ridiculous, and it made me think: his fight with Dad, the note . . . was it possible? God, what was wrong with me? I vowed to stay away from anything "twisty" or "thrillery" from then on.

Dad's treacly rainbow demo and Eugene's eye roll–laugh combo. Because I've seen that since then; as we've been talking to Eugene, truly including him in conversations instead of talking around him the way we used to, his personality has been emerging, and he often does that looking-at-ceiling thing to make fun of one of us (usually John). Every time I see it, I think of that last morning with Dad, and I know for certain—no way they were in a fight.

It's not all or nothing, of course. Every variation, every permutation and gradation between those two extremes of absolute belief and conspiracy-theorist skepticism, forms a dizzying array of narratives. Of the 11,644 possible combinations of the yes/maybe/no answers on the chart, here's the one that keeps me up at night, the one I was convinced was real after I found the paper on our copier the day after the nullification hearing. Shannon asked for a copy of the pages in the manila folder I'd found that first night; she'd wanted them as baseline samples for her handwriting expert, in case Detective Janus wanted to check the authenticity of the two pages from Eugene's shorts (which, of course, she did). I thought I'd left the folder in my room, but I couldn't find it, so I went searching and found it on Dad's desk. Opening the copier lid, I found paper already on the glass, one of Dad's pages from the manila folder.

Here's what I immediately thought: Mom and/or John took this sheet, the page with pretty much all letters of the alphabet in Dad's block print, copied it using the Darken setting, and then used blank paper on top to trace Dad's letters and forge the note in Eugene's shorts. The perfect way to make sure the handwriting matched.

Picturing the note in my mind, comparing it with the sheet on the copier, I realized what had been nagging at me. Anjeli said Eugene didn't like using spelling shortcuts; she had to cajole him to use text-style abbreviations and numbers to make it easier to tell us what happened to Dad. So why did Dad's letter-by-letter transcription of Eugene's spelling, which had occurred two days *earlier*, contain phrases like *LOL, WHY R U, U 2*, and *FAM*? The obvious answer: Mom and/or John created this sheet afterward, having forgotten that

Eugene hadn't used abbreviations before. Was I being too cynical? Anjeli also said she'd been trying to get Eugene to use shortcuts before. Had he started using them with Dad to make that conversation easier?

That's actually when I created the chart, to think this out. And here's what I highlighted as most likely at that time:

| Question | Best Case | Middle | Worst Case |
|---|---|---|---|
| 1. Is Eugene's story true? | Yes | Partly | No |
| 1a. Dad's apology the night before | Yes | Partly | No |
| 1b. Pepper spray leading to scene in video | Yes | Partly | No |
| 1c. First open communication with Dad | Yes | Partly | No |
| 1d. Dad's fall | Yes | Partly | No |
| 2. Was John's/my vision real? | Yes | No | No |
| 3. Did Eugene hear and use John's/my story? | No | Kind of (subconsciously) | Yes (intentionally) |
| 4. Is the 2-page note in Eugene's pocket the real note written by Dad? | Yes | | No |
| IF NO: | | | |
| 4a. Created/planted by Mom, John, or both? | | One | Both |
| 4b. Why created/planted? | | Just in case (insurance) | Don't believe note existed (don't believe Eugene's story) |
| 4c. Does Eugene think it's fake? | No (very similar to real note) | Not sure (knows note exists but thought it looked different or it wasn't in shorts pocket) | Yes |

Maybe it's my long-standing allergy to too-perfect optimism, but it makes sense it would be something in between, doesn't it? Not picture-perfect heroism and self-sacrifice, but also not Eugene pushing him deliberately: just a momentary sensory meltdown, Dad trying to keep Eugene from losing control after bullies hurl insults, and

Eugene doing what he does when he gets like that—shut his eyes tight, shake his head and body in a churn, a visceral and emphatic *NO, GET AWAY FROM ME,* jumping, squealing—and when he's finally calm and opens his eyes, Dad's gone. The panic of not knowing what to do, the uncovering of the mystery, one by one, as the pieces of evidence surface, and then in the haze of sleep in the middle of the night, the answer comes to him in whispers, what might have happened, what could have happened, what he hopes happened. Maybe he knows he made it up. Maybe he doesn't. Maybe he's not sure. And when the two pages appear in his pocket, he tells himself it must have happened.

As for the note, even when I believe the worst, that Mom and/or John forged the note, I remind myself the note's authenticity has no bearing on Eugene's guilt or innocence. Eugene's story could be 100 percent true, and what's more, they could have believed every word of it, and they still might have faked the note. Substantiating proof, like Shannon said. Insurance, to be brought out only if Detective Janus was being unreasonable and unfair, to make sure the police would leave us alone. Would that be so terrible?

I've tried asking—no, not asking or even suggesting, that's too far. I've brought up the issues with John and Mom. I asked John, "Hey, where were Eugene's shorts, by the way? Because I could swear I washed them," and he said they were in the pile of dirty clothes on Eugene's bathroom floor, but it's funny, his yellow shirt wasn't there. I asked Mom, "Do you remember what happened with the laundry? Because I could swear I washed Eugene's shorts," and she said she put a load in the dryer the other day when the washer beeped, she couldn't remember what day that was, but in any case, wow, how lucky I hadn't.

Same with the note on the copier glass, which I showed to Mom and John. "Look what I found in the copier. Strange, don't you think?" Mom shrugged, said Dad must have copied it for Anjeli's file, which I hadn't thought of. They both looked sad at the thought of Dad doing that. Not guilty, not jumpy. Later, I thought, No, it couldn't have been Dad because I remembered seeing the copier-glass page in the manila folder earlier, although maybe I was wrong because it was one of the pages with only random letters, no science or history questions like some of them—harder to tell apart.

I've never said anything to Eugene. If he didn't make it up, if it's all real, he deserves my full faith. He's been doubted long enough.

And if Eugene did make up any part of it, he did it for us and for Dad. If he wanted to just save himself, he could have chosen a different story, one far less generous to Dad. But Eugene knew we were upset with Dad about keeping Anjeli and PPT from us, about doubting him to the point he couldn't communicate freely with Dad, so he chose a story that explains away all the things that had come to taint our memory of Dad. He restored Dad, our baseline non-asshole Dad, back to us. It's a gift, and I'm going to cherish and savor it, not question it or kick it away.

———

LAST MONTH I GOT THE chance to find out for sure about the note, and maybe more, too—and all without doubting Eugene or asking Mom or John outright. It involved Dad's cryptic hint about his 4-digit phone passcode, *add all H & add all Q,* which we'd never managed to figure out.

I think Shannon was glad we couldn't open the phone. We could assume Eugene was safe as long as the phone remained locked. If it weren't for Dad's missing-person case file remaining technically open, our obligation not to tamper with potential evidence, she probably would have urged us to destroy the phone altogether and ensure this line of inquiry will die out. Since Eugene was never tried, Shannon reminded us, nothing prevents the police from pursuing charges against him in the future. (This came up when Mom told her we were encouraging Eugene to write about this whole ordeal. "That's great," Shannon said, "but keep in mind that anything you write, anything you tell other people—it could come out, so be careful." I thought how sad it must be to be a lawyer, to see everything as potentially incriminating.)

Anyway, one day in August I locked myself out of the house after getting the mail and I was entering the passcode on our garage keypad. Dad had created personalized codes, and mine was the numbers corresponding to MIA P. Looking at the letters under each number and entering 6-4-2-7, I thought: Wait. HAPPINESS was 427746377, and QUOTIENT was 78684368. Add all the numbers corresponding to *happiness,* you get 47. For *quotient,* 50. 4750. A 4-digit number.

I was so excited, I got Dad's phone as soon as I got inside to try it. Only the warning in red letters—9 *Password Attempts Since Last Login*—reminded me; this next password attempt would be our last before Dad's phone would automatically erase all data as a security measure. Okay, I thought, it's good I didn't go ahead on my own, anyway. What was I doing? I should wait until everyone was home and share my revelation. Even if 4750 was right, *especially* if it was right, we needed to do this together. In fact, Eugene should be the one to click Photos, show us the last picture of himself with the two-page note. I could picture his proud grin, the way he'd thrust the phone in my face, a nonverbal *See? Admit it. You doubted me, didn't you? Just a little?*

Wait. Was that why I was so eager to unlock Dad's phone? To check if Eugene was telling the truth? Because, at the end of the day, I believed him mostly, but not fully. And I didn't fully trust Mom and John, either. And wasn't that—the almost-but-not-quite-certain level of faith and trust, the need for external verification and objective proof for himself and maybe for me, too—what kept Dad from telling us about Eugene's work with Anjeli, from seeing how much he was hurting Eugene? I'd condemned him for that, but was I doing the same thing?

I thought of what Shannon would say, what she *did* say that first day in the police station. "I don't care if we ever find out what happened; having no answer at all is better than having an answer that implicates Eugene."

I looked down at the phone, the four blank spaces waiting for my input: 4-7-5-0. I knew myself. I wanted answers, desperately wanted them, and here was one, just a few clicks away. If I put away the phone, I would convince myself the next day or the next that it was for the best, no one else needed to know, I would just peek and not tell anyone either way, and if—*when*—I found the corroborating picture, it would safeguard Eugene in the future.

I heard the garage door open, looked up. I saw the blank space on the wall in front of me where Shannon's chart used to be, a piece of tattered tape left from when I ripped it off the wall. I thought of my vow that first day, reading the chart. Dad or Eugene?

The door to the kitchen opened. "Mia? Will you help us bring in groceries?" Mom and Eugene. I was out of time. I pressed 4. 7. 5. My finger went to 0. Hovered over it. The 8 was right above it, and if I pressed that. . . .

"Mia! Where are you?"

I lowered my finger. Pressed.

Red letters popped up. *Phone Disabled. Data Deleted. Contact Customer Service for Help.*

Like I said, I know myself. And I know Dad.

I put the phone down, now a hunk of plastic and metal. An artifact. I ran to the kitchen where Eugene was carrying a ridiculously heavy bag of groceries, about to fall over. I rushed to help and nearly fell over myself, laughed at what in hell could be in this bag—hunks of coal? bars of gold?—and together, we managed to put it in the pantry. (It was huge bottles of soda and a watermelon.) I hugged him. Hugged Mom. Mom frowned and asked what that was for. I smiled and said I was just saying hello, I missed you today. I went out to bring in more groceries.

# THIRTY-FOUR

# Hidden Bright Moon

THE HUNDREDTH DAY CEREMONY IS GOING TO BE SIMPLE. JUST US FAMILY at the park, starting early in the morning before it gets too crowded. By a strange quirk of fate or coincidence or whatever you want to call it, today, the hundredth day since Dad's disappearance, is the day of the harvest moon, the first full moon of fall. In Korea, today is Chuseok, a day for visiting your ancestors' grave sites to pay respect to their spirits. When we lived in Korea, we celebrated Chuseok the traditional way: hiking along the creek to Mom's family's hillside graveyard and then weeding, bowing, and eating at our grandparents' graves. We had originally envisioned the hundredth day ceremony at home, but when we realized it fell on Chuseok, we started considering going to the park, hiking along the river, and spending time at the waterfall overlook, which was as close to Dad's burial ground as we would get. The idea of communing with Dad's spirit at his death site was a little creepy if you thought about it, but no more so than praying over rotting, worm-covered remains of dead people.

Still, we were initially inclined against it for Eugene's sake. It had taken Eugene two months to want to return to the falls overlook spot, which we understood (honestly, it was hard for all of us), and we said he didn't have to set foot in the park ever again, let alone that spot. But he insisted that yes, it needed to be there. Besides, he said, it wasn't like he was going to forget Dad or what happened to him by avoiding this place. And third (God, I loved how Eugene was picking up Dad's/my quirks, like enumerating everything), he didn't want to forget, he *wanted* to remember and spend time here, because it wasn't just the place where Dad died; it was where Dad saved his life and heroically gave his own. A site to remember Dad's sacrifice and say thank you.

I came to the park early. I left a note for Mom, John, and Eugene saying I wanted to watch the moonset and sunrise, and I'd see them at seven-thirty as planned. I took the riverside trail, the same route Dad took that last day, the water lazing downstream, gently building speed and strength, frothing, churning, overtaking the rocks, and then a dam of craggy boulders, a sudden rush, and finally, the force of gravity, the thunderous drop onto the rocks below, once as jagged and rough as the others but now smoothed out by millennia of erosion. I arrived at the overlook just as the full moon was about to set, the perfect circle of white on one side of the sky, and on the other, the orange of the breaking dawn casting a soft glow over the sheer veil of water droplets.

The moonset-sunrise combination is very pretty, but that's not why I came early. I suspected my plan might be illegal (I intentionally didn't look it up; I can honestly claim ignorance), and I wanted to maintain my family's deniability. I stood where I think Dad was standing when he caught Eugene's arm, the last place he stood before he fell. You can see all the way down from here, a good hundred-foot drop, and I felt a momentary tilt of the earth and sat down. Laying my palms flat on the ground to steady myself, I felt a tingle—probably just the height and my nervous excitement, but given Eugene's words about feeling Dad's presence at this spot and my memory of this exact view from my co-vision, it felt significant in an otherworldly sense. I saw what I'd been seeing in my mind for the last three months. Dad's hand gripped tight around Eugene's arm, his tears, glasses askew, depth perception off, a desperate pull to save Eugene from falling, but gravel under shoes, feet sliding closer to the edge and beyond, in the air, can't hold on anymore, need to let go of Eugene's arm, the last touch of his warm skin. And then, before the fall begins, the thud of Eugene's body hitting the ground, and the realization—Eugene is safe; he will live.

I wish I could stretch that millisecond of relief and peace and joy into a lifetime, pause on that beautiful image of Dad in the air, mid-flight, before the fall—the wind blowing through his hair, a flap of cloth, the bright sunny sky, water rushing below—before gravity takes control and terror hits. And when it does, I know Dad, the terror wouldn't just be of the fall, the impact, water, death, but of Eugene. Will Eugene be okay? How will he get home? And Anjeli. She has Covid, is in the hospital. What if she dies, and no one ever finds out about her work with Eugene? I should have told everyone, why didn't I tell anyone, what if Eugene never gets to talk to Hannah, Mia, John? What if I've condemned him to a life of silence and suffering?

I've been worrying about this since last month, when I called this kayaker who nearly died in our park but was miraculously rescued. It happened more than ten years ago, but he described in vivid detail the moment he thought he was going to die. He said it's really true, what people say about accidents, how time slows way down and your life flashes before your eyes, and he remembers worrying about his son behind him, not only his safety but trivial practicalities. "I worried for what felt like five minutes about how he didn't have money so he couldn't buy any food, and then being mad at myself I didn't give him a credit card just in case, and then wondering how my wife was going to get both her car and mine home," he said, laughing.

I can't tell you how much it upset me, picturing Dad and what he would have agonized about, his guilt and worry over Eugene. I couldn't even tell John or Mom about it, and certainly not Eugene; there was no point in them worrying about it, too, and besides, I didn't want them knowing I was continuing to research cases of people surviving falls and near-drownings in our park.

The answer came the other day when we were discussing what we should do for Dad's ceremony. All three of them were very meh on my idea of spreading ashes in the river (not Dad's *ashes* ashes, obviously, but his parents' combined ashes from the urns on our fireplace mantel, which I argued were essentially Dad's in a genetic sense, mixed with ashes from burning hair from Dad's comb and some HQ notebook pages). Of course, everyone loved John's idea—donating a wooden bench in Dad's memory for the overlook and attaching our plaque to the bench during the ceremony. Eugene wanted to give a speech using his new text-to-speech letterboard app "voice," which also got unanimous love and approval. Anyway, Mom thought we should also read passages from Dad's favorite books (more love and approval), and brought some out, one of which was *The Little Prince*.

John and I read *The Little Prince* with Dad when we were around seven, as part of Dad's campaign to increase my "flexible thinking" skills (my teachers apparently thought I was too rigid and disdainful of others' opinions) by discussing stories that invite differing answers and interpretations. When we got to the end where the narrator worries about his pencil-drawn sheep eating the little prince's flower because he forgot to draw straps on the sheep's muzzle and says, "Ask yourselves: Is it yes or no? Has the sheep eaten the flower?," I said this was stupid. The man didn't need to be worried because he could just decide the muzzle was a special one with Velcroed edges that will stick to the sheep's woolen face even without the straps. Dad said that should work under the story's internal logic, except Velcro hadn't been invented at the time of the story. John had a different idea; the man could draw another picture of the muzzle, with straps, and bury it in the spot where the little prince died. "Would that work even though there's no time travel in the story?" I asked Dad, turning my criticism into a curious-sounding open question the way Dad suggested. "Absolutely," he said, explaining about the nonlinearity of time, its circularity, the way it transcends our understanding of "rationality"—all stuff I knew from Star Trek but hadn't thought to try to apply to other fictional worlds.

All this was what I was thinking when I wrote this story of what happened to us after Dad's disappearance. Even the stuff that shames me to remember, the hateful, spiteful stuff I don't think I could say out loud. I tried writing it as a letter to Dad, but thinking of saying this stuff directly to Dad was too awkward. It was easier pretending that I was writing to someone else, someone I don't know. We were running low on paper in the house, so I printed it in tiny font, single-spaced, with no margins, front and back. (I figured the symbolism was what mattered, not readability.)

So here I am. Sitting on the ground at the falls overlook spot, my palms dirty and pockmarked with tiny gravel-pressed dents, our family's story in my hands. I take out the tin can from the bag I brought and put the pages inside. I click on the long lighter from our fireplace, touch the white-hot base of the flame to the corner of the first page. I hold it there until I see the flames eat away the beginning of the story, word by word—*We didn't call the police right away.*

Watching the fire, I think, Dad, this is for you. I want you to know what happened to Eugene, know that he was okay, know he's spelling with us now, the intensity of the joy we feel every day when he communicates with us. I wrote out the story of what happened after you fell, and I'm burning it and letting the ashes fall where you fell, through the same air, into the same water. I know you don't believe this stuff, and I'm still agnostic on whether all our consciousnesses are connected. But if that's true, by its own internal logic, it has to transcend time. And yes, I also realize that by its own internal logic, I didn't need to type out the story, print it, burn it, all that. Transcendence is transcendence. I guess that part was for me. Proof to myself that I did something, didn't just sit around cogitating. If nothing else, writing it all out, confessing my ugly thoughts, felt good. Burning it feels good, too. I told Vic, and he approves, says my subconscious will get the symbolic resonance of catharsis and atonement or what-ever, and it'll end up saving me a ton of therapy in the future. (Also, it's cold right now; the fire is useful *and* symbolically resonant.)

It doesn't take long for everything to burn and the fire to die out. I pick up the hot tin container using the oven mitts I packed (Vic's idea—he was an Eagle Scout; he's very prepared), walk it to the cliff's edge, and pour out the charred remains. It's messier than I expected. The wind scatters it all over. But one clump of black ashes hits the water, spreads like a puddle of ink, and slowly sinks. As the last clump of burned paper hits the water, I see a man's face at that spot—closed eyes, a slight smile, serene. I've just been staring at that spot for too long, I tell myself and blink, and sure enough, it goes away, turns back into shapeless, meaningless shades of gray water, spray, and rocks underneath. I know it was my brain superimposing an image that doesn't exist, a trick borne of evolution combined with my doing nothing but picture Dad since I got here. But it doesn't matter. I know from now on, when I think of Dad's last moments, I'll think of my words coming into Dad's consciousness for that split second before he's gone. Him knowing that Eugene is safe. That he, all of us, will be all right.

I stand and get busy on the second reason I got here early. It's a surprise for Eugene. We decided we'd have a family-ancestral memo-rial breakfast at the picnic table—Boston cream donuts and bacon in honor of Dad, gimbop rice rolls with fried egg, spinach, and daikon radish in honor of our grandparents—and then start the ceremony with Eugene's speech. It's easiest for Eugene to focus when he's fresh, right after breakfast. He's made a lot of progress, but he still has good days and bad, and he tires easily. He's been having trouble transitioning to a letterboard app and touching the letters on the screen with his index finger (a fine motor function), so he decided we should bring the oversized stencil on the stand, which he's most comfortable with. It makes sense, but he was disappointed about not being able to "speak" independently using the text-to-speech func-tion.

That's where my surprise comes in. I've been working on it all summer for his birthday coming up next month, but I managed to get it ready a little early. A gigantic twenty-four-inch touch-screen tablet preloaded with a text-to-voice function and a full-screen letterboard with the same stencil layout he's used to, plus the tablet stylus inserted through a hollowed-out pencil (all courtesy of my CS-major freshman roommate and her Maker lab team). Eugene's getting better with the finger-pointing, but he's fastest using the jabbing motion, and I think he has a lot to say.

I set up the letterboard stand in front of the bench. I sit on it like Eugene will, facing the waterfall, adjust the height, the angle. The moon, huge and bright when I first got to the park, has been setting, that perfect circle of white descending behind the trees in the distance, but I can still see it, just barely, a sliver of white blurring into the pale sky. In a few minutes, it'll dip below the horizon, no longer visible at all, just as the sun peeks up on the opposite horizon. When Eugene's sitting here later, when I hand him the pencil-stylus, I'll tell him about the full moon, how it's still there in our orbit even though we can't see it, still luminous in the sun's light, waiting for sunset to rise again. Eugene will smile and pull his arm back in that familiar fisted jab motion, while Mom, John, and I stand off to the side, holding hands, close enough to touch him but careful not to distract him, knowing how hard it is, this new setting, the heightened emotions of this day at this spot, the new screen and stylus against the dizzying backdrop of the waterfall. We'll squeeze our hands in anticipation, not knowing what letter he'll start with, what he'll say, or how long it'll take. Slowly, carefully, Eugene will bring the pencil-stylus to the stencil-screen and begin.

MY PARENTS AND I IMMIGRATED TO THE US FROM KOREA WHEN I WAS eleven, in middle school. We had been very poor in Seoul, living in one room in another family's house with an outhouse and rusty water pump, and my parents wanted a better future for me, their only child.

Moving to my aunt's house in the Baltimore suburbs, I gained amazing things I hadn't even known to dream of: indoor plumbing (toilets! showers!), my own room (with a bed), a color TV, a refrigerator, a piano I could play for hours every day. Objectively, a better life; I should have been ecstatic. And yet, I was miserable. I missed my old life intensely. I missed the closeness with my parents, whom I rarely saw anymore; they were working 6 A.M. to midnight in a grocery store with bulletproof glass in downtown Baltimore and sleeping in a storage cupboard in the back. I missed my friends, my neighborhood and school, that sense of belonging and fitting in with people who looked, dressed, ate, sounded, and spoke like me.

I was a different person in English than in Korean. Back in Korea, I had been a gregarious girl at the top of my class, constantly talking, whispering with friends, organizing recess games. Here in the US, I couldn't understand or say anything beyond the handful of "essential English phrases" I'd memorized from a book, which didn't help much. "Where is the lavatory?" became "lah-bah-to-dee" in my accent, which the teacher interpreted to mean I loved science (as Asian children were reputed to) and wanted to see the school lab. I felt incredibly frustrated, lost, and lonely, but it went beyond that. Our society—not just the US, but human society in general—equates verbal skills, especially oral fluency, with intelligence. Even though there was a good reason I couldn't speak English, I felt stupid, judged, and ashamed. I became a bah-bo.

This intensified when I learned English to the point where I could understand but still couldn't speak it. When you can't speak, others assume you can't understand and talk about you in front of you. Kids openly made fun of my heavy accent, weird syntax, and "broken" English—even as they were smiling at me, pretending to be friendly. It was humiliating. Even though I became fluent in English within a few years, that experience profoundly impacted my sense of competence and confidence. It's been more than forty years, and thinking about it today, I still feel that burn of shame.

———

MORE THAN A DECADE AGO, I went to a medical conference to learn more about treatment options for my son's ulcerative colitis, including hyperbaric oxygen therapy (HBOT), an experimental treatment featured in my debut novel, *Miracle Creek*. My son's doctor described an incident in which a longtime patient—a nonspeaking autistic teenager who everyone assumed couldn't understand anything, let alone read or write—grabbed his sister's preschool alphabet toy and typed, *Help me it hurts.*

I immediately teared up and couldn't stop thinking or talking about it. The pain and frustration this boy must have endured his whole life, having thoughts and words he desperately wanted to express but couldn't, fearing this might continue for the rest of his life. If my limited, temporary experience—being unable to speak English for a few years, nothing compared to this boy's lifelong condition—was that painful, I couldn't imagine how much trauma it must cause having no outlet in any language or in any format at all, not knowing if anyone would ever discover that you understand, that you have words locked deep within you.

As I told people about this boy, I learned he wasn't the only one. I started hearing stories of people diagnosed with "severe, nonverbal autism" working with therapists who approached autism from a completely different perspective, asking: What if these people can't speak because of motor challenges rather than cognitive deficits? What if we focus on improving their motor skills and sensory regulation so they can point to letters to communicate?

The results were astonishing. Many people who were supposedly "nonverbal" (meaning, *without words*), including children I knew from HBOT, started expressing themselves verbally, by writing. Not just basic wants and needs (like *I want water* or *Head hurts*), but essays about history, literature, science, their own experiences feeling imprisoned in their bodies. These pieces were so beautifully written that I'm ashamed to admit that at first I, along with many others, questioned their true authorship, wondering how much their moms or therapists were "helping" them. These doubts quickly disappeared as I watched videos, observed therapy sessions, and talked directly with them, sitting next to them as they moved their arms to spell out questions and comments in response to my own, with no one touching them. Since then, I've begun teaching creative writing to a group of spellers, and I've been awed as they point to letter after letter, all the thoughts they've been editing in their heads for so long coming out in polished, complete, gorgeous sentences and paragraphs.

I write when I don't understand something, to work through something painful and perplexing. I think this is why I've written about people who have trouble expressing themselves in my fiction: because the bias against them is as painful and perplexing as anything I've encountered. Whether you're an immigrant, you stutter, or you have autism, aphasia, apraxia/dyspraxia, or Angelman syndrome—there are so many reasons why you might have trouble speaking, unrelated to the quality of your thoughts. It's well established that we shouldn't judge a person's internal worth based on external appearance—how many stories are based on this thesis? Why not the same for communication modality? I hope *Happiness Falls* can help to change that. I hope it can build on the brave work of books such as Naoki Higashida's *The Reason I Jump* and Ido Kedar's *Ido in Autismland* and the documentary *Wretches and Jabberers* in interrogating and tearing down our society's deeply ingrained assumption that oral fluency is equivalent to intelligence. Just because you can't speak doesn't mean you can't think or understand.

———

*HAPPINESS FALLS* IS A WORK of fiction. The characters and events in this novel are products of my imagination, but Eugene's story is based on the lives of real people—nonspeakers who overcame the erroneous, lifelong presumption that they were severely intellectually disabled and learned to communicate through spelling and typing. Gatherings of emerging and fluent spellers like the ones I describe at the end of the novel exist, and I've been privileged to observe and take part in a number of them.

The poem in Chapter 33 is an excerpt from "It's Sure Been Quite a Year," a collaborative poem created at one such gathering, the June 2021 Neurolyrical Cafe, and featured at the 2021 SpellX. The annual SpellX and monthly Neurolyrical Cafes, both sponsored by the International Association for Spelling as Communication (I-ASC), are virtual gatherings of spellers who celebrate the unlocking of their words by showcasing their creative work—poetry, essays, videos, and songs. They're open to the public, and I highly recommend them for anyone who'd like to see the spellers at work and/or who wants to be inspired. (You can find out more at i-asc.org.)

The eye-tracking study in the story is based on "Eye-tracking Reveals Agency in Assisted Autistic Communication," by Vikram K. Jaswal, Allison Wayne, and Hudson Golino of the University of Virginia's Psychology Department, published May 12, 2020, by *Scientific Reports*. (You can learn more about Professor Jaswal's research studies at JaswalLab.org.)

I based the manifestations of Eugene's dual diagnosis of autism and mosaic Angelman syndrome (AS) on what I learned from generous families who opened up their homes to me and shared their stories, as well as from research papers and interviews with Dr. Lynne Bird of the University of California, San Diego. Any errors are mine alone. The resources offered by the Angelman Syndrome Foundation at angelman.org are invaluable for anyone who'd like to learn more.

Two caveats. First, I want to make clear that I'm not claiming that spelling to communicate is possible for every nonspeaker; I know parents of children with autism and/or Angelman syndrome who have tried various therapies and didn't get an unlocking of words like Eugene. It's also not easy; the spellers, their parents, and their therapists will tell you how difficult and slow it can be, the often inconsistent progress with backward slides, the difficulty of working with different communication partners.

Second, the communication method in the novel, PPT, is fictional. It's inspired by the two real-life therapies with which I'm most familiar and which I've seen in person—Rapid Prompting Method (RPM), developed by Soma Mukhopadhyay, an inspiring innovator who has made so much of today's spelling community possible, and Spelling to Communicate (S2C)™, developed by Elizabeth Vosseller, whose passion, brilliance, and compassion inspired many of the scenes involving PPT. Rather than advocate for one method over the other, which I don't feel qualified to do, I chose to incorporate elements they share: teaching spelling in the context of academic lessons and working in stages, starting with large-lettered stencils. I've also taken liberties and customized PPT to suit the context of the story. Another reason why I created the fictional PPT is that I did not want this novel to be read as a how-to or training guide. I encourage anyone wanting to learn more to turn to the resources listed and updated on my website at angiekimbooks.com and to work directly with trained, certified therapists.

———

I'VE BEEN FASCINATED BY THEORIES about happiness for as long as I can remember, and many of Adam's musings are based on my own scribblings on the topic (and, yes, spreadsheets attempting to reduce some of those ideas into concrete numbers) throughout the years. The first time I heard about the so-called "lottery-winner happiness study," I recalled my friends in Korea telling me how lucky I was to be moving to America and my parents comparing our family visa to winning the lottery. The disconnect between what I was told I should feel and what I did feel when we immigrated to the US—utter joy versus misery—is something I puzzled over in college as a philosophy major, researching and writing about theories of objective versus subjective happiness.

The discussion of that study in *Happiness Falls,* labeled Counterintuitive Case Study #1, is based on "Lottery Winners and Accident Victims: Is Happiness Relative?" by Philip Brickman, Dan Coates, and Ronnie Janoff-Bulman, published in 1978 in *Journal of Personality and Social Psychology,* as well as follow-up studies analyzed in "Happiness and Memory: Affective Significance of Endowment and Contrast," by Varda Liberman, Julia K. Boehm, Sonja Lyubomirsky, and Lee D. Ross, published in 2009 in *Emotion,* and the fascinating opinion essay, "Happiness Won't Save You" by Jennifer Senior, published in November 2020 in *The New York Times.* Counterintuitive Case Study #2 is based on the story of Admiral James Stockdale in Chapter 4 of Jim Collins's *Good to Great: Why Some Companies Make the Leap and Others Don't.* Counterintuitive Case Study #3 is based on "We'll Always Have Paris: The Hedonic Payoff from Experiential and Material Investments," by Thomas Gilovich and Amit

Kumar, published in 2014 in *Advances in Experimental Social Psychology.*

"Yale's happiness course" in the book refers to Professor Laurie Santos's "Psychology and the Good Life," available to the public through *Coursera* under the name "The Science of Well-Being."

The Blue Brain Project is based on the EPFL Blue Brain project by Ecole Polytechnique Fédérale de Lausanne, a simulation neuroscience project that began in 2005 to digitally reconstruct the mouse brain.

In addition to these sources referenced in the book, I've had numerous conversations with friends over the years who've told me about interesting articles, podcasts, blogs, and books about happiness, which formed the backbone of these ideas. Unfortunately, I didn't record them and can't recount them all here, but several that I returned to during the course of writing this novel include Arthur C. Brooks's articles in *The Atlantic's* How to Build a Life series and the *Happiness Lab* podcast hosted by Dr. Laurie Santos. In addition, the thought-provoking work of Joel Frohlich, PhD, on happiness in children with Angelman syndrome in the blogs of *Knowing Neurons* and *Psychology Today* inspired some of Adam Parson's notebook entries on this topic.

Links, further information, and updates to the resources listed above are available on my website at angiekimbooks.com.

## ACKNOWLEDGMENTS

The list of people who helped me with various aspects of this book is overwhelmingly long. But I have to begin with my incredible agent, Susan Golomb, who encouraged me (with bits of cajolery and occasional loving threats) to finally start writing this novel and then worked her behind-the-scenes magic to bring me to my dream editor, David Ebershoff, whose brilliance, kindness, patience, and enormous faith in me and this story guided me to the finish line. Susan and David, I'm not exaggerating when I say I couldn't have written this book without you. Thank you.

I'm so grateful to the wonderful team at Hogarth and Random House for their hard work and extraordinary support and enthusiasm: Andy Ward, Rachel Rokicki, Maria Braeckel, Michelle Jasmine, Erin Richards, Windy Dorresteyn, Taylor Noel, Erica Gonzalez, Carrie Neill, Isabell Liu, Susan Turner, Cassie Gonzales, Jocelyn Kiker, the entire Penguin Random House sales team, and everyone else who did an amazing job bringing this book out into the world. Kimberly

Burns, you are my rock, and I'm so happy we're doing this together again. My thanks also go to the team at Writer's House, including Simon Lipskar, Kate Boggs, and Peggy Boulos Smith, and to my foreign publishers. Special thanks to Angus Cargill, my UK editor, for his careful, insightful notes, and to the Faber team for nurturing this book's growth across the Atlantic. And to Jason Richman at UTA, thank you for championing me and my work and for your always sage advice.

My heartfelt gratitude to the members of the spelling/nonspeaking, autistic, and Angelman families and communities who generously gave me so much of their time and inspired me to explore deeper levels of this story. Otto Lana, Erin Sheldon (Board member of CommunicationFIRST), Anne Tucker, Professor Vikram Jaswal of UVA, Tauna Szymanski (executive director of CommunicationFIRST), Karen Lager, Shannon Zish (founder of Unspoken Thoughts LLC), Lisa Quinn (executive director of Reach Every Voice), Karen Hoerst, and David Rosenblatt not only shared their experiences and expertise with me, but also read early drafts of this book and provided essential feedback. There aren't enough words to sufficiently express how much you've meant to my writing process. You are the core and heart of this book. Nicky Watkinson, Laura Dragonette, and Julia Henderson also provided meticulous, thoughtful feedback that helped me improve the book tremendously.

I have to single out Elizabeth Vosseller, the founder of I-ASC and Growing Kids Therapy, for serving as an important beta reader for this book and for introducing me to the Spellerverse and the creative writing students I've been privileged to teach. Ian Nordling, Caden Rainey, Ryan Wotton, Benjamin Trendler, Jack Haynes, Ben Carpentier, Benjamin D. McDonald, and Harry R.—you continue to humble, amaze, and inspire me with your ideas, questions, beautiful writing, and thirst for learning. I also have to thank Katlyn Billue, Kelly Berg, and the rest of the staff for their mentorship and guidance. Ethan Tucker, Mike Keller, Jack Allnutt, Matthew Lager, and James Potthast—when I first met you, over fifteen years ago, you had no outlet for your ideas and thoughts. Following your journeys over the years and reading your extraordinary essays and speeches (shared by your warrior mothers) has been nothing short of awesome to witness. And those warrior mothers—Anne, Lori, Amy, Karen, and Brooke, I can't tell you how much I admire you for your faith, courage, and persistence, and how grateful I am for your willingness to share your families' autism journeys with the world.

So many others shared experiences and expertise critical to this book. Mark Bergin, the Sclater family (Michelle, Dustin, Jake, and Bailey), Dr. Lynne Bird of UCSD, Stacy Ruddick, Edith Chen, Elizabeth Zielinski, Donna Shank (founder of Wings to Thrive), Katherine Yoder (executive director of Adult Advocacy Centers), Dr. Kyung-Eun Yoon of UMBC, Katie Hainsworth, Minsoo Kang, Abbey Thompson at Stanford@TheTech's Ask a Geneticist program, Chris Lipscombe (*qurgh* at the Klingon Language Institute), Alafair Burke, and my dear cousins Min-Kyung Terri Kang and Sara Starr-Cho answered my many, many questions about Angelman syndrome, genetic mosaicism, RPM and other spelling therapies, police procedures in northern Virginia, juvenile criminal justice systems, forensic interviews, hospital protocols during Covid lockdown periods, Korean romanization systems, innatism, heuristics, and on and on. Any errors are definitely mine. Thanks also to my hiking and book club gang for introducing me to the trails that inspired this story and for our fun brainstorm-over-wine sessions.

Writing is often a lonely, solitary endeavor, and my writing community was indispensable to my writing process and sanity. Jean Kwok, our weekly deadlines kept me writing, and our feedback/venting sessions rescued me from the depths of the murky middle. I'll always treasure our writing partnership throughout the pandemic. Christina Kovac, our beach writing retreats are such a gift; thank you (and Sharon Taylor!) and I can't wait to write our third books side by side. My Flim-Flam Hive—Alafair Burke and Janelle Brown—what would I do without our daily hundreds of texts on everything from spelling bee and Wordle to plot-hole woes and clothing disasters? (Answer:

definitely never QB and most likely lose my mind!) Fernando Manibog, Carolyn Sherman, John Benner, Dennis Desmond, and Beth Stafford—this is the third book baby of Prosecco & Prose; here's to many, many more! To the authors in my novel-critique group, Danielle Trussoni, Janelle Brown, James Han Mattson, Tim Weed, Jean Kwok, and Chris Bohjahlian, your unflinchingly honest insights helped me see things I couldn't, and I'm so glad to have you in my corner. Lisa Gornick, Julia Phillips, Jamie Mason, Danielle Girard, Amin Ahmad, and Julie Langsdorf also served as early readers, and I'm grateful for their support. I started writing this book during the bewildering times of the pandemic, in the summer of 2020, as part of a silent Zoom writing group. Jamie Mason, Danielle Girard, Jay Shepherd, James Hankins, Christine Kovac, and Kathleen Barber— I'm grateful for all the writing, talking (some of which made its way into this book), and angsting together.

My love and thanks go to my dearest friends Susan Rothwell, Marla Grossman, Mary Beth Pfister, Susan Kurtz, and Jonathan Kurtz for reading this book, but more importantly, for always believing in and being there for me.

To my wonderful 엄마 and 아빠, my parents who sacrificed everything to give me the beautiful life I'm now living, and to my 이모 Helen, my second mother—감사합니다. 사랑해.

To my three sons, to whom I dedicated this novel: It goes without saying that just writing this is making me tear up. (Don't roll your eyes too hard!) I love you so much, and I want nothing but absolute happiness for you. Thank you for letting me steal so many stories and lines from our family life for this book. Thank you for indulging all my fact-checking questions about teenage/Gen Z linguistic and behavioral peculiarities, coding, algorithms, social media tendencies, music composition, and so much more. Special thanks to Steve, who served as an invaluable beta reader, footnote enthusiast, audiobook music composer, and website designer.

And finally and most importantly, my never-ending gratitude and love to my husband, Jim Draughn, who brought me coffee in bed every morning, made dinner every night, did all the house- and childcare-related things in between, *and* read countless drafts and listened to my daily whining throughout the whole process. You're a saint, and I don't deserve you. But I intend to spend the next several decades trying to.

The following is exclusive content for this

Barnes & Noble edition.

# HAPPINESS FALLS

## ANGIE KIM

# Q&A with Angie Kim

**Which came first—the characters or the story?**

Definitely the characters! The Parkson family has been with me since 2010, when I started writing a short story about biracial twins, Mia and John, who try to find their nonspeaking baby brother Eugene's voice, which they believe is buried in their grandmother's graveyard outside Seoul. (In *Happiness Falls*, Mia refers to this story as The Graveyard Incident.) Even as I worked on other stories, these characters stayed with me. I have two notebooks filled with freewriting about them—the family moving back to the United States, the twins getting through high school, the mom going back to work and the dad becoming the stay-at-home parent (which my husband had done). I knew I wanted to return to this endearing, quirky family that I'd fallen in love with. I just needed the right story.

As I wrote in my Author's Note, my experience as an eleven-year-old middle-schooler who moved to the United States not speaking any English has had a profound impact on my writing. I always believed that Eugene had words and thoughts—just no way to say them. When I first learned about spelling and other alternative communication therapies for nonspeakers, I wondered: How would Eugene's family react if they heard about these therapies? Would they try them, given the dad's and Mia's skepticism? What if something happened so Eugene needed to communicate and they had to put aside their doubts and try them? What was that something? The story flowed from there.

**One of the main characters in the novel, Eugene, has a rare genetic condition called Angelman syndrome, and even a rarer form of that. What kind of research did you do while writing his character? What was the most surprising thing you learned?**

I initially thought Eugene had autism, just as his family does at first. I didn't know about Angelman back then, but I'd always seen Eugene in my mind with this beatific smile, even when he's making high-pitched noises out of pain, frustration, or sensory overload.

Several years ago, I was researching a particular type of letterboard-spelling therapy for nonspeaking autistic children, and I saw a reference to it being used for children with Angelman syndrome (AS). I'd never heard of it before, so I looked it up and got chills, because what I read reflected how I'd seen Eugene in my mind for the past decade—his smile, being drawn to water, his motor issues, being a nonspeaker considered by many to have a severe cognitive impairment often misdiagnosed as autism. I instantly knew Eugene had Angelman syndrome and that this would play an important role in his family's story.

I did a lot of research, both in terms of reading the medical literature and meeting (in person or via Zoom) families and experts in the tightly knit Angelman community. I was very lucky to meet extremely generous people who shared their experiences and knowledge with me and even served as beta readers. One of the most surprising things I learned about Angelman syndrome is how many types of AS exist (based on the mechanism that causes the genetic error) and how wide the spectrum is even within each sub-category of AS. One mom with three children with the same type of AS told me how different they are in terms of their skill sets—one completely nonspeaking but very communicative through gestures and expressions, another blabbing constantly, the third amazing at configuring computers and other electronic equipment.

**You discuss the idea that people with Angelman syndrome are considered unusually happy because of the frequent smiling and laughing. Is that where the ideas about happiness in the novel come from?**

The dad's happiness ideas and experiments came first, before I learned about Angelman syndrome, even before the story idea of him going missing. I've been fascinated by theories and studies about quality of life and happiness for as long as I can remember. I think my interest probably stems from my experience as an immigrant—having been really poor but very happy in Korea and then completely miserable my first years in America even though my family was so much better off objectively. I majored in philosophy in college and wrote many papers on the relativity of happiness, objective versus subjective manifestations of happiness, etc. Even though I'm much closer biographically to Hannah, the mom, Adam is much more like me, with these crazy ideas of trying to quantify and maximize happiness for his children.

It wasn't until a good year into the writing process—when I was reading about the debate whether genetic "fixes" for Angelman should be pursued, given that Angelman kids seem so much happier than many teenagers—that I went, Wait! I'm writing about this father who's obsessed about trying to maximize happiness, and his son frequently smiles and laughs but may be in pain. That was a huge breakthrough in the story for me. Everything came together, the three main threads—the dad going missing, his happiness experiments, and Eugene's struggle to communicate—which had coexisted but not been tightly woven before that.

**You just said the happiness thread came before the missing thread. How did the idea of the dad going missing come about, and why did you want that element in this novel?**

When I was still in the freewriting stage, I thought the novel would revolve around the family trying to help the dad conduct happiness-quotient experiments to help him get a nonfiction book deal. The idea of him going missing to start the novel came pretty late, but as soon as it came, I couldn't let it go. Missing-person stories have always fascinated me. On a personal note, one of the most important books to me as a writer is a missing-person narrative: Tim O'Brien's *In the Lake of the Woods,* which I love not only because of its inventive structure and beautiful writing, but because it inspired me to leave the law. (In a nutshell, I had a magical day reading this book from cover to cover, sitting by the ocean, sipping wine, and I realized I hadn't been that happy and relaxed in all the time I was a lawyer, and I decided to change my career in search of something that fulfilled me. It took three more career changes over fifteen years for me to find writing, but I credit that book with starting the whole process.)

Also, I agree with the lawyer, Shannon Haug, in the novel, who says that missing-person cases are the most intriguing and frustrating because they're the deepest mysteries—no one knows anything, and the range of possibilities is infuriatingly wide, from the most horrific (kidnapping, murder) to the most innocuous (took a fun trip without telling anyone). I'm a control freak, and I like knowing as much as possible, as quickly as possible. Waiting for news, not knowing: that's torture to me. So the idea of anyone I know (let alone love) going missing is profoundly upsetting and something I wanted to delve into through this novel.

**Many missing-person novels feature a woman who has disappeared. Was it an intentional choice to have a man disappear in your story? If so, why?**

It was definitely intentional. There's actually a footnote about this in the novel, in which Mia says "Based on my perusal of the genre, most of the missing are girls/women (87.9 percent), with the missing-men stories all being espionage- or mafia-related." (That percentage comes from a spreadsheet I made after discussing this with friends who write crime novels one night several years ago.) The feminist interrogation of women-in-peril stories is nothing new, but I wanted to use this story to explore an additional facet I haven't seen: the stay-at-home father overwhelmed (either physically or emotionally) by the strains of being the primary caregiver to a child who requires a lot of care, like Eugene.

**How does the fact of the missing parent being the father, rather than the mother, change the analysis and the hypotheses? Mia is such a fun narrator for the novel. She has a huge personality and a specific perspective. Why did you decide to write from her perspective instead of another character's or instead of writing in the third person?**

I'm so happy to hear that because I love Mia so much! Her voice has been with me for years. When I started taking seriously the idea of writing a novel about this family, I knew Mia would narrate at least a part of the novel—if for no other reason than that I had so much fun with her voice and I missed it. Also, her curiosity was infectious. Writing in her voice forced me to research anything and everything that popped into my head, to try to make connections between wildly disparate things, which sometimes yielded insights I wouldn't have had otherwise and also often made me laugh.

I did consider switching to the point of view of others, as I did in my debut novel, *Miracle Creek*, which is written in close third-person from seven characters' POVs. I suppose in one sense, I considered it a writing challenge to stick with one POV for the length of a whole book, which I found exhausting. As Mia's family constantly tells her, she can be a lot. (A bit too much, her brother John would say.) Maybe about one hundred pages into my first draft, I kind of fantasized about how nice it would be to be in someone else's head for a while, with the added benefit of enabling the reader to learn more information by switching perspectives, Rashomon style. That's when I realized that staying with a single perspective serves a thematic purpose: its claustrophobic isolation, anxiety, and bewilderment provide a literary taste of what it might feel like to live through a true missing-person case, fearing that you might never know for sure what happened to a person you love.

**_Happiness Falls_ takes place during 2020, a few months into the Covid-19 pandemic. Why did you set your book during this timeframe?**

I don't consider _Happiness Falls_ to be a "pandemic story," per se, and I didn't set out to write one. I placed the story in the summer of 2020 for a purely practical reason: it provided the impetus for me to write. I was having trouble focusing during that time, as the pandemic was all-encompassing, making it hard to think about anything else. Somehow, imagining a family dealing with a crisis during the same quarantine my family and I were experiencing gave me a way into the story and inspired specific scenes and situations. Also, I have some close friends who have autistic children, and they were having an especially hard time with the disruption to routines. Tensions were high everywhere, and my friends were worried about their kids with sensory issues melting down in public, not being able to handle wearing masks, prompting bystanders to call the police or Child Protective Services.

Even though I went into the story thinking that the pandemic merely happened to be an aspect of the setting, I realized how much elements like wearing masks, the racial tensions involving police interactions, and hospital isolation protocols not only added to the plot, but also reinforced some of the themes I wanted to explore. Now, just a few years removed from this time, it seems like a time capsule of sorts. I hope this reminder will help readers to think about how our society's baselines and expectations have shifted during and since that time.

**Tell us about the pacing of the story. Why did you include footnotes throughout—and what do you think they add?**

I'm firmly on the "pantser" end of the pantser-planner continuum for writers, and that was especially true for this novel, where I had no idea what would happen next and had several points in the story when I needed to backtrack to change course. It's definitely not the most efficient way to write a novel, but not knowing what happens next provided a lot of motivation for me to write; I love this family and care so much about what happens to them, and I knew the only way to find out was to get back into my writing closet and write. (Yes, I literally write inside a closet!) After I was done with the first full draft, I made a one-page outline to help me refine the story structure, adjust pacing, reorganize scenes, etc. I ended up cutting out a full third of the story (about 50,000 words or so) with the help of my amazing editor and some other first readers.

As for the footnotes, they just came to me as part of Mia's voice. They help to express how Mia thinks—logically, but prone to going off on tangents she gets excited by. I happen to love footnotes in fiction, but I figured they might be helpful for readers who *don't* love them, because they can simply skip them for a more streamlined, faster reading experience. Some of my early readers have read the book both ways and said they liked both in different ways.

**What about the charts? Why did you include them?**

I love charts and used them in *Miracle Creek* as well, in the courtroom scenes. In my former careers in law and in management consulting, I loved to create simple charts boiling down a bunch of complex information into the most essential elements. I'm a really visual person and seeing something reduced to one page helps me to process it. Shannon Haug (the lawyer in *Miracle Creek* who made a lot of the charts) makes the first chart here, and I thought, of course Mia's going to try making one herself to help her figure out what she thinks really happened.

**What, if any, is the relationship between *Happiness Falls* and your debut novel, *Miracle Creek*?**

I consider them to be companion novels. *Miracle Creek* focused on the parenting angle, the extreme parenting sacrifices involved in medical care and immigration; *Happiness Falls* focuses on sibling dynamics and the experience of the nonspeaking child himself. But they do take place in the same fictional universe, and there are some fun Easter eggs for fans of my first novel (and vice versa).

**What do you hope readers will take away from *Happiness Falls*?**

The primary thing I hope all readers take away from this story is that we shouldn't equate oral fluency with intelligence. A person's inability to speak (or perceived deficits, like accents, syntax irregularities, stuttering, dyspraxia) often has nothing to do with that person's cognitive abilities; just because you can't speak doesn't mean you can't think or understand.

In addition, I hope readers leave the story interrogating their own assumptions about a great many things, such as: Why do we equate things like accents and stuttering with a low IQ even though we know (or should know) that's not how intelligence works? Why do we say that Asians who aren't fluent in English speak "broken English" but we don't say that about, say, French people who don't speak English well? Is happiness the most important goal we should have for ourselves and our children? And what would you do if someone you loved suddenly disappeared?

Finally, I'd like to thank my readers. It's a gift to be able to share this story with you.

1. What were your first impressions of each member of the Parkson family? How did your perceptions evolve over the course of the novel?

2. How would you describe Mia's voice as a narrator? Is she reliable? How would the book be different if Angie Kim had written it in the third person?

3. How did the structure of the book, including footnotes and charts, influence your reading experience?

4. Discuss the relationships between the Parkson siblings—and among the three of them. What do they learn about one another? How do you envision their relationships evolving after the events of the book?

5. Do you think it can be more difficult to see the people closest to us as they really are? Why or why not?

6. As Kim explores in *Happiness Falls*, we tend to equate oral fluency with intelligence (and vice versa). How did the character of Eugene challenge your assumptions about nonspeaking people?

7. In the same vein, how did the novel change your perspective about people who struggle with a language barrier? As Mia notes, "If it was this painful for Mom and me, what was it like for those who have beautifully formed thoughts they can't express their entire lives?"

8. How does race—including the perceived race of mixed-race characters—play into the novel? What biases and stereotypes must each character contend with?

9. Discuss Adam's Happiness Quotient project. Do you agree with his theories? What do you consider your baseline? Do you think it needs adjusting? Do you think it's possible to intentionally lower it? If so, do you think that would make you happier?

10. "For some of us," Kim writes, "the premise that happiness is the end-all and be-all of life is flat-out wrong." Do you agree? Why or why not?

11. Do you think Adam was right to keep Eugene's progress from the rest of the family? Why or why not?

12. "It's depressing, infuriating, and fascinating all at once—the herculean efforts people will exert to not believe what they're seeing": Discuss the ways this quotation plays out in the novel.

13. What did you think of the footnotes? Did you read them or skip them? Why do you think Kim included them?

14. Kim discusses issues of gender dynamics, parenting, cognitive biases, and disability justice, among others. How did these themes reinforce each other? What other themes stood out to you?

15. How did the coronavirus pandemic affect the plot? How did it affect the themes?

16. What did you think of the ending? What do you think really happened—did Eugene repeat parts of John and Mia's conversation, either subconsciously or intentionally? Was the note real? Do these answers matter?